SONGS
in the NIGHT

SONGS in the NIGHT

JO PIAZZA O'MARA

REDEMPTION
PRESS

Published by Redemption Press, PO Box 427, Enumclaw, WA 98022

Toll Free (844) 2REDEEM (273-3336)

Redemption Press is honored to present this title in partnership with the author. The views expressed or implied in this work are those of the author. Redemption Press provides our imprint seal representing design excellence, creative content, and high quality production.

This is a work of fiction. Names, characters, businesses, places, events and incidents are either the products of the author's imagination or used in a fictitious manner. Any resemblance to actual persons, living or dead, or actual events is purely coincidental.

Scripture quotations marked ESV are taken from the Holy Bible, English Standard Version. ESV® Permanent Text Edition® (2016). Copyright © 2001 by Crossway Bibles, a publishing ministry of Good News Publishers.

Scripture quotations marked NKJV are taken from the New King James Version. Copyright © 1982 by Thomas Nelson, Inc. Used by permission. All rights reserved.

Scripture quotations marked NLT are taken from the Holy Bible, New Living Translation, copyright © 1996, 2004, 2015 by Tyndale House Foundation. Used by permission of Tyndale House Publishers Inc., Carol Stream, Illinois 60188. All rights reserved.

ISBN 13: 978-1-68314-324-6
978-1-68314-325-3 (ePub)
978-1-68314-326-0 (Mobi)

Library of Congress Catalog Card Number: 2017938954

Main Characters

Vincent Agosti and Maria Agosti
(deceased)

Joe Agosti	Trina Agosti Lamazo	Angie Agosti Trayor	Lily Agosti Mazzona
(son)	*(daughter)*	*(daughter)*	*(daughter)*
Ellie Agosti	Sal Lamazo	Jake Trayor	Gino Mazzona
(wife)	*(husband)*	*(husband)*	*(husband)*
Anthony Agosti	Vinnie Lamazo	Kevin Trayor	Hope Mazzona
(son)	*(son)*	*(son)*	*(daughter)*
Sammy Agosti		Mia Trayor	Ricky Brando
(son)		*(daughter)*	*(son-in-law)*
Kerri Agosti		Leah Trayor	
(daughter-in-law)		*(daughter)*	
		Cindy Trayor	
		(daughter-in-law)	
		Emma Trayor	
		(granddaughter)	
		Luke Henderson	
		(boyfriend)	
		Matt Bertolino	
		(boyfriend)	

Chapter 1

Joey stood, smiling to himself, as his cold, wet feet dug deep into the shifting sand. This particular expanse of coastline held special memories; many childhood experiences flitted before his eyes while his gaze remained fixed on the turbulent ocean. He couldn't explain it, other than to say the surf and sand were like comfort food for his soul. It would be impossible to enumerate exactly how many times he and his family had come to this place over the years, but this visit was different—very different.

Mama and Papa, the anchors of the Agosti family, had been gone for more than six years, leaving a personal void in each family member. Nothing on this earth could ever replace those two loving, caring parents, but this robust family was determined to move forward in the strength of their family bond, trusting it would honor their memory.

By default, Joey had become the patriarch of the Agosti family, and just as Papa had done, he would faithfully watch over and guard every single member. So now, although he moaned and groaned, it fell on him to rent a beach house for their family vacation. It was no easy task; finding a summer house large enough to accommodate this growing tribe for an entire week proved challenging. Joey's family, plus his two sisters' families had become quite prolific; marriages and a new baby were happy events, very happy events.

Just as he yanked his feet free from the eroding sand that was sucking him down, Trina crept up behind him, covering his eyes just as she'd done countless times when they were kids. "Hey, Joey, lunch is ready. You coming?"

"Sure, I was just about to head up. Have you heard from the rest of the gang?" He turned, nearly losing his balance in the shifting sand.

Trina answered as they walked up to the beach house together, "Angie and Jake should be here in an hour with Mia and Leah in tow. I'm thinking Kevin, Cindy and the baby won't be far behind."

"Good, good. The party never really begins until our crazy sister arrives."

"You got that right, Angie surely hasn't matured with age, and honestly, I hope she never does. Watching her antics with Emma in this new *grandma* role is beyond amusing. She and Jake are bursting their buttons with pride."

"I hear ya, it's so funny to watch! Trina, I was totally lost in my thoughts down there in the surf. Do you remember our family vacation at Salisbury Beach? I think it was in 1968 or 1969."

Trina remained a natural beauty at age fifty-one. Her smooth, olive complexion and warm, brown eyes continued to be captivating. Although she often complained about her unmanageably curly hair, most women admitted to being jealous of it. Only recently, her jet-black hair began to be touched with a bit of silver streaking, giving her a rather regal appearance. With the passing of time, she had taken on a strong resemblance to their mama.

"It was definitely 1968. I know that because I was fifteen and your old friend Lenny planted my very first kiss on these unsuspecting lips."

"Yeah, I seem to remember you telling me that. What a sneak! He cozies up to me so he can take advantage of my little sister."

"It was only a kiss, Joe! I hope you didn't hold a grudge. Do you ever see him?" Trina asked as they climbed the porch steps.

"Yeah, on occasion he stops by the garage. I've taken to calling him *chrome dome.*"

"What?"

"He's as bald as a cue ball, but he takes my ribbing in stride."

Trina gave Joey a playful shove and pulled open the screen door to find Vinnie sitting at the kitchen table, Nutella smeared all over his mouth.

"Whoa, will you look at that face!" Joe exclaimed. "Someone ought to get a picture of that."

"Sal, did your son manage to get his face stuck in that jar?" Trina chuckled.

"Hey, sweetie, it is vacation. I figured every six-year-old should be unburdened of manners while on vacation, right, Joe?" Sal couldn't take his eyes off his son's chocolate-covered mouth.

"Don't get me in the middle of this; you two lovebirds are on your own."

"Okay then, Sal, you have the honor of washing that beautiful little face."

"Aw, Mom, I can wash my own face," Vinnie said with an insulted frown, sticking his hands out for Buddy to lick clean.

Buddy, her faithful golden retriever, was far and away *the* best dog Trina ever had. His graying muzzle hinted at his ten plus years, but still, he managed to muster up enough puppy-like energy to keep up with Vinnie.

"Honey, don't give chocolate to Buddy, it's not good for dogs—remember?"

"Oops, I forgot. Sorry."

"Okay, okay, vacation manners are officially in effect," Trina conceded, kissing the top of Vinnie's head and patting Buddy's, "but with a few necessary exceptions."

Sal and Trina had experienced so much heartache during their first fifteen years of marriage. They both wanted children—desperately. One miscarriage after another finally caused her to accept the cruel fact—it just wasn't going to happen, but then—a miracle! As a social worker, Trina had witnessed many foster children finding their *forever homes,* which was exactly what happened for their son. Vincent, who they respectfully named after Trina's father, had been thrown into the foster care system as a toddler. But through a series of God-ordained circumstances, and tons of bureaucracy, he miraculously found his way into Sal and Trina Lamazo's loving home. They were thrilled, but adopting in their forties certainly kept them on their toes, as well as physically exhausted during their entire first year as new parents. Neither Sal nor Trina regretted it one iota; they were head over heels in love with Vinnie from day one.

"Joe, how did you ever find this place? It easily accommodates all nineteen of us, not to mention that it's right on the beachfront. That alone is impressive!" Sal continued cutting a large stromboli into sections to share.

"It wasn't easy. It took me several months of working with a local Realtor, but voila—here we are."

"I've always thought Massachusetts and New Hampshire have *the* most breathtaking of all our coastlines," Sal added.

"I agree and I think we should make this a yearly tradition; a week at Hampton Beach with the entire Agosti family. What could be better?" Trina declared as she grabbed her section of the stromboli oozing with melted mozzarella cheese.

"Okay with me, but first let's see if we still *like* each other by the end of this week. Keep in mind . . . nineteen people . . . two bathrooms—for seven days. What were we thinking?" Joey laughed with his deep, rich voice.

At fifty-two, Joe was still as handsome as ever, strong and physically fit from countless hours of hard work at the family auto repair business. When people guessed him to be in his mid-forties, he humbly replied, 'good genes'.

"So, what needs to be done before the gang descends on us?" Sal questioned.

"Not a thing. All the gals are bringing towels and bedding for their own families and we agreed to take turns with meal preparations, so we're good until everyone arrives."

"I wanted Ellie to drive up with me this morning, but her boss pressured her into working. She's moving up her company's proverbial ladder, but she's paying a price for it; long hours with too much stress," Joe complained.

"Well, Joe, while you're here together, you should indulge your wife, royally. Let her sleep late, bring her breakfast in bed, give her neck massages on the beach, you know—girly stuff," Trina joked with a twinkle in her eyes.

"Hey, don't get carried away and don't give her any ideas," he laughed, then held his dripping stromboli in the air to catch the stringy cheese in his mouth.

"I was thinking . . . "

"Oh no, we're in trouble now," Joey razzed his sister.

"As I was *saying* . . . I think Kevin and Cindy should take the larger bedroom since it's roomy enough for a small crib."

"That's a good idea, honey," Sal agreed.

"I wish they'd hurry up. I can't wait to get my hands on little Emma. She's the cutest little thing and such a happy baby."

"Yeah, remember what Pops always said, 'happy mothers have happy babies.'" Joey smiled.

Hearing that statement cast Trina's thoughts back to Cindy's tumultuous childhood. By the age of six, that child had all too frequently witnessed her mom being physically—not to mention emotionally—abused by her drunken father. That abuse was on a level that no child should ever be forced to experience. In spite of her horrendous background, she had grown into a beautiful, joyful young woman, now with a child of her own. This gentle wife and mother was a miracle in their midst and the entire family had grown to love her.

Over the years, Trina came to believe it was no coincidence that she was the social worker assigned to Cindy's family, giving her the distinct advantage of helping Cindy and her mom grow past those painful years.

Later, as a teenager, and while her dad was still incarcerated, Cindy became best buddies with Angie's daughter, Mia. Those two young ladies became inseparable and as time passed, she was assimilated into the family, even embracing Mama as her own grandmother. And Mama, being Mama, loved Cindy unconditionally. It came as no surprise when Angie's son, Kevin, began to pursue Mia's best friend; he was totally smitten with this sweet, freckle-faced redhead with sad eyes who, nevertheless, always revealed her joyful spirit.

"Hey guys, we *have* arrived!" Angie hollered from the front porch. "Wow, this place is amazing!"

"Hi, Angie, let me give you guys a hand," Joey pushed open the screen door and saw their baggage. "What the heck? Is all that stuff coming inside?"

"Well, big brother, it's not going next door and before you ask . . . *yes*, it's all necessary," Angie smirked, firmly planting her hands on her hips.

"Sheesh, maybe I should run out and buy us a storage shed," Sal joked.

"All right, enough with the wise cracks you two, now go and make yourselves useful. It's not as much as you think," Angie countered.

"Yeah, right," Leah groaned as she stumbled into the kitchen, her arms laden down. "I could hardly move in that backseat and I think we flattened Mia. You guys better check to see if she's still breathing!" She dramatically flipped her long black hair back over her shoulder and plopped down in a chair.

Leah, the youngest of Angie and Jake Trayor, was definitely more precocious than her siblings; this young lady was vivacious and as witty as they come. The apple doesn't fall far from the tree; Angie and Leah's personalities and temperaments were carbon copies. At nineteen, she was following her longtime passion for photojournalism at Boston University. Like her mom, Leah had always been in love with cameras, the art of photography and—*getting the story*. The family had begun to compare her to a pit bull; there was no letting go once she got her teeth into a story.

"Ugh, I'm so ready for this vacation," Jake whined, opening all four car doors. "Well, come on out of there, Mia," he chortled, as he stared at his buried daughter.

"I would, if I could," she grunted. "Would someone *please* get this stuff off of me?"

"I will, I will," Vinnie excitedly yelled, frenetically jumping up and down. "I've missed you, Mia. You said you were coming over last week."

"I know, honey, I'm sorry. I had to work late every night; I almost missed the last train home—twice. But, I *should* have called you," Mia admitted while tightening her red ponytail scrunchie around her thick, dark hair. Mia favored her dad's family; she was tall and willowy with the Trayors' signature dimples—adorable!

Mia appeared to have it all—beauty, brains and a winning personality. Immediately after graduating from college, she accepted a fabulous job as a computer programmer with a large Boston firm. Angie and Jake weren't always happy with her long days or the train commute, but Mia loved the opportunity to catnap on the ride home, leaving her refreshed and free for the evenings. It worked for her.

"That's okay," Vinnie conceded, "but you have to take me to the boardwalk while we're here."

"I will. I promise, but first can you help get me out of here—*please?*"

With that desperate plea, everyone broke into laughter, teasing Mia unmercifully while working together to free her from the backseat. Leah was right, her sister was indeed packed like canned anchovies in the backseat.

"You guys are *not* funny, I was getting claustrophobic in there!" she exclaimed, finally breaking free.

After unloading the car and piling everything in the parlor, Mia, Leah and Vinnie made a wild dash for the surf. Even though Mia and Leah were twenty-four and nineteen, respectively, they loved spending time with their younger cousin; he brought out the kid in them. Trina and

Angie smiled as they watched the girls swinging the little guy between them. Yanking off their sandals, they waded into the cold, Atlantic surf; Buddy was frantically circling them, barking and jumping, as they jokingly threatened to toss their little cousin into the ocean.

"What a magnificent view," Angie said. "These French doors are wonderful, and that porch is fabulous. This is nothing short of perfection. It suits us to a tee; let's book it again for next year."

"We already talked about that, but Joey thinks we should wait to see how we manage with nineteen people and two bathrooms," Trina reiterated.

"Oh come on, where's your pioneer spirit?" Angie gaily countered. "Remember when we were kids, Daddy rented that little cottage at Salisbury Beach? We managed just fine then; seven of us, including our two friends—and only *one* bathroom."

"How could I forget, it was Polly's Villa," Trina offered. "But Angie, we were hardly ever in the cottage. I seem to remember we spent most of our time on the beach or at *the center,* roaming around the kiosks, checking out the other kids."

"Trina and I were checking out the other teens. *You,* my dear little sister, were just a baby," Joey tweaked Angie's nose.

"What! I was twelve, hardly a baby. But, I do remember you two ditching me more than once when you went to the boardwalk with your friends. *But,* I've forgiven you!" Angie self-righteously proclaimed.

"Hey, Joe, she's forty-nine years old and she's *finally* forgiven us." Trina sniggered.

"I don't mean to change this very sensitive subject, but how about a proper tour of this place?" Jake asked.

"Sure, come on, I'll show you around. Grab those suitcases," Sal suggested. "We'll start with the upstairs."

"This place is right out of an AARP vacation magazine—*not* that I'm ready for any of that yet," Angie chuckled as they climbed the elegant staircase. "I for one am maintaining my Peter Pan mentality, *'I won't grow up, I don't want to go to school',*" she sang.

"Well, you can deny it all you want, Ange, but we are both fast approaching fifty and you *will be* returning to school in a couple of weeks," Jake teased.

"Yeah, yeah, yeah, there's a killjoy in every crowd," Angie grumbled.

Angie's lighthearted, slapstick sense of humor made her the life of every party and a joy to be around. She and her sister shared a strong family resemblance. While their personalities were distinctly different, they were similar in so many important ways. Angie's carefree demeanor was starkly different from her sister's propensity to worry and fret. Still, it was undeniable that they were best friends.

"Holy moly, I was expecting something a bit more—rustic. This is lovely and I'm guessing it was quite elegant in its day," Angie moved around, taking in the beautifully appointed rooms. "Hmm, a posh Victoria home, right on the beachfront, wouldn't you just love to know its history?"

"I wonder what the taxes would set you back on a place like this," Sal commented.

"Now if that isn't a fitting comment from our resident C.P.A.?" Joey said. "And what does our family's social worker have to say?"

"Me, I'm just enjoying the scenery and praying everyone else arrives safely."

"Yup, a perfect social worker response."

As they were finishing their second floor tour, voices drifted up the staircase. "Hey, where is everyone?" came from somewhere in the sunroom.

Angie was the first to make her way down the steps, gently nudging past everyone else. "Okay, guys, hand over that little lady," she crooned, opening her arms to Emma. "Oh, darlin', how's my sweet girl?"

"Oh boy, there goes the gusher," Joey mocked.

"Humph, I can't wait to see how you and Ellie behave when Anthony or Sammy give you a grandchild."

"I won't hold my breath until Sammy finds the right girl and as for Anthony and Kerri, they had better get busy; they're both closing in on twenty-nine years old."

They all cooed over the precious one-year old; even the macho men didn't attempt to hide their love for this newest addition to the Agosti family. The poor little one was confused, sticking out her pouty lower lip as she was being passed from one adoring relative to the next.

"All right you guys, she needs to be changed," Kevin gave his mom a peck on the cheek. "Cindy, where are her diapers?"

"Still in the car, I'll grab them, but first I need to hug everyone."

"Noo—first you need to *destink* that adorable little munchkin," Joey joked. "Phew, some smells you just never forget."

Mia, Leah and Vinnie appeared at the screen door, clamoring to play with the baby. "Hold on, guys, she's got a—load," Kevin cautioned.

"Whoa, I guess so," Mia choked out, withdrawing her arms. "I'll wait," she firmly stated while fanning her scrunched-up nose. Laughter erupted, but everyone did manage to hug Cindy before she ran to retrieve the diaper bag.

"Where are we sleeping, Aunt Trina? I want to unpack and get my camera; there are so many great shots around here. I don't want to miss a single one of them," Leah said.

"Oh, Leah, you have an entire week—pace yourself."

"I wouldn't mind taking over that cute little bunkhouse out back. Has anyone claimed it yet?" Mia asked.

"Actually, it's a playhouse, but it's not really little. It can easily accommodate four people. Believe it or not, it has two separate bedrooms, each with a queen-size bed. But, sweetie, I thought it would be perfect if Lily and Gino took one bedroom; Hope and Ricky could bunk in the other bedroom."

"That makes sense. I'm sure that Hope would be more comfortable with her mom next door."

"Good thinking, Aunt Trina. So, where do want us to crash?" Leah asked again.

"Come on, girls, I'll show you."

Not wanting to be left behind, Vinnie came rushing toward his mom. "I'm coming too," he grabbed Mia's hand.

Trina led them up the classic Victorian staircase, pausing to allow her nieces a minute to peek into the four bedrooms, each lovelier than the previous. They came to the end of the hall and there in the corner was a narrow staircase, almost hidden from view in the hallway. The poorly lit staircase was obviously skipped over when the rest of the house enjoyed a facelift. The well-worn stair treads and dingy walls prompted Mia and Leah to raise their eyebrows at each other, obviously skeptical about what they'd find behind the badly chipped wooden door.

"Hmm, now this is intriguing," Leah whispered, trying not to sound too negative.

When they got to the top of the staircase, Trina pushed the door open to reveal a beautifully decorated attic bedroom. The far wall and the ceiling were a warm, honey-colored wood that gave off a light scent of cedar.

"Wow, what a surprise! This is gorgeous. And it looks newly decorated, so fresh and clean. I'm guessing the bedspreads and curtains are also brand-new," Mia said.

"This is perfect for us, Aunt Trina. I actually like it better than any of the other bedrooms; it's so quaint. Mia, come here, look at this ocean view!" Leah stood before of one of the unusually tall windows.

Turning back to her aunt, Mia asked, "Do you think this was once used for servants' quarters?"

"It's possible. It wasn't uncommon for these old Victorian houses to be used as summer homes for New England's rich and famous. It might be fun to research this particular place; maybe the locals would know some of its history."

Leah sat on one of the beds, then began bouncing up and down like a little kid. "I have dibs on this bed!" she loudly proclaimed.

"Yeah, yeah, I knew you'd stake a claim sooner or later."

"Well, I'll leave you two to battle it out. I volunteered to prepare tonight's dinner, so I'd better get started on it."

Trina smiled as she and Vinnie closed the door behind them, but not before hearing Leah say, "This is going to be a blast. I wonder if there are any interesting guys around here."

"Well, your daughters seem happy with their accommodations," Trina mentioned, as she entered the parlor where her sister was sprawled out on the floor, playing with Emma.

"Oh good, so exactly where *are* they staying?"

"In the attic bedroom, it's darling."

"Terrific, so where are Jake and I sleeping?"

"How about the tree-house?" Trina joked.

"Hey, that's perfect for my monkey-mom," Kevin snickered.

"You two are just too funny."

"Kevin, I gave you and Cindy the large master bedroom. Angie, you and Jake can take the blue room. Joe and Ellie can bunk in the yellow room. And since the sage-green room already has a cot in the corner, Sal, Vinnie and I will sleep in there."

"Wow, I'm impressed with your organizational skills," Angie admitted.

"Oh, yeah, I'm so very impressive! Come on, help me get dinner started."

"Only if you'll help me when it's my turn," Angie retorted, as Vinnie quickly took her place on the floor, anxious to play with Emma.

Trina gave her sister a good-natured nudge toward the kitchen. "So, are you looking forward to heading back to school?" Trina asked.

"Sort of, but you know how my life spins out of control when I start back teaching. I'm in a different stage of my life, my priorities are different now. My heart's desire is simply to spend more time with Emma."

"I understand. Maybe you should mark your calendar before the school year even begins, *Emma-Grandma* dates. Time will slip away otherwise. Who else is going to control your commitments if you don't?"

"You're probably right. Yeah, I'm sure you're right, but let me just say it will take all the discipline I can muster. You know how it goes when September rolls around: a meeting here, a parent-teacher conference there, blah, blah, blah. So, when we get home, the first thing I'll do is pencil in some special days with Emma."

"Of course I'm right. You remember Mama saying, 'time with family is everything.'"

"It sure is. So, what's for dinner tonight?"

"Pulled pork on toasted buns, baked beans and cabbage salad. I wanted to keep it simple, since everyone is arriving at different times."

"That's smart. Guys, did I just hear a car door slam?" Angie yelled to the boys. But before they responded, Ellie was already climbing the front steps.

"Ellie, you're here early." Joe met his wife on the porch steps, pulling her into a warm embrace.

"Yup, I wanted to be with you, not my boss," she spoke in a hushed voice, but loud enough to evoke a chorus of *awws* from the rest of the family.

"How sweet! After all these years, you guys are still gushy." Angie couldn't resist throwing exaggerated kisses in their direction.

"So, tell me, does the Agosti clan approve of your choice?" Ellie asked Joey, while looking around the kitchen.

"Yes, this place is awesome and we all agree it more than meets our needs. He did a great job."

"Well, I have to 'fess up. Ellie also worked with the Realtor," he admitted. "She really deserves most of the credit; she fielded all the phone calls. Thanks, sweetie."

"*No problemo!* By the way, Lily called as I was leaving the office. She and Gino are driving with Hope and Ricky," Ellie said. "They should be here shortly."

"All right, let the party begin!" Trina loudly declared.

Trina absolutely loved it when her family spent time together; their affection for one another is enviable. Over the years, however, Trina fought tooth and nail to keep them from destroying their close bond. But when the dust settled, they remained fiercely protective of one another, and an even stronger family bond arose from the ashes of their conflict.

Joey couldn't help but ponder the abundant blessings that had been showered down on this family. He reminisced, with shame, about how his unwillingness to forgive could have thwarted God's ultimate plan; it would certainly have affected the entire Agosti family.

Thank you, Lord, he silently spoke to God. *You intervened and softened my hard heart. You revealed my rotten attitude before I made a mess out of everything.*

Thinking back to those dark days before Pops died, he still couldn't believe he'd held such bitterness and anger, not speaking to his father for three long years. At the time, Joey felt completely justified in shunning him. After all, Pops' ugly secret threatened to tear his *perfect* family to shreds. The most difficult pill to swallow was the harsh reality that he'd always held his dad up as the moral standard—his idol. They were so close, inseparable, except for those years of emotional torment.

Joe was abruptly pulled back from his gloomy reflections by his sister's voice, "I gave Hope and Ricky one of the bedrooms in the playhouse; Gino and Lily can take the adjoining bedroom. It seemed to make sense for mother and daughter to be together."

"Sounds good to me. Hey, can I see the playhouse before they get here?" Angie asked. "We have plenty of time to pull dinner together before the mob descends on us."

Joey watched his sisters walk down the short path to the playhouse; his thoughts were again cast back to that awful day when he had uncovered the proof of his dad's illicit relationship. That was bad enough, but he then discovered that a child resulted from that one selfish act—Lily.

Three years of conflict followed that discovery. Heart-wrenching torment gripped the family until finally Joe discovered his mom had been aware of it almost from the beginning. She had *chosen* to forgive her husband. That revelation rocked Joey to his core.

I'm still in awe of Mama's ability to extend forgiveness; to live with and love her husband without reservation. She was an amazing woman. We were so very blessed to have her in our lives.

After the initial shock wore off, his sisters were quick to accept Lily into their world—their family. Joey, however, took longer. It was only when those chains that held his heart in bondage were finally broken that he could clearly see God's hand at work. His hand was extended, drawing Lily and her family into the Agosti clan.

That was the most beautiful of days and none of them had ever looked back with the least bit of regret. Lily was Pops' daughter and now she, as well as Pops' granddaughter, Hope, were part of the Agosti family. Yes, tongues wagged in town, even in church, but they were confident they had done right by her.

Mama had fervently prayed her children would enjoy the blessings that would surely flow from the act of forgiving their dad and accepting Lily. Because of Joey's and his sisters' obedience to the Lord's promptings, the entire family was now experiencing those abundant blessings.

Ellie approached her husband, wrapped her arms around him and nuzzled her cheek against his chest. "It's so good to be here with you. I'm glad I left the office early. So, I'm assuming Ricky and Anthony closed the garage early too?" she asked. "Is business slow?"

"Actually, this month has been slow, but remember, I've had this week blocked off in our appointment book for months," Joe answered. "I told them to knock off early today, if at all possible."

After Pops died, Joey honored his father's longtime wishes and took over the Agosti and Sons Garage. Right from the get-go the business flourished and it wasn't long before he brought on his son, Anthony, also a highly skilled mechanic.

Many residents of Lawrence, Massachusetts, were longtime patrons of the garage; switching their loyalty from Vincent to his son and grandson was an easy transition. The business was thriving; it was apparent that a third set of hands would soon be needed.

Ricky, although not a blood relative, became like a son to Joey. Initially he hung around the garage because of his friendship with Mia, but then Lily's daughter, Hope, caught his eye and the guy was hopelessly lovesick. Just before he and Hope married, Joe brought him on board as well. With three skilled mechanics, the Agosti and Sons Garage was doing exceptionally well.

"See, he's not such a hard taskmaster," Angie sauntered back into the kitchen. "I always knew you were a good guy," she chuckled, punching his shoulder.

"Hey, that hurt!" he moaned, rubbing his shoulder. "Remember, we all agreed it was important to take this time together; I'm glad we have."

"That it is, dear brother, that it is," Trina patted his back.

"They're here, guys!" Vinnie yelled from the parlor. "They're here!" he excitedly shouted again.

"Okay, okay, we hear you; the whole Atlantic coastline hears you," his mother chided.

Comically, as though on command, they all traipsed to the door, eager to help Lily, Hope and their husbands. Unfortunately, the doorway wasn't wide enough to allow the excited family to push through at the same time. Each politely made way for the other, but each desperately wanted to be first to greet their adopted family.

"Welcome!" Trina drew Lily into a warm embrace.

Vinnie gave Ricky an exaggerated high five, "I couldn't wait for you to get here. You didn't forget we're going to play football, right?"

"How could I forget, buddy? And that's not all we're going to do; it's going to be a fun week." Ricky lifted Vinnie up then promptly wrestled him down to the ground.

"Joe, your directions were perfect," Lily said. "Whoa, this place is awesome," warmly embracing her half-brother. "Wow, look at all that gingerbread trim. Beautiful, but I wouldn't want to paint it," she remarked.

Joey laughed. "You're here to enjoy the beach, not paint the house."

"Thanks for including us." Gino slapped Joey on the back.

"Hey, we're family. How could we not?"

"And look at you, Hope. You've got a new hairstyle—I love it. It really accentuates those beautiful green eyes of yours," Mia said. Hope responded by spinning around several times attempting to imitate a runway model.

"Come on, everyone! Grab a suitcase, a pillow, something, anything! Let's get these nice folks into vacation mode," Joe yelled.

"Bring everything into the playhouse," Trina clarified.

"Playhouse? There's a playhouse here?" Hope questioned.

"Yup, and it is absolutely adorable. Wait 'til you see it. You four are staying there; you're going to fall in love with it," Angie assured them.

Together, they turned toward the garden pathway leading to the playhouse. Lily's head shot up. "Look, Gino, the playhouse is almost an exact replica of the full-sized Victorian."

"Yeah, I'm thinking the original owners were pretty wealthy," Sal interjected.

"I doubt the playhouse was built the same year as the main house," Ellie was studying the structure. "Take a look at the gingerbread trim, it's slightly different. My guess is that it was custom made at a later date."

"You have a sharp eye, sweetie," Joey hoisted a couple of large suitcases.

"Here, let me help you," Trina said. "I'll carry a pillow," she offered.

"Gee thanks! You're so helpful; I'm completely underwhelmed." Laughing at that playful exchange, they continued their walk to the playhouse.

"Wow, this playhouse is something else! It couldn't be nicer," Hope said. Look, Mom, it has a teeny kitchen and even teenier bathroom. This is so cute!"

"Sure is, and I'm not wasting one minute. Let's unpack and start this vacation," Lily declared.

"Hey, Aunt Trina, I see the meat and the buns, but I'm not seeing any dessert," Kevin whined. "Vacation is not the time for dieting," he admonished.

"Ha, like this family could go one day without sweets!" she fired back.

"So, what's for dessert?" he pressed.

"Oh, Kevin, it won't kill you to do without dessert." Cindy gave her husband a sideways hug.

"Huh, says you. Man cannot live by bread alone," he moaned. "It says that in the Bible."

"I'll have you know, I spent yesterday afternoon making a huge batch of your grandma's scrumptious angeletti cookies. I could hardly keep Vinnie's hands off them," Trina said with a wide smile.

"Oh man, I love those cookies," Joey piped up.

"Thanks, Aunt Trina. Actually, we all love them. So, where did you hide them?" Kevin asked.

"Oh no you don't, they are staying well hidden until dinner."

"Humph! By the way, what time is the rest of the gang arriving?" he asked, while opening and closing kitchen cupboards in search of the delectably light, lemony cookies.

"Ricky just said that when he was gathering up his tools, he noticed Anthony was already locking up the garage, so they shouldn't be too much longer," Ellie informed them. "I know that Anthony and Kerri packed their car last night so they could just head out. Sammy wanted to drive his own car; who knows when he'll get here?"

"He told me he was bringing something from Piro's Bakery, because after all, we need more dessert," Trina chuckled.

"What a good man!" Kevin exclaimed. "You can never have enough dessert."

The Agosti family happily slipped into vacation mode while waiting for the last three members to arrive. Whether lounging in the cool of the front porch or on the hot, white beach sand—it was all good. Vinnie was wired! He was intent on burying Leah in the sand, but that girl was just too quick for him. His attempts usually backfired, ending with her roughly carrying him to the surf, again threatening to toss him, which she never did.

"Here, let me help you with that," Jake said to his daughter-in-law as she struggled down the porch steps. "These contraptions are beyond me, but I suspect every grandpa should know how to set up a portable playpen," he weakly admitted. "I guess I need a refresher course."

"You'll get the hang of it after one or two times." Cindy encouraged him. "Emma doesn't like being penned in, but she needs a safe place. Otherwise, I'll spend the entire week pulling fistful of beach sand out of her mouth. Let's put in right here in the shade," she suggested.

Emma played contentedly for quite a while. Watching the movement of the surf, the diving seagulls and the antics of her crazy family prompted an occasional belly laugh. It wasn't long before she began rubbing her nose with her favorite blanket, signaling naptime.

"Look, Mom," Cindy pointed to her daughter. "Watching all of this activity is lulling her to sleep. I may actually get some free time to relax and enjoy this week."

"Well, honey, you certainly have lots of eager hands to help you," Angie commented from her lounge chair on the porch. "So take advantage of that time while you have—"

"Hi ya, guys." Anthony greeted them as he came from the side of the house. "Kerri and I have arrived and Sammy is right behind us."

"Yess!" shouted Kevin from the screen door. "Hold on, I'm coming around to help you guys."

"Hi, sweetie," Ellie hugged her son and daughter-in-law. "I'm so glad you closed the shop early. You need the break."

"Hi, Mom! He sure does," Kerri agreed.

"Okay, now there's the man I've been waiting for," Kevin declared. Sammy wasn't far behind his brother and he was carrying his promised bakery boxes.

"Man, is dessert all you ever think about?" Sammy laughed, shoving the boxes into his cousin's hands.

"It's not *all* I think about, but it's right up there in the top ten," Kevin admitted.

"Wow, this place is beautiful. I expected something more—earthy," Kerri took in the picture-perfect Victorian home.

"Me too," Anthony added. "This place is quite the find!"

"We're not so small in numbers anymore, so locating this place had to be God's provision for our growing family," Joey said. "Come on, you guys, I'll give you a tour and then show you to your bedroom. So, Trina, where did you say they are sleeping?"

"Anthony and Kerri are taking the pull-out queen-size bed in the sunroom. Sammy, you have the overstuffed pull-out club chair in the office," Trina added.

"These owners knew how to utilize every nook and cranny." Sammy's eyes were moving from one detail of the vintage home, to the next. "Impressive!"

"For sure! As an engineer, I bet you can see all kinds of other possibilities for this house," Sal remarked. "Wait until you see what they did with the playhouse."

With that, the final tour of the day ended with the playhouse. The family could not have been more pleased with Joey and Ellie's efforts to find this rental property.

"This kitchen is wonderful," Angie remarked while helping Trina fix dinner. "It's bright and cheerful; I love this huge work space. If we ever remodel our kitchen, something like this would be on the top of my wish list."

"It certainly accommodates all these bodies milling around," Trina snorted. "I used to call our family a mob, now it really *is* a mob—but not *that* kind of mob," she smiled.

"I got ya! With a couple of married kids and the addition of our precious Emma, we are truly being blessed."

"Honey, this pot of pulled pork will be heated through in about five minutes," Sal yelled from his post at the grill.

"Okay, we're good in here too."

"Do you guys need any help?" Mia asked.

"Sure, honey, would you please finish setting the tables? We'll just use those paper plates for tonight."

"Leah, would you mind cutting those crusty rolls? Then, we're just about ready." Trina walked to the front hall closet and exclaimed, "Hey, what happened to my angelettis?"

"Ha, you really didn't think I wouldn't find them, did you?" Kevin teased as he jogged through the kitchen, stuffing one of Trina's prized cookies into his mouth.

"I don't know how your husband stays so trim," Trina said to Cindy as she threw a wet dishcloth at the back of Kevin's head.

"Hey, you're messing up my perfectly styled hair."

"Ellie, would you please yell out to the playhouse and tell them dinner is ready."

Before she even walked to the door, "I smell food! When do we eat?" Ricky smiled, leading the playhouse guests into the kitchen.

"All right, all right, you maniacs, dinner is served; simple as it may be," Trina announced.

In typical Agosti fashion, everyone stampeded to his or her chair, but quickly quieted down, and waited for the blessing.

Joe stood, just as Pops had done at so many family dinners. He was fully aware of the respect this family had for him as the Agosti patriarch. He became uncharacteristically serious, immediately capturing each person's attention. "I can't tell you how happy I am that we could spend vacation together; hopefully, it will become an annual event. I am honored to ask for the blessing on this food and this beautiful place that God has provided." Joey and each person bowed their heads.

When Joey concluded his prayer of thanksgiving, a symphony of blended *amens* filled the dining room, including one from sweet little Emma, prompting affirming smiles from her adoring family.

A marvelous ebb and flow of conversation, laughter and teasing, continued throughout the meal. Trina cherished each and every family gathering; nothing gave her greater happiness than basking in the warmth of her family.

Later, Ellie brought the bakery boxes to the table, while Angie poured coffee. Kevin reluctantly relinquished his control of the angelettis. To his credit, only one was missing.

"Sammy, thanks for picking up these cannolis," Ellie opened the boxes."Oh wow, we've hit the jackpot, guys. He brought cheese, chocolate *and* vanilla cannolis. Heaven, I'm in heaven!"

All eyes went to Emma as she stretched out from her booster seat until she reached a chocolate-filled cannoli. Quick as can be, she snatched it and shoved it into her mouth in one smooth move. "Now there's a girl who knows exactly what she wants." Angie laughed.

Vinnie was giggling and pointing at Emma's chocolate-covered face when Anthony interrupted the sweet scene. "Mom, there's still something in the oven that you should probably grab."

"What? The baked beans were the only thing in the oven, Anthony, and they're out," Ellie answered distractedly.

"No, Mom, we know for sure—there is something in the oven," this time from Kerri.

Ellie looked rather annoyed, but put down her angeletti and went to the oven. "Humph, there's only a bun in the oven."

Most everyone immediately caught it; laughing hysterically, followed by hugs for Kerri and Anthony.

"What?" Ellie said, looking befuddled.

"Oh, Ellie, don't you know what they're trying to tell us? We're going to be a grandpa and a grandma," Joey said excitedly. With tears in his eyes, he pulled his wife into a big bear hug. "I'm going to be a grandpa?"

"I'm going to be a grandma?" Ellie stood, dazed, with the bun in her hand—wearing a silly grin. "Hallelujah! I'm going to be a grandma!" Ellie finally shouted at the realization of what just happened.

"Well, it's about time!" Angie added.

Chapter 2

"Mom, can I have the car keys?" Mia asked. "I promised Vinnie I'd take him to the boardwalk at Salisbury Beach; I've already cleared it with Aunt Trina."

"Sure, honey, they're in the candy dish on the buffet table. Just you two going?"

"No, Leah and Sammy want to ride along."

"Vinnie, make sure you stay with your cousins. Don't even think about running off on your own. Got it?" Trina sternly instructed.

"Aw, Mom, I'm six years old."

"Exactly my point," Trina responded, pulling him into a deep hug.

"Not to worry, Aunt Trina, I'll keep him on a tight leash," Sammy yanked Vinnie into a playful headlock.

"Have fun you guys and please be home before dinner," Angie yelled after them.

Although the family loved spending the week at Hampton Beach, Salisbury Beach continued to hold so many precious memories, so the cousins couldn't resist taking the short drive along the coast to their old stomping grounds.

"Hey, Kerri, come here," Kevin yelled toward the parlor where she and Anthony were completely engrossed in a book listing every imaginable baby name, along with its meaning.

"What's up?" she sauntered into the sunroom.

"Well, Emma has a full diaper and I thought you'd want to get started—you know practice for the real event."

"*No way*, but thanks for the offer," Kerri shot back with a playful jab to Kevin's ribs.

"Can't blame a guy for trying," he shrugged.

"So, do you already have names picked out?" Joey asked, joining them in the sunroom.

"Naw, we're still tossing a bunch around. We have lots of time. She's not due until March, so we'll have the entire winter to zero in on the perfect one."

Lily and Hope walked up the path from the playhouse and tapped on the screen door. "Hi all, anyone up for walk on the beach? Hope and I desperately need some exercise; all this vacationing won't do my waistline any good. We have dinner duty tonight, so we obviously won't be gone too long."

"Sure, I'm game!" Angie said.

"By the way, what is for dinner?" Anthony questioned.

"We're fixing chicken parmesan, baked rigatoni and tossed salad," Lily answered. "When Hope and I went for a drive yesterday, we found this great little Italian market in Newburyport. I went back this morning and picked up some nice, fresh scala bread. Gino's mom taught me how to make so many Italian dishes, so I'm hoping my chicken parmesan measures up to your grandma's."

"I'm sure it will be delish!" Ellie reassured.

"But, what's for dessert?" Kevin asked as he shoved a breadstick into his mouth.

"Mom, didn't I tell you he'd ask that?" Hope laughed.

"Well, it's the most important part of the meal," Kevin soberly stated.

"Don't worry, Kevin. I could never forget dessert. My Gino also has an enormous sweet tooth. So, I picked up a beautiful ricotta cheese cake and a hazelnut torte. How does that sound?"

"Lily, *you* are my hero!" Kevin bowed before her.

"Yeah right, until the next person promises to stuff your face," Kerri joked. "And, yes, I'd love a walk. Give me a second to grab my sunglasses."

"Don't you overdo it, sweetie," Anthony tenderly touched his wife's tummy.

"I'm fine, exercise is good for me."

"Have a nice stroll, girls. Sal and I had plenty of exercise this morning; walking on the beach sure gave my legs a good workout. I'm just going to settle myself on the porch with Buddy for a while," Trina added as she walked toward the screen door, book in hand.

The blue of the sky and the distant ocean appeared to blend into one humongous seascape. The waves were relentless, pounding the shoreline as they walked along the hot sand. Seaweed was scattered just beyond reach of the waves, as though daring those waves to pull it all back into the ocean.

"So, how are you feeling, Kerri?" Hope asked. "You look terrific, radiant actually."

"Thanks! I feel great, but Anthony treats me like I have some debilitating disease or like I'm going to break."

"He'll relax after a while. Just enjoy the pampering because it won't last long. Once the baby comes, you'll wish you had two minutes to yourself. Have you been to the doctor yet?" Lily asked.

"Yup, last week and everything is fine. He said I'm a healthy twenty-eight-year-old with no medical red flags that he could find."

"Awesome!" Lily said. "I can't wait to see whose genes will win out for this little one—Anthony's coal-black eyes and hair, or your fair complexion and lush blond hair, not to mention your blue eyes."

"Your child will be beautiful—guaranteed," Angie meandered, picking up seashells as she walked a little ahead of them.

"Thanks, we're just praying for a healthy baby!"

"What are you going to do about work? Being on your feet all day will certainly be a challenge," Hope asked. "And will you go back to work after your maternity leave is over?"

"Anthony and I just talked about that. The hair salon is already short-staffed, but I'm not sure I should worry about that. I'm just an employee. I'll put in as many hours as possible, until it becomes a strain, then I'll give my two-week notice. I am sort of concerned, though, about the effects of the hair coloring chemicals I handle every day."

"I can imagine," Hope added. "Why don't you ask one of your coworkers to take those customers?"

"I could, but that's a large percentage of my clientele. For now, I'm just planning to enjoy a nice, restful vacation; I have lots of time to decide about work. But I am in desperate need of help with decorating the baby's room."

"Oh, me, me, me!" Hope excitedly responded. "I'd love to help you with that."

"We all will," Lily added, throwing her arm around Kerri's shoulder. "This is so exciting—another baby in the family!"

"Mama and Daddy would be over the moon with excitement." Angie added.

"Can we play Skee Ball?" Vinnie pleaded, tugging on Mia's tee shirt. "Oh wait, let's get some cotton candy first," he continued, almost hyperventilating.

"Chill out, Vinnie! You're making me crazy," Mia said. "Look, we have a couple of hours, so let's decide what you *really* want to do. What is most important to you? We may not get back here this week."

"Aw, really? Well, then I want to do everything!"

"Yeah, right," Leah ruffled his hair. "Remember we have to be back to the beach house for dinner."

"How about we play Skee Ball for half an hour, then we walk around the boardwalk for a while and *then* get something to eat?" Sammy suggested.

"Sounds like a plan," Leah agreed.

"Okay, let's go, let's go." Vinnie jumped on Sammy's back.

"Whoa, kid! How much sugar have you already consumed this morning?" He wrestled his nephew off his back.

Mia, Vinnie and Sammy briskly walked together in the general direction of the Skee Ball Arcade. Leah, however, uncapped her camera and followed at a slower pace, taking in the sights and sounds of the well-known *center* of Salisbury Beach. To her, every image was potentially an awesome photo, a memory preserved.

Leah had the summer free after completion of her freshman year, however, she couldn't constrain herself from getting very involved in a campus photography club. It was exclusively for enrolled students, but there would be no grading or exams. She did, however, sign up for *the one* assignment that was offered, but not required. She was a perfectionist and obsessed with sharpening her camera skills. The assignment was a simple one, as well as a fun one—a summer collage. Leah probably would have assembled a summer album on her own, but she thrived on competition and the first prize made her salivate. The winner, chosen by the students themselves, would receive a new Nikon camera, loaded with all the bells and whistles that her old camera sorely lacked. This week could provide her with the icing on the proverbial cake.

Leah found herself standing at the far end of the arcade, fascinated by the sight of dozens of weather-worn, upright piers that were some-how—beautiful. *I wonder how long those gigantic piers have supported this old structure.*

Instinctively, she raised her camera and the "click, click, click" of its shutter began. Leah snapped dozens of photos, one after another and from every possible angle—of those *beautiful,* old wooden piers. She was confident these snapshots, printed in black and white, would provide a unique grouping and enhance her summer album. She had the unique artistic ability to see the finished product, before ever raising the camera to her eye.

"The kid did all right for himself," Sammy said to his cousins. Turning to Vinnie, "Maybe you'll be a famous baseball pitcher some day."

"I loved throwing the ball through that teeny hole, but I think I liked Skee Ball better. Can we come back tomorrow?" Vinnie teased.

"I told you, I have no clue what's on the family agenda for tomorrow. Let's just wait and see," Mia responded.

"Aw, come on. I want to come back."

"Don't be a nag! Did it ever occur to you that something even more fun might be on tomorrow's agenda?" Leah asked.

The expression on his face revealed that he hadn't thought that was even possible. He absolutely loved the arcades.

Mia grabbed Vinnie's collar. "Do you want cotton candy or not?" she asked, pulling him toward the food kiosks. "What color do you want?"

"Blue, no pink, no blue. Yes, blue!" he yelled as they approached the cotton candy booth.

"Sheesh! One blue cotton candy, please," Mia, distractedly handed her money over the counter. The clerk made change, never taking his eyes off Mia.

"Here you go," he said to Vinnie, handing over the treat. "And here's your change," he looked directly at Mia. "Hey, don't I know you?" came from the very handsome guy, who appeared to be close to Mia's age.

"Thank . . . uhm . . . I'm not sure," Mia stuttered, suddenly catching a better glimpse of this guy who was smiling at her. "I think you look familiar. No, I know you look familiar."

They stood silently, staring at one another until Mia had to look away, feeling herself beginning to blush.

"Do you work in Boston?" He leaned forward over the counter, waiting for her to respond.

"Yup, I'm a computer programmer."

"That's it! I see you on the train coming home. Hi, my name is Matt Bertolino," he extended his sticky hand to Mia, then quickly wiped it with a dishcloth. He extended it once again.

"Hi, I'm Mia. Mia Trayor. So, do you work in Boston too?"

"Aha, I'm a financial planner. I've been taking that train ride every weekday for the last few years," he said with an easy smile. His wavy black hair fell over his forehead and his stubbled chin gave him a rugged, outdoorsy look.

Mia could still feel the heat in her cheeks and just thinking about it made her blush even more; she couldn't control it. She found herself glancing at his hand for a wedding ring and when she saw none, she coyly smiled. Matt's warm, dark eyes seemed to bore a hole into her, yet she couldn't turn away. *Holy moly, those eyelashes are sooo long—beautiful!*

"So, what are you doing here, selling cotton candy?" she asked, hoping to divert his attention away from her glowing face.

"I'm helping my grandpa out while we're here on vacation. He's owned a cottage and this little business for years. Is that your boyfriend over there?"

"What? No, that's my cousin, Sammy. My whole family is on vacation this week, but we're staying at Hampton Beach," she responded, hoping her pink cheeks were less—pink. *Oh, why did I tell him all of that? Like he cares!*

"Really? That's great! Would you like to get together while you're here? I'm not an axe-murderer or anything; I'm actually a very nice guy—at least that's what my mom tells me," he smiled again, flashing perfectly white teeth and those killer eyelashes.

"Ah, ah—sure," she replied, completely unnerved.

"Awesome! How about I drive over tomorrow night? Maybe we can take a walk on the beach or grab some clam chowder or just build a bonfire and hang out."

"Sounds like fun. Let me write down the address for you," Mia replied, riffling through her purse for a scrap of paper and pen.

"Does seven o'clock work for you?"

"Sure does. See you around seven," Mia called back over her shoulder, walking to the group, keenly aware Matt was watching her.

Leah and Sammy had their heads together when Mia approached them, no doubt trying to guess why Mia was taking so long.

"I love this stuff," Vinnie pinched off piece after piece of his sticky treat, totally oblivious to his cousins' conversation.

"Okay, give it up! What was that all about?" Leah pressed.

"Shh, he'll hear you," Mia hissed, attempting to move the group toward their car, while wiping her sticky hands.

"I was just about to come over and rescue you, but you didn't look like you wanted to be rescued," Sammy needled.

"Quit it, you two. His name is Matt and he rides the train home from Boston every day; we sort of recognized each other—and we have a date tomorrow night."

"Oh, here we go again!" Leah loudly exclaimed. "I hope he's got thick skin and can handle the way you catch and release."

"That's not fair. I just haven't found anyone I like well enough to, you know, keep dating."

"We're just teasing ya. Let's head back to the house; I need some *real* food," Sammy laughed, pulling Mia into a sideways hug.

Chapter 3

"Oh my, Kerri that is *one bad* sunburn," Ellie said to her daughter-in-law, wincing sympathetically.

"Tell me about it. I sure didn't plan to fall asleep in the blazing sun, but I obviously did."

"You'd better get something on your back and shoulders or it's going to blister; it might anyhow."

Leah approached them. "I'm heading to the store, I'd be happy to pick up some ointment for you?"

"Really?"

"Sure. Mom's on kitchen duty tonight and she needs fresh fruit and some veggies."

"Leah, that would be great. Let me give you some cash," Kerri glanced around, looking for her purse.

"Nope, I've got it. You can pay Mom later if you want; I'm spending her money."

"That's very generous of you," Kerri snorted as Leah headed toward the door.

"Why are you bringing your camera? Are you planning to do a veggie shoot in the produce department?" Angie teased, dangling the car keys.

"Hey, great idea, Mom!" she responded. "Actually, there's an awesome seawall near the Italian market. I'm thinking a few angle shots would compliment my black-and-white collage. It's chipped, weatherworn and just about the right height that I'm looking for."

"I have to hand it to you, Leah, you have a keen, artistic eye."

"Thanks, Mom. So, fruit, veggies, some kind of dessert. Anything else?"

"I think that's it, honey."

"Okay, I'm off. See you later, and I won't forget the ointment."

Leah loved to travel the coastline; she was tempted to put her foot to the floor and drive to Kennebunkport, Maine. Maybe she'd run into one of those famous politicians who summered there. *Ah well, I guess that will have to wait for another day. I'd better get those shots first, then head over to the market.*

Leah was familiar with the area; she'd spent many lazy summer days here with her friends and family. She loved the salty breeze on her face, the warm sand between her toes and the breathtaking panoramic views.

She decided to park her car and walk along the seawall until she found the perfect section for her project. It wasn't a long walk, but she had foolishly tossed her sandals in the car, leaving her feet to the mercy of the hot sand. *Not smart, Leah. Not smart at all.*

After deciding on exactly the right section of seawall, and not wanting to stand in the hot sand any longer than necessary, she uncapped her camera and immediately began shooting. It didn't take long for her to capture several great angle shots; the sun shone perfectly on the wall.

Ouch, ouch, ouch! Time to take a break and chill down my burning feet.

After indulging herself in a refreshing splash in the icy cold water, she returned her attention to the seawall. Leah felt confident that three or four of those shots would fit perfectly into her collage. In her mind's eye, she could already imagine her completed project. *Well, time to wrap this up and go shopping.*

Like a kid, Leah spontaneously hopped up on the seawall and began her balancing act, walking back to her car. *Yikes, this wall isn't any cooler on my feet, and, and . . .* In the blink of an eye, she lost her balance and toppled off the seawall, landing hard on the sand. "Oh no, my camera, ouch, my ankle," she whimpered as she grabbed her ankle.

She noticed movement on the other side of her car—a jogger running toward her.

"Hey, are you okay?" came from a young man, who was quickly approaching her.

"I'm . . . I'm not sure. My ankle, oh no, it's swelling."

"Let me take a look. I was watching you, I mean . . . you took a nasty tumble. Yup, swelling fast. If you can stand, I'll help you get it into the water. I think the ocean is cold enough to slow the swelling."

"I'll try, but is my camera okay?"

"It appears to be okay; let's set it over here and get you into the water," he said, yanking off his sneakers.

"Ow, ouch, ow, ow," Leah flinched as he helped her to an upright position.

"Now, don't go passing out on me."

"I'm okay. I need a little more support on this side, please."

They hobbled to the surf and stood there together, for a long time, all the while Leah keeping an eye on her camera at the seawall. It seemed odd to her. Although this young man she leaned so heavily upon was a complete stranger, she felt as though he was an old friend.

Looking down at her with cool blue eyes, he asked, "So, *Madame gymnast*, what's your name?"

"Leah, my name is Leah, and I'm obviously not much of a gymnast. What's your name, kind sir?" she jokingly asked as she looked up, up and further up. *How tall is this dude anyhow?*

"Leah, that's a nice old-fashioned biblical name. I like it! My name is Luke Henderson."

"Huh! *Et tu* have a biblical name, well, the Luke part is biblical," she felt a slight blush rising.

"Ha, I guess we're a blend of Old and New Testament, huh? So, were you taking pictures of the ocean, before your fall from the high wire?"

"No, no, I was shooting the seawall; it's beautiful, don't you think?"

"Ah, I guess, if you say so. Honestly, I'm not much for the arts; I don't think I have an artistic bone in my body. Sorry!"

"Don't be sorry. So, what kind of bones *do you* have? I mean, what do you like to do?" instantly hoping Luke had missed her foolish question.

"Let's see, I obviously love jogging and I may be in the minority here, but I love numbers, finance, stuff like that."

Hmm, finance. So, this guy is not only gorgeous, but smart, too.

"I'm a junior at Boston University in the Business Administration program, with a concentration in finance," he added.

"No way!" Leah exclaimed, just as a series of large waves crashed against them, almost knocking them into the surf.

"Whoa, hold on girl," he laughed.

Steadying herself in his strong grip, she continued, "I'm going into my sophomore year at B.U. and as you might guess, photojournalism is my course of study."

"Really? Well, it's a huge campus, so no surprise that we've never bumped into each other. If we had, I would definitely have remembered you," he brushed his sun-bleached hair aside and warmly smiled at her.

Leah was not a shy girl, by any stretch of the imagination, but something about this guy flustered her, just a wee bit. He was soft-spoken and yet he possessed a certain strength.

"We should probably wrap that ankle, so it doesn't swell once we're out of the water."

"My car is right over there. I'm pretty sure my mom keeps a first-aid kit in the trunk."

"Do you think you can make it to the car?"

"It's not throbbing as much, I think I can."

"Okay, here we go," he supported her as they walked.

After retrieving her camera and his sneakers, they found a makeshift wrap in the glove compartment, then sat enjoying the air-conditioned car.

"How about I drive you home, wherever that is?"

"I'm here on vacation with my family until Saturday, but I have to pick up a few things at the store before heading back to the house."

"I'll take you to the store, then drive you home. What do you say?"

"Are ya kidding? You *must* have something better to do than grocery shop with a gimpy girl."

"Oh, but you're not just *any* girl?"

"All right! You *do* have a driver's license, I assume."

"Of course and I don't have a single moving violation. Feel better?"

Luke was even more helpful than she'd expected; helping her maneuver the store in a motorized shopping cart made their stop so much easier. With only a few items to pick up, they were done and back in the car in less than thirty minutes.

"So, where to, Leah?" he asked, jangling the keys as he helped her into the car.

She wasn't even halfway through giving him directions, when suddenly he cocked his head slightly to one side. "Oh, you mean the old *Sea Mist Bed and Breakfast*? I know exactly where it is."

"Huh, when was it a bed and breakfast?"

"It was very popular at one time; booked a solid seven months out of the year for, I'd guess about twelve years. The owners retired several years ago and sold it to the present owners. They're an older couple with several adult children. It's unfortunate that the kids and grandkids live on the west coast; they rarely visit."

"How do you know so much about it?"

"I live next door," he softly answered with an engaging smile.

"What?"

"It's our summer home. Actually, my grandparents bought it when they were newly married, so my dad spent his summer vacations there. Then, after grandpa died, we inherited it."

"So how often are you here?"

"As often as possible; I love the place. We live in Andover the rest of the year."

"How is it possible that you've been next door for the past few days and I never saw you? I mean—not that I was looking for you—I would have noticed you."

"Well, Leah, we'll have to remedy that situation, immediately. What are you doing tonight?"

Hearing the crunch of tires in the driveway, Mia and her mother looked up at exactly the same time. Suddenly they lost all interest in the magazines they'd been absorbed in just seconds ago.

"Who is that driving your car," Mia asked, tossing her magazine aside and moving to the porch railing. "Whoa, he's cute!"

"Cute? Why is he driving your sister in *my* car?"

"Let's find out," Mia was already walking down the porch stairs toward the car.

Luke was helping Leah out of the car when Angie and Mia approached. "Hey, what happened to you? Are you limping?" Angie asked.

"Yeah, stupid me, I fell off the seawall. But Luke, oh this is Luke; this is my mom and sister, Mia. Anyhow, he was jogging by and rescued me. He took me shopping and drove me home."

"Well, thank you, Luke, for being there, even though I always tell my girls not to talk to strangers," Angie reproved.

"He's not a stranger, Mom, he lives next door."

"No kidding. What a happy coincidence," Mia teased.

"Well, I was glad to be of assistance. So, Leah, what time tonight?"

"How about seven?"

"You're getting together tonight? What do you say we double date? Matt is coming by again tonight; let's do something together," Mia suggested.

Leah and Luke exchanged glances and nodded. "Sure, sounds like a plan," Leah enthusiastically answered.

Chapter 4

Jake and Angie walked along the beach, each lost in their own thoughts. The steady, but gentle breeze lulled them into a peaceful, quiet place in their spirits. Without speaking a single word, they communicated volumes to one another. Jake hadn't been convinced that a week at the beach would work out very well for him. He wanted—no, he needed—a time of solitude and although he loved his crazy in-law family, he wasn't sure he'd find the rest he needed during this vacation. He was happy to admit, that he had been dead wrong. They were halfway through their week and he already felt refreshed.

Taking Angie's hand, he drew it to his lips and gently kissed her fingertips. "Sweetheart, I'm so glad we came; it's been much more than I'd hoped for."

Angie stopped, faced her husband and gently cupped his cheeks. She searched his face, "I'm so happy you're enjoying it, you look a teeny bit more rested. I was beginning to worry about you."

"Worry—why?"

"If I remember correctly, it was only a couple of weeks ago that I told you that you looked pale? And you've been a bit lethargic, don't you agree?"

"No, sweetie, you told me I looked *pukey*."

"I didn't say that, did I?"

Jake loved his wife's personality. "I guess you're right. I *have* felt a bit off my game this summer and I'm not sure why. But I need to get back to my old self, coaching is right around the corner."

"Do you think it's wise to continue coaching? It's such a rigorous schedule on top of your teaching responsibilities."

Wrapping his arms around his wife, Jake softly whispered, "I'm fine—and I can still keep up with you." Unexpectedly, he dragged her into knee-deep water then ran for his life. Angie was a *forgive and forget, but get even first* kind of gal. Predictably, she was off like a shot, chasing him down the beach with a vengeance. She caught him all right, jumping on his back and dragging him down into the wet sand. They crouched together in the sand, laughing and taunting one another.

When finally their little escapade ceased, Angie, huffing and puffing, said, "So what do you think of your little girls meeting these two young men this week? They both seem like nice guys."

"They do, but it's way too early for me to judge. Of course, my primary concern is whether or not they're Christians. Let's wait and see. We don't know if either of our girls will continue to see them once we've returned home."

"True, especially Mia, our oh-so-fickle one. She may toss him away in a week or so—along with all the others."

"So, is this Luke guy from *the Henderson family?* You know the one. They're continually splashed all over the society page, not to mention dominating the business section."

"I'm familiar with them; I taught a couple of the children before they transferred to private schools. The family is heavily involved in the arts and finance, and I believe the oldest brother was instrumental in renovating one of the old textile mills into business offices and posh apartments."

"Posh, huh? Well, I guess we'll find out sooner or later." Brushing off the sand, "Come on, let's head back to the house." They started walking hand-in-hand, but looked back over their shoulders in time to catch squawking seagulls, swooping and diving for their dinner. It was a sight that held them totally spellbound.

Joey was again gripped with a wave of nostalgia as he grabbed his Bible and settled himself on the porch glider; it had swept over him numerous times during the past few days. He was enjoying this vacation, but kept drifting back to his childhood and those carefree days. Not that he wasn't happy, he couldn't feel more blessed. But there was something indefinable about this week's vacation, something that kept him on his knees. He wondered if being together in these close quarters had birthed a fresh concern for each of them? He was acutely aware that they looked to him as the head of this family and Joey being Joey, couldn't help but take that seriously. *God, help me to guard this family, to watch over them and never shirk that responsibility or take it lightly. I want You to be glorified by how I live my life—make me safe to follow, as I follow You.*

"Hey, Uncle Joe, let's toss the pigskin for a while before dinner," Kevin yelled from the beach. "I need to work up an appetite."

"Now that is the funniest thing I've heard all week," Joe responded, already moving toward his nephew. "Sure, I'm up for it, but when do you ever have to work up an appetite; you're a bottomless pit."

One by one, the guys found their way to the sandy beach and the good-natured game of flag football that followed. The girls watched from the porch, cheering them on and sometimes laughing at their horseplay.

One particular maneuver caused Trina, Angie, and Hope to cover their eyes simultaneously; Sammy and Anthony collided—hard; they shook it off and jumped right back into the game.

"Ugh, my knees will never be the same," Jake muttered after his marathon run along the beach. The younger men mocked him, each pretending to hobble on canes.

"Yeah, go ahead and laugh, but your day will come—smart guys!" Jake huffed and puffed, while gripping his knees. Then, "I'm done!" he exhaled deeply and surrendered to the cold surf.

"Okay, let's quit, I'm getting hungry," Sammy said.

Hope took the hint, and retreated to the kitchen; it was her turn to fix dinner. Angie lingered at the porch railing, staring at her husband.

"Hey, what's up?" Trina nudged her sister. "Why the big scowl?"

"Huh? Oh, I was just watching Jake. Does he look a bit pale to you? I mean the guy just ran around like a wide receiver and yet he looks pale instead of flushed; he's not been himself lately."

Carefully studying her brother-in-law, "I think you're right, Ang. He does look a bit peaked or maybe even gray. Maybe he's coming down with a cold or he might be anemic. When was the last time he had a checkup?"

"I don't think it was all that long ago, but he's definitely going when we get back home."

"What are you trying to do?" Ellie asked as she rushed to Anthony who was struggling to carry a huge armful to the beach. "Let me help you."

"It's all light stuff, Mom. How much can a bag of marshmallows weigh?"

"Cute, but you're carrying a lot more than one bag of marshmallows. Have you invited every Hampton Beach resident to our bonfire?"

"Nah, but have you noticed how ravenous this crew can be? I'm not even sure I bought enough hot dogs or hamburgers to fill up their bellies. It's scary, watching them pack away tons of s'mores!"

"Oh, stop. I'm certain there will be plenty and when it's gone, then they stop eating. Right?"

"I guess you're right. I thought a dinner bonfire would make it easier for Kerri's turn in the kitchen. She's so tired these days."

"Well, we all think this was a great idea and it's looking like a perfect night. I've put out some cheese and crackers to hold everyone until we can get the bonfire going."

"Thanks, Mom. I figured we could cook all the meat, then wait a while for the s'mores."

"I can't believe we only have tomorrow night before rejoining civilization. Ugh!"

"I know, but it's been a great week and it's not over yet, so let's get the rest of the stuff down to the beach." Ellie grabbed a few more bags. "Oh, by the way, Luke and Matt are coming tonight."

"Oh great, now I'm sure there won't be enough food."

Cindy kept the baby far away from the smoky pit; everyone else seemed impervious to the swirling smoke. Anthony and his dad worked feverishly to keep a steady flow of cooked burgers and hot dogs, making sure every mouth was well fed. It was no easy task; most everyone had worked up a good appetite playing volleyball all afternoon. Still, Joe was better than most short-order cooks. He was a pro, turning, flipping and moving the meat around on their improvised grill until—perfection.

Every so often, the sea breeze would lift a handful of paper plates and float them across the beach. Vinnie was a spectacle, erratically running in circles attempting to catch them, giggling in his determination not to lose one single plate.

"Hey, Luke, if those are your folks sitting there on the porch, please tell them they're welcome to join our beach party," Joe flipped yet another burger.

"It is, but I seriously doubt they'd join us," he sheepishly responded. "But thanks for the invitation."

"Oh?"

"Dad really doesn't like the sand. I know, I know, it's weird; they have a place right on the beach—with lots of sand."

"That is definitely odd, but to each his own."

"Dad's a strange bird. He's most comfortable in a suit and tie."

"Now, *that is strange.* I personally hate wearing neckties, but love my greasy old coveralls," Joey snickered, shoving a hot dog in Luke's direction.

"Oh, no more for me. I was just about to find Leah, but thanks."

Joe watched Luke as he walked barefoot in the sand toward his niece. Lowering his head, he mumbled, *no sand . . . suit and tie . . . you have to be kidding.*

"Leah, I'm stuffed. I could use some exercise. Would you like to go for walk along the beach? I need to make room for those s'mores." Luke rubbed his belly in a circular motion.

"Sure!"

"Would you like to swing by our cottage to meet my parents on the way back?" he asked.

"I would, but just for the record *that* is not a cottage. That, kind sir, is a gorgeous beach house."

"Yeah, I know. Is it too much, over the top?" he asked as he took her hand.

"I'm just busting you. It's a beautiful home. So, it's hard to believe this week is coming to a grand finale. Soon we'll be back on campus."

"True. Do you think, I wonder if . . . "

"Ah, you do realize that I don't bite. Just spit it out."

Running his hands through his sandy blond hair, he blurted, "Right! I was wondering if we could still see other when we're back at school?"

"Luke, I'd love that."

They walked together gathering seashells and trading stories about their experiences and friends at B.U. until Luke stopped, looked up at his beach house and said, "Well, we're here. Just so you know, my mom is terrific; you'll like her and she's going to love you."

"What about your dad? Is he terrific too?"

"Dad is—different."

"That sounds ominous. Here goes nothing," Leah joked, pulling her long hair into a ponytail and marched toward the house.

"So, where is this happy foursome off to tonight?" Trina asked while washing the dinner dishes.

"Just wondering the same thing," Angie added. "You guys were certainly welcome to join us for dinner."

"We know. Thanks, Mom, but we're trying to decide between a nice dinner or the concert. We wanted to make our last night here—special," Mia glanced at Matt for affirmation.

"Well, personally, I think it's a no-brainer," Luke confidently interjected. "Do we all like the Dave Matthews Band? Because that's our only choice at the Casino Ballroom. If not, then I can suggest an amazing seafood restaurant."

"What are the odds we'd ever get to see Dave Matthews again? I cast my vote for the concert," Leah firmly stated.

"Me too," added Mia as she high-fived her sister.

"I'm in," Matt agreed.

"Awesome! If we're all in agreement, I'm going next door to call for tickets," Luke responded.

"Is there a chance we won't be able to get tickets this late?"

"No worries, I'll get us tickets. Be right back."

"He's pretty confident," Mia said to her sister. "How can he be so sure?"

"I guess his father has some connection to the concert hall; pretty sweet, huh?" Leah winked as she popped a handful of cashews into her mouth. "Let's wait for him on the front porch."

⁓

"Humph, I guess Luke *is* one of those well-known Hendersons," Angie whispered to Trina.

"Huh? What are you talking about?"

"Come on, you must know about *the* Henderson dynasty? That family has their hands into everything in Lawrence, Lowell, Andover and pretty much the whole Merrimack Valley. Jake and I were wondering if Luke was connected to that family. Guess so!"

"Oh yeah, The Henderson Foundation assisted with grants to benefit projects my coworkers were working on. I don't remember what it entailed, but somehow the social workers in my company magically got whatever they wanted."

As Angie began stacking dishes into the cupboards, she heard the two couples on the front porch enthusiastically cheering. "Ha, from the sound of that, I guess *they* all got what they wanted too. Poof—tickets!" Angie laughed.

"So, I'm assuming you were able to get those concert tickets?" Trina inquired, pushing open the porch door.

"Yes, ma'am! They're being held for us at the box office." Luke puffed out his chest just a tiny bit.

"Wow, that was a stroke of good luck at this late hour."

"Not really. My mom is a board member of a couple of local theatres."

"Really? And we are oh so happy that she is," sang Leah.

"Where is everybody?" Angie asked as she picked up a magazine and plopped onto a porch chair next to her siblings.

"Sammy and Vinnie are tossing the ball around back. Kevin and Cindy are settling Emma down for the night and Anthony and Kerri are walking on the beach. And of course the foursome are at the concert," Trina recited. "I think the rest of the gang went back to the playhouse to start packing."

"Well, girls, I think this has been a successful test of how much we like each other." Joey folded his hands behind his head and leaned back on the porch chair. "Yup, nineteen people, two bathrooms and we're still talking to each other. Remarkable!"

"It's been more than successful; it's been a blast," Angie said. "The memories we've made here this week will bless our kids for years to come."

"I think I've gained five pounds, but it's been totally worth it. What do you say we just go ahead and book it for next year?"

"Like now?"

"Well, as soon as possible. You know it will get snapped up; these houses rent quickly."

"I may be daydreaming here, but wouldn't it be nice to own a family summer home? Not one of us lives more than forty minutes away, so the entire family could enjoy it throughout the year," Ellie chimed in from her place on the porch steps.

"Really? I mean really? That would be awesome! But can we afford it and its maintenance?" Trina asked, sitting up straighter and leaning in toward her brother.

"I dunno, let's get some expert advice from our resident financial guru," Joey said. "Hey, Sal, come out here for a second; you too, Jake."

The guys pushed through the screen door and were met with three Cheshire-cat grins. "I'm not sure I want to know the answer to this question, but, what's up?" Sal warily asked.

"No, no, relax, nothing to be afraid of, but we had a terrific idea and wondered if you could lend your financial expertise."

For the next forty-five minutes the three couples offered educated guesses on what the house would sell for in the current market. They tossed around ideas on how to make the purchase financially equitable for each family member. Then they drilled down and seriously discussed practical ways to handle the purchase and the maintenance of this dream house. The final verdict was that they could well afford it and its upkeep, provided the purchase price was within their mutually agreed upon number.

"What if the owner doesn't want to sell?" Ellie asked.

"Then we rent it every year until . . . until we wear them down," Joey replied. "And then I make them an offer they can't refuse," in his best imitation of Don Corleone. Laughter erupted and fresh excitement was in the air.

"This may be even more exciting than the last Patriots *Super Bowl* win," Sal said.

Joey and Jake looked at each other and together responded, "Naw!"

"Nothing could top that! That win over the Eagles was sweet, I mean, just plain sweet," Jake emphasized. "Do you think they can do it again?"

"Absolutely, I wouldn't be surprised to see Brady lead them in a couple more wins," Sal said.

"But guys, I've got to tell you, that Patriots victory parade in Boston was one for the books. The crowds were electric; can you believe three Super Bowls wins? There are no fans quite like New England fans. Am I right, guys?" Joey asked.

***

"Well, tonight has been a perfect ending to a perfect week," Trina smiled. "And again, we need to thank you and Ellie for your hard work. We appreciate that you both took the time to find us this jewel."

"You don't have to thank us. I'm just happy it turned out so—"

Screech! Screech!

"Oh, dear God, what was that?" Trina yelled. Bolting out of her chair, she raced around the side of the house.

"Vinnie, Vinnie!" Sal frantically yelled, running toward the stomach-dropping sound.

Trina was the first to reach her son, pulling him into a fierce embrace; he was sobbing uncontrollably. She couldn't believe her eyes, there was her Buddy, lying in the sand—bloodied and lifeless. "Oh no, Buddy!" she screamed and she began to weep, dreadful sobs. Trina cradled his head on her lap and whispered, "Buddy, Buddy . . . " but she knew he was gone.

Chapter 5

Hope called through the screen door, "Hi, Trina, can I come in? I thought you could use some cheering up so I've brought your Mama's secret weapon—biscotti."

"Oh, Hope, you're a sweetie. Come on in, I'll put on some tea. I'm so glad you stopped by. These look delicious and you're right; the house is so quiet without Buddy, especially with Vinnie now off to school. It's just that I had him since he was a pup and you know how he shadowed me and Vinnie. I miss him so much, but Vinnie is beyond devastated."

"I can imagine."

"Getting him up and off to school has been a daily battle and it's already been three weeks since Buddy died. Sal and I think he's blaming himself."

"Well, that's another reason why I stopped by. It wasn't his fault, it wasn't Sammy's fault; the truck driver told me that it was brake failure, just like he claimed that day."

"What? How do you know?"

"We visited him. It's been killing me to see Vinnie so joyless. For whatever reason, Ricky got the guy's telephone number right after the accident, so we decided to follow up. We didn't blame or accuse the poor guy, we just wanted more details."

"And?"

"Let me just tell you that that trucker is also bummed out; he feels horrible about it. But here's the deal, I think you can honestly tell Vinnie that Buddy was a hero. The guy told us he saw Sammy and Vinnie tossing the football when he was coming around the turn; they were pretty far away from the road, but he soon became aware that his brakes were failing. That must have been when we heard a horn blasting—remember?"

"Yes, I do remember, followed by that horrific screeching sound."

"But here's the thing, he distinctly remembers Buddy running toward Vinnie and forcefully jumping against him. Trina, he was trying to get his best pal out of the truck's path. And he did it; he saved your son."

"Oh, Buddy," Trina whispered almost inaudibly.

"Apparently, right after the incident, the company's mechanic went over it with a fine-tooth comb and discovered intermittent brake failure. The truck has since been fitted with an entirely new brake system—whatever that entails. I guess in all the confusion and emotion, we never gave him any contact information; maybe he would have called us sooner."

"I always knew he was the best dog ever and in light of what you just told me, I'm not only grateful for the eleven years of enjoyment he gave us, but now . . . now I'm so thankful that he saved our son. Thanks for taking the time to talk to that driver. Thank you," she whispered with a husky voice.

"Hey, I have an idea! Why not have a family ceremony to honor Buddy. I'm sure one of us could create a certificate of valor and also find some kind of medal; we could present Vinnie with Buddy's medal. I'll bet that would really perk him up. What do ya think?"

"Oh, that's a terrific idea. It would be so much more meaningful than just me or Sal telling him. Let's do it!"

"Great! I will handle everything. You won't have to do a single thing. Pass me a biscotto, please," Hope proudly smiled.

The train sped along the track as Mia, halfheartedly, flipped through a ladies magazine. She was considering a shorter hairstyle, but which one? *Ooh, I like this new cut on Meg Ryan. I haven't had short hair since I was eleven. Hmm, but this one might be too radical a change.* She caught something from the corner of her eye and looked up to find Matt looking down at her with that irresistible smile.

"Hi, Mia, I guess we both got stuck working late, huh? What are you looking at?" He dropped heavily into the seat next to her.

"Hi yourself, I was hoping to see you. Oh, just thinking about cutting my hair."

"Oh no! Please don't. I love your hair," he tenderly leaned over and nuzzled his face into her thick, black hair. "It is so beautiful, shiny, and—it smells so good," he grinned.

"I'm just thinking about it. So, why are you late?" she closed the magazine.

"Monthly client meeting, nothing exciting. How about you?"

"My team had to test our newest beta rollout; the program isn't scheduled to go live for quite a while, but the testing has begun."

"Are you doing anything tonight?"

"I'm getting together with my sister. She wants my opinion on her summer collage, like I know anything about photography. I think Luke is coming, want to join us?"

"Well, I was going to ask if you'd like to go to the movies, but maybe we can do both? What time is your thing with Leah?"

"I think she said around seven-thirty. So, what movie?"

"How about *Miss Congeniality* at the nine o'clock showing?"

"I love Sandra Bullock and I haven't seen it yet. Is it okay with you if I invite them to join us?"

"Sure is. And, your hair is perfect just the way it is," he winked and sniffed her hair again.

Leah stood back, then circled around like a cat stalking its prey. She stepped side to side, studying her black-and-white collage from every possible angle. She liked what she and her camera had produced. The collage made a strong statement; it appeared to be well-balanced and was definitely well thought out. The final submission day was Monday, just three days away, but Leah was a perfectionist and would take every available minute; she wanted to be absolutely sure that her final project met her own high standards. *I probably don't have a chance of winning, but that grand prize makes me drool. Oh, what I could do with that Nikon.*

"Leah, Luke is here," Jake yelled from the foyer.

Within seconds, he ambled into the living room, flashing that smile she'd grown to love. "Hey, looks like you've made good progress," he nudged her shoulder.

"I have, but close your eyes—don't look yet. I want you to get the full effect."

"What? Okay," he covered his eyes. "Whatever you say."

"Now back up and stand still for just a second."

With his eyes covered, he spoke in a stage whisper, "You do remember that I have no artistic bones, don't you?"

"Shush, just wait one more second."

Leah looked around, trying to decide on the best place to display her collage; she wanted to create an art-gallery first impression for her prized work. "Hmm, not there, not here either. Yes, perfect! Okay, open your eyes," she commanded.

Luke didn't have to fake it or let her down gently. He was totally and completely impressed with the collage displayed on the mantel. "Whoa, and I mean whoa! Holy cow, Leah, you are *really* talented."

"Really? You like it?" she asked, wringing her hands.

"It is perfect, absolutely perfect. I've been in a lot of galleries because of my mom's involvement and I'm betting your collage is right up there with those pros."

"Do you think I honestly have a shot at winning?"

"You have my vote," he smiled broadly.

"Thanks, you're the first one to see it, but Matt should be here—" Just then, they heard the front doorbell, followed by the sound of Mia sprinting down the stairs.

Leah hurried to the doorway, blocking Matt and Mia from entering the living room. "Wait, guys, hold on a second. Cover your eyes, I'll guide you into the living room."

"What? Why?" her sister protested.

"Just do it! I want you both to see my collage at the same time and give me an honest critique, okay?"

"Okay, okay," Mia impatiently responded, but complied.

"I love the intrigue," Matt teased as he stumbled into the living room.

"Hey, bro," Luke yelled from the other side of the room.

"Hey!"

"Okay, now stand right there and when I tell you to uncover your eyes, look at my collage—it's displayed on the mantel. Got it?"

"Yup," they said in unison.

"Now!" Leah almost shouted.

They were both silent, but began walking in the direction of the fireplace. Still silent.

"Well? What do you guys think?" Leah nervously asked.

"You did this?" Matt asked.

"Aha! It's going to be my entry into B.U.'s summer school photography contest."

"It's awesome, really. I'm impressed," Matt studied the piece with genuine interest.

Turning to her sister, "Mia, what do you think?"

"Leah, I am speechless."

"Now there is a rare phenomenon—Mia without words," Angie remarked as she joined them. Then her eyes locked on the collage. "Wow, honey, your project turned out so well."

Mia gave her sister a fist bump, "I'm proud of you, kid."

Leah let out a long, slow sigh as she smiled at the black-and-white collage displayed before them. "So, is the frame okay? Should I put it into a brushed silver frame? Do you really think I should submit it?"

"Leah, it's perfect just the way it is—go for it," Angie reassured her youngest daughter. "Perfect!"

Chapter 6

Despite working long shifts at the hospital, Hope was determined to pull this ceremony together for Vinnie's sake. She further complicated her life by hosting dinner for the entire family at her home, which previously was Mama and Daddy's old homestead. Her plan was to follow dinner with the surprise ceremony. At first Ricky thought it was kind of sappy, but soon warmed up to the idea when he realized just how devastated the little guy was, moping around the house and even crying at bedtime.

Vinnie was the kind of kid everyone enjoyed having around. His energy was endless and his corny jokes kept the entire family in stitches. They would bend over backwards for him.

"So, did you invite the two new guys?" Ricky asked his wife.

"Sure, the more the merrier. Luke and Matt seem to fit right in with this whacky bunch. Besides, Mom's not working so she offered to help me. I just hadn't planned on giving Lawrence General so much overtime this week, but I shouldn't complain. The extra cash is nice and I really do love my job."

"And you are such a good nurse," he planted a kiss on her cheek. "Just let me know how I can help, I gotta run. Joey asked me to open the shop and, of course, today's scheduled repairs are heavier than normal. I hope he's not too late."

"Did he say why he's going to be late; that's not like him."

"The beach house just went on the market; He and Anthony are meeting with the Realtor. Joe wants to bring the newest beach house information to dinner, since we're all going to be here."

"Oh, this is getting exciting, imagine our own beach house. See you later, sweetie," she yelled as he rushed out the door. She was already dressed and ready for work, but figured she had a couple of minutes to squeeze in a quick phone call.

"Hey, Mom, I can only talk for a few minutes, but I wanted to get your opinion on my menu for Saturday's dinner."

"Sure, filet mignon and lobster tails, right?" Lily joked.

"Yeah, right! Actually, it's going to be easier than that, and a whole lot cheaper."

"I was just teasing."

"I got that, Mom. But let me just tell you, it's a really scary deal to prepare a meal for all you experienced cooks."

"Aw, come on, honey, you are an excellent cook."

"Well, I *have* made this awesome chicken risotto dish for Rick several times and he loved it so I figured it might be a safe choice. Of course, I will have to make several batches for this crowd, but I can grill the chicken ahead of time and then all I have to do is prepare the risotto. Ricky will pick up some fresh Italian bread to round it out. For dessert, I've decided to make those ricotta cookies; remember, they were such a big hit last Christmas. So, what do you think?"

"It all sounds delicious. Great choices."

"Oh, I forgot, Trina is making an antipasto and both Ellie and Angie are bringing appetizers. Appetizers always help to slow those guys up a bit, if that's even possible."

"Perfect, how about if I bring some gelato to compliment the cookies?"

"Now that does sound perfect. Thanks, Mom! I've got to get going, I'm working overtime again tonight. Love you."

Hope's thoughts drifted, *Perfect, yeah perfect. Oh brother, how do I get myself into these things? Who am I kidding? Wasn't the risotto gummy the last time I made it? Me—cooking for the Agosti family? Really? Well, if disaster strikes, Napoli's Pizzeria is only a phone call away.*

Joe and his son left the Realtor's office and walked together to the car. It was a beautiful day and they both had a spring in their step. "Well, Anthony, what do you think?" Joe asked as he fanned the stack of papers. "The price is right, which makes me think the seller is motivated to move quickly on this."

"I don't want to go out on a limb, and I sure don't want to speak for anyone else, but Dad, I personally feel confident that our family can easily swing it, provided there is no radical change in the future that will affect our total income."

"My thoughts, exactly. So, we'll explain everything to the family and see where the conversation leads. Mom and I don't want Aunt Trina's or Aunt Angie's families to feel any pressure. And since Lily and Hope already decided not to join us, that means the six of us will be carrying the lion's share of financial responsibility."

"Yup, I agree, but the rest of us can certainly share the maintenance and upkeep costs. You're smart to clearly spell out all these details. And if someone can't pitch in, I don't think that should exclude them from time at the beach house. Do you agree?"

"I sure do. So, we'll lay it out and stress that fact; I don't want any hard feelings. Family is family, regardless of their ability to share any of these costs."

"Agreed."

"Okay, we'd better get to the shop, we're already an hour late. Ricky's probably got his hands full."

"Yeah, hopefully with a wrench," he quipped.

"What do you say we make a quick stop at Mann's Bakery for some of those orange cappuccino muffins he likes? That should appease him," Joey chuckled as he pulled into the main flow of traffic.

"Always works for me."

"No, Matt, I'm telling you, you don't need to bring a thing," Mia spoke into the phone. "You don't understand, wherever and whenever we get together, there is food, mountains of food, all kinds of food."

"I get it, I get it, I just don't feel right coming empty-handed, especially on my first family visit."

"Well, you're not going to be empty-handed! You'll have my hand in yours," she teased. "But I would like to get there a bit early to lend my other hand to Hope. Can you pick me up by five-thirty?"

"Yup and you're sure I can't bring—"

"Matt, nothing, absolutely nothing," she cut him off.

"Sal, I'm so concerned about Vinnie. Yesterday was the second day he came home from school crying. He didn't want to talk about it, but I'm almost certain that he's being bullied," Trina said.

"Bullied? About what?"

"Believe me, some bullies don't need a reason; they often target younger or smaller kids."

"Maybe we should set up a meeting with his teacher next week, what do you think?"

"I have no problem with that, his teacher is terrific. Let's see how he reacts to Hope's ceremony. I just pray it doesn't backfire and make him feel worse."

"Oh, I doubt it will make things worse, but I was kicking around an entirely different idea. Now this is just an idea."

"What? I'm guessing this is going to be a life-changing idea," she smiled.

"Tell me you haven't had the same idea?"

"You say it first."

"No, you say it."

"Now we're acting like five-year-olds."

"A puppy," he whispered so softly she could barely hear him.

"Yes! A puppy!" she shouted and then roughly hugged him.

"Hold on, Trina. It may be a bit too soon for the little guy. We don't want him to get the idea that Buddy can be replaced. Let's just take this slow, agreed?"

"Okay, I really do agree. But, Sal, a puppy would be so much fun—and extra work."

"Honey, calm down. They are not going to disown you if your risotto isn't perfect. Just relax and enjoy the day."

"I know, I know, Ricky, but they are all up there in a class with *Chef Giada De Laurentiis*—and me, I'm more of a Mickey D's kind of foodie."

"You are not! I love your cooking and especially your baked junk."

"Junk!"

"No, no, I mean baked *stuff*," he quickly pulled her into a calming hug. "Sweetheart, just be yourself and do your best. They are family; they're our loving, accepting family. Got it?"

"Okay, I'm sorry and I'm being totally irrational, huh? I love you and thanks for picking up the scala bread. Now, would you mind slicing it and covering it with plastic wrap so I can keep going on my risotto?"

The sound of the doorbell just about sent Hope through the ceiling. *Oh my gosh! They're starting to arrive already!* Taking a quick look around her kitchen, she murmured a quick prayer and started toward the front door. *This is going to be fine, just fine. Anyhow, it's all for Vinnie.*

"Oh man, does it ever smell good in here," Matt said as he and Mia entered the kitchen.

"Thanks, Matt," Hope suddenly felt a surge of confidence.

"Mom wanted me to bring her appetizers ahead of time so we'd have time to bake them here. Is that okay?"

"Oh yum, sausage-stuffed mushrooms. Your mom is a regular *Giada*, isn't she, Ricky?" Hope suddenly turned pale and again felt totally inadequate.

"Nah, they couldn't be easier. A five-year-old can make them. Can I preheat your oven?"

"Help yourself."

"Oh, risotto, now there is a *Giada* kind of dish. It looks wonderful and I'm sneaking a taste."

Before Hope had a chance to stop her, Mia scooped a spoonful and loudly exclaimed, "Mmm, delish!"

"Really?"

"Yes, really, *Giada*," Ricky winked at his wife.

Finally, Hope felt her shoulders relax; she just might enjoy this party after all.

"Knock, knock, can we come in? Hi, guys. You all remember Luke Henderson, don't you?" Leah came into the room with Luke two steps behind her.

"Of course, come on in. Welcome to our home, Luke."

"Thanks. Can I—can we—help you?" he asked.

"Sure, would you two mind setting the tables? Everything is on the buffet."

"You got it," Leah playfully dragged Luke into the dining room.

"And what have we here?" Hope asked Matt as he handed her a familiar box. "Oh, torrone, we love this candy."

"I told him he didn't have to bring anything, but as long as he did—I have dibs on the first piece," Mia snorted.

For the next forty-five minutes, the kitchen door repeatedly swung open and closed, as the family trickled in. The noise level quickly escalated from a low, pleasant murmur to a not-so-pleasant roar that was comparable to the sound of a Blue Angels flyover. Hugging, teasing and loud conversations filled the old homestead. Everyone was talking at once, making it virtually impossible to follow any one conversation before yet another topic of conversation nudged out the previous.

Rick and Hope Brando were thrilled at the opportunity to live in her grandfather Vincent's cozy Cape Cod-style home. Although Hope had never met Maria Agosti, she shared her love of gardening. Many of Maria's days were spent in the backyard, which she lovingly called her garden of hope. After both grandparents passed away, the entire family believed it was God's desire for Hope and her new husband to live there. She loved the house, but her real passion was obviously for the garden; the garden of hope was just as beautiful and lush now as it had been under Mama's skilled hand.

Trina found herself wandering around the old homestead, realizing there was something different. "Hey, Hope, you've made some changes. I love your new curtains. They pick up the colors in your sofa and club chair perfectly. Did you recover the window seat?"

"I did."

"It looks awesome. You have a real eye for decorating."

"To be honest, I was worried you guys might be offended that I changed some things."

"What? Never! It's your house, yours and Ricky's. Make it your own, however you'd like."

"Thanks, Trina. That's a relief, because I have some ideas for the master bedroom."

"Have at it, girl, and I'd be glad to help if you need it."

Vinnie was still a bit sullen, but playing with his cousin, Emma, seemed to perk him up. "Vinnie, you're very good with her; she likes you," Kevin playfully chucked Vinnie under his chin.

"Thanks, I like her too and she smiles at me."

"Why wouldn't she smile at you? You're a handsome dude?"

"Well, not everyone thinks . . . some kids . . . never mind," he abruptly stopped, went out to the garden and sat on the ground alone.

"Aunt Trina, what's up with Vinnie?" Kevin said. "He just took another nosedive."

"Yeah, I overhead. At first we thought it was just the loss of Buddy, but now Sal and I think he may be dealing with bullying at school, on top of his grief."

"Man, that stinks. I'm telling you, Aunt Trina, I've recently seen statistics that there is a significant spike in serious bullying cases. I'm not talking tiny infractions, I'm talking serious physical injuries and even one death."

"Really? That is so sad and frightening."

"Most of them never get into the courtroom, but still it's not to be taken lightly."

"Oh, we aren't taking it lightly, Kevin. We were already planning to set up a meeting with his teacher next week if these emotional red flags persist."

Kevin had almost always known he was destined for the courtroom. He was only twenty-six years old, and he was already regarded as a promising lawyer—one to watch. Naturally, Angie and Jake were very proud of him, but he flinched whenever they introduced him as "my-son-Kevin-the-lawyer." It was embarrassing, but he loved them both so he did his best to make light of it. He did have to admit that he was equally as proud of Emma. *Look at that kid, already playing peekaboo and blowing kisses—genius. Yes, she's headed for the courtroom or maybe even the bench,* he mused to himself.

"So, Leah, when are you going to hear on that art contest you entered?" Sammy asked.

"Oh, Sammy, I don't think I have a chance in a million of winning, but it was a good summer project and I don't regret doing it. Anyhow, the name of the winner will be posted on Monday."

"Do you want me to go with you on Monday?" Luke asked as he shoved one of Ellie's bruschetta in his mouth.

"You'd do that?"

"Sure, what time should I meet you?" He grabbed another bruschetta from the tray. "Wow, these are terrific," he said with a juicy grin.

"You're too funny. How about we meet at ten, if you're free then?"

"Works for me."

Leah wouldn't admit it, but this contest was making her as nervous as a cat on a raft. She certainly was not counting on winning, but she could not stop thinking about that awesome camera. She was grateful for Luke's sensitivity to the emotional roller coaster she was riding and that he was considerate enough to make the time to be with her to ease her pain when her name didn't appear on the announcement board. She liked that about him.

This particular family gathering was a carbon copy of so many past get-togethers—perpetual motion, nonstop talking and gregarious laughter—and food, lots of Italian food. The hallmark of the Agosti family never changed; they were truly interested in one another, protective of one another and deeply committed to one another. The spiritual lessons they had learned following Mama's and Pops' deaths, served to only knit them more tightly together.

A high-pitched whistle suddenly pierced through the din. Every voice was instantly silenced by Ricky's ear-piercing attention-getter. "Hey, guys, dinner is ready, but first we want to thank you for coming and for bringing such great food—"

"Yeah, yeah, yeah," Kevin interrupted with a taunting smile. "Let's eat!"

"Sheesh! Cindy, I think your hubby has a tapeworm. Okay, okay, I can take a hint, let's eat. Joey, would you say the blessing?" Ricky asked.

"I'd be honored."

Joey, not only prayed a blessing over the food, but more importantly over this precious group. Later, he couldn't take his eyes off them as they moved through the makeshift buffet table, laden with scrumptious foods. He couldn't help but smile at the heartwarming sight. They were nudging one another, passing Emma around to one another and needling one another, all the while incessantly chattering until each reached the end of the buffet table. This was family, and family was everything to him. He was abundantly blessed!

"Wow, this risotto is amazing! Is it Mama's recipe?" Angie asked as she shoveled another spoonful into her mouth.

"You got that right!" Sal added. "You deserve a standing ovation."

"Oh stop it," Hope weakly protested. "You guys are just being nice."

"Uh uh, it is to die for," Trina added. "I know excellent risotto when I taste it—this is excellent and the chicken is grilled to perfection."

Hope outwardly appeared cool, calm and poised, but inside she was jumping up and down—secretly doing the happy dance. She was thrilled that it had gone over so well. *Phew! Thank You, Lord.*

After the dinner dishes had been cleared away, Lily—hoping to draw him in—asked Vinnie to please serve the ricotta cookies while Hope poured coffee. He loved those pastel-colored frosted treats and he'd already devoured a pink one and a mint-green one—when he wasn't being watched. Pink was his favorite. Even though Trina told him they were all the same flavor, he was convinced that the pink ones were the best.

The room suddenly got very quiet and Vinnie looked around, trying to figure out if something had just happened. They were all looking at him, just staring at him with goofy smiles on their pastel-colored lips. "What?" he stammered. "I only had two," he sheepishly confessed. He blushed when they laughed at his admission.

"Vinnie, we have a surprise for you," Hope enthusiastically motioned for him to stand with her in front of the fireplace. The entire family drew close, encircling them, not unlike a flock of sheep witnessing the birth of a lamb.

"Huh? What kind of surprise," he appeared to be rather bewildered.

"Well, we all loved Buddy and all of us miss him, just like you do," Hope said as she gently placed her hand on his shoulder. "But here's the thing, Vinnie—he was a true hero. Remember the day, that awful day, how he jumped on you and pushed you out of the path of that truck. He saved your life because he loved you more than he cared about himself. That is a hero!"

"Yeah, I remember how he jumped really hard at me," he sniffled and wiped his eyes with the back of his arm.

"That's right. He wanted to save your life. Do you understand, Vinnie?"

Now his tears were freely flowing, "Wow, my Buddy saved me?"

"Yes, he sure did, and we have this special certificate that says that."

"A what?"

"A certificate is an important piece of paper that tells everyone that Buddy Lamazo was a hero," which prompted the entire family to hoot and cheer. When they settled back down, Hope continued, "We think that Buddy would want you to have this medal—his medal."

Trina and Sal came forward, just as they'd planned and pinned the medal on Vinnie's shirt. Then each gave him huge hugs.

Vinnie was silent for several minutes, causing Sal to briefly worry if this whole thing was a good idea after all. Then he jumped into his father's arms, "Can I wear this medal to school, Dad?"

"Sure, if you want to."

"I do 'cause Buddy is a hero and I want all the kids to know. Thanks, everyone," he said with a sniffle. And then it happened—his face lit up brighter than a night game at Fenway Park. "Thanks," he whispered again, looking down at the shiny, gold medal on his chest.

Chapter 7

Leah scrambled away from her first class, hoping to grab a strong cup of coffee and a bagel before meeting Luke. With every gurgle and growl from her stomach, she had caught sideways glances from her classmates, but she ignored them, pretending to concentrate on the professor's lecture. She had been too unsettled to eat a single thing before class. She pushed open the heavy door and hurried out into the crisp, September morning. *I can't remember being this nervous about anything. Leah, get hold of yourself.*

Tossing her gum wrapper into a trash bucket, she started jogging, but was quickly stopped by a large hand on her shoulder. "Hey, Leah, are you running to me or away from me?" Luke laughed, making effortless strides to match her jog.

"Oh, Luke, I was just heading over to meet you. Did you go to your eight o'clock class?"

"I did, but I already stopped back at my dorm to dump my books. I don't have another class 'til three. So, are you ready?"

"No, not really. I don't know why I ever entered that contest. It seemed like a good idea at the time, but I don't have a chance to win third place, let alone first place. What was I thinking?"

"Cut it out. You have as good a chance as anyone else. I loved your collage. Come on, let's go," he ordered.

Leah temporarily forgot about the contest as they walked together, totally immersed in their conversation—until they entered the arts building. Her heart began pounding and she felt a rush of blood in her ears. *What was I thinking?*

"Luke, will you do me a huge favor?"

"Sure, anything."

"Just go over and check out the board, I'll wait here."

"Oh no, give me your hand, we'll check it out together. You *do* know that it won't be the end of the world if—"

"I know."

"Take my hand, close your eyes. I'll tell you when to open them."

"I'm being silly, let's get this over with." Leah grabbed his arm, drew herself up to her full height and said, "Lead the way." Luke smiled when he noticed that her eyes were indeed closed.

Leah couldn't believe how disoriented she felt; unintelligible voices and echoing footsteps of both students and professors swirled around her. She wondered if any of them were staring at her childish behavior. Luke turned and studied her face; he thought she was the most beautiful girl in the world and couldn't help but feel proud to have her on his arm.

"Stop," Luke said. "Now, take three steps forward. Stop," he commanded, with both hands on her shoulders. "Open your eyes."

"No, just tell me."

"Open your eyes, Leah," he firmly stated.

It took her a couple of seconds to focus, let alone search for that one posting among all the other sticky notes and more official types of announcements. Then her eyes sharpened and fell on an ivory-colored sheet of paper with her school logo on top. Before she fully took it in, Luke lifted her up and swung her in a circle.

"You won, Leah! You won! I'm so happy for you."

Students were still milling around and now, for sure, were staring at the spectacle before them.

"Luke, I won!"

"Yup, you won! I knew you would."

"I can't believe it," she mumbled. "I'm numb."

Together they read the details, explaining the criteria used by the student judges to distinguish second and third place winners from *the* winner. On the bottom of the sheet, in very small print, she found what she was looking for—the time and location where she would pick up her brand-new Nikon camera.

"Hey, Ellie," Trina spoke into the telephone, while wiping down her countertops. "Are you calling from work?"

"Yes, I am, but your brother wants to nail down a date for the six of us to get together since we really didn't have a lot of time at Buddy's ceremony to talk in-depth. He'd like everyone's thoughts on the beach house—you know, see where we all stand."

"Sure, Sal and I were talking about that this morning over breakfast. We like what he shared last Saturday. It was kind of hard to really discuss anything with all the commotion, so a meeting is a great idea. When are you thinking?"

"I haven't firmed this up with Ange yet, but how about Friday night for dinner?"

"Works for us. Is it okay to bring Vinnie?"

"You don't have to ask, of course it's okay. By the way, how's he doing since last week's ceremony?"

Trina laughed into the receiver, "Well, we were prepared to make a school visit this week, but he's come home every day—happy as a clam. Sal and I are taking him to Findeisen's for ice cream after school today. We thought a trip to his favorite ice cream shop would set the atmosphere for him to talk, hopefully."

"That's a great idea."

"And get this, he's worn that silly medal to school every day. I think Hope's idea was a stroke of genius."

"It was. Hopefully the other kids aren't picking on him."

"So, what can I bring?"

"We're a small group, so how about if I make Mama's scacciata?"

"Oh yum, Sal and I love her scacciata. I'll bring a salad."

"Okay, let's say around six o'clock? I'll give Angie a call when she gets home from school.

"How did Kerri's doctor appointment go? What is her due date?"

"Doc said she's doing good and the baby is growing normally. I'm so excited I can hardly stand myself. Joey warned me to stay out of baby departments. I've already bought a bunch of stuff since we came home from the beach. She's due March twenty-seventh and we cannot wait to be grandparents."

"You are too much, Ellie. Now listen up, we gals are planning to give her a baby shower, so give me a couple of possible dates for late February or early March."

"That's so nice of you guys. I'll have to thank them."

"Well, they don't actually know yet, but they will." Trina laughed. "It will be so much fun! Another nut on the Agosti family tree."

"So, Vinnie, what flavor do you want?" Sal asked at the serving window.

"Uhm, chocolate mint chip, I think. No, wait, peanut butter cup. Wait, no I definitely want chocolate mint chip in a sugar cone." Vinnie smiled at his dad.

"You got it, champ!" He affectionately tousled his son's hair. "Trina, your usual?"

"Yup, a strawberry milk shake. Vinnie, let's grab that picnic table over there. Can you manage our order, Sal?"

"Sure, you guys go ahead and claim your table."

It was a beautiful, unseasonably warm September afternoon, but it wouldn't be long before this and every other ice-cream stand in the area would close for the season. Not many people craved ice cream during the long, snowy New England winters. But for now, they would enjoy their luscious treats.

Hoping to draw out her son, Trina asked, "So, Vinnie, how was school this week?" in the most nonchalant manner she could muster, even purposefully looking away.

"Okay."

"I see you're still wearing that beautiful medal," trying not to put him on the spot.

"Yeah, it makes me think of Buddy."

"I can imagine. I think of him all the time," she said.

"You do?"

"Of course, don't forget he was my buddy for eleven years—even before we had you. He was the best dog," she said, trying to crack open the door for him to talk.

"Yeah, I know." Then he was quiet and walked away from them, still eating his ice-cream cone.

Trina and Sal looked at each other, but let him go. It wasn't long before he did an about-face and walked back to them. "The kids at school know that he was a hero too."

"Do they?"

"After Buddy got hit by that big truck, some kids kept calling me a crybaby; it just made me cry more. Brett even pushed me down on the playground a couple of times."

"Honey, why didn't you tell us about that?"

"Aw, Mom, I'm not a wimp. But then on Monday, I came to school wearing my medal and told everyone that Buddy was like an army dog and that he saved my life."

"Really, what did they say to that?"

"They wanted me to bring in pictures of him and then kept bugging me to let them take turns wearing my medal."

"Wow, that's awesome, sport," Sal said.

"Did you let them wear it?" Trina asked.

"Yeah, I did. Now they don't call me crybaby anymore, but sometimes I still feel like crying."

"I know, honey. Me too. So it was a good week then?"

"Yup, it was a good week. This ice cream is really good. Thanks for bringing me," he said, licking the treat that was dripping all over his wrist.

"Mia, your dad and I are heading to Uncle Joey's tonight for dinner. Can I whip up some dinner for you or are you off with your friends?" Angie asked.

"Have fun, Mom, but I'm going out with Matt tonight. I think we're going to The Loft for a burger. Thanks anyhow."

"Leah hitched a ride home from school with Jenny, but she was right back out the door clutching my car keys. Any idea what your sister is doing tonight?"

"Nope, none, but she mumbled something about taking full advantage of every second of daylight or shadows, or something like that."

"Yeah, she seems to be on a mission with her new camera. I do believe that girl has a bright future in photojournalism."

"I'll say. Her work is fabulous and she is so passionate about it. I can't really say that writing code trips my trigger that much anymore," Mia said rather wistfully.

"Really, I thought you loved being a programmer."

"I did, I do. I guess I'm sort of in a slump right now. The company is great and my coworkers are terrific. It's just that writing this particular type of code has lost its challenge."

"Have you considered checking out greener pastures, new opportunities, new challenges?"

"Actually, I have . . . oh, Leah's home."

"Hey, where has our resident photographer been with that handy dandy new camera?"

"Hi, Mom. I truly do love this camera." She planted a kiss on her new Nikon, turned and stuck her head in the refrigerator. "I'm starving, anything good to eat?"

"Now that's weird!" Mia ribbed. "Who kisses a camera?"

Completely ignoring her sister, Leah plopped herself down at the breakfast bar with an apple in hand. "We have a new assignment, so I've been driving around, trying to decide what to do."

"Decide? What's the assignment?"

"Well, our professor—who by the way is a really awesome guy—gave us one assignment, but three possibilities within that assignment. That's what I love about him. He always encourages individuality; he's not looking for cookie-cutter results."

"So, what are the choices, honey," Angie asked again.

"Well, first of all, you have to understand that this guy is a radical history buff, so naturally that's reflected in his assignments. He hammers on 'our rich history' in practically every class."

"Sounds like an interesting guy and he's right. New England certainly does have a rich history."

"He is interesting, for an older guy. So, we have to compile a portfolio of old churches, old schools, or old textile mills."

"Those are great options. You shouldn't have any trouble finding subjects for any one of those. Are you limited to Boston?"

"Nope, he suggested staying within a thirty-mile radius of B.U., which is perfect because I want to stay local."

"Great, maybe we'll see you more often."

"I'm thinking the mills offer almost endless possibilities. What do you think, Mom?"

"Talk about *rich history*; we have it all right here."

"I remember stuff about the mills from high school, but I need to do research for the paper. Oh, yeah, we have to write a three-page overview of our chosen subject."

"You do realize that at one time Lawrence was a leader in the textile business. All of those mills along the banks of the Merrimack River were operational and thriving businesses," Angie said.

"I find it very sad to see how they've deteriorated over the years," Mia added. "I remember something about a Bread and Flower strike that was a really big deal."

"No, honey, it was called the Bread and Roses Strike," Angie clarified. "And it really was a big deal at the time. The National Guard was even called to the site. I don't remember exactly which mill was the site of the strike, but the guardsmen had their bayonets fixed on the protesters, which included a lot of women who worked in those factories."

"It's kind of an odd name for a strike, isn't it?"

"Well, if memory serves me correctly, it came from a poem that was read and later chanted during the strikes. One of the lines in the poem that impressed many of the female workers went something like, 'they need bread but must have roses too'; that's my paraphrase."

"Wow, good to have a teacher for a mom," Leah laughed. "So, what else do you know about the mills?"

"You really do need to research it, but the textile mills were built in the early 1900s and the Wood Mill alone was the largest mill in the world at the time. And that huge clock tower on the Ayer Mill is the world's largest *mill clock* and the glass faces are only a few inches smaller than Big Ben in London—isn't that something?"

"Get out! Really?"

"Yup, and did you know that Lawrence was a planned city?"

"Look out, now she's on a historic roll," Mia teased.

"What does that mean?" Leah questioned.

"Well, the city didn't just spring up, willy-nilly. Wealthy, influential developers who were smart and forward-thinking, designed it from the city's inception. They had housing built for their mill workers and they even influenced where churches and parks would eventually be built. It's sad to see how Lawrence has declined, but it was very prosperous in its day, along with the Lowell mills. I believe both were modeled after mills in England."

"Well, Mom, you have confirmed my choice. I think I'll focus on the urban redevelopment of those old mills; maybe I can capture some of the old and some of the new."

"Hey, Leah, do you and Luke want to join Matt and me for a burger?"

"This double dating thing is getting to be a habit, but sure, sounds like fun. I'll give Luke a call and, Mom, thanks for the history lesson." Leah planted a kiss on Angie's cheek as she picked up the phone.

Chapter 8

"Whoa, who drives a Lexus?" Matt taunted as he hopped into Luke's silver car.

"What? It's just a car," he responded rather flatly.

"Yeah, just a car, right. What does a machine like this cost?"

"No clue. I just drive it whenever my dad's in a good mood, which isn't very often. He's a workaholic, so I hardly ever see the guy and when I do, his attention is somewhere else, definitely not on me."

"No kidding. What does your dad do, I mean what's his job?"

"That's a bit difficult to answer. Suffice it to say, his greedy little fingers are sunk into everything. But I'd rather not talk about him."

"Okay, man, sorry. So, how's it going with you and Leah?"

"Ah, my favorite topic—Leah. She's the most beautiful girl in the world and—"

"Nope, Mia is and she's not only beautiful, but so intelligent and gentle and those dimples—"

"All right, all right, I get that you're nuts about Mia, so let's just say that we both lucked out at Hampton Beach this summer when met the Trayor sisters. Agreed?"

"Agreed!"

"So, I'm majoring in business, but I'm not sure *exactly* what a financial planner, like yourself, does all day." Luke inquired.

"You're kidding, right? I can tell you that it's definitely not brain surgery." Matt laughed. "If you want the textbook definition, I'd tell you: 'It's long-term profit planning, aimed at generating greater return on assets, growing market shares and solving problems.'"

"Ha, did you memorize that just for me?"

"No, but in plain language, I work with couples and individuals, focusing heavily on retirement. My goal is to ensure my clients will have adequate monthly income for their golden years or rusty years if it doesn't go as planned."

"That sounds like an honorable profession. So, at what age do you suggest someone like me should start all this planning?"

"Luke, as soon as you graduate and are raking in a weekly paycheck, then come see me. The earlier you start, the more successful you'll be in squirreling away enough to live on—when you're no longer pulling down a regular paycheck."

"Sounds like a plan—no pun intended."

They pulled up to the Trayor home and before either walked to the front door, Mia ran out of the house and jumped into the backseat. "Whoa," Matt laughed at her impish grin.

Within seconds Leah pulled the front door closed behind her and yelled to her sister, "Hey, were you born in a barn? Can't you close the stink'n door?"

Luke was already walking toward Leah. "Hey, are you guys okay with each other?"

"Huh, oh sure. This is normal for us; we're always jabbing each other."

"Come on guys," Mia yelled from the backseat. "We're hungry. Let's get this show on the road."

"Sheesh, never get in the way of a hungry Trayor," Matt laughed as he bumped shoulders with his girl.

Luke and Leah were already into a conversation as they backed out of the driveway and headed for The Loft restaurant. "Nice car, Luke. Is it new?"

"Nah, it's Dad's, but I don't get to drive it very often. My sister, the favorite child, gets the honor much more often than I do."

"Well, she works with him and lives local, so I guess that makes sense, don't you think?"

"I guess. But she has a decent car, I'm the poor college boy who drives a clunker."

"Yeah, right! Poor college boy, now that's almost laughable," Matt blurted, whacking the back of Luke's head.

"So, exactly what does Michelle do at your dad's office?"

"She's their financial manager, which is a perfect fit for her since she has an International Business degree from Merrimack College."

"Sounds like a big job."

"It kind of is, but I think she's feeling boxed in, rather unchallenged right now. I think she'd really like to travel. She went through a nasty divorce and it changed her. She keeps alluding to 'seeing the world' and I think she will someday. But Dad holds tight reins on her, like he does on everyone and everything. Well, enough about the Hendersons."

"Right, let's talk about food," Mia interjected. "I'm starving!"

"We know, we get that," Luke laughed as he drove down Union Street, past some of Lawrence's historic textile mills.

"Okay, here's another subject, I have a new assignment in one of my classes and I think it's really, really cool. I will be photographing these mills, well, I'll probably zero in on just one mill. I can't wait to get out there and catch the shadows and angles. Aren't these mills beautiful?"

"Hmm, I don't know if I'd describe a mill as beautiful, but they are definitely *woven* throughout the fabric of our lives—get it? Woven in?" Luke sniggered.

"We get it!"

"Leah, when you get into this project, you might consider meeting with my dad, or at least my sister. I'm positive she'd be willing to give you some background information. One of Dad's construction crews just finished renovating a huge block of one of those mills into really nice offices and very upscale apartments. I toured it last month, very impressive."

"My focus will be on the exterior, but it would be nice to do a walk through. Besides, I'd like to meet your sister," Leah said.

They pulled into a very crowded parking lot and drove around it three times before finding an open spot.

"Like my dad always says, 'crowded parking lots equals great food'," Mia stated.

"Wait 'til you taste these burgers, they are amazing," Matt said.

"Oh yeah, we know," Leah and Mia sang out.

Chapter 9

"Come on in, guys," Ellie yelled to Angie and Jake.

"Wow, smells really good in here," Jake said.

"It's Mama's scacciata recipe and it's almost done. So, Angie, how'd it go with Emma today? I heard you babysat your little angel."

"Aha, I took a personal day and it was so worth it. She is such a love and getting more verbal and demonstrative every day. Jake worked, so I had the little darlin' all to myself. She kept me so busy that I didn't have time to bake, so we stopped at Piro's Bakery." She handed the bakery box to Ellie.

"Ooh, what did you bring?" Joey preemptively yanked the box out of her hand.

"I declare, this family has one giant sweet tooth. It's just a little sampler of Italian cookies—roman tricolored cookies, s-cookies and macaroons. Something for everybody," Angie rubbed her tummy, "Mmm, mmm good!"

"Well, I never met a cookie I didn't like," Joey joked. "I'll have one of each."

"So, where are your girls tonight?" Ellie asked.

"They're still gaga over Luke and Matt, at least for the moment. They're double dating again tonight. I like both boys, they treat the girls well, so I'm not complaining," Angie responded.

"I can't complain either, as long as Leah keeps her focus; she still has lots of school ahead of her," Jake heavily plunked himself into Joey's recliner.

"Oh Jake, your memory is failing you. How long did we go together in college?"

"That's different, we were very mature," he quipped.

"Mature? Me? Right!" Angie crossed her eyes while pushing up her nose, causing the group to laugh at her antics.

Ellie pulled the meat pie out of the oven just as Vinnie banged on the door. "Aunt El, can we come in?" he yelled as he bolted through the kitchen door.

"Sure, come in." Ellie laughed at the little guy. He was definitely back to his old precocious self and they were all thrilled.

"Did you bring your folks or did you drive yourself?" Joey asked as he snatched up his nephew and raised him high over his shoulders.

"Aw, Uncle Joey, I can't drive. The pedals are too far down." He giggled.

"You're kidding! Well, you know I'm a mechanic and I work on cars, so maybe I can fix that for you."

"Nah, it's okay, Uncle Joey. I like when Mommy and Daddy drive me."

"Oh, okay, I get it, bud."

"Hi, guys, sorry we're late. Okay to put the salad right on the table?" Trina asked as she and Sal trailed behind their son. "That kid is always ten steps ahead of us. I guess his old mom and dad are slowing down."

"How's everyone?" Sal asked, exchanging hugs. "Your scacciata looks and smells exactly like Mama's, doesn't it, Trina?"

"She taught us well. Her recipes are among my most prized possessions." Trina moved her salad to make room for the meat pie.

The three men and Vinnie made a beeline for the living room television. Not even the lure of Italian meat pie would coax them away from their beloved Red Sox, at least not just yet.

"Sorry, I totally forgot about the game when I set this up," Ellie confessed.

"Not to worry. We're all Sox fans, so let's watch for a while, then we can eat, okay?"

"Sure, the scacciata is better when it sets up for a few minutes. Let's grab drinks for everyone," Ellie agreed.

This family was hard-core Red Sox fans. As a matter-of-fact, they were fans of every single New England team. There were no more loyal Patriots fans than the Agosti family and they passed that loyalty on to their children. They rarely missed an opportunity to gather together in front of the television or even better, cheer on their teams at Fenway Park or Gillette Stadium.

It didn't take long before all of the adults were totally engrossed in the game, coaching and, cheering from their seats.

"Who's the other team?" Vinnie innocently asked.

"New York."

"New York what?" he asked again.

"New York Yankees!"

"I like their striped suits."

"Aha."

"Who's winning?" came from the little guy, yet again.

"Vinnie, the Sox are winning five to three, and it's the bottom of the eighth. Could you just watch the game—please?" Sal chided.

"Mom, I'm hungry."

"Vinnie . . . "

"Come on, girls, I think that's our cue to get dinner on the table. I guess we'll have to wait a couple of years for his love of baseball to develop."

"Dinner was delicious, honey. Once again, you outdid yourself. Can I help you with coffee and dessert?" Joe asked.

"I'm okay, why don't you grab your paperwork so your sisters can start looking everything over. I'll be right in. On second thought, would you carry that plate of cookies to the table?"

"Sure thing."

"Cookies! Mom, can I have two?"

"Sure, then please take your Legos into the living room so the grownups can talk?"

Joe dropped the stack of papers in the middle of the dining room table. "Have at it, guys," he said.

It was obvious that he'd done his homework on the ocean front property. He'd taken the time to gather every pertinent piece of information he could think of, hoping to answer as many questions as possible.

"So, guys, let me just start by saying this meeting is strictly informational; we don't need to make any decisions. On the other hand, the Realtor said this house could get snapped up fairly quickly. After we review all this stuff and if one of us is not on board, then we table it. Agreed?"

"Well, hold on. What if two of our three families want to move forward?" Sal asked.

"I guess that's fine. I just don't want anyone to feel bulldozed into this purchase. If someone can't or doesn't want to take on an extra financial burden, then please feel free to say so."

After a couple of hours of shuffling papers, posing questions, and calculating the finances, all three couples were in complete agreement to take the next step.

"I think we can well afford this house at the asking price. It's really a steal compared to similar houses in that location. But still, I'd like to offer ten percent less or at least negotiate the inclusion of the furnishings. That alone would save us several thousand dollars, not to mention that all those extra sleeping accommodations are perfect for our tribe," Jake reasoned.

"I believe God wants us to be good stewards of our finances, so what's the harm in offering less and also inquiring about the furnishings?" Trina ventured.

"I agree. What's the worst thing the seller can do? Say no? Take our first born?" Angie laughed, popping a macaroon into her mouth. "This is getting exciting and I love Anthony's idea of our kids helping with upkeep, but we can't assume all the kids are on board with shouldering the responsibility for maintenance."

"True, but when the rubber meets the road, haven't we always stepped up to the plate and helped one another?"

"I think we should run this whole deal by Kevin before we make any formal offer. If he thinks it's *a go* then let's ask him to represent us through closing," Joey offered.

"I'm sure he will. I know they're home tonight, I'm going give him a call right now," Angie was already reaching for the phone.

Chapter 10

"Hey, Kev, very fancy office," Joe said, leading the parade into the office suite. "I'm proud of you, kid."

"Thanks, Uncle Joe. The Wood Mill renovations have been a great boon to Lawrence. One of the rental agencies told me they can't gut and remodel fast enough to keep up with the local demand."

"I just read that in the Tribune. It's nice to see our history being preserved in this way."

"I agree, impressive digs," Trina added as she looked around her nephew's office. Kevin's massive cherry desk was perfectly centered in front of a wall of windows. She took special notice that every window was sparkly clean. *I wish someone would grab a bottle of Windex and go to work on my windows.* The other three walls were just as impressive, showcasing modern artwork by local artists. The carpeting, a rich hunter green, was beyond plush. Trina had an urge to remove her shoes and wiggle her toes in it. "So does all this mean that my nephew, attorney Kevin Trayor, has made it to the big time? We are honored to have you as our family *consigliore*. May I kiss your ring?" She snickered.

"Very funny, and I will be honored to represent my family, if you decide to go forward with this deal."

"Thanks, honey," Angie proudly added.

"Sit down, guys. Okay, I looked everything over and I have to concur. It is a fabulous deal at the asking price. Have you talked to the Realtor since Friday?"

"No, we wanted to get your opinion first," Joey replied.

"Well, if you're all in agreement to move on this, I'd do it today. If this was summer, this property would be gone by now. It's a gem. The taxes are a bit high, but oceanfront property tax is always on the high side."

"Okay, so . . . "

"So, call the Realtor and make your offer; she'll do most of the work, but I'll work with you on the closing," he handed the phone to his uncle.

"Now?"

"Sure, let's get the ball rolling."

Not a sound was heard in Kevin's office for the entire conversation between Joey and the Realtor.

"Well?" Trina asked the second the receiver hit the cradle.

"Well, she's going to present our discounted offer and also ask about the furniture. She'll call us as soon as the seller gets back to her."

"Be prepared for a counteroffer. It's pretty normal. As a matter of fact, it's part of the real estate game," Kevin advised.

"Thanks, kid. We'll get out of your way and make room for all of your paying clients." Joe lightly punched Kevin's arm.

"Wait, didn't I tell you we're running a special. For you guys, it's double the fee," Kevin chortled as he closed his office door behind them.

Mia knew that she was just going through the motions. Her job had become mind-numbing, presenting very few intellectual challenges. She loved writing code, testing it, tweaking it and then basking in satisfaction when it went live without any glitches. But her assignments had become repetitive and boring. Despite her frequent requests for more complex projects, they never materialized. And so she'd begun to put out feelers, networking and submitting her resume when something piqued her interest.

"Hey, honey, how was your day?" Angie asked as Mia walked through the front door.

"Hi, Mom. Same as always. Nothing ever changes in that office. I'm getting a bit discouraged."

"Well, I don't know if this is good or bad, but you just missed a call—a Mr. Gardner? His number is next to the phone."

"Really?" she was already racing toward the phone. "It's from Mr. Gardner?"

"I just said that. So, who is this Mr. Gardner that has put a smile on your otherwise grumpy face?"

"I'm not grumpy! Anyhow, he's the Human Resource Director for a company I've been checking out; they must have received my resume. Do you think it's too late to call him back? Wait, you said he *just* called? I should probably call, right?"

"Holy moly, Mia, just call him." Angie laughed, gently nudging her daughter toward the phone.

Just then the front door opened and Leah made an exceptionally loud entrance. "Hi, guys," she yelled, noisily dropping her book bag on the floor.

"Shh," came from Mia.

"Shh," then came from Angie. "Come here," she whispered.

"What? What is going on? Did someone die?" Leah said with a genuine look of concern.

"No, no, nothing like that," her mom answered in a hushed tone. "Mia is phoning back on a possible job opening."

"Oh! Yeah she was moaning about her boring job the other day. If you ask me, I'd like to have the money she's making on her *boring* job." Leah responded as she peeled a banana.

"Mark my words, someday your bank balance will have a few more zeros at the end. You have great promise, honey. Your work amazes me. So, tell me, how are you doing with your mill project?"

"Great! I feel really good about it; I've already got tons of ideas. I'm planning to spend some time at the Wood Mill this week, whenever I can fit it in."

"You know your brother's firm is in that mill; you should stop in to see him. He might be able to help you on—"

"Mom, Mom, I got an interview! I can't believe it!"

"That's wonderful, Mia, and why can't you believe it? You're an excellent programmer. So, when is this interview?"

"Tuesday, the eighteenth, at one o'clock. I'll work half a day and take the early train. It will be close, but I'll make it."

"Where is the interview?"

"Can you believe it's in the same building as Kevin's firm, except that it's the block that's all the way to the other end of the mill."

"Why don't you have Dad pick you up? You don't want to risk being late for an important interview."

"Hmm, I'm sure I'll have plenty of time, but thanks. I am so excited! He briefly outlined the job description and it does sound challenging, but I think I can handle it."

"It would be nice to eliminate that train commute, especially when you work late," Angie said. "I am thrilled those renovated mills are now serving our community instead of simply deteriorating and giving our city a black eye."

"It's ironic, Leah photographing the mill, Kevin's new office at the same mill and now you interviewing there as well."

"Well, it is a humongous building. Didn't you mention that in its day, it was the largest mill in the world?"

"I did indeed."

"Dad's home!"

"So have you heard anything on the beach house yet?" Leah asked as she watched her dad pull in the driveway and disappear into the garage.

"Actually, the Realtor thinks that we should hear by tomorrow. Uncle Joey gave the guy and his wife an extended response time; the poor guy has been in the hospital for quite a while."

"That was nice of him, but then again, Uncle Joey is a super nice guy."

"We doubt the seller will accept our offer, but we figured it wouldn't hurt to try. None of us want to take unfair advantage of the man, especially since he's dealing with recent medical issues. Apparently the maintenance is falling on his wife's shoulders and they're anxious to get out from under that burden."

"Hi, honey," Angie walked to her husband. "How was your day?"

"It was good. Well, look at this, all my girls are here at the same time! I'm a blessed man," Jake leaned in to kiss Angie on the forehead. "Is there something special going on this weekend or are you just eager to spend time with your dear old dad?" he joked, chucking Leah under her chin.

"We just couldn't stay away, Dad—you're *the man*! Leah guffawed.

"Ha, I know better. You probably both have dates. Am I right?"

"Well, it is Friday night," Mia responded sheepishly.

"I just thought we could all go to Salvatore's Restaurant tonight."

Mia and Leah looked at each other with questioning eyes. "I guess the boys can wait 'til tomorrow night," Leah said.

"Nah, that's okay. Your mother and I will go, we can do it another time. What do you say, Ange?"

"I'd be honored. But, Jake, I think your daughters really would like to come tonight, right girls?"

"Yup, we would."

"Sure would, Dad. It's a date and their food is amazing; I love their eggplant parmesan."

"All right then, it's settled. I'm dining with the three most beautiful girls in New England."

"Dad, that's a bit of a stretch."

"If it's okay with everyone, I'll just go ahead and make a reservation for six-thirty," he said.

He went into the family room and settled in his favorite chair to make the call. Mia hadn't had the opportunity to share her good news, so she followed, sat down across from him to wait. However, he wasn't actually making the call; he seemed to be hesitating. He was looking—strange. "Dad? Dad?"

Angie looked up at the urgency of Mia's cry. She was in front of her husband within seconds. Something was definitely wrong. His eyes seemed droopy; his mouth was moving, but he wasn't making an audible sound. "Jake?"

Suddenly the phone slipped out of his hand, and crashed to the floor. "Dad?" Leah yelled.

"Jake? What's wrong? Jake?"

"Mom, he looks weird. What's happening?"

Chapter 11

Ellie sat on the sofa, hanging onto Joe's every word. She was trying to guess what was being said on the other end of the conversation. They hadn't expected the Realtor to call until tomorrow. She didn't have a clue what was transpiring during this conversation and she sure didn't want to get her hopes too high.

"Well, that's great news. And they're absolutely sure that's all that is important to them? Sentimental, maybe?" Joey pressed.

Ellie's face lit up and she couldn't resist giving her son a silent thumbs up. Sammy smiled at his mom's excitement as they sat, neither uttering a word, waiting for Joe's conversation to end.

"Okay, what's next?" he asked the Realtor. "Wonderful, I'll pass the word along to my sisters and get back to you right away. Thank you."

Joey hung up the phone and gave an unexpected victory shout. "We got it! The guy and his wife just want out. Oddly, their kids want nothing to do with the house; geographically, it's not practical for them. I guess they live on the West Coast and rarely make it back east."

"Dad, that's awesome!"

"What about the furnishings?" Ellie asked.

"They only want to remove a few items, hardly anything at all."

"So, the ball is rolling. I'm going to call the girls."

The girls, that is hysterical! I guess they'll always be his little sisters, Ellie thought.

"Trina and Sal are over the moon; she sounded like a schoolgirl, giggling uncontrollably. She's already planning our first family beach party."

"What did Angie say?"

"No answer. They're probably shopping or out to eat. I'll try to . . . "

The telephone rang and somehow, deep in Joe's gut, he just knew it was a *bad* call. His family had a history of sensing *bad* calls from the everyday *good* calls. Sammy picked up the phone, "Hey, how are you? What? Slow down, hang on, he's right here." Turning to his father, "Dad, quick, grab the phone. Something happened to Uncle Jake. Mia needs you, she's almost hysterical."

"Oh no, a car accident?" Ellie suspected.

"No, I don't think so."

"Hey, honey, what's going on?" Joey listened with great concern.

"Uncle Joe, we're at the hospital, something's wrong with Daddy. We don't know what yet. Uncle Joey, I'm afraid."

"Hang in there, kiddo, we're on our way. Wait, is he at the General?"

"Yes, Lawrence General. He's in the emergency room right now. We just got here. Please hurry."

"On my way, sweetie," he quickly disconnected from their call.

Ellie was on her feet, "What's going on?"

"I'll explain in the car—let's go!" Joe frantically answered. "Hold on, let me call Trina real quick."

"I'll call her. You guys go, Aunt Angie is going to need you. I'll be right behind you," Sammy said.

⁓

The Agosti family was as tightly knit as an old-fashioned sweater. Their lives were woven together, creating a beautiful life pattern. It was often hard to tell where one life started and the other left off, especially in times of family crisis. The emergency wing's waiting room was filling up fast; word went out that one of their own was hurting, that's all any one of them needed to hear.

Joey sat with his arm around Angie's shoulder; Ellie settled on her other side, holding and patting her cold hands. Kevin was pacing the floor, desperate to hear something about his dad. He frequently glanced up at the triage nurse, silently willing her to look up at them; he needed answers. Cindy had enough forethought to toss Emma's stroller into the trunk of their car, which now came in very handy. She walked the short hall, back and forth, attempting to keep her little one as calm as possible; Kevin's mom didn't need the additional stress a fussy baby would add.

Hope was nearing the end of her shift when she got Ricky's call, so immediately after punching out she hurried directly to the E.R. waiting area. "Hi, sweetie. Do you have any news on your dad?" she asked Mia, completely out of breath.

"Nothing we didn't already know. It's been quite a while since our last update?"

"Sometimes these things take much longer than you'd expect, but I'm confident it will be soon."

Vinnie was sprawled on the floor with his coloring book and crayons, the ever-present staples in his travel toy bag. Trina frequently struggled to keep her active six-year-old amused, so together they had filled one of Grandpa Vincent's old soft-sided bags from the garage. Vinnie proudly carried his grandpa-toy-bag, as he liked to call it, to any and every grown-up gathering.

Oh, Lord, that floor has to be crawling with germs—probably superbugs. I don't even want to guess what evil bacteria is living in that ratty old rug, but Trina was unable to politely pull herself away from her distraught niece's death-grip. She needed the closeness at a time like this; they all did. Finally, when Trina could no longer bear to watch her son playing on that grimy floor, she caught her husband's attention. "Sal, could you get him off that filthy floor?" she whispered, not wanting to make an issue out of such a small thing.

Sal gave her a knowing nod and quickly pulled Vinnie onto the two-seat vinyl bench. "How about a cuddle with your old dad?"

"Aw, Dad, you're not all that old."

"Thanks, honey," Trina said in a hushed voice, when her little man climbed up into an equally grimy vinyl chair. *Oh good, at least the germs will slide off that chair.*

Lily and Gino returned from a cafeteria run, carrying trays of hot coffee and several bottles of water. "Here ya go." Gino handed the cups to Angie and Ellie, then passed the remaining beverages around the waiting room.

"No word yet?" Lily asked.

Angie and Mia shook their heads in response, but didn't utter a word. Kerri, Anthony and Sammy sat together at the far corner of the room, silent, but together. The entire family was uncharacteristically quiet; it was unnerving.

Mia, obviously deep in thought, stood and began pacing. "We probably should have called Matt and Luke to give them a heads up," Mia said to her sister.

"I know, but I didn't want to leave Mom."

"Me either. I'm sure they'll understand when they hear what happened."

"Joey, remember when our whole family was in this very room?" Angie sadly looked at her brother.

"Yes, unfortunately. I'll never forget the day Pops died," he frowned.

"Me, either. This place never sparks any good memories, does it?"

Kevin stopped pacing when he noticed a doctor walking in their direction.

"Mrs. Trayor? Which one of you is Mrs. Trayor?" he asked, scanning the group.

"Here!" Angie jumped up to face the doctor. "I'm Angie Trayor. How is my husband?"

He stared at her for just a few seconds too long. She steeled herself for the worst possible news. "I'm Dr. McGraw. Mrs. Trayor, can we sit and talk alone over there?" he asked, pointing to a small conference area just off the waiting room. "I'd like to explain exactly what has happened to your husband."

"This is my family," sweeping her hands around to include everyone. "We are very close and I'd rather they be with me. We have no secrets, if you're okay with that."

"Sure, sure, it's your choice."

The doctor was a soft-spoken, distinguished looking middle-aged man. His long nose gave him a rather aristocratic appearance. His gray eyes suggested sadness to Trina, as she attempted to study his body language. Was this news going to overwhelm her sister? She immediately began crying out to God on their behalf.

Angie and her children sat together on the largest sofa in the room; Dr. McGraw pulled up a chair in front of them, their knees almost touching. The entire Agosti family quietly clustered around them, not unlike a protective cocoon.

"Mrs. Trayor, I'm sorry you had such a lengthy wait. We were waiting for all the test results to come back. I didn't want to be premature in my determination of his condition."

"And have you received all of his tests back?"

"Yes, yes we have. I have also consulted with one of my colleagues and we concur on his diagnosis. Before I get into that, I'd like to ask you a couple of questions."

"Sure, anything," she responded, nervously twisting the fabric of her blouse.

Glancing down at his clipboard, Dr. McGraw asked, "Has Jake experienced any unusual symptoms lately?"

"Nothing major, but he did admit to being rather lethargic. I scheduled an appointment with our family doctor for next week. Actually, the appointment was scheduled for last month, but my husband changed it—due to a conflict at school. He's a teacher and a coach. Why?"

"And, Angie, remember how pale he was at the beach?" Trina interjected.

"Yes, that's right. Tired and pale, that's what prompted me to make the initial appointment."

"Can you think of anything else? Blurry vision, dizziness, anything like that?"

"Yes, yes, now that you mention it. When we were carrying in groceries last week, he had to sit down, he complained that he was light-headed. And then at Joe's house, he had another spell, but didn't tell me about that one until later."

"Well, all of that makes sense. Of course, we did blood work on him, which revealed the determination of our final diagnosis."

"Which is?" Mia asked, sitting forward just a bit.

"Your dad has a disease called *polycythemia*. I know it sounds very scary, but let me explain. Simply put, a person with polycythemia has a high red count in his blood; it can become *thick*, for want of a better word. When the blood is too thick, like your husband's," he explained, focusing on Angie, "it can cause a transient ischemic attack or TIA. In other words, a ministroke."

Angie inhaled and put her hands to her face, which brought Kevin's protective hand to her shoulder. "Oh no, is he . . . "

"It was a very mild ministroke, so I doubt he'll have any permanent damage. But the symptoms can actually be similar to a regular stroke. The good news is that TIA symptoms often go away within twenty-four hours without treatment. That may be because a blood clot broke up, thus allowing blood flow and oxygen to be restored, or it can mean that other arteries have compensated by supplying blood to the brain. But you have to keep in mind—it is a warning sign and we're not going to ignore it. We're going to treat him with certain medications that should keep his red blood cells level."

"Okay. Will you be treating him?"

"No, I'm the primary hospitalist. I'm going to send your husband to a specialist; he's one of the best."

Angie's face revealed her hidden fear, and Dr. McGraw gently placed his hand on her trembling hands. "Mrs. Trayor, Jake is strong and otherwise healthy. He is going to be just fine; this disease will not likely take his life. I anticipate he'll live a normal, long life and live to play with his grandchildren," he said with a warm smile. "Polycythemia is highly treatable when discovered early."

The entire Agosti family simultaneously exhaled; their relief was palpable. Smiles were beginning to breakout on every face.

"Can we see him?" Kevin asked.

"Sure. I want to keep him overnight, just to be on the safe side. But I anticipate his discharge will be tomorrow. I'd like to go over some information with you now, if that's okay?"

Angie nodded her head as she blew her nose. "Yes, it is and thank you for being so kind."

The physician went over Jake's discharge information, tentative treatment information and the name and address of his new specialist. "Our nurse will call to schedule his appointment; she'll give you that information tomorrow. I think it's a good idea to also keep that appointment with your primary care physician; we'll forward a report to his office."

"Thanks, Doc," Joey interjected. "We all appreciate it."

"You're welcome. You can see him now, but only three at a time and with this mob, that might take awhile to rotate through." He smiled as he made his way back to the emergency triage room.

Chapter 12

Leah and Mia returned from church to find their folks snuggling on the sofa. "Hey, you guys, quit it! You're too old for that stuff," Leah jokingly covered her eyes.

"What are you talking about? Just be thankful your dad and I are still madly in love," Angie chuckled, hugging Jake a little tighter.

"I'm just ragging on you, Mom." Leah smiled. "I love that you guys are still gushy with each other."

"Yeah, keep hugging. I hear it's good for overall health," Mia snickered. "I plan to have a marriage just like my dear old mom and dad's."

"How are you feeling, Dad?" Leah came over and sat close to him.

"I'm doing great, honey. I am so grateful that we caught this early. And look," sliding a piece of paper across the coffee table toward her. "I've been practicing my signature; you'd never know I had a TIA."

"Your writing looks exactly the same, no deficits whatsoever. That's incredible, Dad."

"Everyone at church was asking for you, but I discouraged visitors until next week. You need your rest; you've only been home for a couple of days."

"Yes, *nurse*," he looked at his daughters. "But I'm pretty confident I'll be back to school by next week. Remember? The doctor clearly stated—no permanent damage."

"Jake, we've already talked about this, you're going to wait until after your doctor checks you over. Agreed?"

"Man, nothing like living with a house full of nursemaids."

"Oh stop! You know you love being pampered."

"Come on, Leah, let's start dinner," Mia was already dragging her sister backwards by her collar.

When they reached the kitchen counter, Mia's countenance changed. "You know what? I think Dad is a walking miracle."

"For sure. I've never seen Mom so scared. It scared me too," Leah admitted.

"Yeah, like our entire world was rocked in one split second. But he's good now, and I'm sure the worst of it is behind him—I hope."

"I hope so too. The doctor seemed pretty positive, so that's a good thing. By the way, Luke was very understanding about being stood up. How about Matt?"

"He was a prince. He totally got it. Leah, I really, really like this guy. Grab me that box of rigatoni, please. Hey, would you and Luke like to join us for a drive this afternoon?"

"Where to?"

"We thought we'd head to the White Mountains?"

"Whoa, that's a pretty long drive. I hope you're not planning to hike Mount Washington; we'll be calling out the park rangers for a search mission."

"Nah, no hiking today, just a quiet drive to check out the fall foliage."

"I'm pretty sure the foliage is past its peak, but you guys go and have a nice time and thanks for the invitation. I'm spending the afternoon at the mills. I've got to keep this project moving."

Angie came into the kitchen and gave a warm smile to her daughters. "Looks like you girls have everything under control here. Do I have time to take a shower? I didn't want to leave Dad alone while you were out, but I truly need a shower."

"Please, do take a shower." Leah pinched her nose and grinned at her mother.

"You're too much. I'll have you know I take a shower once a month, whether I need one or not," she fired right back at her daughter.

"You have plenty of time. Pasta will be done shortly, but then I have to make the salad. Go ahead."

"Okay, keep an eye on your dad; be right back."

Leah waited a few minutes, then peeked in on her father; his head was back, his eyes were closed. She watched his motionless body for a minute. She was just about to run to him when he scratched his eyebrow. After she finished setting the dining room table, she came back to help Mia. "You know what? I think Mom is blaming herself for Dad's ministroke. Twice, twice, she mentioned she should have pushed him harder to get into the doctor's office. I guess she's been worried about him since summer vacation."

"It's not her fault. It's nobody's fault," Mia firmly stated, as she bit into a piece of hot rigatoni. It must be al dente; the entire family disliked overcooked pasta.

It was a beautiful day, sunny, cool, and ideal for a photo shoot. Leah was determined to get a good start on her portfolio. She packed up her Nikon, some notebooks and grabbed the car keys. "I'll see you later, Mom. I'm heading to the mills," she yelled up the stairs, as she hurried toward the front door.

She'd recently developed the habit of jotting down notes relevant to her subjects. Sometimes, when she reread those notes, they made no sense whatsoever. But thankfully, more often than not, they proved invaluable to the stories and bylines her professor was looking for, so she continued to record her thoughts and impressions.

When the traffic light changed, she turned onto Merrimack Street, a street she'd been on a thousand times before. But today she was seeing the long expanse of mills through different eyes and definitely from an entirely different perspective. The old Wood Mill building seemed to go on forever. She drove alongside it until she reached her target area and pulled into the newly paved parking lot. The lot struck her as a stark contrast to the old brick structure.

This particular mill now housed many modern offices and medical facilities, as well as restaurants; her mom warned that it was nearly impossible to find a parking spot on the first go-around. However, it was Sunday, so she caught a break and easily found a spot close to the block that most interested her.

Before Leah unloaded her equipment, she leaned back against the car and looked up; the sunlight cast across the brick facade seemed to evoke all sorts of thoughts and emotions. Leah reasoned it was silly, but she was emotional, standing in the shadow of this huge building. How could this mill that was built in the eighteen hundreds possibly matter to her? It seemed to come alive to her—in her. It beckoned thoughts of its glory days; days when immigrants filled every square inch of every single mill that was nestled along the banks of the Merrimack River. Each laborer performed backbreaking tasks for a measly take-home pay.

She remembered Grandpa Vincent telling stories about the hard-working bobbin girls, and the skilled weavers, many of whom were young women. It was no secret that those monstrous machines were extremely dangerous to operate. Accidents were commonplace, but the workers didn't have the luxury of picking or choosing the easiest or safest jobs. They desperately needed to work and work they did, spending countless hours bent over machines in the worst possible conditions. Young children were not exempt; they too were expected to help the family unit by spending long hours in frightening surroundings.

Leah brushed off the malaise she was feeling and went to work. She was torn between *then and now*; much of this block's renovation was completed, but a portion of it stood still in time. Her desire was to capture the contrast of the old and the new and this particular location was exactly the right spot.

The Lawrence textile mills were primarily brick with lots and lots of windows. She moved around the parking lot focusing on the rich, red brick that had stood the test of time. Next, she focused on the old window frames. She marveled at the interesting designs created by the sunshine on the old, oily glass. She was cognizant that before long, what she was looking at today would be gone forever. Leah was determined to capture this precious piece of history that stood proudly before her; she vowed to do justice to it and maybe even honor those hardy workers who flocked to the well-known *Immigrant City* in hopes of a wonderful new life.

"Hey, there's my girl," came a voice near her car.

Leah quickly turned around and saw Luke smiling back at her. "Hey, yourself."

"Your mom told me you'd be hard at work on your project, so I drove around until I spotted your car. It helped that she assumed you'd be zeroing in on the Wood Mill, otherwise I'd still be driving."

"I know, this one mill alone is humongous."

"Can I wait for you? Maybe we can grab something to eat?"

"Actually, I'm almost done and I'd love that. Just give me a few minutes to catch this last bit of sunlight."

Luke went back to his car and listened to the radio while watching her work. He liked what he saw. *This is one amazing girl. I love her intellect and that amazing sense of humor. I don't think I want to let this one get away.* When she began packing up her gear, Luke hopped out of his car and walked in her direction. "Can I help?"

"Thanks, but I don't have much—I'm good. So, should I leave my car here while we're gone or drop it off at home?"

"Hmm, why don't you pull it over there in front of my dad's office, best to leave it wherever they'll be good lighting."

"Where's your dad's office?"

Luke gently put his hands on her shoulders and pivoted her to face, 'Henderson Realty and Development Company'. It was, without question, the most distinctively upscale-looking facade in the entire complex."

"Oh, wow! How could I have missed that?"

"Oh and Leah, I wouldn't leave your camera."

"Really? Is there a lot of crime here?"

"Enough. I'd hate to see you lose your prized possession."

Driving out of the parking lot, Leah turned to Luke, "I should call my mom. She doesn't need to be worrying about me."

"You could, but I already told her that I was taking you to dinner, so she'll put two and two together," he smiled. "So, how is your dad?"

"He's actually good, but it was definitely a warning sign. Mom will stay on his case from now on; I'm sure of that."

"Good. Where do you want to go?"

"Surprise me."

"I'm craving a bowl of good chowder. How about Markey's?"

"Excellent! Luke I'm so excited about this mill project. It's one of my most challenging assignments so far. The history of these buildings is so intriguing. It was hard for me to narrow myself to just one mill, but I guess I'm not the only one to choose the Wood Mill. How long has your dad occupied office space there?"

"Well, as I told you before, he's been heavily involved in huge sections of renovations near where you just photographed; I guess I should say that his construction company has been heavily involved."

"He has his own construction company?"

"Aha, and real estate company, and art galleries, and theatres and financial institutions. Suffice it to say, he's got his fingers in everything."

They talked more about his dad and his place of prominence in the community, but Luke didn't give her the impression they were all that close. When she pressed, he closed up. So Leah changed the subject to his mom. It was obvious that he loved and admired his mother, proudly sharing many of her accomplishments as well as a few stories highlighting her loving personality. Then the conversation turned to Michelle. He only had one sibling and while he loved Michelle, she had lots of problems and those problems affected their family.

He opened up over dinner, telling her about his sister's nasty divorce. "I remember going through the acceptable motions when she got engaged and then witnessing their sham of a wedding. My dad spent oodles on that fiasco. I knew from the beginning that it was all for show and, sadder still, I knew it wouldn't last," Luke said wistfully.

"That must have been awful."

"He had a violent temper, but she wouldn't listen to me when I warned her. Predictably, her ex-husband became abusive, but she hid it from my folks and especially from me. He severely damaged not only her physical body, but her once sweet temperament." Luke went on to say that he felt helpless as he watched her close up like a dying flower. "It was pitiful; I guess I became kind of protective of her."

"So, does Michelle date now or is she still gun-shy?"

"I've not heard her talk about dating at all. As a matter of fact, all she does is work and watch sappy chick flicks. She's become a loner and that's definitely not good for her overall health."

"No children?"

"No, and I'm not sure if that's good or bad. But it is what it is."

Leah was quiet for a while, silently reflecting on how blessed she was to have such a loving family. "This chowder is the absolute best in the area," Leah popped another oyster cracker into her mouth. "Or should I say *chowdah?*" she smirked.

"No matter how you pronounce it, it's the best," he smiled. "Say, would you like to meet Michelle? She could sure use a friend. After the divorce, her married friends dropped her like she had leprosy."

"I'd love to. I'm a few years younger, but if she doesn't mind, neither do I."

"That would be great. You'd be a good influence with your perky personality and wonderful sense of humor." He leaned far enough forward to grasp her hand.

Oh, those blue eyes of his get me every time. "Sense of humor, huh?" She deliberately crossed her eyes at him. "Don't forget mature, I'm so very mature."

Luke introduced Leah to his sister the following week; he was pleased that they connected so quickly, but he often felt left out of their conversations. These gals conversed on so many levels and subjects: clothes, music, movies, shoes—especially shoes. Leah began stopping by Michelle's office whenever she'd finished a shoot at the mill; they enjoyed each other's company, chatting for hours on end.

Leah spent part of every weekend at the mill, right up until Thanksgiving break. The days were getting shorter and she needed to take full advantage of every precious minute of daylight. She snapped hundreds of pictures, from every possible angle. As the project due date pressed in on her, she hitched rides home with her friend, Jenny, who had had enough of the dorm life and was commuting for her senior year.

At one point Leah wondered if it would have been more practical to have chosen a subject closer to school. But when all was said and done, she confessed to being captivated by this particular old mill and the many historical accounts she'd read about it. Those long-ago stories were woven into the very fabric of the entire mill era and Lawrence's glory days. She sensed that many of those colorful stories still lingered within the walls of the Wood Mill. She'd hoped her paper would do justice to those immigrants, the sacrifices they made and the part they played in growing this city.

Chapter 13

"To what do I owe this honor," Kevin smiled, moving around his desk to hug his sister.

"Well, I just came from my second interview for that job I told you about, so I thought I'd drop in to say hi—Hi!"

"I'm glad you did. They're moving pretty slowly on filling this job, aren't they?"

"Tell me about it. I expected an answer after the first go-around."

"Well, a second interview is always a good sign. How do you think it went?"

"They brought in the big guns, the senior project manager and the vice president. Oddly, I didn't feel at all nervous, considering they grilled me on every imaginable aspect of coding that might pertain to this particular position."

"Did they give you any indication of when they'll be making a decision?"

Mia paused for a long time before yelling, "They already did—I got the job! Kevin, I got the job!" She laughed, jumping up and down.

"You stinker! And here I was about to set you down nice and easy just in case you didn't snag it. Well congratulations, sis, I'm so proud of you."

"Yeah, now you'll have the distinct honor of occasionally buying me lunch. I know the building is a mile long, but we should still see each other."

"Sure, sure. My treat for a celebratory luncheon at Salvatore's. Did you tell Mom and Dad?"

"Nope, just left the interview and I'm on my way home now. Did they hear anything on the house closing yet?"

"Aha, I called them a couple of hours ago with the date and time. If all goes well, they can take possession before Thanksgiving."

"That is absolutely fabulous," she enthusiastically responded. She gave her brother a huge bear hug, then scurried out the door like a schoolgirl. "I'm gonna burst. I have to get home to tell them—then call Matt."

"Sal, Sal, listen to this one," Trina excitedly began, "'Golden retriever pups, ready to meet their forever families. This litter was born on September seventh, both parents are on the premises and have excellent temperaments. Worming and shots are up-to-date. These puppies are perfect for younger children. Call for an appointment.'"

"That would make them around eight weeks old, which is just about right, but do you want to train a puppy in the winter?"

"I hear ya, but I'm getting so anxious to hear the pitter-patter of four little feet around here, so winter toilet training seems a small price to pay. I'm lonely when Vinnie is in school and nooo, I don't want to go back to work," she beamed.

"Where is that breeder located?"

Looking back down at the newspaper, she answered, "It's a Salem, New Hampshire exchange. Do you want to sneak out there tomorrow while he's in school, take a look around—just check it out?"

"Are you sure you're ready for stained rugs, walking him in the frigid temperatures, chewed up sneakers and—"

"I get it, I get it. Yes, I'm sure. The real question is, are you okay with it?"

After several long, nerve-wracking minutes of silence, Sal wrapped his arms around her and kissed the side of her neck. "I'm more than okay with it and it will be good for Vinnie to have a pal. I was just playing hard to get."

"Yay! I'm so excited. So, male or female?"

"I think male, but neutered when he's old enough. Right?"

"Yes, agreed. We could never replace good old Buddy; he was a perfect dog, but it's time to move on."

Luke and Leah were fast becoming a couple, seeing each other on campus and on weekends. They were together whenever they weren't studying—and sometimes when they were studying, they managed to occupy their favorite spot in the library. While Leah loved spending time with him, she was a pragmatic person. She had a lot more schooling ahead of her, so her tendency was to keep the brakes on. Luke, on the other hand, completely infatuated with her, pressed to spend more and more time together. That was Luke's personality, full throttle ahead in everything. In the three months they'd been steadily dating, they became comfortable in their relationship; each said they felt like they'd known each other their entire life.

"I still can't believe your family is buying the old *Sea Mist Bed and Breakfast*. What a weird coincidence. You know my dad had his eye on it on a couple of different occasions."

"So, why didn't he purchase it?"

"I don't know, it seems there was always some kind of obstacle. Plus the guy gets wrapped up in so many deals at the same time. Some days I wonder how he finds his way home."

"He was cordial, when we met at the beach," she haltingly remarked, with a sideways glance.

"He's okay, but if I have to use just one word to describe him, it would be—cold. I haven't seen him hug my mom in ages. He gives Michelle a hard time every stinking day."

"And with you?"

"Me? I'm oblivious to his insults."

"Insults? Your dad insults you?" Leah sort of overreacted.

"I don't really want to go there."

"I'm sorry, but I don't understand. Why, what could he possibly say that was negative about you?" she responded forcefully.

Looking around her family room, he winked at her, "Leah, you are so lucky, or as you would say, blessed. You have a wonderful family and parents who are way above average in parenting skills. Not every family is quite that lucky—blessed."

"Honestly, I have to confess that I'm guilty of taking them for granted."

Luke put his head down, taking a while to respond to her. "Don't get me wrong, he's not a monster. He's just so entangled with raking in the big bucks, building his business, that he forgets about his family."

Leah moved closer to him. "I really am sorry. Maybe he'll come to his senses; he's certainly missing out, because I think you're terrific."

"Thanks, I'm not looking for sympathy, it's—"

A knock on the front door interrupted him, "I'll get it," Mia yelled as she scurried from the kitchen.

"Uncle Joey, come in," Mia hugged him tightly.

"Hey kid, you get more beautiful every time I see you."

"Oh, come on."

"Are your folks home? I have good news."

"Mom," she loudly yelled from the top of her dainty lungs.

Joey covered his ears and mocked a dizzy spell. "You just shattered my glasses."

"Uncle Joey—you don't wear glasses."

"But if I did—shattered," he laughed, pulling her long, black hair.

"You're messing up my hair!"

"Hey, why are you beating on my child," Angie feigned disapproval by separating them, but then laughed as she hugged her brother. "And what brings you here, oh family patriarch?"

"Knock it off with that patriarch stuff. I'm not ninety years old," he joked. "Anyhow, I was talking to Trina this morning and we had an idea."

"Oh no, those four words coming out of your mouth are some of the scariest words I can think of," she snickered.

"Funny, but since we're closing on the beach house in a few days, we thought it would be fun to celebrate Thanksgiving there. We already know it will accommodate the entire family. We can officially christen it and give thanks for it and each other—at the same time. What do you think?"

Leah piped in before her mother had a chance to answer. "Awesome! That sounds like a blast."

"That's a great idea, Uncle Joey," added Mia.

"Well, Luke, would you also like to add your two cents?" Angie teased with her hands on her hips. "And yes, I think it's a super idea. Sometimes you surprise me."

"I must confess, it was Trina's idea. There, I said it."

"It figures. So, we gals will get right on that and make our plans, same way we do when we celebrate here."

"Okay, I'm outta here," Joe turned and saluted his sister, then reached for the doorknob.

"You could've just called, not that I don't love seeing your smiling face."

"I was only a street over, picking up stuff for Ellie, so I thought, why not?"

"Okay, bye. Love to your crew," Angie closed the door behind her brother.

Luke and Leah walked back to the family room and he whispered, "See, that's exactly what I mean. That little scene would never happen in my house."

Leah looked up at him with sympathy. "Hey, why don't you help me sort through my mill photos? I have so many that I need to start eliminating the bad ones."

"I doubt there are any bad ones. Are you done shooting?"

"Oh no, I'm guessing I have several more trips. If I were a pro, I'd be done by now, but until then, snap, snap, snap," she mocked, taking his picture.

"Okay, grab your laptop and let's see what you've got."

───────

Trina and Sal drove to the kennel a couple of times that week. They were impressed that it was so clean and well-run, but in reality, she just wanted to visit the puppies. Their plan was to surprise Vinnie on Saturday during a country drive. Trina's only concern was that he'd want to bring home more than one of those irresistible puppies. Secretly, she'd accumulated all the necessary items needed for this new adventure. Puppy chow was hidden in the guest room closet, dog dishes and brush were tucked away in her closet and the crate was well-hidden in the garage.

"Vinnie, grab your jacket, we're going for a ride," Trina sang up the stairs. "Vinnie?"

"What?"

"We're going for a ride, get your jacket."

"Aw, Mom, I wanted to go play with Ronnie today."

"Vinnie, listen to your mother. Let's go."

Trina could hardly conceal her excitement, discreetly reaching across the seat to give Sal's hand a knowing squeeze. They drove on winding back roads for quite a while, eventually finding their way to Salem, New Hampshire. Vinnie asked, "Are we going for ice cream?"

"Hmm, ice cream, maybe," Trina smiled back at him.

"Isn't it kind of chilly for ice cream, champ?" Sal looked back at his son in his rearview mirror.

"Yeah, it is. How about pizza?"

"We just had lunch. Let's just ride."

"It's kind of boring, Mom."

Sal and Trina smiled at each other while Vinnie occupied himself in the backseat with his action figure heroes. He soon got so involved with his imaginary game that he didn't notice when they slowed and pulled into the kennel parking lot.

Sal parked the car and turned around, calmly asking, "Son, would you like to have a puppy of your very own?"

Instantly, Vinnie's head jerked up. He looked around and it hit him, "Dad, are we gonna get a puppy?"

"If you want to," Trina said. "A new puppy will never replace Buddy, but I think he'd like you to have a new friend. What do you think? Do you want to go in and check out the puppy we picked out for you?"

"You really picked out a puppy for me? Yes, yes, I do want one," his eyes were tearing up as he fumbled with his seat belt.

Vinnie was ten steps ahead of them, almost running; his eyes were fixed on the bright red double door ahead of him.

Sal pushed open the door; they were quickly assailed by puppy yelps and the smells associated with a large kennel. Mama and daddy quickly made their presence known, pushing their full body weight against them, sniffing and wagging. Vinnie ignored the adult dogs and walked directly to the litter, grinning from ear to ear. "Oh, Mom, can we take two, please?"

"Honey, we can't; the others are already spoken for."

Just then the owner walked in. "And you must be Vinnie?"

Vinnie never took his eyes off the litter, but nodded, "Yup, I'm Vinnie."

"Well, young man, are you ready to take good care of this little guy?" she knelt to lift up one of the pups. "Would you like to hold him for a minute, while I talk with your folks?"

Again, Vinnie just nodded, holding out his arms; Trina was certain she saw tears slip from his eyes.

As she watched her son, Trina was thrown back to images of Buddy and Vinnie running in circles around the house—at the time, driving her nuts, but—now, a precious memory. She was welling up herself at the sweetness of this moment. Vinnie was nuzzling his puppy and giggling, almost uncontrollably.

After closing on the beach house, most of the family gathered at Sal and Trina's home. They were always up for a celebration. Besides, they wanted to meet Vinnie's new puppy. "Kevin, you did a wonderful job today, very professional." Joe patted his nephew on the back. "It's good to have a lawyer in the family."

"Right, in case he has to keep one of us out of the slammer." Sammy laughed.

"Thanks, but I'm not a criminal lawyer. You do the crime, you do the time," he smiled, pointing his fake finger-gun at his cousin.

Angie sat on the floor, cuddling Vinnie's puppy. "He's the cutest little guy and what did you finally decide to name him?"

"Well, we've changed it three times, but I do believe we've settled on Lance—right, Vinnie?"

"Ha, Lance as in the mascot for Lawrence High School—the Lancers?" Angie asked.

"Hey, you're pretty astute," Sal responded. "Yes, that's exactly right. Vinnie saw an old Lawrence High School yearbook and was quite taken with the image of the Lancer on the cover. So we went round and round until we, or he, decided on Lance. It's catchy, different, don't you think?"

"Well, little Lance, you are in a good home and we all love you already. Oops! Vinnie, I think you're adorable little puppy just wet my jeans. Oh no, I'm really, really wet."

"I got it, Aunt Angie," Vinnie covered his giggle as he began wiping up the puddle. "Auntie Angie wet her pants, Auntie Angie wet her pants," he impishly sang out, prompting her to grab him from behind and spin him in circles. Lance thought that was his invitation to jump in and nip at Vinnie's stocking feet.

"Hey, everyone. Anthony just brought the pizza so come on and help yourselves," Trina announced, setting out soda and paper products.

As usual, the noise level came down to a murmur while the family shared yet another meal together. Lance was struggling to get some traction on the hardwood floors, scampering from one person to another, sniffing their pizza and begging for treats.

As they were finishing, Joey brought out a small paper bag of keys. "Listen up, people. I want each of you to have a set of keys to the beach house. We'll figure out some kind of schedule for our family vacation, but you should each feel comfortable in running out there for a weekend getaway."

"Joe, I personally think you should be aware when someone wants some personal family time there," Trina said. "I mean, who wants twenty of their closest relatives showing up during their romantic weekend? Do you all agree?"

"Yup, makes sense to me," Angie said.

"I volunteer to keep a calendar, so Joe doesn't have to be bogged down with all those details," Ellie reached for a slice of pizza. "If you're planning to go, just check with me first. I'm a good secretary."

"Thanks, honey. So, I have keys for all us old married folks. Don't throw anything at me, but I'm not comfortable handing over keys to our single kids just yet—agreed?"

"Aw, Uncle Joey, you're such a killjoy; I was planning a wild raucous party for the weekend," Leah snorted, pretending to dance.

"Dream on, little girl," her father said sarcastically.

"We can work out all the maintenance details later, but I do think we need to get out there for a quick once-over before our Thanksgiving weekend. Is anyone free to drive out with me Sunday after church?" Joey asked.

Almost everyone nodded, raised hands and generally agreed. "Okay then, we'll spend a couple of hours Sunday afternoon to get the place in shape for our Thanksgiving feast."

"I wish Grandma and Grandpa could be with us for this," Mia said. "They'd love it."

"They sure would, honey."

The gals went into planning mode. They discussed and decided on the tiniest of details; nothing was left to chance. The one detail that was impossible to plan for was the weather. New England's winter weather was unpredictable and often treacherous. Even their massive snowplows were, on occasion, no match for those well-known nor'easters.

"So, Uncle Joey, what if it snows and we can't get there? That would be a disaster," Leah lamented.

"Well, I guess we'll see if this family still has that old pioneer spirit Pops always talked about."

"Let's not worry about that now; we'll be smart and keep an eye on the forecast," Angie said. "When is everyone planning to be there and for how long?"

Trina looked at Sal, Ellie looked at Joe, as did the others. "Okay then, let's just wing it; come when you can, go when you have to. My kind of lifestyle!" Angie stood with arms akimbo.

Chapter 14

"Are you busy?" Leah asked as she poked her head around the door and winked at Michelle.

"Leah, come in. I'm not as swamped as I was last time you dropped by. Have a seat."

"Thanks, I'm wondering if I can treat you to lunch?"

"What? A poor college girl like you, springing for lunch for the rich office nerd? No way, I wouldn't feel right about that. How about I just pour us a fresh cup of coffee?"

"Okay, works for me."

Michelle came around to the front of her desk and poured coffee from a beat-up old coffee maker that was wedged between stacks of paperwork on a corner buffet. Leah noticed Michelle's hands weren't very steady as she poured the coffee. "And—" searching the small refrigerator, "I have these!"

"Ooh, what is in that Tripoli's box?" Leah asked with great anticipation.

"Luke stopped by the bakery this morning and gifted me with these two giant éclairs. He's always force-feeding me with these creamy, fattening desserts."

"He's a good brother and he's worried about you, Michelle. And yes, give one of those over to me."

"He's the best, but no need to worry. I'm doing—okay. The divorce is behind me and I've got my work to keep me busy."

"Well, you know what they say, all work and no play . . . "

"Oh great, now I have the two of you hovering over me."

"Actually, you have four, your mom and dad should be added to that list."

"Maybe my mom, but Dad's in his own little world: money, deals and connections. Humph, if it weren't for his criticism, he'd never talk to me at all," she complained. "Enough about me. How is your mill project going?"

"Great! I think today is my final shoot. I should have been done ages ago, but every time I'd review them, I just wasn't completely satisfied. But I think I'm good now; I've been here on Saturdays, Sundays and every daylight hour in between."

"I know you've put lots of hours into this project, you deserve an excellent grade. I'll miss your impromptu visits. When is this project due for submission?"

"Right after Thanksgiving, then I can concentrate on my finals before Christmas break. This assignment has sapped so much of my energy that now I need to play catch up on my other classes, but I'm not too worried, my grades are right up there."

"Good for you."

Just then the outside door opened and Mr. Henderson appeared, sucking the oxygen out of the small office. There was no doubt that this man was a dominant figure, an alpha male among his pack.

Without so much as a hello, "Michelle, what's going on?" glancing at his watch as if to say, 'You're still on my time.'

"Dad, you remember Leah Trayor, Luke's friend from B.U.?" Michelle couldn't hide the obvious quiver in her voice. Her eyes were darting back and forth between Leah and her father.

"Of course I do, we met at the beach house in August." He turned to face Leah. "How are you?" Not waiting for an answer, "I hear you've purchased the Sea Mist?"

His eyes were as blue as Luke's, but they were nothing like his son's. They were icy and seemed to bore into her as he quickly sized her up.

"Yes, our family is planning to be there for Thanksgiving," she responded, sounding to herself like a frightened little girl. This man was not quite as tall as Luke, but much stockier and he certainly lacked the warmth that she admired in Luke.

"Yes, yes, that's nice. Michelle, do you think you could find the time," he stated sarcastically, "to put together a couple of reports for me? I'm sure your little friend here will understand if you have to get back to work. I'll pick them up in an hour," he flatly stated. He scribbled down the report titles, or maybe he was telling Michelle to get rid of her guest.

"I'll let you get back to work. Besides, I'd need to get moving on this final shoot. Talk to you later," Leah nervously responded, leaving her untouched éclair on the buffet.

Through sad eyes, Michelle watched as her new friend hurried out the door.

On her drive home, Leah went through all sorts of mental gymnastics. What had just happened? It was almost impossible to keep her composure; she couldn't shake those icy-blue eyes. Leah went straight to her bedroom, intentionally avoiding her mom. She honestly tried to give this guy the benefit of the doubt. Maybe he was having a bad day, maybe he was disappointed he'd lost the Sea Mist, maybe he even received some horrible news just five minutes before walking into Michelle's office. *Who am I kidding? The man is a rude, self-centered, cold fish. Who does he think he is—looking down his long nose at me?*

"Hey, sweetie, can I come in?" Angie asked from the other side of her bedroom door.

"Sure!"

"Are you okay? You have *that look* on your face?"

"Huh? What do you mean—*that look?*"

"Hmm, I guess I'd describe it as the 'I'm hurting look,' or maybe the 'I want to clobber somebody look,' Angie snickered, as she plopped on the bed.

"How about the 'I'm hurting *and* I want to clobber somebody look,'" she gruffly responded.

"I'm sorry, can you tell me what happened?"

"Mom, I really like Luke and I'm getting to know his sister, Michelle. She's kind of cool, but their dad is a beast. Oh, that was unkind. Sorry."

"I didn't realize you knew the beast, I mean—father."

"I stopped in to see Michelle before my final shoot this afternoon. We were having a normal conversation and he marched in and pretty much dismissed me. He's seriously deficient in the manners department."

"I realize you and Luke are just beginning a friendship or maybe even a relationship, but it's wise to keep this in mind—for the future: 'You don't just marry a man, you marry his family.'"

"Whoa, who said anything about marriage? Sheesh, I'm not ready for that."

"Well, neither am I, but I thought I'd pass on Grandma Maria's words of wisdom."

"So, I'm giving Dad a humongous hug when he gets home; he is the absolute best dad and I'm so thankful to have him."

"Aw, that's sweet and you are right. He is the best and I'll bet he'd love to hear that from his favorite youngest daughter."

"His only youngest daughter! And how is Daddy doing, you know with the polycy-thingamajig?"

"You're too funny. It's called polycythemia and he's doing excellent. It was frightening to watch him have that TIA, but it was a blessing in disguise—it warned us before a big one hit. The medicine is keeping the disease in check."

Both of them heard the front door at the same time, they smiled at one another. "Well, there he is."

"I'm going down to hug my favorite daddy—right now."

Chapter 15

"Grab him, grab him, Vinnie! Lance is chewing my sneaker."

"I got him," Vinnie yelled, yanking the sneaker away from his puppy. "Hey, Mom, now it matches your other sneaker." Vinnie covered his mouth to hide a laugh.

"It's not funny, I can't afford new sneaks every week." Softening, she continued, "Oh, it's not your fault, honey. I should have kept them out of reach until he grows out of this stage."

"Lance, come here," scooping up the irresistible ball of fur and planting a kiss on his nose. "You had better behave," Trina admonished.

He stuck out his long, pink tongue and swiped it across her face, which really got Vinnie giggling. "Lance loves you, Mama."

"He does, huh? Come on, let's crate him for now. We're going to be late, Aunt Ellie and Aunt Angie are waiting for us."

***

"Nice sneakers," Angie raised one eyebrow as she looked down at Trina's chewed Nikes.

"How could I have forgotten exactly how much a puppy chews? Huh? Tell me."

"Relax, sis, it doesn't last forever."

"I know, it's just that I just bought those sneakers. So, how does Mia like her new job?"

"So far, so good. She never expected to be functioning in the role of project manager, but apparently it's the challenge she's been looking for."

"Well, that girl has the smarts and maturity to handle whatever they throw at her," Ellie pulled the whistling teakettle off the burner.

Trina set her plate of biscotti on the kitchen table and began helping Ellie with the tea. "Every time I bake these, I have a *Mama flashback*. I still miss her."

"You are not alone," Angie replied, fixing her own tea. "Vinnie, come get a biscotto," she yelled.

"Can I have two?"

"Vinnie, why do always ask for two of everything? Isn't one enough to start with?"

"Nope, I have two hands. I don't want the other one to get lonely," he blurted and ran back to the family room with a biscotto in each hand.

"That kid is a smarty-pants."

"When I watch his antics, I can hardly wait for our little one to make his or her appearance," Ellie admitted.

"Speaking of that bundle of joy, we should set a date for the shower, otherwise the time will slip right by us."

"Let's see," Ellie studied the calendar on the wall. "She's due at the end of March, so should we set it for February?"

"Hmm, February weather is brutal, but March can be wicked too," Angie conceded.

"Well, why don't we take a chance on the end of February and if we have to postpone it, then we just have to postpone it," Trina ventured.

"Before we set the date in stone, you should probably run it by Kerri, unless you want to surprise her."

"Oh no, no, no! She hates surprises; besides, those two are always on the go. I'm thinking it would be a real challenge to trick that gal."

Ellie held up the calendar and asked, "If we're planning to do it on a Friday, what do you think about February twenty-fourth or March third?"

"Either works for me; why don't you call Kerri right now, so we can nail it down," Trina suggested.

Ellie was already walking toward the phone. "Okey-dokey."

"Mama, can I have another cookie?"

"Vinnie, you already had two. I think that's plenty."

"While Ellie is calling, let's talk about our Thanksgiving menu," Angie suggested.

"I think we should do it the same as always. Why change? Sal and I can take care of the turkey, if you guys are okay with that? We can plan the side dishes and pies today, then ask the gang who wants to do what."

"Exactly what I—"

Just then Ellie walked back from the phone, waving her calendar. "She's thrilled that we're doing this and suggests we go with February twenty-fourth and hope for an unseasonably warm day."

"Terrific, I'm glad that is settled, unless of course Mother Nature throws us a curveball."

"Well, since it's set for a Friday, we could use Saturday as our rain date—or snow date."

"I think the kids would love to be involved in planning this shindig, don't you, guys?"

"Sure do."

"Speaking of rotten weather, did you hear the latest? There's a chance we're going to get socked with a storm over Thanksgiving," Trina grumbled.

"I did. Do we have an alternate plan if we can't make it to the beach house? I mean, I don't even know if they plow that road in the dead of winter. Do you?"

"I have no clue. But I'd suggest we just switch to my house if the roads turn nasty. Okay with you guys?" Trina inquired.

"Sure, makes sense. We'll have lots of time to enjoy the place. No sense taking any chances."

"If the entire gang is coming, I should probably roast two smaller turkeys. I want to have enough leftovers for sandwiches," Trina said. "I was just wondering about Matt and Luke?"

"Don't plan on Matt, he's having dinner with his family. I guess some other relatives are joining them for a huge dinner and reunion," Angie told them. "He's a gem! Jake and I really like him. He's been spending a lot of time at our house, plus the two of them frequently double date with Leah and Luke."

"What about Luke? Will he be having dinner with us?" Trina asked.

"Nope, not him either. He's taking his mother and sister out to dinner."

"What about his dad?"

"I guess Mr. Henderson has some business trip lined up and is flying out of Logan on Thursday."

"What? On Thanksgiving Day?"

"Aha, Luke didn't elaborate, but from what Leah tells me, he's not very close to his dad."

"Well, I think that's a shame and I bet the business tycoon will regret it someday."

"Leah has been spending time with Michelle because Luke thought his sister needed a friend. And you know Leah, she's so perky and compassionate, she was bound to step up to that plate. One friend coming up! I guess Michelle is nice enough, but definitely Leah's opposite. She's a few years older and without a doubt a rather melancholy type. But that's understandable as she went through a pretty difficult divorce."

"Any children involved?" Trina asked with genuine concern.

"No, so maybe that's a plus. Michelle is a loner and our Leah is trying to get her to enjoy living again."

"She's always been a sweet, caring kid," Ellie said, "so I'm not surprised that she's taking Luke's sister under her wing."

"Mr. Henderson is, according to Leah, a *cold fish* and rude. I guess he's also pretty tough on his children."

"He's very well-known in the community and I might add, pretty wealthy. Maybe he doesn't think manners apply to him," Trina remarked.

"I just hope my girl isn't getting in over her head." Angie scowled. "She's very trusting and fairly naive for her age."

Chapter 16

A light snow actually did begin to fall on Thanksgiving morning, but it would take more than a few flurries to keep these pioneers from enjoying their family celebration. One by one they trickled into the beach house, each carrying enough food to sustain them until a spring thaw. Joey often joked that everyone of them was too young to possess a *Great Depression* mentality and yet, there they were stockpiling once again. "Are you kidding me? Do we really need thirty rolls of toilet paper?"

"It is definitely better to be safe than—"Angie scoffed, immediately cut off by her mocking brother.

"Are ya expecting Montezuma's revenge to darken our door?" Joey yanked his sister's hair.

Sal was unloading grocery bags and held up one of the rings of dried figs he was stacking in the cupboard. "Hey, if we eat all five of these rings, then that toilet paper will definitely come in handy."

The entire family squeezed themselves in two rooms, bumping into one another, laughing and telling stories. The ebb and flow of their conversations was energizing and they undoubtedly drew strength from one another.

Trina, sounding like a drill sergeant, began handing out jobs. Sammy and Kevin, elbowing each other, began saluting their aunt and shouting, "Yes, sir!"

"Oh, stop being so snarky. You'll thank me when our feast is on the table, hot and delicious."

"Oh. Look! The snow is really starting to come down now." Kerri smiled, leaning against the French doors.

"Well, sweetie, it would really look funny going up," Anthony teased.

"You're hysterical," she responded. "I'm glad this little one will arrive in the spring. I have nightmares about not making it to the hospital in time."

Anthony embraced his wife. "Don't you worry, I promise to get you there in plenty of time; you and our baby will be just fine."

"By the way, Kerri, when are you going to start on the nursery? Remember I'd like to lend a hand," Lily said.

"Just give us a date and we'll come with paintbrushes and whatever else you need," Angie reassured.

"We'll probably start on it after the holidays; we still have lots of time."

"Hey, Mom, please tell me we didn't forget to bring whipping cream. I don't see any," Mia was pushing food around in the refrigerator. "My pumpkin pies will be a big fat flop without whipped cream."

"Calm down, I know we have it somewhere." Angie began rummaging. "It's a good thing we brought along those coolers. This refrigerator is packed to capacity. Oh, here's the whipping cream."

"I'm glad we decided to drive in yesterday," Trina said. "I had to cook the turkeys, one at a time. We should think about replacing that oven or building in a second one—somewhere?"

"Like where?" Sal asked.

"I don't know, somewhere. This family needs either a gigantic oven or two ovens. Am I right, Angie?"

"Yes, indeed you are. That one is too wimpy to accommodate all of us. We did a lot of cooking outside over the summer, so we squeaked by."

"All right, all right, girls, I'm on it," Joe interjected. "The boys can help me with that in the spring."

"Thanks, Joe," Trina and Angie responded simultaneously, fist bumping as they walked past each other.

"You know what, Joe?" Sal asked.

"What?"

"I don't know how you stood a chance, being raised with those two divas. How did you ever survive it?"

"Oh, please! Joe was the golden boy. He never did anything wrong, so we girls had to point out all his flaws, just to keep his feet on the ground," Angie scoffed.

"What are ya talking about? I had no flaws; end of conversation."

"Dream on, big brother," Trina jumped in. "What about when Daddy grounded you for skipping school; you waited until he was snoring away in his recliner before you crept out the window—somehow ending up at a Central Catholic dance. You were just lucky neither one of them checked your room before they headed up to bed. I'm still amazed you didn't get caught."

"That was no big deal."

Angie piped in with, "Yeah, well, what about the time you took your first girlfriend for a ride in Daddy's car—without his permission."

"Mama gave me his keys," he reasoned.

"Oh, sure she did. But then, didn't you run over a cat that same night?"

"What? Uncle Joey, you killed a kitty?" Vinnie jumped in.

"No, Vinnie, I didn't. The kitty ran right under the car and out the other way. She was fine," he answered soberly.

"Oh good," Vinnie said distractedly, as he chased Lance into the sunroom.

"See what you did? The kid is going to hate me."

Trina and Angie were laughing hysterically at their brother's fidgeting. "Vinnie adores you," Trina reassured her brother. "But I can't for the life of me figure out why."

"Mom, do you need any help with dinner or do we have time to get our room set up?" Mia asked.

"We're good for the time being. You and Leah can go ahead and do your thing."

Leah and Mia trudged up the stairs with luggage in tow. They settled themselves in the same attic-bedroom they'd shared on summer vacation. They loved the room; it was beautifully appointed and to them, more homey than any of the fancier bedrooms.

"This room is perfect. It's cozy and peaceful. Isn't it amazing that we can't hear the chatter going on downstairs? It feels like a hidden getaway," Leah spread her arms and dropped herself backward onto the bed.

"You got that right. I'm tempted to stretch out for a little nap," Mia followed her sister's lead and also plopped onto her bed. "Leah, isn't that bureau beautiful?" lifting her chin in its direction. "Dad said it was tiger maple. I guess that species of wood is not all that common and it's definitely an antique."

"Well, it's huge. Look, it's bigger than the doorway. How'd they get the thing in here?" Leah wondered.

"Maybe it was here before the renovations. Remember this was just an open attic at one time."

"Oh, right! I forgot about that. Luke knows a lot about this place. I'll have to ask him."

"So, how's it going with Luke? You guys seem good together."

"He's terrific, really terrific. But, honestly, his dad is a royal pain and his sister is—very needy. I like her and all, but there's something about her that's hard to warm up to; it's like she throws up a wall. You know what I mean?"

"I guess. Like she's not friendly?"

"No, no, she's friendly enough. Sometimes she's even kind of clingy and then she does an about-face and she's aloof. It's crazy. I can't figure her out."

"Well, just be careful. You've got a lot on your plate with school and all. Help if you can, but don't get swallowed up."

"She's hurting from that wicked divorce. I think she just needs some TLC. Really, I don't mind spending some time with her, although I'd rather spend it with Luke."

"That's exactly what I mean. Don't let her devour you or suck you dry, if you know what I mean?"

"If I remember correctly, you were there for Cindy when she needed a friend. Am I right?"

"You're right, but I felt God's leading to help her out and she was respectful of my time. I'm just saying—big sister to little sister—be careful."

"Okay, got the message, loud and clear, and I appreciate your concern."

"You're welcome. Do you want to go for a walk?"

"In the snow? On the beach?"

"Why not? It's not exactly a blizzard out there, just a nice steady snow."

"Okay, sure, let's do it."

"If you don't need our help right now, Aunt Trina, we thought we'd brave the snow and go for a nice, brisk walk."

"Dinner won't be ready for at least an hour. Why don't you grab Lance's leash and walk him for a few minutes. Maybe he'll be tired enough to sleep through our dinner. I swear, it's like having a newborn in the house."

"You got it. Hey, Vinnie, we're taking the puppy out for a walk. Want to come?" Mia was already pulling their parkas out of the closet.

"Nah, I'm playing with Emma. She likes it when I do this." Vinnie crossed his eyes, stretched out his lips and wiggled his tongue.

"Okay, we'll be back shortly, but be careful, kid—your face may stay like that," Leah laughed, as she scooped up Lance and went to the door.

What started with light flurries was quickly turning into heavy snow, but they would not be deterred. They were surprised at the strength of the sudden squalls. "Let's walk him to the bend in the road." Mia wrapped her scarf a bit higher around her neck.

"Those gusts can take your breath away and it's hard to see. I'm predicting this is going to be a short walk. Hey, Mia, look," she said, pointing to Luke's beach house. "Does it look like their door is open?"

"Looks that way from here, but it's kind of hard to tell in this wind. I can hardly see. Let's walk over there."

The girls jogged to the house, hoping their eyes were deceiving them. "What in the world?" Leah almost shouted. "Why would that door be open?"

"Do you think they had a break-in or maybe they just didn't push it closed; the ocean winds are pretty stiff and could easily have blown in that door."

"Let's check it out."

"I don't think we should go in," Mia warned. "Let's call Dad."

"Why don't you get Dad? I'll wait here to guard the open door."

"Are you sure?"

"Sure, what's the harm?" Leah laughed. "I have this vicious guard dog to protect me. Right, Lance?"

"Okay, be right back." Mia turned and fought the gusts as she ran to their beach house.

Leah was being pummeled by the heavy gusts; her eyes were watering profusely. "Come on, Lance. Let's stand on the porch out of the wind."

Leah felt sorry for the little fur ball, so she picked him up and snuggled him against her chest, leaning against the door jamb. "Come on, Dad. What's taking you so long?" she pleaded to no one.

"Hey, I thought Mia said you were waiting outside the house," Jake yelled as he approached Leah.

"I was just on the porch; I had to get out of this whipping wind. It's brutal out here."

"Okay. So, I've called the local police. They'll be here in a few minutes," Jake said to his daughters. "Let's go back to the house and wait there."

The words were no sooner out of his mouth when a Hampton police cruiser pulled up. The car had hardly stopped when the driver's door swung open. Both of the girls' eyes were riveted on the driver. He could have easily been the lead actor in a movie or television show with those beautiful hazel eyes and that strong jaw. Even with his bulky winter uniform, it was obvious that he was extremely muscular. They let their dad do the talking, probably because they knew this guy's presence would tongue-tie them—guaranteed. The police officer made them wait while he went inside and checked out each room, just on the chance a vagrant or thief was hiding. He came out within five minutes and announced the *all clear*. But he came close to interrogating them. He wanted to know whose footprints were on the porch near the door.

"The squalls were beating me up, so I squeezed myself close to the house to block the wind until my dad came." The heavy gusts were causing Leah's eyes to water.

Satisfied, he said, "Okay then, I'm going back to the station now. I'll call the family and give them a report. You have a nice Thanksgiving and welcome to Hampton Beach. By the way, it's much nicer in July." He smiled, closed his notebook and walked back to his patrol car.

Mia and Leah weakly waved as he backed out. "What a hunk!" Mia whispered.

"Tell me about it," Leah agreed.

"Come on, girls. Wipe the drool off your faces and let's get back to the house." Jake laughed, shaking his head as he took long strides back to their house.

Thanksgiving at the beach house was nothing like Thanksgiving at the old homestead. The novelty of their new place was an adventure—for each of them. The old Agosti homestead held so many warm memories, all of them included their mama and daddy. While they couldn't say for sure that every Thanksgiving going forward would be celebrated at the ocean, Joey told his sisters that this was symbolic of their family moving on together, but never forgetting their roots. *Pops would have fallen in love with this place. I can picture Mama working at that kitchen counter, whipping up one of her scrumptious Italian dishes.*

"The previous owners were smart to install this gas stove," Jake warmed his hands over it. "It's not only practical, but sure adds to the ambiance of the place."

Angie walked to him, wrapped her arms around him, saying, "It does make for a cozy atmosphere, but it's lots better when *you* keep me warm."

"Oh gag me," Kevin shouted. "You guys are too old."

"We are not dead, young man," Jake laughed as he twirled Angie in a mock waltz.

"I think they're cute," Cindy smiled as she rocked Emily side to side.

Jake planted a huge kiss on Angie's lips and said, "See, we're cute!"

"Honey, your hands are like ice cubes. Are you feeling okay?"

"Yup, I'm fine. I just got a bit of a chill out there. The temps are definitely dropping."

It was like an arctic blast when the door blew open. Lance lumbered in with the snow-covered girls right behind him.

"You're tracking snow all over the floors," Sammy scolded.

"Sorry! We're wet, cold and starving," Mia announced. "We just worked up a huge appetite out there; we couldn't resist making a couple of snow angels, but the wind is too much."

"Vinnie, your puppy is hysterical in the snow."

"I thought you were coming in right behind me," Jake commented. "How about you dry off and help Aunt Trina in the kitchen. I think she could use a few more hands."

"Lance, you're all wet. C'mere, so I can dry you," Vinnie coaxed. With that, Lance scrambled away, fast as his little legs would carry him. "Lance, c'mere!" Somehow that ball of fur flattened himself and shimmied under the sofa, poking his nose out just enough to tease Vinnie.

"Give it up, son. He's not going to let you catch him, he'll be dry in a few minutes."

Everyone laughed, but Vinnie was insulted that his very own puppy would not come to him, no matter how many times he called.

Trina came out of the kitchen in time to watch the antics. "You know what I think? When your puppy is a little older, we should send him to obedience school. Then you'll have an easier time with him. What do you think?"

"Mom, that's a great idea. Then I can make him do everything."

"Well, maybe not everything, but it will help. Hey, everyone? Guys!" Finally she had their attention. "Dinner is served!" And true to their normal form, they raced to the dining room; *ohs, aws* and *mmms* came from their lips as they salivated over the bounty set before them.

"Whoa, you girls have certainly outdone yourselves." Joey clapped and rubbed his hands together. "This is a feast fit for a king. And since I'm the king of the family, I get first dibs," he joked.

"Right, everyone take a seat. Shall we ask *King Joseph* to say the blessing?" Angie mocked.

"Oh groan, I'm stuffed. I say we wait a couple of hours before serving dessert," Ellie suggested.

"Perfect! Let's get the dishes out of the way and relax before we're overwhelmed by the sugar-shock that's certain to come," Angie suggested. "Trina, you've done enough. Go sit for a while."

"No arguments here," she conceded. "Vinnie, how about you and I take a little snooze before dessert?" Oddly, he didn't fight it.

The clan was rapidly slipping into their annual tryptophan-coma. Predictably, each person nestled into whatever nook or cranny they could find in their comfy beach house. The wind howled, whipping against the French doors, but they were warm and cozy. The snow continued to fall heavier and heavier well into the night.

Leah and Mia piled mounds of quilts over themselves, then settled in for a nice long nap. Thanksgiving seemed to be the one day of the year that napping was almost a necessity. After all, they needed their strength for round two of their eat-a-thon.

"What time is it?" Leah rubbed her eyes as she tried to shake off the slumber.

Looking down at her watch, Mia sleepily responded, "Looks like six o'clock. I can't believe I slept that long." She dangled her legs over the edge of her bed. "Obviously, that little outdoor escapade tired us out."

"We should have invited that nice police officer in for dinner," Leah chuckled.

"He sure was *nice*," Mia agreed.

They both chortled, but Leah grew quiet. Mia noticed her sister staring at the bureau. "Hey, what's up? What are you looking at?"

"I was thinking my vision was blurry from sleep, but . . . " Leah stood and walked toward the antique bureau. The dresser was very old; it was probably used by either a country doctor or a pharmacist. While the bottom half of the chest had two full-sized drawers, the top half had three rows of very small drawers, likely used for herbs, powders and the like. "But," she continued, "this little drawer looks crooked."

"So, it's ancient, it's not going to be perfect."

"No, no, can't you see, it's different from all those other drawers. It looks as though someone shoved it in too far."

"Big deal, it jammed. Just pull it out and slide it back."

Leah was already trying to pull it out, to no avail. She then began pulling out each and every one of the other drawers, just to be certain they were functional. They all moved freely, only the one would not budge.

"Leah, leave it alone. Who cares if it's stuck?"

"I do. Maybe it was put in the wrong opening. That would keep it from sliding properly. I'm just going to wiggle it a bit." Nothing seemed to budge the drawer, which only made Leah more determined to release it and fit it properly.

"You're a nut job. Let's go down and break out the desserts."

Just then, Leah yanked just hard enough that the swollen wood moved a tiny bit. "Ah, there, it's moving." She pulled with all her strength, when suddenly she was holding the small drawer in her hands—free from the dresser.

"Well, now you did it," Mia started to chide her but they'd both heard a clink.

They looked at each other, then looked around them, wondering what that sound could have been. The light from the table lamp illuminated something on the floor, something that was wedged against the leg of the bed.

Leah dove for it, and Mia said, "What is that? Is that a ring?"

Grabbing it, Leah said, "Indeed it is. I think it was wedged behind that drawer. It must have fallen out of the top drawer, and got stuck on the edge of the bottom drawer, preventing it from moving."

"Look at that diamond. It's huge; and those smaller diamonds on the side are stunning. It's so beautiful and it looks like it could be one-of-a-kind. Do you think it was someone's engagement ring?" Mia inspected the ring.

"That would be my guess. But why leave it behind? Don't you think any woman would have coaxed her husband or fiancé to pull that chest apart until the ring came out?"

"You'd think! Let's show it to Mom."

The family was moving around, slowly but surely. The wonderful aroma of brewing coffee filled the kitchen. Angie had already pulled out dessert plates and was resetting the table with all of their luscious desserts. Mia made two pumpkin pies, Ellie brought a decadent pecan pie and Angie made a classic apple pie.

"Can I whip the cream for you?" Jake asked.

"Sure, that would be terrific. I knew I brought you along for something," Angie winked. The girls stood before their mother, waiting to get her attention. "What?" she responded.

"Mom, take a look at this?" Leah held out the diamond ring.

"Whoa, did you?" Angie was afraid to finish the sentence.

"No, I'm not engaged!" She laughed. "I found it upstairs. Can you believe that?"

"What do you mean, you found it?"

"It was wedged behind one of those small drawers in the apothecary chest."

"Really? Well, it's beautiful and that center diamond alone has got to be at least a carat, maybe more. Those smaller stones on each side really set it off."

"It's not a carrot, Auntie Angie, it's a shiny ring," Vinnie blurted, causing a ripple of laughter.

"Yes, honey, it is indeed a ring."

"So, what do I do about it, Mom?"

"Well, for starters, I think we should contact the previous owners to ask if they lost it. How does that sound?" Angie asked?

"Okay, good, I'll guard it very carefully until we get an answer. Mom, don't tell them what it is or what it looks like. They should tell you. Am I right?"

"Good thinking," Jake added. "We want to verify ownership by their description of the ring. One step at a time."

"Dessert's on!" Trina yelled.

Vinnie was the first one to the table. "I want two pieces of pie," he smiled at his mom.

Chapter 17

Thanksgiving weekend tested the Agosti family's patience with one another in close quarters. The snow persisted throughout Friday and into Saturday evening, forcing all nineteen of them to be house-bound. The ocean roared and the wind was relentless for more than forty-eight hours. Fortunately, they never lost electricity and the house stayed cozy. The previous owner left several beat-up old board games in one of the closets; Vinnie stayed occupied jumping from one game to another. He cornered most everyone to play with him, at least once.

Back in October, Cindy complained to Kevin that the shovel he'd stashed in the back of the van took up too much space; now she thanked him for his foresight. That one shovel went from hand to hand until all of their cars were freed from the grip of those deep snowdrifts. They never saw a single plow until Sunday morning when the sun finally broke through, giving them a beautiful day. In spite of being snowed in together for several days, it was a precious memory that the family would long cherish.

"So, guys, what did your better halves think of our cottage retreat last week?" Joey asked as he slid under an old Chevy. "Personally, I didn't mind the storm at all. As a matter of fact, I enjoyed my afternoon naps."

"First off, that place can hardly be called a cottage. Kerri absolutely loves that house and it was a great opportunity to spend *quality time*, as she puts it, with the other gals," Anthony added, while wiping his greasy hands.

"That was actually the first time Hope had experienced a snowstorm at the beach; she was mesmerized by the awesome power of the roaring ocean," Ricky added. "I must say that I prefer a hot summer day, but it was a great time together and I do mean together."

"What, too much *togetherness* for you, Rick?" Joey laughed.

"Nah, you guys are great. I thank God every day that I married into this nuthouse, I mean family," he punched Anthony in the shoulder.

"We don't get to spend enough time just hanging out and once the baby comes, we'll have even less time."

"Don't kid yourself. Once that baby arrives, the girls will descend on your household like locusts, whether you want them there or not." Joey rolled out to grab a wrench. "Just ask Kevin next time you see him. The girls smothered them after Emma made her appearance. I'm guessing your mom will be your most frequent visitor. She cannot wait to be a grandma."

"What about you, Dad," Anthony asked his father. "Are you looking forward to being a grandpa?"

"You bet I am and I'm going to spoil that kid *rotten*, just like Grandpa Vincent did."

"Hey, look who's here," Ricky yelled. "Hi there, Trina. What brings you to the Agosti and Sons Garage on this fine, sunny day?"

"Wow, what a greeting! Did I interrupt anything or are you guys actually working?"

"We're always hard at work."

"Well, I'm a bit early to pick up Vinnie from school, so I thought I'd drop off some goodies for three of my favorite guys." She handed Ricky the familiar white Tripoli's bakery box.

Joey freed himself from under the car. "Hey, kid, that's so thoughtful of you. Mama taught you good," he chortled.

"Mama taught you *well*," she corrected.

"Whatever! We were just talking about our weekend adventure. None of us seem any the worse for wear and tear. We're in agreement that it was a huge success."

"Sal and I loved spending time with all you goofballs. It was lots of fun, but I think I gained five pounds. We've been kicking around the idea of getting bikes."

"You mean, *vroom, vroom* bikes, leather jackets kind of bikes?" Ricky imitated riding a motorcycle with his hands.

"Right, you dingbat! Can you just picture me on a Harley? No, I mean trail bikes or ten-speed or whatever they're called these days. I think they'd be fun and good exercise."

"Now don't go giving Ellie any bright ideas. I'm not interested in bicycle riding," Joey chastened.

"Too late! I probably should get going, but I wondered if you were able to provide Leah with any information on the previous owners, because of the ring that was left behind?"

"I gave Jake the seller's telephone number; he already contacted them, but they knew nothing about it. According to them, two of those drawers have always been jammed shut. The bureau was already there when they bought the place, so it might even date back to the owners prior to when it was a bed and breakfast."

"Hmm, it's a beautiful ring. Angie wants her to have it appraised, which is probably smart. I mean it's silly to spend a lot of time tracking down its owner, only to learn it's from a Cracker Jack box."

"Oh, I'm certain it is not from a candy box; it's the real thing," Joe added, walking toward the dessert box.

Abruptly, Trina stood. "Well, I'm off to get Vinnie. Love you all. Bye!"

"Hey, wait a sec, how come there's only two cream puffs in this box?"

"Ah, I weakened on the drive over here. Sorry! Fight over them."

"No wonder you gained five pounds," Joey yelled after her as she giggled all the way to her car.

She'd never get tired of playing practical jokes on her brother.

"Phew, I am mentally depleted," Mia sighed, dropping her briefcase on the dining room table. "My brain hurts. I am so ready for the weekend."

"Aw, honey, was it a tough day?"

"It was, but I have to tell you, the challenge is exhilarating. This job change was a very good move."

"I've never doubted that you have what it takes to get the job done. We're so proud of you; and we couldn't be happier for you."

"Thanks, Mom." Mia sat at the kitchen counter for a while, twirling her hair around her fingers while lost in her own thoughts. "Mom, do you mind if Matt comes to dinner some night?"

"Not at all, any or every night, is fine with me. I would have asked him to join us sooner, but I was under the impression that you two liked to be out and about town. Any particular reason for inviting him this weekend?"

"I don't know. I'd kind of like you guys to get to know each other a little better, but don't jump to any conclusions. We're not eloping or getting engaged, nothing that serious. But I really do like him, well maybe

I *more* than like him. But you know my track record, *love 'em and leave 'em,* so I don't want to mess this up. I'm determined to take it slow."

"I think that's very mature and smart of you; there's nothing wrong with being cautious. Mia, just so you know, Dad and I think he's a great guy."

"I think so too. He wants me to meet his family sometime over Christmas week."

"Sounds nice. I'm making chicken piccata this weekend. Why don't you see which day works for him. I'm flexible."

"That sounds terrific and I love your recipe."

"Mmm, did I just hear you say chicken piccata?" Leah waltzed into the kitchen.

"Hi, sweetie, how was your week?" Angie embraced her daughter. "Did you take the train?"

"Yup! I don't love getting up at the crack of dawn for class, but I do love finishing up early on Friday's and getting a jump-start on the weekend."

"Good for you. How is the mill project going? You must be pretty close to your submission date."

"Yeah, it's Monday, which is why I hit the lab right after lunch. I'm going to spend most of the weekend assembling my portfolio. I finished the article, but I'm not exactly thrilled with my photo collection." Leah stood in front of the refrigerator's open door, searching. Finally she decided on a bowl of hummus and crackers. "I'm starving."

"I'm surprised to hear you say that; all the photos that I saw were exceptional. I'm sure it will all come together before you head back to school."

"It has to. So is chicken piccata on the menu for tonight?" She glanced around the kitchen looking for evidence of one of her favorite dishes.

"Not tonight, but Mom's going to serve it when Matt comes for dinner."

"When is Prince Charming coming?" She tilted her head, popping another cracker into her mouth. "And would it be okay if Luke joined us?"

"Sure, the more the merrier." Angie turned away, smiling to herself.

"Awesome. I haven't seen much of him at school this week. We're both so busy, but his sister has managed to call me twice this week."

"Really?"

"She was moaning about the break-in at their summer house. She kept asking me questions: Did I see anyone? Did I hear anything? Did I go into the house? Talk about interrogation!"

"What's her problem?"

"I don't know? I'm going to grab a shower. By the way, how's Daddy?" Leah offhandedly asked as she moved toward the stairs.

Angie looked at her rather seriously, but didn't answer.

"What? Mom, how's Daddy?" Both girls turned to study their mother's face.

"He's been extremely tired, which is very normal for his disease, according to the oncologist."

"Oncologist!" Leah and Mia shouted at exactly the same moment.

"You guys never mentioned that Dad was seeing an oncologist. When did that happen?"

"This morning. Remember the primary hospitalist said he was sending him to a specialist? Well, we had an appointment earlier this morning. I took a personal day, but you know your dad. He headed straight to his class after the appointment."

Both girls sat at the breakfast bar; Mia pulled her mom's hand, guiding her to sit with them. "Tell us what the oncologist said—tell us everything."

"There is no reason for you girls or Kevin to worry. Remember when this happened, the hospitalist told us that polycythemia was very manageable."

"Yes, but exactly *how* will it be managed?"

"Well, this morning Dr. Glenn started your dad on a medication called hydroxyurea, which is a type of chemo. He's also going to be scheduled for regular blood work. I guess each time blood is drawn, it shows the levels of his red blood cells. I think the doctor explained that monitoring his red cell count, as well as his platelet levels, will dictate exactly what dosage of this medication he will subsequently prescribe. So, whenever blood is drawn, Dr. Glenn will read his hematocrit levels, and stuff like that, adjusting or tweaking the specific dosage based on that regular blood work."

"So how often will he have his blood drawn? And for how long?" Mia questioned.

"To start, every eight weeks and, honey, it will be for the rest of his life."

"Mom, please don't keep important medical information like this from us. We need and want to know about this stuff," Leah pleaded.

"You do know that we're big girls now? We can handle it and besides, don't you want us to all be praying?" Mia added.

"You're right, I was just trying to protect you and your brother from worrying. From now on, I'll try to keep you in the loop. Oh, he's also taking a daily dose of baby aspirin. But girls, promise you won't hover over him. You know how he hates that, even from me, especially from me. Are we good now?"

"Yeah, we're good, Mom." Mia hugged her.

"Okay, Mia, go call that dude of yours so I can get Luke to pile on for dinner," Leah lightly pushed her sister toward the phone.

Chapter 18

"Hi, Matt, she'll be right down. I sort of hogged the bathroom, so she's running late," Leah laughed as she closed the door behind him.

"Oh, little sisters! I know all their tricks."

"It wasn't a trick, really. I hate those dorm showers, so when I come home, I tend to dominate our bathroom. I don't always play nice," Leah admitted. "So, you have a younger sister?"

"Sure do. Most of the time she's the best, but occasionally I'm tempted to wring her neck. She's a prankster and sometimes her tricks get pretty elaborate." Looking around, he asked, "What smells so amazing?"

"Ha, I like your sister already. And *that* is chicken piccata you're smelling. It's Mom's signature dish, wait 'til you taste it."

"Oh, I've had it lots of times and I always clean my plate. I'm a good little boy."

"Yah right, little. Do you lift weights?"

"Aha, we have a well-equipped gym at work; I take advantage of it during lunch or sometimes stay late, just to work out."

"It shows. Oh, was that bad to say?"

"Nope, I'm good with it. Oh, I almost forgot, actually I did forget. Be right back."

Matt ran out to his car and retrieved a small package, but kept it to himself until Mia appeared. "Hey, there you are," She smiled at him.

"Hi! I brought something for you." He handed her a familiar blue and silver box.

"I adore Baci chocolates. How did you know?" she asked.

"Come on, is there an Italian on the face of this earth doesn't love Baci chocolates? It's in our DNA."

"Yes, well, I am a chocoholic and that hazelnut in the center is to die for."

"Did you know that it means *kiss*?" he whispered, placing a tender kiss on her cheek. "Plus those sayings on the wrappers add to their enticement."

"I don't remember exactly which holiday it was, but my cousin Sammy and I kept unwrapping, reading the sayings and stuffing our faces until we turned green."

Leah piped in, "It was Christmas. Grandpa Vincent brought one of those boxes for me and you guys swiped it. Serves you right that you got sick."

"Ah, Leah, it's time to get over it. We were little kids."

"Yeah, well you still owe me a box," Leah teased, as she walked to the kitchen. "Hey, Mom, do you need any help?"

"Guess I opened old wounds."

"Nah, she's joking and yes, she's a pest sometimes, but I still love her."

Just then Leah hurried past them at the sound of the doorbell. "I got it," she yelled.

"Good Lord, Leah, could you please turn it down a notch. We're not deaf, although I soon may be." Jake smiled and shook his head as he extended his hand to Matt. "Hi there, glad you could make it for dinner. Have a seat. It's not always this noisy."

"Thanks, sir. I appreciate the invitation; I hear Mrs. Trayor is an excellent cook."

"That she is, son, that she is." He turned and was startled to find Luke standing behind him. "Oh, hey there. Nice to see you again."

Matt stood up, greeted Luke and returned to his place on the sofa. "Good to see you, man. How's it going at the prestigious B.U.?"

"Good, good, but exams are bearing down, so I'm feeling the pressure."

"How are your grades so far?" Jake asked.

"Somewhere in the 3.85 range."

"I don't think you have anything to worry about, son."

Luke grunted and responded, "Ha, you don't know my dad. According to him, 3.85 is miles away from a 4.0 G.P.A."

Jake suddenly felt sorry for the kid; he identified with this young man. His own father kept the screws tightened down on him all throughout high school and college. All these years later, it was painfully clear to Jake that he never measured up to his father's unrealistic expectations.

"Well, Luke, it seems to me that he's raised a wonderful young man and you've got your head on straight. He'll come to realize that someday."

"Yeah, someday . . . " His voice trailed off.

Matt was not unaccustomed to meals like the one set before him. Both his parents were Italian-American, so he'd grown up enjoying every imaginable old-world dish. Also, his grandparents lived next door, so as a youngster, he often visited in time to grab the first of Nana's fried pizza dough or pizza fritta, as she called it. But tonight's dinner was right up there with the best his mom had ever made. Angie's chicken piccata on a bed of parmesan garlic orzo was out of this world.

"Mrs. Trayor, that was delicious. Thank you. I won't need to eat for a week." Matt said as he pushed himself away from the table.

"He's right. I've not often sat down to a home-cooked meal like that one." Luke added. "You are an excellent cook and I've eaten in lots of metropolitan restaurants. My mom is not much of a cook, really doesn't spend much time in the kitchen at all, so we frequently eat out or we order in. But I have to say, that Italian cream cake was decadent. Thank you."

"Oh stop with the buttering up. I'll still let you guys see my daughters," Angie chortled. "Now you guys go relax in the family room. Jake will help me clear, won't you, dear?"

"I never argue with the boss. I do whatever I'm told."

———

"Ugh, I may never eat again," Luke groaned, yanking at his belt.

"Luke, if you're going to hang around my family, you've got to learn how to pace yourself. There is always a second or third course, always. We are serious eaters." Leah chuckled.

"I totally get that, but it is a miracle you all are so trim."

Matt and Mia moved to the sofa at the far end of the family room, already lost in a private conversation.

"Would you like to see my collection of mill photos?" Leah asked Luke. "I have way more than I can use and tomorrow is my deadline. I've got to decide which ones to eliminate from my portfolio."

"Sure, I'd love to see them."

Leah powered up her laptop, opened her mill file and set it to slideshow.

"Wow, you *have* been a busy little girl, haven't you?"

She shrugged. "I guess I'm an overachiever."

"Ya think?"

Luke studied her as she methodically scrolled through her work. It was apparent that she knew exactly when each picture was taken, organizing them according to the subtle variations of light and shadows. To him, they pretty much all looked the same, but he recognized talent when he saw it. This girl was going places, he just knew it.

"Leah, I have to tell you, you have a unique gift, you really do. I have been exposed to hundreds of artists through Mom and Dad's art galleries, so I am serious when I tell you, you have a very bright future."

She stared at him as though he'd just handed her a check for a billion dollars; she was taken aback. "Luke, are you joking? You're not pulling my leg, are you?"

"I am definitely not pulling your leg, or stroking your ego, or anything else. After you get your final grade, would you consider displaying your work at the Methuen gallery—if my mom agrees to it?"

"Would I what?" Her hand went to her throat. "You're serious, aren't you?"

"Sure am!"

"If your mom is on board, then how could I say no?"

"Great!" Luke looked down again, studying each photo more closely. "Hey, that's my sister's car," he laughed. "Will you have to crop any of these?"

"I don't like to crop when I'm telling a story. That's why it takes me forever to get the angles exactly right. But, see how the parking lot also tells a story?"

"If you say so," he said, shaking his head.

"Oh look, a few more shots with her car," he pointed to three more photos.

"That girl sure puts in a lot of hours."

"She does and Dad encourages it. It drives my mom nuts, but Michelle doesn't listen. Hey, I see you're wearing that ring you told me about. It really is very pretty."

"It is, isn't it? And since you brought it up, can you tell me any history of our beach house?"

"Just what I already told you, but my dad would definitely know more; he spent every summer there since he was a little kid. I'll ask him—next time we bump into each other," he sarcastically responded.

"Okay, that would be great, because so far, the previous owners have been dead ends."

"Did you consider that it may have been left by a guest of the bed and breakfast?"

"I did. And in that case, I'll never be able to track down the owner. But it doesn't make any sense to me. Would a woman knowingly leave her rather large diamond ring behind? I surely wouldn't."

"Leah, if it hasn't been claimed by now, I think it's safe to assume that it's yours." He took her hand. "It does look like it belongs on that hand."

The phone rang, but Jake yelled that he'd grab it; within seconds Angie appeared in the doorway, "Leah, it's for you."

"Luke, will you excuse me?" She returned in a few minutes, looking perplexed. "Your sister wants to get together with me."

"Now?"

"No, tomorrow. We're going to meet for coffee, right after church. She sounded stressed, more stressed than normal. I'm sorry, that didn't sound very kind. It's just that tomorrow is crunch time for me. I have to finish this project before heading back to school."

"Hey, she's my sister, but I hear you. She's got some major issues; don't let her drag you into her problems."

"What issues? Is there something I should know about before we meet tomorrow?"

"Not that I'm aware of. She probably wants to boohoo about her ex-husband. Honestly, sometimes she's a bit hard to take, but she *is* my sister."

"I get it, but I don't think I'm the best person for her to lean on. Maybe she needs professional help."

"I think she does, but I wouldn't suggest it if I were you. She'll flip out on you."

"Great!"

It was uncomfortable for Luke to speak negatively about Michelle; he felt like a traitor even though the reality was, she did need professional help. He secretly regretted that he'd encouraged this sweet, naive girl to befriend his troubled sister. It certainly wouldn't be fair if Michelle managed to suck Leah into her vortex of emotions.

After they had reviewed Leah's pictures, Luke said, "I almost forgot, my dad needs some help at the office tonight, so I probably should take off now."

"I understand."

"Thanks for a nice dinner and the good company. Do you need a ride back tomorrow night?"

"Sure, that would be terrific."

"I'll come by around seven, if that's okay?"

"Seven is good. I'll be ready."

Leah continued to work on her portfolio after Luke said his good-byes to everyone, but she couldn't shake the feeling that his sister was trouble. Big trouble!

The sun broke through Sunday morning, and although cold, it promised to be a beautiful day. The Trayor family had regularly attended services at a little white church on a knoll, set way back from the main road. It was the same church that Mama and Daddy had attended for years. Unlike her friends, Leah never had to be coaxed or chided into going. She loved everything about her church; those people were extended family. Pastor Rainey was getting up in age, but his messages were still powerful and relevant to his congregants' lives. Mia often remarked that the Holy Spirit used him to minister mightily to this congregation, often speaking *life* back into the heavyhearted.

Leah was desperate for a word of comfort this morning and she was not disappointed. Pastor spoke from *Joshua 1:9: "Have I not commanded you? Be strong and courageous. Do not be frightened, and do not be dismayed, for the Lord your God is with you wherever you go."* Those words from Scripture both pierced and comforted her soul. She was ready to meet with Michelle.

Leah quickly changed into a pair of well-worn jeans, along with her favorite royal blue sweater. She took a few minutes to stuff her duffle bag with the clothes she'd need for the next week; she'd be heading back to campus later in the day and wanted to spend the entire afternoon on her project. "Mom, can I borrow the car?" she yelled from the hallway. "I'm meeting a friend for a few minutes."

"Sure, honey. Lunch will be ready in an hour, if you're eating with us?"

"I'll be back by then." She left, feeling upbeat and positive. She pointed the car in the direction of the Dunkin Donuts on Pelham Street. She and Michelle had stopped there for coffee a few times. It was a short drive and she found herself singing, *Great is Thy Faithfulness* the entire way. Leah thought to herself, *It's true, Lord, Your faithfulness has always be great and abundant to me and my family.*

She pulled into the parking lot and immediately spotted Michelle's car. The lot didn't appear to be very crowded; she had her choice of spots. Unexpectedly, her stomach began doing flip-flops. *What on earth could she possibly want? Lord, protect me from any possible ambush or trap of the enemy. I like her—I just don't trust her.*

She spied Michelle sitting in the far corner of the room, but she barely acknowledged Leah until she was standing directly in front of her.

"Hi, Michelle. How are you on this beautiful Sunday?" Leah half sang, trying to keep a positive attitude. She plopped herself down and started to peel off her jacket but noticed Michelle hadn't bothered to remove her own. *Guess this is going to be a quick meeting.* She kept her jacket on.

"Hi," she whined back, which immediately conjured up thoughts of Eeyore from Leah's old *Winnie-the-Pooh* books. She'd always loved Winnie, but couldn't figure out what Eeyore had to be so gloomy about. He was always in a funk. She never wanted to view life in such a pessimistic or anhedonic way. Life was worth living! There was happiness and joy all around, if people were just willing to grab hold of it. She liked to think of herself more as a Tigger personality, at least she hoped she was.

"I can't stay long; my folks are expecting me for lunch. What's up?" Again Leah tried to maintain a cheerful persona.

Although Michelle was very pretty, today she looked hard or maybe even cold. *Oh no, that's how I described her father—a cold fish.* There she sat, just staring at Leah with hooded eyes.

"My father cornered me last night while Luke was out of the house."

"Why would he have to *corner* you?"

"He's a very dominating man, not to mention—persuasive."

"Persuasive? I don't get what you're trying to tell me."

"Leah, I'm talking about Thanksgiving afternoon, during the storm."

"Okay, what about it?"

"My father is convinced that when you were waiting for your dad, you pushed in the door of our beach house."

Leah was now on the defensive. "Why would I do that?"

"Leah, he told me that you took money he'd left in that old Chinese keepsake box."

"What? Are you kidding me? I did no such thing."

"I wish I was. He had me so upset, I didn't want to believe him," she moaned.

"So, you believe him?"

"No. Definitely not! Luke and I talked this morning—"

"Wait, he talked to Luke too?"

"Yes, they met late last night at Dad's office. My brother isn't afraid of him, so he fights back. They had a terrible argument, they called each other hateful names. But I think they ended on a civil note."

"They argued over me?"

"Yes. My father doesn't think anyone is good enough for his children, so he denigrates whoever interests us."

Nice guy.

"Anyhow, Luke filled me in on the details. Don't worry, he somehow managed to talk Daddy out of pressing charges. But my father didn't bother to tell me that, leading me to believe he was going to call the police. He was testing me to determine where my loyalties were. Can you believe that?"

"No, not really. I mean, I believe you, but why would he do that to you?"

"Ha, you don't know how vindictive he can be. I mean, I love him, but sometimes I can't stand to be in the same room with him."

"I'm sorry to hear that. So, what now?"

"He doesn't want us spending time with you. Neither Luke nor I were able to convince him that you just were not capable of doing something like that. But, apparently, he's convinced you're a bad influence on his precious children."

Leah could feel her blood boiling, she had to get away—now. Abruptly, she stood, signaling the end of their conversation. She was determined to get to her car before the tears started. "So, Michelle, I guess this is good-bye." She turned without another word and walked to the door, not once looking back. But she was certain she heard Michelle whisper, "I'll miss you."

Leah turned the key in her ignition, looked in the rearview mirror and watched the tears rolling down her cheeks. There was Eeyore, looking back at her.

Leah couldn't remember ever feeling so dejected. The short drive to her home seemed like an eternity; she struggled to see the road through her tears. At first she didn't notice, through her relentless tears, but then she spotted the familiar car. Luke was sitting behind the wheel with his forehead leaning on the steering wheel; he bolted from his car when he spotted Leah. It was obvious that he wanted to head her off before she made it to her front door. Leah's stomach lurched and she began to step up her pace, but Luke's long stride was no match for her.

"Leah, wait up!"

At first she ignored him, then abruptly turned to him. "I don't think I can talk to you right now."

Luke's face darkened. He avoided making eye contact, then said, "Leah, do you think we could go for a short walk, I need to talk to you."

She stared at him, then silently nodded her head. She shoved her hands deep into her parka as they slowly walked down the quiet street. Leah loved her neighborhood, especially in the evening when bursts of lamplight shone from almost every house. She knew every family on this street; it was not unlike an extended family and it gave her a sense of security.

They walked in silence for a few minutes, an awkwardness building between them. "Luke, why are you here?"

She was painfully aware that he was wrestling with something, maybe something big, but she held her tongue and waited until he was ready.

"Let me start from the beginning. After I left you last night, I went to meet with my father. I was under the impression he needed my help with a project, but . . . " He rubbed the back of his neck. "When I arrived, he was in a foul mood. To make a long story short, we had words and it escalated into a wicked argument, and I mean *wicked*."

"Michelle just told me . . . "

"Let me finish, please."

Leah fell silent. Hands shaking, she fumbled with a tissue to blow her nose, as the tears kept coming. She could see compassion in Luke's eyes.

"I didn't sleep last night. I kept playing his words over in my head. This morning I grabbed Michelle when he wasn't around, but apparently, he'd already raked her over the coals pretty good. She was still a basket case from last night. I knew you guys were meeting for coffee, so after she took off, I decided to try to intervene—maybe help you get through this."

"Luke, there is no *through this*. Your father accused me of stealing. Stealing! And why would he leave a large sum of cash in an empty house for months, anyhow? It seems very foolish to me."

"Well, apparently my father was *foolish*. He said that he'd forgotten about it when he was closing up for the winter and when he did remember, it was too much bother to drive out there. Besides we've never, ever experienced any crime or vandalism." He let out a long sigh, "My father said the police report stated 'nothing appeared to be tossed or damaged', but . . . "

"But, what?"

"The policeman told him there were footprints in the snow that led to the door. He told my father that he questioned you and your sister about it."

"He did and I told him I simply squeezed in close to the house just to get out of the high winds."

Luke attempted to take her hand, but she stuffed them down into her pockets again.

"So, what now, Luke?"

"I don't know what to tell you. He's convinced that you quickly entered the house and reached into the decorative box that was on the little table; it's only eight or ten feet from that door."

"I'm telling you that I did not go in! And I most certainly would never steal from him or anyone else."

"I know you wouldn't. But he can be very persuasive and—"

"And what?" she almost shouted.

"I talked him out of pressing charges."

"I cannot believe your father was going to have me arrested!" Leah was so upset, she was trembling and began pacing back and forth.

Luke didn't know what else to say or what to do. He knew that his father was a powerful man and had a lot of pull in the community. Who would the authorities believe? He hoped he had truly convinced him to let it go; that it must have been a drifter or some local kids—not Leah. Why was nothing else touched—nothing, and there are so many valuables in that house.

"Luke, I think you need to leave now. I'll see you at school, I just need to be alone now."

"Leah, please, I know you didn't do it. Don't punish me because of my father."

"I'm not, I wouldn't, but my stomach is sick about this."

Reluctantly, he walked her to the front door. "Okay, I understand. I'll see you tonight at . . . " he said weakly as Leah closed the door, retreating to the security of her home.

"Hey, where've you been?" Mia asked, knowing something was bothering her sister the second she laid eyes on her. She discreetly followed Leah up the stairs, waiting until they were both in the bedroom. Leah closed the door and flopped on her bed. Immediately Mia went to her. "Leah? Are you okay?"

The floodgates burst open. Leah was now sobbing, almost hyperventilating, which made Mia press even harder. "Did Luke do something to you? Did he break off with you? Tell me what's going on?"

It took a few minutes before Leah composed herself enough to speak clearly. With her head snuggled into her sister's shoulder, she began, "His father . . . he . . . "

"What the heck? What did his father do?" Immediately thinking the worst.

Through intermittent sobs, "Mia, remember Thanksgiving Day when we went for a walk in the snow?"

"Sure I do, it was cold, windy and generally unpleasant," she tried to lighten the mood.

"Well, the police report determined that it really *was* a break-in at the Henderson's house. There was no damage, but money was stolen; I guess it was a large amount of cash."

"But, that hunky policeman told us everything looked fine."

Raggedly exhaling, she said in hushed tone, "Well, apparently it wasn't fine. Luke's dad accused me of stealing money."

"Are you kidding me? That creep! You didn't even go in the house."

"I didn't, but there were no witnesses to confirm that; I was alone on the porch, waiting for Dad to come back."

"We have to tell Mom and Dad. What if he calls the police?"

"Hold on, Luke talked him out of pressing charges, so hopefully it ends there. But, how can I keep seeing Luke with this mess hanging over me—over our relationship? And here's another quirky thing, because Michelle and I have become *friends*," she exhaled a bitter laugh, "he's pressuring her to stay away from me. I guess he's afraid I'll defile his children. I'm way too low on the social ladder for him."

They sat on the edge of her bed, Mia desperately trying to soothe her sister's hurt. "You're every bit as good as they are; you're a daughter of the King and don't you forget that. I still think we should tell the folks."

"Can we just wait on that, I really don't feel like rehashing this right now."

Mia gave her a mournful look and hugged her a bit tighter. "Got it. When are you headed back to school?"

"Luke offered to drive me back tonight, but forget that."

"I'll take you. Matt and I aren't doing anything special tonight. Okay?"

"You're the best, most of the time." Leah pushed her sister onto the floor and smiled down at her. "Mia, thanks."

Chapter 19

"I'll, be right back, Joe. I need a few things at the store," Ellie leaned down and kissed her husband. She had done exactly that same sort of thing a hundred times before, and he thanked God for her—she was a gift to him. They've made a wonderful life together; it never ceased to be exciting, fun and, yes, sometimes complicated. *From the very first day that we met—I knew she was my soulmate. And after all these years, she's still the love of my life.*

Yielding to this wave of nostalgia, Joey folded his newspaper, melted into in his recliner and allowed his mind to drift back to his younger days when life was—simpler.

"It's not fair!" Angie whined to her mother. "Why does Joey get to spend a week at the beach?"

"First of all, it's not a week, it's a few days. Don't you remember the year we invited Lenny to join us on our vacation? Now his folks are doing the same thing, they've asked your brother to come to the beach with them."

"I remember, but this is different."

"How is this different? If my memory serves correctly, Trina's best friend, Donna, was with us for the entire week. Angie, stop thinking only of yourself, you should be happy for your brother."

"I am, but . . ."

"Listen, why don't we ask Daddy to take some time off from the garage for a day-trip to the beach? I haven't been to Salisbury Beach all summer.

Angie's face lit up, "That sounds fun. Can my friend come?"

"Sure and if Trina isn't tied up with her summer job, she can invite one of her friends too. Are you happy now?" Mama smiled that warm, comforting smile.

"I'm going upstairs to help Joey pack."

At nineteen, Joe was feeling his oats. High school and one year of community college were behind him and he'd already been accepted into a two-year apprenticeship upon completion of his second year of college. He had a natural inclination for anything mechanical or automotive; after all, for the past ten years he had functioned as his father's right hand garage man.

Angie adored her older brother; he was generally kind to everyone. She didn't know of a single soul that did not respect him. The girls at school were falling all over him, which annoyed him to death. But it was easy to see why they were so enamored with him; he was movie-star-handsome with that dark, wavy hair and friendly smile. She was proud to call him her big brother.

She paused at his half-open door. "Joey, do you need any help with packing?" she asked. At nineteen and sixteen years old, these siblings were close, but that didn't mean he'd pass up any opportunity to harass or tease his youngest sister.

"I'm only going for a few days; how hard can it be to pack my toiletries and a couple of bathing trunks?"

She pushed the door opened and dropped into his well-worn side chair. "I think you'll need more than that. You don't want to use up all their towels and you should have several changes of clothes. I'm sure you'll go to the arcades and kiosks at night."

He looked at her sad eyes and guessed that she was feeling left out. "Look, Angie, I can't ask them to take you along. It would be rude. Tell you what, how about I take you and Trina to Canobie Lake next week or even Salisbury Beach—whatever you want."

"It's okay, Joe, you don't have to do that. I understand," she sulked.

"Cut it out, kid, you're making me feel like a creep." He pulled her into a headlock and ruffled her hair. She hated when he did that, so her recourse was swift and deliberate. She shoved his chest with all her might.

"Okay, okay, I give," he laughed. "Tell you what, I'll bring you and Trina some salt water taffy."

"That's nice, but what I'd really like is—could you to teach me to drive? I am sixteen, you know."

Joey laughed at her; he should have known she had an ulterior motive. "As soon as you learn all the stuff in that driver's book, I'll take you for driving lessons."

She ran toward him, nearly knocking him into the closet. "Really, you will? You're the best! See you in a few days. Have fun!"

"We will, " he smiled, shaking his head, as she retreated to her own bedroom.

"I'm not moving to another continent," Joey mocked, as the whole family walked him to his father's beat up old car. Technically the car belonged to Pops, but Joey and Trina frequently drove it since their father had recently purchased an older Ford with low mileage. He already had it running like it just rolled off the assembly line.

"Yes, yes, but we're the farewell committee," Mama hugged her son. "Oh, and I told Lenny's mom that I'd send something," handing him a box.

"What's this?"

"Just biscotti and a few fig squares. Don't eat them on the drive to the beach," she warned.

"Thanks, Mama, I'm not promising anything. Pops, your car keys, please," he held out his hand.

"Drive careful, son, and behave yourself while you're a guest."

After Joe drove away, Trina looked at her younger sister. "Come on, Ange, I'll treat you to a lemon ice."

Joe would arrive at Lenny's cottage long before lunch, but his stomach was rumbling and the smell of those anise biscottis were starting to tempt him. Still, he resisted that temptation. This familiar drive triggered so many wonderful memories. His thoughts drifted back to his family's summer vacation, just four years before; they were just kids. Since then, his sisters had both blossomed into dark-haired beauties. He watched the boys watching them, and didn't like it one bit. He was protective of his kid sisters, even if they drove him completely berserk at times.

Many of the older oceanfront cottages along this coastline were built very close together; sometimes only a walkway separated one cottage from another. Recently, owners started painting their cottages in a wide variety of pastel colors—lavender, pale blue, soft yellow were just a few in one grouping he couldn't help but admire. Throughout their childhood, Joe and his sisters had laughed at the whimsical and creative names displayed on some of these cottages. At the moment, he was following Lenny's directions while looking for a cottage named *Sandy Britches*. Trina would definitely add that quirky name to her list of *funniest beach house names*. Just then he spotted his best buddy, sitting on a porch rail, wildly waving his arms to catch Joe's attention. These two were thicker than thieves since grade school, and Lenny's antics never ceased to amuse him.

Lenny jumped the rail and was at the car within seconds. "Hey, bud, you made it. Let the party begin! Well, maybe not *party* exactly, but let the vacation begin," he laughed, lifting Joey's only duffle bag from the backseat. "Come in and say hello, then we'll head down to the beach."

"Hey, this is a nice place, and I love that it couldn't be any closer to the water." Joe grabbed the desserts, breathing in the salty ocean air. *I love that smell. It feels like home.*

"Yeah, they already decided to rent it again next year. Hey, I already scoped out the landscape," he said with a wink.

"Oh, really? I'm assuming you mean—girls?"

"What else? Hey, Mom, Joey's here," he pushed through the front door.

Lenny was taller than Joey, but not as muscular. His mother, who appeared dwarfed next to her son, greeted Joey with a casual wave. "Welcome, it's nice that you could spend a few days with us. How is your family?"

"Thanks for inviting me. They're all good. Oh, this is for you." He handed her the box of desserts. "My mom is a fantastic cook, so I'm betting you'll like them."

"Blah, blah, blah, come on, get changed and let's get on that beach," Lenny pressed, throwing the duffle bag in the guest room.

Within minutes they were stretched out on a blanket, watching the seagulls swoop and dive for their lunches. The local weather station was forecasting that temperatures would soar into the high nineties throughout the entire week. After all, it was August, and today was a perfect day to catch an ocean breeze while relaxing on the beach.

"So, Joe, I met three really cool girls yesterday. I mean, really cool and they're here for the rest of the summer."

"Where are they from?"

"One is from Boston, but the other two are from North Andover—they're cousins. Their parents rented the *Sea Side*. It's six or seven cottages down," he pointed in the direction of their house. "Did I mention they were really cool?"

"You did," Joe laughed, pushing Lenny into the sand. "Let's go for a walk," he returned the knowing grin.

They very quickly regretted their decision; they were barefoot and the sand was scorching hot. Joey did an exaggerated jog, but Lenny moved much slower. He began to resemble a flamingo, standing on one leg at a time in an effort to cool down the other foot. To say that they hotfooted it to the walkway would be an understatement.

"I feel like a dork," Lenny lamented when he noticed two of the girls sitting on their porch, watching them.

"Well, that's because you *are* a dork, my friend," Joey caught sight of the girls. "Oh, now I see what you mean, they are beyond *cool*," he agreed, as they approached the porch.

"Hey there," Lenny called to them. "Mind if we sit for a while, my feet are just about medium well-done," he guffawed.

"Sure! So where are your sandals?" one of the girls asked.

"We weren't thinking," Lenny admitted. He then turned to squeeze Joe's shoulder and said, "This is the friend I was telling you about."

Joe couldn't take his eyes off the smaller of the two girls. Her long sandy-brown hair was sun bleached and gave her a surfer-girl appearance. Wispy bangs accented the most beautiful gray eyes he'd ever seen. He felt his mouth go totally dry, like it was stuffed with cotton; he was tongue-tied and that was beyond unusual for him.

He'd casually dated throughout high school, but never met anyone then or at college who 'tripped his trigger', as he liked to explain. Lenny knew his friend so very well. One glance at his face and he was convinced that Joey was interested in this girl; he was silently staking his claim. That was okay, because Lenny was more attracted to her friend.

Finally, Joey found his voice, "Hi, I'm Joe Agosti, from Lawrence," flashing a winning smile in her direction.

She was amused and appeared to be mutually interested. "Hi, my name is Ellie, I'm from North Andover."

"Hello," the second girl sang. "In case anyone's interested, my name is Gloria." She nudged Lenny, both aware their two friends were destined to get better acquainted.

The foursome spent the rest of the day at the water's edge, intermittently running through the frigid, foaming surf, then retreating to the warmth of the blanket to thaw out their toes. They became fast friends, never at a loss for conversation.

"You're getting a wicked sunburn," Joey warned Ellie. "Maybe we should go back to the porch."

"I hate to break this up, but my folks are expecting us for dinner," Lenny interjected. "Why don't we meet up after dinner, maybe hit the arcades?"

"Are you good with that?" Joe directed his question to Ellie.

She shrugged her shoulders and looked at Gloria for affirmation. "What do you think?"

"Sounds like fun."

"What about Boston girl?" Lenny asked.

"Her boyfriend drove in today. I guarantee she won't want to join us."

"Okay, it's settled. We'll pick you girls up at seven," Joey blushed slightly. He shook out the blanket and turned toward the *Sandy Britches*.

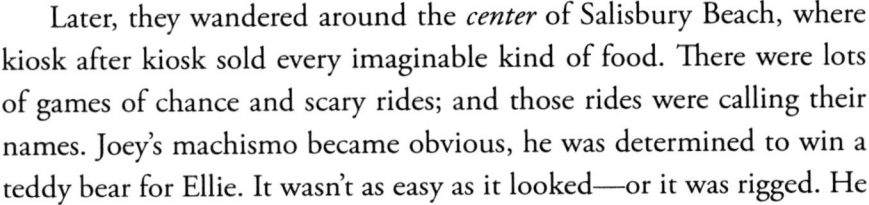

"Man, I don't think I have ever seen you blush—ever."

"I didn't blush, I've got a sunburn," Joe said defensively.

"We all have sunburns—*that* was a definite blush," Lenny insisted, while changing into clean shorts and a tee shirt.

"Aw, lay off," Joey chortled, giving his friend a hefty shove.

"Can I pick 'em or what?"

"You can indeed. She's—they—are great gals."

"Don't give me that—*they stuff*, you are so hopelessly hooked on Ellie. Even a blind man can see that?"

Joey raked his hands through his thick, black hair, looked up at his best buddy, "She's a keeper, for sure."

"Come on, Casanova, it's almost seven, we don't want to keep the girls waiting," Lenny mockingly blew kisses across the room.

Later, they wandered around the *center* of Salisbury Beach, where kiosk after kiosk sold every imaginable kind of food. There were lots of games of chance and scary rides; and those rides were calling their names. Joey's machismo became obvious, he was determined to win a teddy bear for Ellie. It wasn't as easy as it looked—or it was rigged. He doggedly tried, but finally gave up, shrugged his shoulders and said, "Anyone want to go on the Ferris wheel?"

Ellie looped her hand into his elbow. "I'm with ya!" Somehow, that little gesture eased the pain of his humiliating defeat.

High above the buildings, food stands and other rides, Ellie and Joe swayed in a Ferris wheel pod. Ellie kept nuzzling closer to Joe. "I don't think this was such a good idea," she shakily whispered.

"Are you okay? You're not afraid, are you?"

"Honestly—yes! I don't like being stopped on top like this. When is it going to start up again?"

"It's only stopping to let more passengers into each pod," he tried to reassure her. Realizing she was still nervous, he pulled her toward him in a protective hug. "It will be okay." And he was right, just then the wheel began moving, but she stayed close for the remainder of the ride.

"Anyone ready for some beach pizza?" Lenny shouted as Joey led Ellie away from the ride.

"Ah, not yet. My stomach needs to settle down a bit." She looked slightly green.

Beach pizza, aptly named, was loved by the locals, as proven by the extremely long lines in front of each booth. Although there were several pizzerias in the center of Salisbury Beach, Tripoli's also had a bakery in Lawrence, thus the distinguishing label. Diehards, however, sang the praises of the beach pizza, compared to regular in-town pizza, claiming it had sweeter sauce and thinner crust.

"I promised my sisters I'd bring them some salt water taffy, so I'm heading over to Willey's. Are you guys coming?"

"Definitely, their fudge is to die for," Gloria said.

"That's so nice of you to think of your sisters," Ellie remarked. "How old are they?"

"They can bug the life out of me sometimes, but most of the time they're okay. Trina is eighteen and Angie is sixteen."

"Well, I think you're sweet."

"Speaking of sweet," Lenny mocked his buddy, "there's the candy store."

Almost every Salisbury beachgoer was familiar with Willey's Candy Shop. It had been making huge assortments of candy since 1913 and it was located on a corner lot, making it almost impossible to pass by without stopping. Famous for their delicious salt water taffy, Willey's boasted a large variety of flavors, leading many to say that you haven't truly experienced Salisbury Beach unless you return home with a bag of their delicious candy.

The store was small, but packed with every imaginable confection. "I have to get out of here," Ellie joked. "I'm taking on a pound a minute just by inhaling."

Predictably, the temperature dropped as the sun set, making the walk back to the cottages much more comfortable. Pulling off their sandals, they walked in the wet sand, roughhousing and chasing one another. Joey kept stealing secret glances at Ellie. *I feel like I've known this girl my entire life. I wonder if she feels the same?*

Joey loved the ocean, he loved everything about it. The sound of the ocean at high tide was hypnotic, relaxing. He respected its awesome power, there was no doubt that it could be treacherous; the pull of the undertow could be a frightening experience. Yet, there was no place he'd rather be. "Isn't it beautiful?" he nudged Ellie.

"Huh? What?"

"The ocean, silly. I love that salty, sort of fishy smell, the roar of the waves at high tide and the gentler flow at low tide," he clarified.

"It is awesome. I'd love to have a place on the oceanfront—some day."

"Me too," he gave her a knowing smile. "Me too."

"Ellie, I wish I could stay for a few more days, but Pops needs my help at the garage. But, do you think . . . "

"Do I think what?" she teased as she playfully walked backwards in front of him.

He felt his face flush, grateful for the darkness. "I'm pretty busy once classes start up, and I'm sure you are too, but I'd like to see you again."

"I'd like that and I'm not all that busy." She pushed him and ran ahead.

They walked the girls to their cottage; on their way back to the *Sandy Britches* Lenny began to dance around, patting his chest as though his heart was wildly thumping. He began to sing a poor imitation of Carole King's hit song, "'*I Feel the Earth Move*.' Oh man, you're a goner, buddy, a goner!" he mocked and jeered his best friend.

Joe woke to the sound of seagulls. He lazily rolled over and pushed the curtain aside to take in another beautiful morning. He heard noises, activity coming from the kitchen. He bolted out of bed, wondering what time it was. Just then Lenny dashed through the door, "Hey there, Sleeping Beauty. I was just about to check for a pulse."

"What? What time is it?"

"It's only nine-thirty."

"You're kidding. I didn't want to waste the day. Why didn't you wake me up?"

"Because I just got up ten minutes ago," Lenny admitted. "Mom's got breakfast on the table, let's go, Romeo."

"Knock it off."

"Why? You are hooked, bro, hooked. I can see it in your eyes. Come on, today's your last full day. Let's not waste it cooped up in here."

They bounded down the stairs, pulled along by the smell of sizzling bacon. "Aw, you didn't have to do all this." But Joey salivated as he eyed the bacon, eggs and cinnamon buns.

"Sure I did. Enjoy!" Lenny's mother stepped back, smiling and remembering those two inseparable youngsters who'd grown into these wonderful young men. *Where had those years gone?*

They didn't want to fritter away one minute of their last day; within minutes after finishing up breakfast, they were on the beach, keeping an eye on the girls' cottage—waiting. Before long Lenny lifted his chin in their direction, whispering, "Here they come, be still your heart."

"Shut up!" Joey growled. "She'll hear you."

"Hi guys," Gloria yelled, running toward them. As they got closer, Joey noticed how badly sunburned Ellie really was. "It's going to be another scorcher."

"Ellie, that's a nasty burn. Does it hurt?"

"It does, but my mom just slathered me with some kind of greasy cream. I'll live."

Joey smiled and shyly responded, "I'm planning on it, but I don't think you should be out in the sun today. Why don't we spend most of the day at the center or at least in the shade somewhere?"

Lenny jumped up. "Hold that thought. I'll be right back," he began jogging toward their cottage.

"What was that all about?"

"No clue, but you have to know Lenny. He's one of a kind and I think that's a good thing."

It wasn't more than a few minutes before they saw Lenny awkwardly trudging toward them, carrying a huge beach umbrella. "I totally forgot about this thing, it was just lying on the front porch. It should help a little." He jammed its pointed end into the sand and pushed the canvas covering up. "Voila! Instant shade," he proudly declared.

"Thanks, that will definitely help."

They tried to stay protected from the sun under the umbrella, but the ocean was at low tide and they couldn't resist running back and forth, instantly cooling themselves. Every half hour, Lenny readjusted the umbrella for maximum shade; by lunchtime they were ready to check out the activities at the center. The kiosks were now open and ready for business.

"I'm going to get changed before we head to the boardwalk," Joey announced. "Do you girls want us to pick you up or would you rather meet us there?"

The girls exchanged glances. "We'll meet you at the arcade in an hour," Gloria said. "We should check in with the folks."

They actually did not want or need to check in with their folks, but being typical teenage girls, they wanted to primp a bit so they looked their best. "So, what do you think of Lenny," Ellie needled her friend as they shared the bureau mirror.

"I like him. He's a gentleman and very considerate. That whole umbrella thing—that was so sweet of him."

"Yes, it was."

"I don't have to ask what you think of Joey. It's plastered all over your face," Gloria couldn't control her laughter.

"Is it that obvious? I think he's—well, he's a head above any other guy I've dated," Ellie admitted.

"Listen to you, you've only dated twice that I'm aware of."

"Come on, they'll be waiting for us. How do I look?"

"Beautiful! Red, but beautiful."

They laughed and chatted in hushed tones as they walked close to the beach front homes. As they got closer to the center, the smell of fried onion rings, fried clams and French fries tickled their senses. "All that fried stuff sure smells good and I'm not really even hungry."

Their conversation stopped when Ellie noticed four young men leaning against one of the houses; they were smoking and talking loudly to one another.

"Oh boy," Ellie whispered in a shaky voice. "Ignore them. Let's just walk past—don't talk to them."

"Do you know them?"

"Aha, that blond guy has been harassing me. I'm sort of—afraid of him," she said in a husky voice.

"Well, well, well, look who we have here. If it isn't Princess Eleanor." The more muscular one of the group wasted no time in coming to stand directly in front of them. "If I didn't know better, I'd think you've been ignoring me, Princess Ellie," he said with a sardonic grin.

The girls did, in fact, try to ignore them, but it became evident that this sun-weathered, bully was not about to let that happen. Still, the girls stayed silent as they attempted to walk into the sand to go around them.

"Not so fast, Ellie. I am dead serious. Why haven't you returned my phone calls?"

When she realized he was determined to get some answers, she steeled herself, "Perry, I'm sorry I haven't called you back. I probably should have."

"Should have? Should have?" he impatiently pressed her.

"I've been busy," she responded, but not wanting to give him any false impressions or lead him on in any way, Ellie weakly said, "Honestly, Perry, I'm not the right girl for you. So, please stop calling me; let us go by—please"

He was noticeably humiliated and that humiliation quickly turned to rage. "Ohhh, Princess Eleanor is too good for the lowly Perry," he growled. Without any warning, he grabbed both Ellie's wrists and pushed her hard against the porch.

"Let go, you're hurting me!"

"Hey you jerk, leave her alone," Gloria screamed, attempting to pull him off her friend. "Tell him to stop," she frantically yelled at the other three boys, to no avail.

"Back off," he snarled at her, giving his friends the eye, which signaled their intervention. Two of them pulled Gloria to the stairs, "Sit there and shut up," one of them barked.

"I will not shut up. Leave her alone!" she yelled as loud as she could muster. The same guy crowded her in an attempt to shut her up; people on the beach were now turning to watch.

"Perry, let us go and *you* leave her alone," she loudly yelled, creating quite a commotion.

Out of nowhere, Joe and Lenny appeared and they didn't hesitate to jump into the fray. "Hey, you—get your hands off of her!"

Perry appeared temporarily disoriented. "Yeah, and who exactly is going to make me do that?" he snarled, turning to see who was threatening to spoil his fun.

"I will," Joey grabbed the guy from behind and spun him around. "That is no way to treat a lady."

Before he could say another word, all four of the punks were on top of Joe, viciously beating him. Lenny jumped on one guy's back trying to subdue him, but still it was four against two and they were being pummeled badly.

"Stop it! Stop it!" Ellie cried. "Help them!" she pleaded to anyone on the beach who'd listen. And listen, they did. Several guys attempted to break up the fight—it briefly turned into a free-for-all; fists were flying and some were confused, not knowing who exactly started the fight. Eventually the boys separated, giving the onlookers time to clarify. Four teenage boys had watched the whole thing escalate from the beginning and placed the blame squarely on Perry's shoulders. He didn't apologize, probably never would, but he did back off.

Joe declined someone's offer to call the cops, but he stood firm against Perry, warning, "If you ever touch Ellie again, you'll not only hear from the police, but you'll deal with me one-on-one."

"Come on guys, let's get those cuts cleaned up," Ellie suggested, as they walked away from the group that was already dispersing. "Thank you, really, thank you," she said to the ones who'd come to their assistance.

Trying not to alarm his mom, Lenny quietly snuck their first-aid kit out of the cottage and let Gloria clean up their wounds. "There, that's better. You guys hardly look like you were beat on," she snickered.

"Let's go back to the arcade."

Ellie took Joey's hand as they started back. "Joey, I don't know how to thank you; I was really frightened back there, that is until you came to rescue us," she shyly whispered as they walked close together.

The four of them were soon laughing again, feeling relieved as they wandered around the beach center. "Hey, I'm just wondering about something. We were supposed to meet you at the arcade, right? What made you walk back toward the cottages?" Ellie questioned.

"I was going back to get some sunblock, for you. I'd hate to see that burn get any worse," he smiled. "But I never made it back."

"That's okay, your timing was perfect; anyhow, I'd say you really *creamed* those guys," she joked.

Joey heard a familiar voice as they walked. "Joey, Joey, over here."

He turned to see his family at the fried clams booth. "What are you doing here?" he asked, bewildered.

"Daddy took a day off—you know, family time at the beach," Angie excitedly answered, as she gazed at his face. "What happened to you?"

Mama was also taken aback by her son's battered face. Tenderly taking hold of his chin, "Joseph, who has done this to you? Are you all right?" showing typical motherly concern.

Joey started to answer, but Ellie interrupted. "Your son is a hero! He and Lenny saved me and my friend from a group of thugs. Truly, he's a hero," she repeated, looking at him with admiration.

"Aw, it wasn't that much. These punks were trying to hurt Ellie and Gloria. We stopped them, that's all. Then a bunch of kids on the beach jumped in to help even out the numbers."

Mama put her hand to her mouth, "Oh my that must have been awful."

Papa finally spoke, "It was the right thing to do, son. I'm proud of you boys. And now, I'd like you to please introduce these two lovely ladies."

After the introductions were made, they sat together on the park benches that were located throughout the center of the beach.

"So, did you just get here?"

"No, we drove to Plum Island and then to Hampton Beach. We thought it was a lovely day for a drive along the coast. But, did you hear about that poor girl?" Mama asked.

"What poor girl?" They looked at each other and shrugged their shoulders.

"Apparently, a teenage girl drowned over at Hampton Beach. It just happened this morning, so the roads were still blocked; there were so many police and rescue vehicles. We never did complete our drive, so we decided to come here for the rest of the day," Papa explained. "And I'm glad we did or we might never have met your lovely ladies."

"A bystander told us she lived in one of those beautiful beach front homes during the summer months," Trina added. "It's so sad—poor girl."

Abruptly, Papa announced, "Well, we're going to leave you young ones to enjoy your day. See you tomorrow, son," he turned and walked away.

Mama looked at the girls, "It was so nice to meet you and I'm thrilled that my son and his friend were able to assist you. They're good boys," she proudly smiled at Joey, then at Lenny. "See you tomorrow," she turned to catch up to her husband, giving them a backward wave as she rushed along.

"Oh, can't we stay with them," Angie pleaded.

Trina rolled her eyes at her younger sister and said, "No, we're going. Have fun guys and it was nice to meet you, Ellie, Gloria."

Angie wasn't happy. She wanted to stay where the action was, but she conceded and caught up to her family, but yelled back, "Bye, guys!"

"Well, *that*, my friends, is my crazy family." Joey laughed.

"They are great and your sisters are beautiful."

"Yeah, tell me about it. I keep close watch over them, but not as close as Pops does," he snickered.

"Let's get some Italian Ice. I'm hot and thirsty," Lenny said.

They only had one night left at the shore, so Joey was already making plans for their next—or maybe first—actual date. Later that night, as they sat on the cool sand, stoking their bonfire, Joey blurted out, "So, Ellie, how about I pick you up Saturday night? Maybe we could go to the movies and then head up to Joe's Bungalow for a chicken barb. What do you say?" he shyly asked out of earshot of his friend.

"I'd love that, Joey."

"Really, you would?"

They both chuckled, but his was a very nervous kind of laugh. *She said yes. She actually said yes! Man, this girl is a keeper.*

Chapter 20

Christmas 2005 had come and gone, but it was always the happiest of holidays for the Agosti family. Mama and Daddy, even during their leanest financial years, never failed to make wonderful memories for their children. Christmas was holy and special to both Maria and Vincent Agosti; they instilled in each of their children the value of keeping family traditions alive.

Christmas had been celebrated very much like every other preceding year. There was no shortage of Italian food on the dining room table. Mama's ravioli recipe was always the family's favorite; they were served at every Christmas dinner. Trina, Angie and Ellie carried that torch by meeting together each year, just prior to the twenty-fifth. They had the process down to a culinary science; their efficient production line cranked out more than two hundred cheese raviolis. The Agosti family never failed to make an impressive dent in that number.

Perfectly seasoned sauce, made only with San Marzano tomatoes, happily simmered to perfection. The commercial-sized stockpot was also filled with homemade meatballs and braciole. It was almost impossible to keep the self-appointed *taste-testers* away from the stove. Antipasto platters, fruit, nuts and a delectable assortment of desserts also graced every holiday meal. Yes, it was tradition!

Angie hosted the family gathering and she did it with her usual flair and slapstick humor. Her antics amused young and old, with the exception of her youngest daughter. Finally, Leah, with Mia by her side for moral support, divulged the reason why Luke hadn't been around for several weeks. She hadn't seen him on campus, neither had he called during their entire Christmas break. Jake was not happy with Mr. Henderson's accusation and was preparing to confront him, but at Leah's urging, he let it drop.

With the holidays behind them, Leah would soon be heading back to school for her January semester. She was beyond nervous that she would run into Luke on campus; then again maybe he'd simply decided to avoid her. Leah assumed he was being a *good little boy* by obeying his father's wishes since he hadn't called. Yet, he was the only one who seemed to stand up to the brute; he'd related many situations where he'd gone toe-to-toe with dear old daddy.

It had been snowing all day—a winter wonderland. Leah sat on the window seat, taking in the beautiful picture-perfect New England scene. Several inches had accumulated since she and Mia last shoveled. The snow was blowing and swirling against the window; she was spellbound by the rhythmic motion of the flakes. She hadn't seen a car on their road in quite some time, but it was Saturday so her neighbors were likely hunkered down for the day.

"Hey, Leah, are you up for another round of shoveling?" Mia yelled from the hallway. "I'm getting cabin fever; I need some fresh air."

"Sure, let me grab a dry pair of gloves and I'll be right there." She jumped up from the window seat, but caught a flash of something silver from the corner of her eye. She turned back to the window and there was Luke, getting out of his father's silver Lexus. With those long legs, he was almost to the front door when Leah half-whispered and half-shouted to Mia, "Luke is out there. What should I do?"

"Ah, answering the door would be a good start," Mia sarcastically answered. "I'm going to be right out there," she pointed to the door, "if you need me. Okay? Mom and Dad are upstairs—do you want me to call them?"

"No, no! I'm fine. You go."

Mia opened the door to find Luke just about to knock on the door. "Hey, Mia, how are you? Is Leah home?"

"Of course she's home, we're in the middle of another snowstorm and why are you out in this? Never mind!" she answered rather curtly.

Leah approached the front door—cautiously. "Luke?" she struggled to utter that one word.

He brushed the snow from his hair, but silently stood at the door, obviously just as uncomfortable as she was. "Leah, I know you hate me—and my family, and I don't blame you."

"I don't hate you."

"Can I come in or would you rather walk? I need to talk to you."

"I think it would be better if you came in." She gave her sister the raised eyebrow as Mia picked up the shovel to begin her third driveway pass.

Mia was conflicted. Should she stay out of their way or go in and provide a buffer between her sister and any hurtful words he might throw at her? In the end, she decided to mind her own business, not easy for her.

"Give me your coat and have a seat. I'll just let my folks know you're here and that we need to talk privately."

"They know?"

"Of course they know." With that she ran upstairs and asked her parents to give her and Luke a few minutes alone in the family room.

"Sure, honey, but we're right here if you need moral support," Jake folded over the newspaper he had been reading, giving his daughter full attention.

"I know, Daddy. Thanks."

Luke was clearly as jumpy as a wet cat. He was rubbing his hands, raking them through his hair, looking around and appearing to be on the verge of hyperventilating. She'd never seen him behave quite like this. Leah couldn't imagine why he was here, especially when the driving conditions were so poor. *What is so important that it couldn't wait another day?* she wondered, pulling her legs up under her in her favorite wingback chair.

"Would you like some hot cocoa?"

"Not right now, thanks. I have to tell you something, and it can't wait."

"I'm listening."

He took a huge, deep breath, locked eyes with Leah and slowly began. "I'll try not to stretch this out and bore you with any needless details."

"It's okay, take whatever time you need. Obviously I'm not going anywhere in this storm."

"Well, suffice it to say you're aware of the stolen money situation."

"Painfully aware," she replied, more snarky than she meant to sound.

"Well, it got worse—much worse."

"What does *much worse* mean?"

He let out another deep sigh and continued, "My father came to me last week to tell me that a huge amount of money was also missing from the business."

Defensively, Leah quickly stated, "I haven't been anywhere near—"

"Leah, stop! I know that and I never thought you took the beach house money either—just for the record."

"I'm sorry, that was uncalled for. Continue."

"Well, we couldn't determine if it was poor accounting, erroneous entries or cash that was actually taken. It was rather skillfully done."

"So, what did you determine?"

"This kills me to admit, but the bottom line is—either my mom or my sister seems to be responsible for company cash that's gone missing. No one else has access to that office, except for a couple clients or maybe a few construction bosses, but they are never alone in the office. Most of them typically come in and are quickly gone after they get whatever information they need."

"You're serious, aren't you?"

"Dead serious."

"But your family is loaded, they'd have no need to steal. Besides that, your mom and your sister, wouldn't do that. They're family! There must be another explanation."

"Leah, you're being sweet, considering how my family has hurt you. Listen, you are fortunate to have a loving family, but you do realize that not all families are quite so *Little House on the Prarie-ish?*"

"So I've been told."

"I came because, well, for one thing—I've missed you," he looked at Leah with sad eyes. "But also, I wanted you to know that my father now realizes you must be innocent. I just want to warn you that he's planning to personally apologize."

"Really? He doesn't need to."

"Yes, he does. He's arrogant and leaves carnage wherever he goes. He has always used people for his own advantage; I hate that about him. Maybe, just maybe, this incident has humbled him a little bit, but I have to admit I'm not betting on it."

"Okay, thanks for the warning. So what are you going to do about his business finances?"

"It's not up to me to do anything. But before he confronts Mom or Michelle, I have to ask a favor."

"Shoot!"

"Before I ask my favor, did you get a good grade on your mill portfolio?"

"Huh? Yes I got an *A*, but why are you thinking about that now?"

"That's great. I knew you would, it was terrific."

"Thanks."

"And, I'm wondering if those photos are *time and date stamped?*"

"The actual photos aren't, but there's a setting in my camera that allows me to check that information. It's very accurate, but I didn't want it showing on my work. Why?"

"Well, remember how several photos captured Michelle's parked car in front of Dad's business? I'm just wondering if we could zero in on exactly which family car was in the parking lot on specific dates. Hopefully, that would give me solid answers before making any accusations. I really don't want to risk damaging my family any more than necessary."

"I hear ya."

"Dad seems to think he will be able to pinpoint some possible dates where discrepancies showed up on the books."

"Well, sure I can help you with that, but I've already discarded some photos. Not every one of them worked for my portfolio. But, Luke, why not just ask them?"

"You don't understand how fragile our family relationships are right now. Mom is threatening to leave Dad because he never spends time with her. Apparently he's grown very cold to her."

Hmm, cold fish! What a surprise!

"And Michelle, well, she's gone off the rails. I'm guessing she's gotten herself back into pain meds. She's in la-la-land half the time. She's been aloof—no, more like downright rude. Not the Michelle I grew up with, that's for sure. No, I'd rather have something a bit more solid to tell my father before he lands all over either one of them. Better if he doesn't destroy two lives—one is bad enough."

"Oh, Luke, I'm so sorry to hear all of this. You must feel caught in the middle of this mess," she said, now taking the seat next to him on the sofa. She patted his arm, "Truly, I'm sorry for what you're going through."

"Thanks, Leah."

The front door swung open and Mia stumbled in, looking like an abominable snowman. "Hey, thanks for the help. It's okay, I've got it," she joked, shaking the snow off her purple, knitted hat and all over the foyer floor.

Jake and Angie apparently felt they'd given the kids enough private time, because they marched down the stairs in sync with Mia's grand entrance. "Well, now you have another mess to clean up," Angie teased, pointing to the wet floor.

"Anyone up for some hot cocoa and Italian pepper cookies?" Mia cleverly changed the subject.

"Sure," everyone except Luke answered.

"Hello, Luke," Jake extended his hand. "It's been a while since we've seen you, son."

"Hello, sir," he cautiously responded, reaching for Jake's warm handshake. "I'm truly sorry about everything that happened."

"Luke, let me fill them in on what you just told me—if that's okay with you?" Leah interrupted.

"It is."

Taking their seats, she proceeded to share what Luke had just unfolded. Mia was back by the end of the story, carrying a tray of hot cocoa and cookies.

"So what now?" Angie questioned as they tried to relax with each other.

"Well, if Leah is willing to share her camera's original date and time stamps, then I'm leaving it up to my dad."

"This is terrible. I feel so heavyhearted for you, Luke," Angie said. Leah sensed that her mom was touched with compassion for him.

"Before you get your camera, do you think we could pray with you," Jake suggested, turning his full attention on Luke. "This situation could devastate your family."

"Sure, I'd appreciate your prayers. As a matter of fact, I've been going to church for the last few weeks. I'm beginning to realize there's absolutely nothing *I can do* to keep my family from disintegrating."

"You're right, son. Nothing, except to bring the Lord's hand to bear on this whole mess. This is not a burden you should carry on your shoulders. Let's give it to the Lord, right now."

As they prayed, asking the Lord to remove this weight from Luke's shoulders, a sweet peace filled their family room, casting out fear and anxiety. As Jake was ending his prayer, he lifted his eyes and asked Luke if he would like to give his heart to Jesus; Luke was weeping, but acknowledged that he needed Jesus to become the Lord of his life.

It was quite possibly the sweetest moments of Leah's life. She was thrilled that Luke was now equipped to walk this difficult—if not impossible—walk he had so unfairly inherited.

"I wish my family could learn a few lessons from yours," he finally said after blowing his nose multiple times. "Thank you. I believe the weight of this whole mess has somehow lifted from me."

"Indeed it has," Angie smiled.

A short time later, Leah retrieved her camera and began fiddling with the settings. "I don't use time and date stamps very often, so it usually takes me a minute to find it. Ah, here we go."

"Can we just scan the photos first?"

"Definitely! Are you ready?" she looked at him, wondering if this was such a good idea after all.

"As ready as I can be when I'm about to point a finger at either my mom or my sister," he sighed heavily.

"I'm sorry, Luke. Maybe there's some other explanation. Well, here goes!"

They sat together, scanning every photo she'd taken at the Wood Mill. Luke had no idea that she'd shot so many; her tenacity was impressive. He could almost guarantee no other student would even come close to her portfolio. They examined each photo, eliminating the majority of them, until they were left with seven photos that captured any vehicle that belonged to the Henderson family.

"Can I have a sheet of paper? I'd like to record each car along with the date and time."

"Sure," stretching backward to her dad's desk she grabbed a notepad and pen. "What now?"

"First of all, if I need them, can I get copies of these?"

"No problem, as long as you give me a heads-up."

He jotted down the seven dates, ranging from October to December, notating the exact times to the right, as well as the specific vehicle. "Now comes the hard part. Dad will have to sift through the books for possible matches of the dates with any discrepancies."

Leah set her camera aside, closed up her laptop and turned to Luke, "It's still snowing, would you like to stay for dinner?"

Chapter 21

Trina pushed the curtains aside to get a better look at Lance and Vinnie playing together in the snow. She couldn't restrain her laughter. Vinnie had managed to single-handedly build himself a fort and it was pretty impressive. Lance, on the other hand, was bent on destroying it; he pranced, circled and pounced on any part that Vinnie wasn't actively defending. Finally, her son had just about enough. "Lance, cut it out! It's *my* fort, stop doing that," the poor kid whined. "Mom," he yelled to the door. "Can you bring Lance in?"

"What's the problem?" she questioned, but knew, pushing open the backdoor.

"He's wrecking my fort."

"Well, maybe he's just wanting to play with *you*," she reasoned. "All right, come here, boy."

Lance ran indoors, circling the kitchen island, dropping tiny snowballs that had managed to cling to his fur until the heat had its way. "You poor guy. The little man doesn't want your help, huh?" she crooned to him as she struggled to towel dry his thick fur. "Come on then, sit with me by the fire."

Trina loved this newest addition to her family. He was every bit as sweet as her old pal, Buddy, but this puppy was Vinnie's. He cried to be with him every waking moment. Not even ten minutes passed and her son was standing at the backdoor, asking for hot cocoa.

"Come in, you must be freezing." Trina smiled, peeling away the layers of Vinnie's snow clothes.

"Nah, I'm not freezing. It's just no fun without Lance out there."

"I thought he was messing up your fort?"

"He was, but it's okay. C'mere, Lance," calling the clumsy puppy to his side.

"Mom, when will the snow be gone?" he asked as Trina pulled his boots off.

"Well, it is still February, so we have several weeks to go. We do live in New England, you know. Why do you want to know?"

"Just wondering if I'll see that lady when the snow is gone and we can go on the playground again."

"What lady?" Trina distractedly asked.

"I don't know her name, she comes around the schoolyard sometimes, but not since the snow got piled against the fences," and he was off, running after the puppy.

Hmm, he must be talking about a neighborhood lady. "Do you want some cheese crackers to go along with that hot cocoa?"

"Yup, and can I have some of those little marshmallows too?" he begged.

"You got it," she smiled, so grateful that this little boy had come into their lives.

"I don't think you'll have another snow day off school tomorrow, bud. The forecast is sunny and cold, so enjoy the rest of today."

"Mmm, that's okay. I like school now. I have two friends, they're nice to me," he slurped his hot cocoa, then chased the marshmallows around the mug with his spoon.

"I'm glad you have nice friends now. Would you like to have them come for an afternoon play-date sometime?"

"Sure! Thanks, Mom."

"So tell me about the lady?"

"What lady? Oh, the one that stands at the fence?"

"I don't know. Does she always stand by the fence?"

"Yup. She always says hi to me and asks how I'm doing?"

Trina was beginning to feel a bit uncomfortable, but reasoned that it was just a friendly person who lived somewhere around the school; possibly walking a dog or pushing a stroller.

"Does she talk to all the children?"

"Nope, just me."

"Is she alone?"

"Yeah, she was crying one day."

"Oh, that's too bad. Do you know why?"

"She said her little boy went away."

Trina's blood turned cold; the room began to spin. "Honey, did the playground monitor see her or talk to her?" she asked as casually as possible.

"No, the lady went away when Miss Wright walked near me. She did that two times."

"Oh, really? Can you tell me what the lady is like? I mean, is she young, like Leah."

Vinnie cut her off, now losing interest in the conversation. "She's nice. She always smiles at me. She's kind of pretty. Mom, sometimes she doesn't have a coat on. Can I watch TV now?"

"Sure, just finish up that cocoa. I'll turn on your show for you." Trina, full of questions, walked slowly into the family room. She was desperately trying not to assume the worst, but she'd spent most of her adult life in social work. She knew that things happen—that are not supposed to happen. She needed to talk to Sal—right away.

Chapter 22

"Listen to this, guys! You are not going to believe it," Leah loudly announced, rushing through the front door, allowing yet another arctic blast to enter the house.

"Whoa, close that door. It is frigid out there," Angie protested.

"I know, I know, I'm sorry."

"So, what's your big news," Mia questioned her sister.

"Wait, where's Dad? Everyone, please come here!" she excitedly insisted.

When finally her sister, mother, and father were gathered around her, she pulled a box out of her purse. "I was almost afraid to ride the train home alone today," she blurted.

"Girl, what are you babbling about?" Mia almost shouted.

Leah carefully opened the box and pulled out the ring she'd found at the beach house.

"Yeah, we've all seen it before, remember?" Jake was smiling at his precocious daughter.

"No, listen to me, I finally had it appraised in Boston. I went to two different reputable jewelers and you are not going to believe its estimated value."

"Well, come on, spit it out," Angie snickered as she playfully attempted to swipe it out of her daughter's hand.

"Drumroll, please—and the mystery ring's current value is estimated to be approximately forty-two hundred to forty-six hundred dollars."

"Whoa! Are you serious?" Mia questioned, taking a closer look at the ring.

"I'm dead serious. Look, they even gave me written appraisals. I'm not sure how they know, but both jewelers thought it was probably twenty-five to thirty-five years old."

"I thought you'd given up on finding its owner or getting it appraised," Jake asked.

"I was just so busy with school that I forgot about it until my roommate picked it up off my dresser to admire it. I decided to check it out, I was totally blown away. I've honestly exhausted every single lead to find the owner, so I guess I'm the proud owner of a beautiful diamond ring," she smiled, slipping it back on her finger.

"I guess you are. Congratulations!"

The group turned at the sound of the front door opening, again letting in a blast of cold air. "Knock, knock," Trina yelled as she and Vinnie walked into the front foyer. "Sheesh, it's bitter out there."

"Hi, Aunt Trina! Hey, Vinnie, give me a hug," Mia grabbed him and spun him around. "Wow, you're getting too big for me to do this anymore."

"No, I'm not!" he argued. "I like when you spin me."

Leah was still bubbling over with excitement, so she just had to retell the entire diamond ring story to her aunt. "Well, you just may start a new tradition."

"Huh? What do you mean, Aunt Trina?"

"Well, when you do find that lucky guy who is destined to become your hubby, just tell him you already have a ring—no need to purchase another."

"No way! Whoever *he* is, he has to do it the old-fashioned way. This one is simply a bonus," she smiled, holding her ringed finger out to admire it yet again.

Trina dropped several bags of party items onto Angie's dining room table. "I brought some possible ideas for shower favors. We don't have to use any of them, but you can check them over to see if they'll work."

"That's great, thanks. I've just started to think about this, so it's good timing. How about a cup of tea?"

"Love one, can we talk, privately?"

"I can take a hint," Leah pulled her sister's sleeve, nudging her toward the stairs. "Bye, Aunt Trina, don't talk about me while I'm gone."

Vinnie was already sitting next to Jake, watching a *guy* show on television, so he was oblivious to the conversation that was about to unfold.

"Angie, something has me rattled, really rattled."

"What's wrong?"

Trina retold the entire conversation she'd had with Vinnie, trying not to blow it out of proportion, yet not missing any significant details. Angie listened intently, her facial expressions changing in response to her sister's emotions.

"Am I nuts or should I be concerned?" Trina asked, looking over her shoulder to be certain her son was still preoccupied.

"I definitely don't think you're nuts, well, not more nuts than you usually are," she snickered. "What was Sal's reaction?"

"Well, that's partly why I'm here. He thinks I should talk to the playground monitor and first confirm that there actually was a *pretty lady* who visited at recess. That's where you come in. Do you personally know Miss Wright?"

"Sure, she's a single mom, very sweet. She volunteers at the school at least once a week. I don't socialize with her or anything like that; she's much younger than me. I'm sure she'd be helpful and approachable. Do you want me to call her, set up a meeting?"

"Yes, definitely. I'd like to keep this from Vinnie and do it as soon as possible?"

"I'll do it tomorrow if she's on duty."

"Thanks, Ange. The idea that someone might be stalking him gives me the creeps."

"I can imagine. I'm way on the other side of the building during his recess, so I can't watch over him or I certainly would."

"I know. Vinnie told me that they don't go on the playground when there is heavy snow."

"That's true. If it's snowy or really cold, they have recess in the gym. But if we hit an unseasonably warm, sunny streak, they just might allow the kids to get some fresh air. But even when they have indoor recess, they still use monitors, so she's likely to be around one day this week."

"Thanks, Angie. I can meet her at the Dunkin Donuts right down the street from school or you can just give her my number in case she doesn't want to actually meet with me."

Leah walked across campus, pulling her scarf a little tighter around her neck against the stiff wind. She and Luke were back to seeing each other fairly regularly, but his father still hadn't given him a clue what was going on regarding the missing money. Maybe it just wasn't worth splintering their already damaged family relationships. Still, she'd hoped that they'd get to the bottom of the whole mess.

"Leah!" came from just outside the campus café. "Do you have time to grab a coffee?"

"Hi, Luke. Sure, I'd like that."

They made their way through the crowded café. Books and coats were scattered on the floor next to occupied tables. It was busier than she'd ever seen it.

"Are they giving away free stuff or something?" she chuckled.

Luke laughed, "Yeah, it's crazy in here. Oh, there's a table in the corner. Why don't you grab it and I'll get us some coffee? Do you want anything to eat?"

"Nope, just coffee, thanks," she hurried to the table before it was stolen out from under her nose. She watched Luke as he waited in line, towering over every other student, including most of the guys. *I really do like him, but that family! Sheesh!*

While she was lost in her thoughts, a guy started to take the other chair. "Ah, excuse me, but my friend is coming."

"Yeah, but your *friend* is not here, *now*," giving her an up and down stare that made her uncomfortable.

"Please, put the chair back," she yanked on one leg of the flimsy chair.

"Hey, is there a problem?" Luke asked as he set two cups of coffee on the table.

The intruder took one look at the size of Luke and weakly responded, "No problem," then slinked away toward his friends.

"Who was that?" Luke asked, looking over at the group.

"No idea. But you were almost without a chair."

Luke leaned back and stared at Leah, as though seeing her for the first time. "You look extra beautiful today," he smiled.

"Really? Must be my extra pink cheeks. I'm probably wind-burned."

"No, Leah, you are beautiful inside and out." Clearing his throat, he began, "I have something awesome to tell you."

"Well, thank you. So, tell me what's going on?" she looked at him, while blowing on her hot coffee.

"You won't believe this, because I'm still trying to wrap my head around it."

"What? Tell me."

"Well, you know that my dad's been procrastinating on the missing money issue for weeks now. Every time I've asked about it, he just dismisses me or makes light of it. But I know, from a business standpoint, that he couldn't just let it go. I couldn't figure out why originally he was so insistent on getting to the bottom of it and then doing a complete about-face and seeming not to care."

"Okay."

"So, yesterday, out of the blue, he informs me that he's been attending my church. I never even saw him there because he went to first service and I went to second service. Our paths never crossed."

"Wow, that's a shocker; that's actually fantastic."

"It is, and get this—Mom went with him last Sunday. I mean, I haven't seen them interact with each other very much so, I'm in total shock. My mom and dad inside a church—my church."

"How did this all come about? I mean, how did he even know about your church?"

Luke leaned back, his eyes flooding, as he self-consciously wiped his eyes and began to speak. "After your family prayed with me, I decided to talk to the pastor. I guess, I now consider him to be *my* pastor. He is a great guy, very compassionate and caring. I told him that I'd just become a Christian and then unloaded all the nasty stuff about my dysfunctional family."

"Was that hard for you? To share so much, I mean."

"No, not really. He made it very easy."

"My pastor is awesome too. I can go to him or his wife with anything," Leah added.

"Well, here's the kicker, I was totally unaware that he and my dad go way back—back to college days. So, a few days after we met, he took it upon himself to pay Dad a visit."

"What? I bet your dad wasn't too pleased with that."

"Actually, he was happy to reconnect with his old college pal, who is now my pastor. And get this, at the end of their visit, my pastor prayed with him. I was totally blown away when dad told me that it was a *nice* prayer."

"A nice prayer?"

"I think, and I sure hope I'm right, that Dad gave his heart to the Lord, but he doesn't quite understand what's happening to him."

"Really? I mean, really?"

"So, they are meeting on a regular basis, just the two of them."

"That is super! But still nothing about the missing money."

"Oh, this gets better," Luke excitedly said. "Well, maybe not exactly better, but—"

"But what, come on, tell me," she interrupted, wiggling impatiently in her chair.

"Okay, okay! Hang on to your seat. Dad and I were sitting in the office before the day got busy. Michelle was late, which has become the norm for her. We both looked up when she walked in and I immediately knew something was up with her."

"What do you mean, *up with her?*"

"She looked like she hadn't slept in a month and she smelled—stale or maybe dirty. She dropped her purse into the desk drawer without saying a word or even acknowledging us. Dad was surprisingly quiet, you might even say he was pleasant to her. I think that unnerved her."

"I can imagine. Then what?"

"Well, Dad and I continued our conversation about one of his museums, trying our best to include her in the discussion. She remained aloof, probably hoping we'd leave the office. Then Dad stood, walked to her chair and stood there, not saying a word. I'm sure Michelle thought he was going to yell at her or demean her in some way."

"So, he just stood there?"

"No, all of a sudden, he embraced her and began to sob."

"Are you kidding?"

"Leah, he was so broken, crying and asking her forgiveness for his past behavior. He clung to her for the longest time, sobbing like a baby."

"What did she do? How did she react?"

"She broke down in his arms, hysterically weeping."

"Oh my goodness, Luke. I can hardly believe that happened." Tears were welling up in Leah's eyes.

"Believe it! Then, without any prompting or pressure, Michelle confessed to stealing thousands of dollars from the business. She admitted to being in a dark place for a long time; she'd become so despondent that she was popping pain meds and drinking heavily. She even stashed bottles in the office. Between the pills and the booze, she was circling the drain and she knew it."

"And then, stealing?"

"Yup, she figured she had nothing else to lose and her habits were getting quite expensive."

Leah drew her chair closer to Luke and placed her hand on his back. "Luke, that is God! He's obviously working miracles in your family. I'm so happy for all of you."

"Well, I don't yet know where Mom stands, but it's true, God is at work in my family. I never, never, never could have predicted this."

"So what about Michelle? Is there a chance she'd consider checking herself into a rehab program?"

"She and Dad are talking about that. He is willing to pay anything to get his little girl back."

Just then, the same guy who'd given Leah a hard time, walked by, pretending to stumble as he spilled his coffee on Luke's shoulder. "Oh,

I'm sorry. I didn't see you sitting in that chair," he smirked again, probably trying to provoke a confrontation.

Luke almost jumped out of his chair, but calmly responded, "No problem, buddy. It's all good."

Leah covered her mouth and giggled, causing the instigator to give her a puzzled glance. She reached for Luke's hand and smiled. "Fasten your seatbelt, Luke. This is just the beginning of your new life. Jesus loves your family and desires restoration—I'm sure of it."

Chapter 23

Trina, despite Sal's voice of reason, continued to be concerned about the pretty lady Vinnie claimed visited him during outdoor recess. She trusted the Lord to protect her son, and yet she was unsettled. God had made a way for Vinnie to transition from being their foster child to being their very own adopted son. As she sat in the donut shop, she wracked her brain trying to figure out exactly how Vinnie's biological mom could have tracked him down, if indeed that was the case.

The door opened and a lovely young woman walked in. Scanning the customers, she quickly locked eyes with Trina. Miss Wright was a modern-day Maureen O'Hara; her flaming-red hair was long and lush. Vinnie talked incessantly about this lovely school volunteer, and Trina now understood why.

Trina waved, calling her to their table. "Miss Wright, thank you so much for meeting with me, I really appreciate your time."

"It's nice to meet Vinnie's mom, he's a wonderful little boy. And it's Mrs. Wright, but I am widowed."

"Oh, I'm so sorry to hear that. Please accept my condolences."

Lowering her head while removing her gloves, she said, "Thank you. He was killed in Iraq and—I'll miss him forever."

"That must have been awful, beyond awful. Besides your son, do you have any family in the area?"

"I do and they have been very supportive. I don't think I could have walked through this without them."

"I'm glad to hear you say that. My family is everything to me; we're blessed to have them. Mrs. Wright . . . "

"Please, call me Ginger."

"Ginger—now that is an appropriate name," Trina smiled, pointing to her new friend's gorgeous red hair.

"Yes, well it's actually Virginia, but *once tagged, always tagged*. So I stopped fighting it and answer to both names."

"I think it suits you. Maureen would have also suited you, but you're too young to know who Maureen O'Hara was."

"I know exactly who she was; my dad was in love with her." She leaned back and laughed, then said, "So, Mrs. Lamazo . . . "

"Please, call me Trina."

"Trina, how can I help you?"

"Well, my sister may have given you a brief overview of my concerns. To start, I'd just like to know if there actually is a *pretty lady*, as my son calls her, that visits him? Truthfully, I'm hoping it's just a neighbor, out walking."

Ginger seemed somewhat reluctant to respond, but then related, "I understand, but your son is being truthful. I have seen a young woman standing on the other side of the fence two or three times, but it could have been more often than that. It gets so hectic when all the kids are running around that I could have easily missed another time."

Trina slumped back in her chair and raised her hands to her forehead. "I was hoping our conversation would end here."

"She doesn't appear to be threatening at all, but I did report it to the vice principal, just in case."

"Oh you did? Thank you for doing that, but I never got a call."

"Probably because there was really nothing to report. The gates are locked, she was pleasant and nonaggressive and Vinnie appeared to actually have a relationship with her."

"Can you describe her to me?"

"Sure. She's quite young, I'd guess early twenties with blunt-cut dark hair. She certainly is pretty, but rather unkempt and she looked unhealthy. Also, she's quite thin and the last time I saw her, she wasn't wearing a coat and it was cold. That's one of the reasons I started walking toward them, but she waved to Vinnie and took off down the street. I don't think you have to worry about abduction or anything like that."

"No, maybe not, but Vinnie is adopted and I'm afraid his biological mother may be regretting her decision to sever rights." With that Trina choked up and had to stop.

"Oh, I certainly hope not. Does Vinnie know he's adopted?"

"He does. We've been truthful and open with him, sharing as much as we felt he'd be able to comprehend."

"But how would she ever get her hands on his private records?"

"I'm a longtime social worker and I'm sorry to say that I've seen it happen. Somehow, it happens," Trina said wistfully.

"We haven't had recess outside in a while, so maybe she has given up."

"Maybe—I hope so. Please, Ginger, keep a close eye on him. I'm heading over to the vice principal's office to ask the same of him and the other volunteer monitors. Thanks so much for your time, I really appreciate it."

"You're more than welcome. Say, do you think Vinnie would like a playdate with my son, Billy?"

"He'd love it. You have my number, so please call when you've got a free block of time."

Ginger stood, and obviously feeling compassion for Trina, placed a comforting hand on her shoulder. "It's going to be fine. He will be fine."

Trina looked up at this beautiful young woman who had been through so much pain and loss. Experientially, this single mom knew about needing a comforting touch.

Trina paced the floor, waiting for Sal to return from work. She was desperately trying to remember every single detail in Vinnie's records. Before they had considered adoption, she'd just about memorized his case study file. His history was nothing out of the ordinary: underage biological mother, drug usage and child neglect. Without any effort at all, Trina could close her eyes and visualize the teenager's signature, agreeing to the *termination of parental rights* clause.

There was no named father and no grandparents who were willing to take responsibility for the toddler. Apparently, to her credit, the mother attempted to care for him for a short time, but soon got sucked into the drug culture, leaving Vinnie to inconsistent feedings and inadequate care. It was not an uncommon story.

It amazed Trina's family that in light of all he'd experienced, he was such a good-natured, happy little boy when he came into their home as a foster child. It wasn't long before they submitted paperwork, expressing their desire to begin the adoption process, eventually making him their own.

Trina's head shot up when she heard Sal come into the family room. "Hey, there's my beautiful wife," he cheerfully yelled, dropping his briefcase on the floor. Sal was still the cool-headed, charmer she'd been attracted to so many years ago. He seemed to know exactly how to calm her; he was always the voice of reason.

"I'm so glad you're home," she greeted him with a warm hug.

"Where's our little—"

"Hey, Daddy, look at the picture I made for you." Vinnie came running down the stairs with Lance scampering behind him.

"It's beautiful, partner, just beautiful. How about we put that one on the fridge?"

"Good idea," and Vinnie was off to the kitchen, eager to display his latest work of art.

"We have to talk."

"I gathered. Let's get the little guy occupied first so we're not interrupted."

Sal and Trina briefly talked about the *pretty lady* situation, but Vinnie was continually barging in on their conversation, so they postponed it until he was in bed. After Sal tucked him in and together said their nightly prayers, he joined Trina in the living room.

"Sal, I need your wise counsel on this; I'm turning into a basket case with every passing hour."

"First of all, settle yourself down. We don't actually know anything with any certainty. What did the vice principal say?"

"All the normal stuff. 'They'd keep a close eye and call us if anything unusual occurred.' I already called one of my most trusted former coworkers. I explained this whole situation to her, but she had no idea if or how Vinnie's records would have been compromised."

"So maybe this is all for nothing. I mean maybe she is just someone who wandered by the school yard."

"Three, four or five times, Sal? I don't think so. I have an awful feeling in my gut."

"What do you think we should do?"

"I was hoping you'd have that answer?" she sniffled, leaning into his chest, needing a comforting hug.

"Honey, I'm sorry, I don't have a clue what to do next. I just think we should make Vinnie aware that he shouldn't go with anyone, except family."

"Let's talk to him in the morning. Now, here's my big question. Should we tell him that his *other mommy* might be out there?"

"Not yet. It might arouse unnecessary curiosity. Don't you think?"

"I agree. Let's wait and see if she shows up again. I guess we have to trust the school to be on top of this."

Trina and Sal quietly sat together, lost in their individual thoughts. Trina could not imagine her life without that little boy who slept upstairs, completely unaware of the turmoil swirling around his family.

Chapter 24

The Agosti women were feverishly finishing up on the decorations for Kerri's baby shower. Excitement escalated as each detail was completed. Each gal contributed in some way, either by decorating, food preparation or both. Most showers served light refreshments, but not this family. Kerri laughed as Ellie recited the many, many foods that would grace the table. She didn't try to dissuade them. She had learned years ago that food was an expression of their love. And love her, they did!

In a few weeks, they would all know if pink or blue blankets would lovingly wrap their bundle of joy, but for now, the theme was mint green. The girls stepped back and nodded to one another; they were more than pleased with every detail of this lovely shower.

One after another, invited guests began to fill the house. The beautifully wrapped shower gifts were piled high in the corner under a fancy paper umbrella.

"I cannot wait to be a grandma," Ellie loudly proclaimed with each and every gift her daughter-in-law unwrapped. By the time the last gift was passed along to the enormously pregnant guest of honor, the onlookers chanted back to Ellie, "We know, we know!" It was such a joyful time, even New England's weather accommodated their plans.

Anthony appeared at the backdoor. "Is it safe yet for the *other gender* to enter?"

"Sure, we are just about done; your baby is going to be the best-dressed child in town, or maybe the state." Trina smiled.

"Terrific! Was there more pink or blue?" he curiously asked.

"Neither, the ladies stayed with mint green, lavender and yellow; we know how to play it safe." Angie hugged her nephew. "I'm so happy for you guys."

"Well, as long as you're here, why don't you start loading these beautiful gifts into our car? I'm exhausted," Kerri admitted. After really looking around the room, she remarked, "Come to think of it, I don't think one car will handle all of these wonderful gifts; we'll probably need two more cars."

"Ellie, I'm going to divide up this food for everyone to take home," Cindy said. "You and Anthony will never eat all of this. Is that okay with you? It is your shower."

"Of course it's okay—Oh! Oh!" Kerri grabbed her back and lower stomach at the same time, dropping the box she'd been holding.

Ellie was the first to notice blood running down Kerri's leg, "Sweetie, oh no!" and with that, her daughter-in-law passed out—falling hard.

"Oh, Lord! This is not normal," Hope yelled. For the past couple of years, she worked as an R.N. in the obstetrics and gynecology wing of the hospital. "Let's lay her flat on the floor; can we get some towels under her hips? Anthony, is she at thirty-seven weeks yet?"

"No, not yet?"

Hope, kneeling by Kerri's side, shouted, "Anthony, call her doctor—now. Explain what just happened," trying to remain calm. "Hurry, make the call."

Anthony's hands were shaking, but he managed to get through on the first try. His family was trying to listen to the one-sided telephone conversation, yet attentive to the activity swirling around Kerri.

"Mia, get me a damp washcloth, please."

"On it!"

Anthony returned from the phone, explaining his brief conversation with a physician assistant. "When she comes to—we need to bring her to the emergency room." He gripped Kerri's hand, trying to keep his emotions in check.

The tone of the party had abruptly changed from pure unadulterated joy to frenetic activity and concern for the expectant mother and baby.

Kerri's eyes began to flutter, her face was chalk-white. "Stay still," Hope instructed. "You and your baby are going to be just fine. We're driving you to the hospital as soon as you feel steady."

"No, I don't need . . . "

"Stop it," Anthony firmly answered. "You're going to be checked out, for our baby's and for your sake. No arguments."

"You're right, you're right, Anthony, please stay with me."

"Of course I will."

Anthony drove, while Hope tended to Kerri in the backseat. "We're almost there, sweetie," he reassured, hoping to calm her fears, as well as his own.

Ellie and Joe paced the waiting room, hardly talking to one another. Sammy sat close to his brother, trying to maintain an upbeat demeanor.

"Hey, thanks for coming here," Anthony turned to his younger brother. "It means a lot to me."

"Are you kidding? I drove over as soon as Mia called me. We're family," he squeezed the back of Anthony's neck like he'd done a hundred times before.

Anthony didn't want to leave his wife, but one of the doctors insisted he wait outside. He promised he'd only be a few minutes. Being part of the hospital staff, Hope was allowed to stay close to Kerri.

Trina and Sal sat with Angie and Jake, lending whatever support they could. "It was sweet of your girls to watch Vinnie for us," Trina said to her sister.

"Are you kidding? They love being with your little guy. By the way, I meant to ask if anything new had developed on the playground."

"No, thank God! Nothing new at all. And I'm taking that as a good sign."

"Yes, that is good. Maybe, just maybe, it was some kind of fluky thing."

Anthony looked up, Hope was poking her head around the door behind the triage desk. "Anthony, the doctor wants to talk with you again," she spoke in a stage whisper. The family stood, but quickly realized that only Anthony was being allowed back in with his wife.

This feels like bad news. Trina watched her nephew close the triage door, leaving the rest of the family behind. *I'm just being a worrywart. Lord, please, Lord, please!*

The doctor looked at Hope, then Anthony, "Would you prefer to speak in private?" he asked.

"No, no, she's family, doc, she can stay."

As you wish," the hospitalist said, sounding like a British butler.

The distant elevator bells and rhythmic sounds of opening and closing hallway doors were setting Anthony's teeth on edge, "Doc?" he pressed.

"First, let me ease your worries, your wife is doing fine. She is strong and thus far she's had a normal pregnancy. She's in labor and because she has not reached her thirty-seventh week, we are considering this to be a premature birth. There was an ample amount of blood in the amniotic fluid, which is never a good sign. It could be related to many different things, but we are focused on delivering a healthy baby."

"Can I be with her?" Anthony nervously asked.

"Certainly. She's asking for you." He smiled, then added "I would suggest that the rest of your family go home and wait there. This could take several hours."

"Sure, but what about her passing out, doc?"

"I think her blood pressure plummeted in combination with the sudden onset of pain. I haven't found any specific reason to be concerned. We'll know more over the next few hours. Her OB/GYN doc should be here shortly; she'll take over the delivery."

"That's great. Thanks so much," Anthony said. "Where is she?"

"If there are no other questions, I'll take you to her."

"Hope, please let the family know what's going on; I'll call them later."

They were more than relieved, but still, they were well aware that a preemie could present with many medical issues. It was time to activate the family prayer chain.

Whenever the family was happy, whenever they were sad and just plain whenever—they would take any opportunity to gather together around the dinner table. There was plenty of leftover food from the shower, and after all, it had to be eaten. Being together somehow made waiting a lot easier.

"Is the nursery ready, Aunt Ellie?" Mia asked. "I'd be happy to spruce it up, do laundry, whatever is needed. Just let me know."

"That's sweet of you, but your mom, Aunt Trina and I finished it up last week. Now I'm glad we did."

"For sure, we all thought we'd have several more weeks," Ellie said. "So, Mia, how are you and Matt doing?"

"Fabulous! He's a gem and I think he's *the* one," she whispered.

"Well, I for one am not surprised. He's a fine young man, has his head on straight and it's clear that he's crazy about you."

The room fell silent as Joey ran to the ringing phone. "Hello, yes, aha, really? Okay, are you sure? Say that again. Really? Wait, let me write this down. Are you sure?" he asked again, as the group began moving toward him like a bunch of zombies.

"What?"

"Uncle Joey?"

"What? Come on!"

Finally, he hung up the phone, turned to Ellie and pulled her into a huge embrace, spinning her around, while he obviously was fighting back tears.

"Will you please talk!"

"We have a grandson! Anthony Jr. is four pounds, four ounces and is seventeen inches long."

The whole group broke forth into boisterous cheers usually reserved for their beloved Red Sox or Patriots, but today, baby Anthony was their reason to celebrate.

"Oh, Joe, I couldn't be happier. How is Kerri doing?"

"He said she's doing fine; even though the baby is small, he is well developed. He'll have to stay in the neonatal unit until he reaches at least five pounds, provided there are no complications."

"Can we go see him, them?" Ellie pleaded.

"Anthony said we could come, but we should only stay for a short visit. Kerri is exhausted."

Ellie was beaming like a new bride.

Joey was lost in thought, *Mama and Pops would be thrilled! There was nothing they loved more than this family—they would be so proud.*

Chapter 25

Winter was well behind them and Vinnie couldn't wait to build sand castles at the beach house. He talked incessantly about the last day of school and his summer plans. Trina and Sal could not keep straight faces as they watched him struggle with composing his very own *to do* list—playing with Emma and baby Anthony consistently graced the top of his list.

Anthony had reached the magic number of five pounds rather quickly, so his hospital stay was remarkably short. Fortunately, he escaped many of the common health problems associated with premature births. Infant jaundice was the one issue the little guy fought and won during his neonatal care. Kerri and Anthony rejoiced on the day of his homecoming, as did the rest of the family.

Meals came to their doorstep from the women of their church, as well as their own family; Kerri was grateful to have time to spend with her little one. Although it could potentially be a financial strain, they had decided she would give up her job at the hair salon.

"Vinnie, don't forget that I'm picking you up early today."

"Aw, Mom, do I have to go to the dentist?"

"Yes, young man, you do. I thought you liked our dentist?"

"I do, but I like playing kickball better and I'm going to miss the big game today."

"I'm sorry, honey. I didn't realize you had a big game," she remarked.

"Well, maybe not a *big* game, but it's still fun."

"Tell you what, you can go on outside and play for a while. I'll get you signed out first, then I'll come out the side door to get you. That will give you a little extra time to play. How's that?"

"I guess it's okay, but it would be better if I could play the *whole* game."

"Next time I'll be sure to make your appointment later in the day. Okay, let's get this show on the road."

"What show?" he ruffled Lance's furry head, kissed him on his snout, then slung his small backpack over his shoulder.

Later in the day, as Trina was about to leave the house to pick up her son, the dentist's receptionist called. She apologized profusely, but asked if they could move Vinnie's appointment back one hour; the doctor had an emergency. Trina smiled to herself, agreeing to be there a bit later. *Vinnie will be thrilled. That kid leads a charmed life. The extra hour would also give me time to run a couple of errands.*

It was turning into a beautiful day; the warmth of the sun seemed to give her an energy boost. Trina managed to accomplish more than she'd expected in that extra hour. She glanced at her watch. Realizing she'd be a bit early, she decided to sit on one of the benches outside the playground. It would be fun to watch her son interact with his playmates.

He'd had a rocky start in school, but he proved himself to be a problem solver; he soon learned how to disarm the class bully.

Trina settled onto the splintered old bench, wondering how many years it had occupied that very spot. The sun was so bright that it prompted her to dig into her purse for her scratched-up old sunglasses. It wasn't long before she needed to remove her scarf. *What a wonderful promise of spring.* The kids poured out of the double doors and onto the playground, pushing one another, yelling and otherwise being children. Trina didn't see Mrs. Wright, but another playground monitor kept a watchful eye over her charges.

I should do this more often. Trina enjoyed watching Vinnie become a leader on the playground. His behavior was so animated, barking orders and waving his hands. *A future general! Wait, where is he going?*

When Vinnie disinterestedly dropped the ball and began walking toward the fence, Trina instinctively followed his line of sight; within seconds she realized a young woman had moved close to the fence and appeared to be calling to Vinnie. *What is he doing? Oh no, the pretty lady!* Trina decided not to call out to Vinnie. Instead she quietly walked up behind the woman, hoping to speak with her.

"Miss?" Trina spoke softly, as she reached her, but got no response. Vinnie saw her and started to wave, whether at his mom or the stranger. "Miss?" she repeated, but the woman stood perfectly still, either not hearing or ignoring the voice over her shoulder. Vinnie was almost to the fence, so Trina moved to the woman's side, gently placing her hand on the woman's forearm, "Please don't run away, I'd like to have a word with you after my son goes back into the building. Please, it will only take a minute."

"Hey, Mom, are we still going to the dentist?" Vinnie asked, his eyes darting between the two women. He was obviously confused that this lady just stood wordless, next to his mother.

"Hi, honey! Yes, we're going, but you have time to finish up your game. I'll meet you in the office to sign you out, after your game. Okay?"

"Okay," he said. "Hi," he innocently waved at the lady and turned back to his friends, but not before looking over his shoulder at the two women.

They stood there together, neither speaking as they watched the children play ball. "Miss, please, sit with me for a minute," Trina coaxed. She could tell that this was the woman Mrs. Wright described to her. She was extremely thin, her hair was dull and matted. It was obvious that her clothes hadn't been washed for quite some time. Trina felt a tug on her heart. She wanted to embrace her and assure her that everything would be just fine. But would it?

"My name is Trina," extending her hand for a handshake. For the first time, the young woman lifted her head; she pushed her hair away from her face and locked eyes with Trina. Clearly, she was a very pretty young lady, but whatever addiction had hold of her was stealing those good looks.

"I know who you are," she snarled. "You're his mother," she spat, lifting her chin as if to point to Vinnie.

"Yes, I am," Trina responded firmly. "And who might you be?"

"I'm . . . I was his mother," her facial muscles tightening.

Although Trina suspected as much, still it was like an arrow had just pierced her heart. "How did you, how were you able to . . . "

"It's wasn't that difficult; I knew my son went into your home for foster care; I've stayed away all this time, but—"

"But what? You know he's been legally adopted. He has a good home and a loving family."

"I'm sure he does," her voice seemed to soften.

"Then why are you coming here to see him?"

Then she fully turned to face Trina. "I have been in and out of rehab and I'm still not in a good place. I know I can't give him a fancy house and a good education, but I just had to see him."

They sat together quietly, both unsure what to say next. "So, what are your plans? You just can't keep showing up here?"

"I just wanted to see him. You can't understand what it's like to lose a child. Even when I'm high, I'm hurting, especially when I'm high."

"Miss, ah what is your name?"

"Darlene."

"Darlene, you're wrong. I know exactly what it's like to lose a child. I've had several miscarriages and the pain was just awful."

"I have to go," the woman nervously responded. "I'll try to stop coming here. I'll try." She jumped up and began walking away.

"Wait, do you have a phone?"

"No, no phone," and with that she was gone.

Trina was so rattled at this point that she didn't know whether to run after Darlene or call the authorities. She decided to sit quietly and seek the Lord. As she prayed, her eyes followed Vinnie's every move, every step. *Lord, watch over my son. I pray You'll put a hedge of protection around him. Keep him from any evil plan or intention. And, Lord, watch over Darlene and heal her broken spirit and her emaciated body.*

"Is there a special occasion that I don't know about?" Mia asked her mother. "It's not like you to fuss over the table setting."

"What? Does there have to be a special occasion for me to spend an evening with my sister and brother?"

"No, I think it's great that you guys are so close and you care enough to set a pretty table. I was just wondering if you were having a party and forgot to invite your favorite daughter." Mia snickered.

"You sound like your Aunt Trina; she was always proclaiming that Mama and Daddy liked her best. But, of course we all know they liked me best," performing a slight curtsy.

"You're too funny, Mom."

"So, are you going out with Matt tonight?"

"Sure am! Mom," Mia said wistfully, "I really do like him. He's a gentleman, he's smart and funny; and he never fails to make me laugh."

"Are you guys dating one another, exclusively? I mean, are you serious about each other?"

"Well, yah! I thought you knew that by now."

"Honey, I've had a hard time keeping up with you and your fast-changing love life, but it does seem like this one is different."

"He is, Mom, he is."

The doorbell rang and the door swung open simultaneously. "Hi, Auntie Angie." Vinnie ran to her and wrapped his arms around her waist.

"Hey, Vinnie. So, where's your puppy? You know he's always welcome. Oh my—" Angie exclaimed as Lance jumped at her. "You are one big oaf."

"What's an oaf?"

"Someone who's big and clumsy. Maybe this guy just hasn't grown into his big boy feet yet," she laughed, ruffling his thick fur. "But, Vinnie, you really should leash him in this neighborhood. The cars don't drive very slowly in our development."

Trina and Sal followed behind their son. "Vinnie, I told you not to open the door until I had the leash on him."

"I forgot," already distracted by his cousin. "Hi, Mia, will you play with me?"

"Hey, buddy, I'd love to, but I'm going out with Matt tonight. How about I give your mom a call and we do something fun—real soon," she twirled him around, although she could barely get him off the ground.

"Aunt Trina, what are you guys feeding this kid?" She poked him. "You'll soon be bigger than me."

Just then Joe and Ellie pushed in the door, saying, "Knock, knock! We are here and we come bearing food."

"I told you guys not to bring anything," Angie scolded. "So what do you have there?"

"I know, I know. But it couldn't be helped, my car automatically turned into Mann's Bakery. I had no control, whatsoever," he chuckled, planting a kiss on Angie's forehead.

"Yeah, right!"

Jake, Sal and Joe wasted no time in making their way into the family room, leaving their wives to prepare dinner. "Hey, Jake, how are you feeling these days?" Sal asked. "You look better than you have in months; those treatments must be doing the trick."

"I'm finally regaining my strength and the dizziness has completely stopped."

"Don't kid me, you've been dizzy ever since I've known you," Joey ribbed. "Nah, seriously, I'm glad you're beating this thing, *poly* . . . whatever."

"It's called polycythemia, polycythemia," he repeated, enunciating slowly for his brother-in-law.

"Okay, okay, I got it. Anyhow, glad you're back to normal," Joe responded. "So, how about we make our annual plans for Fenway?"

"Sure, I'm in. Just let me know when."

The diehard Red Socks fans had attended as many games as their schedules permitted over the years. But it didn't stop there; they frequently also found their way to Patriots and Celtics games. Angie often teased Jake for owning every Patriots tee shirt and every Sox baseball cap that had ever been sold.

Trina waited until Mia and Vinnie left the kitchen before blurting out, "Can we talk a minute before dinner?"

"Sure, what's wrong?" her sister's facial expression instantly turning sober.

Ellie stepped closer to them in an effort to catch every whispered word.

Trina began, "You both know about the *pretty lady* that supposedly visited the playground a while back?"

They nodded as one, listening intently.

"Well, I was early to pick up Vinnie the other day, so I sat on that old bench outside the fence. I thought it would be fun to watch him play without him showing off for me. It wasn't long before this very sad young woman appeared. She was so focused on Vinnie that she wasn't aware I'd walked up to her, at least I don't think she was aware."

"Trina, are you serious? Did she look threatening?"

"I don't really know if she is a danger. What I do know, is that she is his biological mother."

Angie put her hands to her mouth and inhaled sharply. "Did she say that?"

"Yes, yes she did."

"How did she know where to find him? Aren't those records sealed?" Ellie pressed.

"She said that she knew he'd been placed in our home under the foster care program; she just assumed from there. Unfortunately, this kind of thing has happened more than I'd care to admit. By the way, her name is Darlene."

"So, what does she want? Did you tell the principal or the authorities?"

"Apparently, she's recently felt compelled to see him—to be with him. Yes, I actually did have another meeting with the vice principal. Sal and I thought about home schooling him, but I can't shelter him forever."

"No, you can't. I realize that Vinnie knows he's adopted, but are you planning to tell him about—Darlene?"

"I don't think we should, at least not yet. I'm scared. I haven't slept for the past few nights. Actually, I'm a wreck." She began to tremble.

"Why didn't you call me?" Angie sounded hurt, but still wrapped her arms around her sister.

"I should have. I've gone to the school every day since it happened, but I can't keep doing that."

"No, you can't, but my job has become pretty flexible; I can go with you or instead of you to give you a break," Ellie offered, sympathetically.

"What does Sal think?"

"Sal and I both think we should try to draw her in, get to know her, find out her motives, if she has any hidden agenda."

"But she hasn't returned," Angie said.

"No. And *that* makes me even more frightened."

Just then Leah bounded down the stairs and into the kitchen. "Hey, smells good in here," she said before noticing her aunt's red-rimmed eyes. "Aunt Trina, do you have a cold? If so I'm staying far away." She teased, but kept a questioning eye on her aunt.

"Hi, sweetie. No, I don't have a cold. How are you doing?"

"Great! I'm gearing up for the end of yet another semester. I've got a shot at a summer internship."

"What sort of internship?" Ellie questioned.

"It's an *unpaid internship*," Angie interjected. "But that's okay if it gives her a well-rounded resume."

"I don't know for sure yet, but it will be in the field of photojournalism. I'm excited about it."

"And you should be," Trina remarked, hugging her niece.

Angie realized that Trina was done discussing her concerns for now; she wouldn't want to say more in front of the kids. She winked at her sister, their private communication that conveyed, 'I'm here for you.'

The weeks slipped by and after much prayer and counsel from their pastor, Trina and Sal had decided against involving the authorities. The playground monitors were on high alert, keeping a close eye on the playground perimeter. Although Vinnie never knew it, he was well-guarded from the time Trina or Sal dropped him off, until he was safely back in their care. Darlene never once reappeared and the school year was finally coming to a close. Trina was breathing more easily, eager to resume her normal lifestyle. She assumed that Darlene's addiction had predictably sucked her back under and into the shadows of her lifestyle.

Chapter 26

As schedules allowed, each individual family visited the beach house. Getting it spiffed up and ready to accommodate their crew for their first summer gathering was a priority. *Hampton Beach, here we come*, was their often-heard mantra. Joey and his sisters set aside an afternoon to shop together. Purchasing the few needed pieces of furniture was an excellent excuse to get away for a few hours and enjoy some sibling time.

As the three wandered around the furniture showroom, Joey's mind wandered back to a time when his sisters insisted on decorating *his* tree house. Joey and Lenny, with Pops' help, built themselves a magnificent house. Well, it was magnificent in their eyes. Trina and her best friend, Donna, used poor Angie to spy on the boys. The girls badgered them nonstop, until finally the boys relented, allowing entrance to their *new home*. It didn't end there. Soon those sweet girls attempted a takeover. Joey smiled to himself as he recalled with fondness the antics that ensued. In the end, they struck a deal, a lopsided deal, but a deal.

"Hey, what are you smirking at?" Angie shoved her brother, bringing him back from his mental wanderings.

"You wouldn't believe it if I told you," he snickered.

"Try me," Angie pressed.

"Remember my tree house?"

"You mean *our* tree house, don't you?" she snapped back.

"No!" he firmly retorted. "I mean *my* tree house—the one you girls commandeered."

"Oh, please! Commandeered! We simply decorated it to make it spiffier—more livable."

"It was just fine before—"

"Okay, kids, let it go!" Trina laughed. "Sheesh!"

"Those were fun times, weren't they?" Joey conceded. "Life was so simple."

"It sure was," Angie agreed. "Hey, let's find a sales clerk, get a delivery date for this stuff and then you may have the honor of treating your gorgeous sisters to lunch?" she teased.

As the siblings were finishing their lunch, Angie said, "So, did Leah tell either of you that Luke invited her to his home for dinner on Friday?"

"No, I haven't talked to her lately," Trina responded. "How do you think that will go?"

"Well, Luke did say that his home life has greatly improved since his dad surrendered his life to the Lord and they've been going to church together. I'm really praying they are gentle with her; she was badly wounded by Mr. Henderson's accusation."

"I know—poor kid. Well, I certainly hope he's learned a valuable lesson from that mistake."

"Luke's sister, Michelle, will be in rehab for quite some time; I think she's in a facility near Boston."

"So, are we all going to the beach house on Memorial Day?"

"Why not? It's a great way to kick off the summer. Remind your kids to let me know if they're planning to ever be there alone so Ellie can maintain a schedule," Joe said. "I think it will be great for them to have that special family time together, don't you guys?"

"Yup, I agree." Trina smiled at the waitress as she placed the check on their table.

"And, just for the record, we *did not* commandeer your little tree house," Angie firmly stated, as she boldly slapped down the check in front of Joey.

Mia watched her sister fumbling with the clasp on her necklace. "Here, let me get that for you. Are you sure you're okay? I mean, you don't have to go, you know."

"I'm fine, just a little nervous. That man can be so arrogant and cold." *Cold fish*, she reminded herself. "I'm just praying that he's softened a bit since our last meeting."

"I hope so."

"I really don't think Luke and I have a future. Remember, his dad is convinced that no one is good enough for his kid. They have the best of everything and who can compete with that; who wants to compete with that?"

"Yes, I remember. But, Leah, you are a child of *the King*! Don't you ever forget that and don't sell yourself short."

"You know you're really lucky to have someone like Matt. He's the salt of the earth and doesn't put on any airs."

"Luke doesn't put on airs either, Leah. He's not like his dad, so give him a break."

Leah's eyes welled up. "You're right. I shouldn't judge him just because he was born into that family. Honestly, I am a tad hopeful they're changing."

"Oh, there's the doorbell. Are you ready for this?"

"Yup, fine! How do I look?" she asked, abruptly leaving her bedroom.

"You look great," Mia called after her.

"Hey, how's my girl?" Luke asked when she opened the front door.

"I'm good—I think," she tentatively responded.

"Are you ready to go?"

"Luke, I don't think this is such a good idea," she blurted.

"Listen, Leah, I'm going to be right by your side. I won't leave you for one second and I will not let my family be anything but kind to you. You deserve that and more. Besides, they've changed."

Leah exhaled raggedly. "All right then. I guess I'm ready. Let's get this show on the road."

He smiled, pulling her into a deep embrace. "You are amazing!"

The drive to Luke's Andover home was a short one, but Leah found herself wishing they were driving to another state. She nervously picked imaginary lint off her jeans, twirled her hair around her fingers and talked incessantly.

"Leah, it's going to be all right. Honest!"

"I know, I know! No, I don't really know." Her head jerked up only to fix her gaze on the mansion-like house that rose up in front of her. "We're here? Is that your house?"

"It is."

"Four people live in that house! I mean—it could accommodate a small army," she stated.

"That is a slight exaggeration. Come on."

Leah hesitated for a few seconds, then jokingly asked, "I'm guessing we're not having hot dogs and beans for dinner?"

"Probably not. Let's go in."

Leah had a death grip on his arm, likening this walk to a funeral procession. *I'm being foolish! I'm a child of the King!*

They hadn't yet reached the front door when it swung open to reveal a diminutive middle-aged woman wearing an old-fashioned floral print apron. She had lovely skin, very curly hair and sparkling, dark eyes. "Hello, Mister Luke," she welcomed. "And who is this lovely young woman you have brought home?"

"Hey, Nina, I'd like to introduce you to my good friend, Leah."

Leah extended her hand, "I'm happy to meet you, Nina."

Nina ignored her hand and pulled her into a mama bear embrace. "I'm honored to meet you, Miss Leah. Please come in. Dinner will be ready in a few minutes. Your parents are in the living room, Mister Luke."

Leah whispered to Luke as they walked together toward the formal living room, "You never told me you had a maid."

"What? You mean Nina, she's more of a friend-housekeeper. I don't think of her as a maid."

"Hmm, whatever! I'm just saying, knock at my door and you'll get me or my sister or—"

"I get it, I get it." He shook his head as they entered the living room.

Leah's head began spinning as she attempted to take in the beautifully appointed room. It was clear, at least to her, that a very expensive interior decorator had created this exquisite, yet warm space. She was beyond impressed, but kept silent, at least for the moment.

"Hi, Mom." Luke approached his mother, while protectively holding Leah's hand. "Do you remember my friend, Leah Trayor?"

The woman that stood before Leah was the epitome of elegance. Her clothes, her demeanor, everything about her shouted *sophistication*. Luke certainly didn't inherit his height from his mother's side of the family;

she was of average height and weight. Despite Mrs. Henderson's polish and sedate manner, Leah immediately liked her. Her smile completely and totally set Leah at ease, for now.

"Hello, dear. Luke has told me so much about you and your lovely family. I am pleased that we are finally able to spend some time with you and not just a quick hello at our beach house. That hardly counted as an introduction," she teased her son.

"Where's Dad? Nina said he was home."

"He is. He'll be down in a minute. I hope you're hungry, Leah. Nina is an excellent cook and she's outdone herself tonight. I'm embarrassed to admit that if it wasn't for her occasionally taking over the kitchen, my family would have starved long ago. The kitchen is not where I shine," she admitted, with a warm smile.

"I'm famished." *And a little bit queasy,* she thought, not at all looking forward to Mr. Henderson's appearance.

"So, how are your studies coming along?" Luke's mother asked. "My son tells me you are a very gifted photographer."

Leah looked at Luke, feeling her face flush. "Well, I love what I'm doing. Actually, I've loved photography for as long as I can remember."

"You'll have to bring her to one of our galleries, Luke. I'm sure she would thoroughly enjoy the experience."

"I'd love that."

"We showcase local talent, as well as world-recognized artists. I'm quite proud of our galleries and our museums."

"Leah is waiting to hear on an art internship," Luke boasted to his mom.

"Really? Exactly what is entailed in that internship?"

"I don't know if I even have a chance, but it would offer me the opportunity to work in the world of art, all facets of art, including photography. Learning under the guidance of an experienced curator would be invaluable—and thrilling."

Mrs. Henderson seemed deep in thought, then said, "Leah, dear, would you be willing to share some of your work with me? Maybe I can help you along in your chosen field. If your work is as good as my son claims it to be, I'm sure I could find some wall space in our Andover gallery—no promises until I see your portfolio," she cheerfully teased.

Leah remembered Luke's idle comments about the chance to display her works, but that was before that horrendous accusation was thrown her way. She had since dismissed the whole idea, not giving it further thought in light of the happenings of the past few months.

"I wouldn't want to be any bother and I certainly wouldn't want to put you in an awkward position."

"Leah, I'm a businesswoman. I will have no problem saying *no* to you, if I must. On the other hand, I find it so rewarding to help up-and-coming artists, if it's within my power. I don't want to ever brag, but I'm certainly aware that the Henderson name wields a lot of influence and I'd like to use that influence in a positive way."

Leah didn't know what to say or how to respond, so she simply smiled. Her mind was already in high gear; she was imagining how she could reorganize to create the Henderson Gallery Portfolio.

"There you are," Mrs. Henderson turned to her husband as he joined them. "Rodney, you must remember Leah?" she waved her hand as though unveiling a new work of art.

"I certainly do. How are you?" he said in a velvety soft voice, which totally disarmed Leah.

Despite Luke's stories about his changed family, she expected the same cold, hard response she'd previously received from him. She wasn't about to relax just yet; she'd proceed gingerly hoping for the best. Dipping her toe into icy water was smarter that jumping in and experiencing the shock of her life.

"I'm just fine, thank you." Leah extended her hand that was warmly received. "Thanks for inviting me."

The room grew silent, revealing an obvious awkwardness between them. Attempting to smooth things over, he asked, "And how is your family enjoying their beach house?"

"Well, we are just beginning to get it in shape for summer. I have a large family and we're working on a schedule so each individual family gets to enjoy it. We'll also all be there together, whenever we can work it into our calendars." Leah felt as though she was babbling, so abruptly stopped.

"I'm thrilled to see life and activity there. It's a beautiful house with good bones," Mrs. Henderson added. "I'm anxious to meet your entire family over the summer."

Mr. Henderson plopped himself in an oversized wingback chair that she guessed was his favorite. It was a luxurious shade of wine and when she looked more closely, it showed wear around the piping. *I'm guessing he sits there every day, reading the Wall Street Journal, with a cup of steaming Oolong tea, while puffing away on his pipe, if he even smokes a pipe.*

"Do you spend a lot of time there?" Leah asked, hoping the answer was *no*.

"We are there as often as possible, considering both Rodney's and my own schedule."

"I've spent every summer there, since I was a boy, in that very house," he quickly added.

"You're fortunate. You've probably seen a lot of neighbors come and go in your lifetime," Leah added.

He grew pensive, as though picturing one face after another. "Yes, indeed I have," he quietly replied. "How long before dinner?" he abruptly asked.

"It shouldn't be long. Rodney, we were just discussing Leah's photojournalism talents."

Luke jumped in, "She's already won several photography contests. I'm amazed at what she can do with that fancy camera."

"I hope you'll share what you've accomplished with that *mill project*. I think that was rather ingenious of you to set your sights on those old mills. I, too, find value in their architecture and their rich history."

"We're going to see her work shortly. Isn't that right, Leah? I'd like you to bring everything you've done to our Methuen gallery whenever you are free to do so."

"Splendid!" was all he said in response, causing Leah to wonder if he approved of the idea.

"That would be awesome—I mean I'd be honored."

"Dinner is ready," Nina yelled, in a rather undignified voice.

Leah kept waiting for the other shoe to drop, but she was pleasantly surprised. The evening went by without so much as a sarcastic or rude comment. Luke, just as he'd promised, never left her side. Mr. Henderson entertained them with stories surrounding the mill renovations. *He really can be quite charming.* Leah's eyes grew wide when he told them that some of his construction crew believed the mills were haunted. He leaned back in his chair and guffawed. "I couldn't convince them otherwise, but to their credit, they showed up for work every day, regardless of the so-called ghosts."

"I never heard that," Leah laughed, covering her mouth as she hiccupped. "Excuse me," she giggled.

Leah felt a bit self-conscious when she noticed Mr. Henderson staring at her hand. *I guess it's not good manners to hiccup at the dinner table.* She immediately and gracefully folded her hands, placing them back in her lap. *Am I imagining it or has he become noticeably quiet?*

Mrs. Henderson began to share with Leah how their family had recently experienced a wonderful spiritual renewal. She was obviously delighted that the atmosphere in her once-divided home was being healed. "You're aware that our Michelle is still in a rehab facility and she's doing quite well, making great strides. We're proud of her turnaround, aren't we, Rodney?"

"Yes, we are," he quietly responded.

Nina moved around them like a whirlwind, removing plates and serving dishes. "Who is ready for my lemon meringue pie?"

She was the epitome of efficiency. Within minutes, the table was cleared and she'd managed to carry in a serving tray with four dessert plates. She had assumed they wouldn't turn down her offer of homemade pie—and she was right.

As Leah reached for her dessert plate, she noticed Mr. Henderson's eyes were fixed on her hand or was it on her ring? They locked eyes and he seemed flustered, rattled. "Leah, I'm sorry if I was staring, but that is a lovely ring you're wearing."

"Thank you. I love it."

"Was it a gift?"

"Oh no. You won't believe it, but I found it at our beach house."

"You found it?"

"Yes, my sister and I were in the attic bedroom and noticed one drawer in the antique apothecary chest looked odd, somehow it was crooked. So, being the curious person that I am, I attempted to pull it out so I could reset the old drawer properly. Well, I worked at it for a while and suddenly when I yanked, it came free and this ring flew out. Do you believe it?"

"I see. Well, it's lovely. It certainly must be one of a kind, very unique."

"Thank you. I haven't had any success in finding the owner. We think it may have belonged to a guest at the bed and breakfast."

"That's possible," Mrs. Henderson agreed.

After their delicious dinner, they enjoyed some light conversation, signaling the evening was winding down. Mr. Henderson became a bit jittery when finally he said, "Leah, I asked Luke to bring you to our home because—I want to apologize for my poor behavior. I treated you badly and made a wrong judgment. Can you ever forgive me? I am dreadfully ashamed of myself and so very sorry."

Leah shouldn't have been flabbergasted. After all, Luke did tell her that his dad had become a Christian. Still, she was somewhat surprised by his admission.

"Mr. Henderson, I will not lie to you, I was hurt and angry by your accusation. I'd never had anyone, ever, think so poorly of me. I'm so thrilled that you've given your heart to the Lord and of course, I forgive you."

He reached across the table and took her hand. "Thank you, Leah. You have lifted a great weight off my shoulders, thank you."

"Well, my dear," Mrs. Henderson interrupted, "before you kids run off, I want to remind you that I truly would like to see your work at your earliest convenience. Luke will give you my number so we can set up a proper time."

"I won't forget. There is no way that I could forget." Leah smiled and breathed deeply.

Chapter 27

"Mommy, I think Mia is here!"

"I know, I heard her car. Vinnie, you'd better open the door. I'll be right there," Trina said, smiling to herself. Vinnie loves his cousin; she's always been so kind to him, making time for his crazy games. *This girl is one in a million.*

"Okay, I'm coming," he yelled, racing down the steps. When he reached the door, he swung it open so hard that it banged against the interior wall. "Oops!" he sheepishly said, then quickly looked for damage on the wall. He was grateful for the doorstop on the baseboard. "Phew!"

"Hey, buddy," Mia greeted him with her usual exuberance. "Are ya ready for an afternoon with your old cousin?"

"Aw, you're not that old. Where are we going?"

"Well, that's up to you. I thought we could go to Findeisen's for a giant ice cream cone."

"Yumm!"

"Or we could go to the zoo or maybe bowling? What do you think?"

"Hmm, I think we should go to the zoo."

"Okay, the Stoneham Zoo it is! But I have to make a quick stop at the mall. I need to pick up a birthday gift for my friend, but I know what I'm getting her, so it will be quick."

"Mom," he shouted, "we're going to the zoo!" But Trina was already walking into the room.

"That's great! Please don't yell. The neighbor will think I'm torturing you." Turning her attention to her niece, "Hi, Mia. Are you sure you're up for an afternoon with this wild guy?" She laughed, ruffling her son's hair.

"Sure, and I haven't been to the Stoneham Zoo in ages. I'm kind of looking forward to those monkeys," she imitated a monkey while chasing Vinnie. "Aunt Trina, we won't be too late, but maybe we'll stop to eat on the way home, depends on what this guy packs away at the zoo."

"Give your old mother a hug," Trina pulled Vinnie to herself. "Now listen—you behave and listen to Mia. Got it?"

"I got it. Bye!" He was already running out the door.

<hr>

Once at the mall, Vinnie boldly reminded his cousin, "Don't forget, you said you'd be quick. I hate shopping for girly stuff."

"I know you do, buddy. Come on, this will only take a minute," she said as she grasped his hand and began leading him to the department store.

Vinnie shook his head and said "Naw, go get it. I'll just sit here." He sat down on a beat-up old bench that was right outside of the department store. From only a few feet away, he watched Mia at the jewelry counter, moving from one glass display to another. *Right, only a few minutes.*

He'd seen lots of old men sitting there, probably waiting for their wives to finish shopping. He just couldn't figure out why girls liked to shop; he thought shopping was boring.

Mia was disappointed that the necklace she'd seen last week had been sold. *I should have grabbed it then. No big deal, I'll find another one.* She had to; the birthday party was tomorrow night. The sales clerk wasn't very helpful; she was slower than molasses in January, pulling out each piece for Mia's inspection. Finally, she selected a necklace, paid for it and was ready to make Vinnie a happy little guy.

With her gift bag in hand, Mia hurried out of the store. *He's been so patient. He deserves an extra special treat.* Her smile quickly changing to a frown. "Where did that prankster go?" she said to no one. "Vinnie!" she half yelled, looking back to the jewelry counter. "Vinnie," she called louder, scanning the fronts of several kiosks. She couldn't have been more than fifteen feet away from him; he was right here the whole time. "I'm going to strangle that kid," she growled under her breath. *I bet he's trying to get back at me for making him wait more than a minute.*

Mia stood next to the bench, confused, wondering what to do next, when she spotted a mall security guard. She wasted no time in running to him. "Sir, I need your help. My cousin was waiting for me on that bench while I was right there," she nervously pointed to the entrance of the jewelry kiosk, "and he's disappeared. I've been calling for him and—I'm scared."

"Calm down." Quickly taking out a notebook, he asked, "Can you tell me what he was wearing, color hair, that sort of thing?"

"Yes, yes," Mia rattled off all of that and much more. She was a detail-oriented person, so she was able to give specific and accurate information.

"Stay here, Miss. I'm going to report this immediately and check the footage of the mall's security camera for the last half hour."

"He was sitting there ten minutes ago." Tears welled up as she pointed to the empty bench.

"We'll find him, Miss," and he took off running.

Oh, dear Lord, please keep him safe. I'm so sorry for taking my eyes of him. Mia was an emotional wreck and what made it even worse—she had to call her Aunt Trina.

Mia saw her aunt running toward her. The guard had not yet come back to her, so she had stayed at the bench, in case Vinnie returned. She was expecting her aunt to yell, chastise, admonish, but she did none of that. Instead, she pulled Mia into a fierce hug, "Any word? What is happening?"

"Aunt Trina, I'm so sorry. I should have *made* him come into the store with me. I only looked away for a couple of minutes and he was so close to me, but . . . "

The security guard was approaching them, "Miss, please come with me," he calmly said.

"This is Vinnie's mother, Mrs. Lamazo." They were already moving quickly alongside the guard.

They walked a short distance and were escorted into a tiny office, where he indicated they should take a seat. Trina looked up; there were six monitors mounted on the wall. It was obvious that they were actively scanning every mall exit, as well as the main walkway.

He didn't waste one second. "Is that your son?"

"Oh, good Lord, yes it is—and that woman is his biological mother." Trina's hands flew to her mouth. "How could she have followed them here? I doubt she has a car?"

"A lot of these types hang out on the side of the mall, near the Dumpsters. Please, try to stay calm. Time is of the essence. I'm calling our local police and sending his picture."

Trina threw herself against Mia, sobbing. "Mia, she's stealing him from us. Why wasn't I more proactive?"

"It's my fault, Aunt Trina. I shouldn't have left him for one second." She wept along with her aunt. They were beside themselves.

"Mrs. Lamazo, why don't you go on home? The police will handle it from here. They have all your information. I'm sure . . . "

"You're sure what? That's he'll be okay? His birth mother is a drug addict. She lives in a very dangerous world," Trina frantically snapped.

"I understand, I'm sorry," he responded.

Mia put a calming hand on her aunt's arm, "Aunt Trina," she whispered.

Trina looked at her niece, then back at the well-meaning guard. "I'm sorry, it's not your fault. I apologize for lashing out at you. You've been very helpful—forgive me."

"Nothing to forgive. Here's my number, please feel free to call me."

Trina and Mia dragged themselves to the parking lot, weeping and catching stares from curious shoppers. "Aunt Trina, can I come to your house? I just can't go home. I need to be there with you."

"Of course. Uncle Sal should be home shortly; I really don't want to be alone either. Where's your car?"

"Right over there. I'll be right behind you. Are you okay to drive?"

Wiping her nose, Trina was already walking toward her car. She was not okay. *Why would Vinnie walk away from Mia with the pretty lady when I've warned him a hundred times about talking to strangers. Technically, she wasn't a stranger to him, but still, what was he thinking?* She pulled out of the mall parking lot and started for home. She was having difficulty focusing, the tears were flowing uncontrollably. At the first traffic light she pulled her purse close and fumbled for a tissue. When she looked up, less than a block from the mall, she saw Vinnie and Darlene, sitting together on a bench; they appeared to be waiting for the next bus. *Where was she taking him?* Trina looked in her rearview mirror. Mia was right behind her. She quickly punched her hazards, trusting her niece would catch what she was about to do. She slowed her car and pulled into the spot that said, 'No Parking—Bus Stop.' Mia was right behind her and Trina knew she'd also spotted Vinnie.

Before Darlene had a chance to react, Trina was standing two feet away from her; Mia followed within seconds.

"Mommy!" Vinnie jumped at Trina, wrapping his arms around her hips. "I didn't want to go on the bus, but she said you told me I had to. Is Daddy okay?"

Confused at that statement, "Daddy is fine, he'll be home in a few minutes."

"He wasn't in an accident?"

Trina glared at Darlene. "No, honey, he's fine—no accident."

"Mia, please take Vinnie home and call the authorities. I'll be home in a few minutes."

Mia took her cousin's hand, wanting to squeeze him into a big bear hug, but this was not the time or place. Trina waited until Mia pulled into the flow of traffic, knowing the police would be there shortly. It didn't take a professional to know that this young woman was stoned. Again, her personal appearance was dreadful, and she never attempted to apologize. Trina felt a tug on her heart for this very sad young woman—Vinnie's birth mother.

"Darlene?"

She looked up with great effort and through glazed, bloodshot eyes. "I wouldn't have hurt him," she slurred.

"You can't know that; you're out of control. Please, let me help you. I have connections with many rehab centers and counselors."

"I've tried all that. I just wanted to be with my son."

"Darlene, listen to me, you relinquished your rights. You can't see him, especially in this condition. If you get clean and stay clean, we'll talk—maybe."

The flashing lights and wail of police sirens ended their fragile interaction. Two policemen exited their cruiser and approached the bus stop, hands resting on their firearms. "Mrs. Lamazo?"

"I'm Trina Lamazo. This is the young woman who abducted my son, but he's safe now. I just sent him home with my niece."

The two officers alternated in asking her questions. Trina almost felt as though she was being interrogated, when finally, "You'll have to come down to the station to press charges, paperwork, you understand," the older policeman said rather cavalierly.

"Yes, I understand. Thank you, officer," she responded. "Darlene?" but Darlene didn't give her the courtesy of making eye contact and never uttered another word.

Trina stood there for a few minutes, along with a few curious onlookers who had gathered, and sadly watched Darlene stumble into the car and eventually be driven away.

Thank You, Lord, for allowing us to rescue our sweet boy from living in that dark world of addiction and hopelessness. Thank You, thank You!

Chapter 28

Trina's heart was heavy. Intellectually, she knew that Darlene had made her own choices, but emotionally she was heartbroken for this young woman. Her compassion spurred her to reach out, trying to help in some way. Her years of working within the social service and legal system opened some doors, but this charge was, after all—kidnapping. Sal had pleaded with her to leave it alone, but Trina went ahead and arranged meetings with several of her former colleagues. The least she could do was petition for rehab, on Darlene's behalf; then she'd leave it in the Lord's hands.

Entering her sister's home, she called, "Angie, I'm back."

"Hi, I thought you'd be gone longer. I hope you didn't rush."

"No, things moved right along. Thanks for watching my little man. I really appreciate it."

"No problemo! He's fun to have around. So, how'd it go?"

Vinnie was out of earshot. "I guess it went well. I met with the right people, I laid it all out, made my request for rehab rather than incarceration. The ball is in their court now, we'll see."

"Were you able to visit her?"

"She doesn't want anything to do with me. Besides, Sal thought I should stay away."

"Trina, you're a good old gal. I'm proud of you for trying."

"What do you mean, *old gal?*"

"Well, you are older than *moi.*"

Trina was so thankful for her sister and best friend. Angie was a light-hearted, happy person; she never failed to cheer up her *older*, more serious siblings.

"We're heading to the beach house this weekend. Would you like to join us?" Angie asked.

"Sounds like just what the doctor ordered. I'll check with Sal and call you later. Is anyone else going?"

"Just Mia and Leah. But wherever they are, Matt and Luke can't be far away."

Trina laughed. "They're good boys, so that can't be a bad thing."

"No it's not. Matt is away on a men's retreat with his church this week, so he may not be ready for another getaway, but I know Luke will be next door, for sure."

"I should get going. Vinnie . . . " she called to her son, "let's go Lance will be crossing his legs if we don't get home soon."

"Oh, Mom, you're silly. I never saw Lance cross his legs. Bye, Auntie Angie." After giving her a quick hug, he took off running toward the door.

Smiling back at her sister, "Thanks again. I'll call you later."

Leah couldn't believe that Luke's mother had actually made good on her promise to view her portfolio. Everyone affirmed her work—said it was good, including her professors, but was it good enough to be considered art-gallery-worthy? She stayed up until two in the morning, fussing, rearranging, and brutally second-guessing herself. Some of her confidence had evaporated when the coveted internship fell through. But later, when she honestly scrutinized the whole situation, she concluded that the recipient was far more worthy than herself, and yet that did not mitigate the hurt. She was truly happy for her classmate and told him so. But now, she was given this awesome opportunity to show her work to Luke's mom, a real-life curator, in the hopes of securing a coveted piece of wall space in one of her well-known art galleries.

"So, are you ready?" Mia asked, leaning against Leah's door.

Jolted from her concentration, she realized her sister was talking to her. "Oh, Mia, I'm a nervous wreck," she admitted.

Mia walked into the bedroom and studied Leah's portfolio. "Why? Your stuff is beyond amazing. Trust me, you have nothing to worry about."

"Yes, yes I do. The competition is stiff and I'm not sure I'm in their league."

"Listen, just because you didn't get that internship does not mean you don't have talent. Did you consider that it just wasn't the right internship for you?"

"Hmm, I hear you. Will you come with me—please?"

"Sure, but I thought Luke was going with you?"

"He is, but I'd like you to be with me too."

"Okay. When?"

"Uhm, we leave here in twenty minutes."

"What? Twenty minutes? Look at me; I desperately need a shower." Just then the doorbell rang. "That would be Luke."

"Okay, you're off the hook. Go take a shower, I'll go with him."

"Are you sure?"

"Yeah, I'm a big girl—right?"

Mia gave her sister a quick hug and whispered, "You'll be fine."

Leah was fidgeting, squirming and probably quite unaware that she was chewing her lip during the short drive to the gallery. "Why are you so nervous? My mom doesn't bite. Now, Dad on the other hand," he snickered.

When she didn't laugh or even smile, Luke knew she was really struggling. Without warning, he pulled into a parking lot, turned off the engine and stared at her.

"Why did you stop? We're going to be late," she reasoned.

"We have plenty of time and we don't have to punch a time clock, you know."

"Yes, I know, but I want to make a good impression and . . . "

"Leah, you've already knocked my mom's socks off. She thinks you're terrific and so do I. Can I pray with you right now, right here?"

That simple gesture touched Leah's heart. Luke was changing before her very eyes. She thought of the scripture from 2 Corinthians 5:17 that says, *Therefore if anyone is in Christ, he is a new creation; old things have passed away; behold, all things have become new.* "Luke, I love the new you." She smiled as she took his hand. "Yes, please pray for me. I need His peace." Together they sat, heads bowed, praying for peace and minutes before Luke concluded his prayer, that once elusive peace had settled in her spirit.

The gentle tinkling of an old-fashioned bell that hung over the door announced their arrival. Leah spotted Mrs. Henderson sitting at a gorgeous, cherry-finished antique desk at the rear of the gallery. She didn't immediately look up, but kept her eyes down as though compelled to finish reading the final chapter of an excellent novel. Still half-focused on the stack of paperwork, she stood. "Hello there. I see you made it all right."

Once again, this woman was impeccably dressed and Leah thought she carried herself like royalty. "Yes, we did and thank you again for taking time from your busy schedule," Leah commented.

She could hardly maintain eye contact with Luke's mom, she was so taken with the variety and sheer number of pieces of art being showcased. The lighting, the wall colors, even the slight scent of cinnamon in the air, all screamed—*upscale.*

"Oh, don't be silly, sweetheart. I live for this kind of thing. Well, let's see what you have here." Mrs. Henderson carefully placed Leah's treasure on a large display case. "Hmm. Yes. Aha," rolled off her tongue. They were *nothing* words, but to Leah, they were scary words. She stood silently, fidgeting with her watchband as Luke's mother studied every single image. The annoying ticking of a grandfather clock on the back wall exacerbated every passing minute. Luke stole a quick glance at Leah, who appeared to be maintaining her composure. He tried to distract her, but Leah's eyes were locked on her portfolio.

Finally Leah decided to walk away from Mrs. Henderson to take a closer look at the display of beautiful paintings. Luke grabbed a soda from the small refrigerator in the back room. "Leah, are you thirsty?" he yelled.

"No, I'm good. Thanks."

Just then, Mrs. Henderson looked up as though coming out of a trance. "Leah, my dear, please step over here."

To Leah, it sounded like a command and an ominous one at that. "Sure," she said, trying to appear as matter-of-fact as possible as her palms began to sweat. Mrs. Henderson took a deep breath and looked into her eyes as though seeing her for the first time. "My dear, you have a rare talent for one so young."

"Mom, she's not that young," Luke interjected.

His mother smiled at him and continued, "As I was saying, you have an uncanny ability to capture light and shadows in such a powerful and sometimes subtle way. I'm very excited about what you've put together here. I would like to see more."

Leah thought it was impossible for her to smile any broader or to feel any more excited than she did at that very moment. She was elated, thrilled. "Thank you. I'm humbled by your assessment of my work. So, I'm on the right track?"

"You certainly are, indeed you are. Leah, I wonder if you'd consider accepting an internship with me? I have several galleries and I could use the help, but more importantly, I would like to advance your career. You would be exposed to up-and-coming artists, as well as some very well-known and respected ones, many of whom reside right here in the Merrimack Valley."

Leah's hands flew to her face in response to the offer. She had never expected this, never dreamed she'd get this kind of opportunity.

"Of course, you may need some time to think it over. Maybe you'd want to talk to your parents, but I'd be delighted if you'd seriously consider coming on board."

"Oh, Mrs. Henderson, I cannot thank you enough and I will talk with them tonight and get back to you tomorrow."

"Please don't feel hurried. I can assure you that I'm not looking at anyone else for this internship and I will speak to the Chair of the Art Department at your school. We are old friends and I think she'd agree with me that you should also get academic credits for your time spent here."

"You could do that? I mean, is that standard protocol? I guess you know what you're doing. Thank you so much."

Trina and Sal lingered over their morning cups of coffee. They both were looking forward to a few days at the beach house. Hampton Beach had become their home away from home; the sounds and smells of the ocean recharged their batteries. "Aren't you glad that we both love the same things?" Trina asked.

"How so?"

"Well, the peace and quiet of the beach. The comfort of having family around us? Stuff like that."

"I'm with you there," he smiled, hooking his pinky finger in hers. "But I think we'd better get our old bodies moving if we want to get to the beach sometime today."

"Okay, I just have to throw a few things in my overnight suitcase. Vinnie is packed; the food is put together and ready to go. Let's do this," she declared, pushing away from the table.

"Vinnie, brush your teeth and let's get a move on."

"I already did, Dad. I'm ready and so is Lance."

The jarring sound of the phone interrupted their conversation. "I'll get it," Trina yelled from the next room.

Sal rinsed their cups and began pulling items out of the fridge to be loaded into the car. When he returned from his second trip, Trina was standing in the kitchen, white as a cloud. "Honey, what's wrong?"

"Sal, something terrible has happened."

Vinnie ran into the room. "Mommy, can I bring my new sleeping bag? Please!"

"Sure, honey. Go on upstairs and get it." When Vinnie was out of the room, she turned back to her husband. "Sal, Darlene has attempted to take her own life. She's in rough shape, hanging on by a thread. That phone call was the hospital social worker; Darlene is asking to talk to me. What should I do?"

Sal exhaled deeply, then pulled her into a deep hug. "I was afraid your compassion would suck you into her life, but in light of this, well, you have to go. You just have to go. Do you want me to go with you?"

"No, why don't you guys go on ahead to the beach. I'll catch up with you there. And, Sal, please pray for me; pray that I have God's words to share with her."

Vinnie bounded in the room, "I'm ready!"

Trina helped her boys load up the car, kissed them good-bye and then picked up the phone. "Joey, I'm glad I caught you at home." She explained what had just happened and asked him to please cover her in prayer for the next couple of hours. She really didn't know if Darlene was going to pull through; the social worker conveyed a sense of urgency and this frail girl was asking for her. How could she not respond?

Trina had walked through these hospital doors more times than she'd like to count. Her job frequently brought her to this place, not to mention episodes of family sickness and even death. She pressed the elevator button, impatiently tapping her toe, wondering what awaited her. Stepping off the elevator, she was immediately greeted by an old friend; this chaplain covered the care of psychiatric patients and was one of the most compassionate women Trina had the privilege of knowing.

Their embrace was spontaneous and heartfelt. "It's so nice to see you," Trina greeted her, "but I wish it were under different circumstances. Please, can we talk for a few minutes before I see Darlene?" She needed to get as much accurate information as possible. "How could this happen? I mean, she hadn't been incarcerated all that long?"

Her friend did not paint a pretty picture. "Trina, you know as well as I do that if an inmate is desperate enough, they will succeed in acquiring whatever they want, drugs included. Apparently, this young woman was plenty desperate; she had ingested enough dope to kill a moose." The chaplain went on to explain that the guard who found her said the ambulance attendants almost lost her twice before finally pulling into the emergency room entrance.

"What's she like now?"

"Presently, she's drifting in and out of consciousness; in her more lucid moments she repeatedly asked for Trina Lamazo—that's you, honey."

Trina's shoes echoed on the well-worn flooring as she made her way down the long corridor leading to Darlene's room. She lingered at the doorway; the room was dark and had an unpleasant odor. She gingerly stepped across the threshold, cognizant of a wizened old woman in the adjacent bed. The woman shifted slightly when she became aware of Trina's presence, but remained silent.

Darlene's form appeared to be that of a discarded rag doll; she was thin and completely disheveled. *Why hasn't the staff washed her hair? She looks terrible.* Not wanting to wake her, she stood silently at her bedside. She didn't know exactly how much time had passed as she wordlessly shifted from foot to foot before Darlene began to move. It took a while before her bloodshot eyes opened and focused on Trina.

Despite her many years as a social worker, Trina felt completely tongue-tied. Her head knew all the right words to recite, but her emotions were a tangled mess. Finally, "Darlene, how are you feeling?"

Clearing her throat, Darlene turned her face away, responding, "I've been better," attempting a limp smile. "Thanks for coming."

"Do you want to talk about what happened to you?"

"No. Definitely not."

"Okay, then why did you want me to come here? You didn't want me to bring *my son*, I hope," sounding a bit harsher than she'd meant.

"Of course not. I now understand that chapter of my life is over. I made my bed, now I have to lie in it."

"Then why? How can I help you?"

Clearing her throat again, "After I OD'd this time, my mind was really messed up. I couldn't remember my name or that I was in lockup. I did have one vague recollection—delivering my baby boy. Bits and pieces of the last six or seven years were all muddled in my head. I felt like I was being sucked down a deep, hole—it was so black. Then someone, probably a guard, called 911. I'm convinced I would have died if they'd left me there. And on some level, I think that may have been better for everyone. Just be done with it," she said in a hushed voice.

"Oh, Darlene."

"I heard the staff whispering that you'd gone to bat for me, in spite of what I've done and *not* done. I thought I should say thank you for trying to help me, but I don't deserve another chance. I've done horrendous things. You really have no idea what kind of the things I've done in my life. My stepfather was right, I'm worthless. It's a waste of time for those rehab people to try to fix me. I know that now. So, thank you, but don't be offended if I don't accept your helping hand. And don't be afraid because I won't come around your son anymore."

Trina was stung by the words of this pathetic young woman. *I can't begin to imagine what kind of home life this girl has endured?* Torn between risking her son's well-being and helping his biological mother, she silently prayed for God's words and direction.

After a long, awkward silence, Trina blurted, "That is nothing but a bunch of lies. You are not worthless. Yes, you've had a rotten life so far, but my God is in the business of fixing broken lives, and He redeems them back to Himself."

Darlene looked away, but Trina was certain she'd seen a tear stream down her cheek. It was then that she stepped forward to take her hand. "Darlene, I'm sure you're not interested in me laying a bunch of Bible verses on you, but please allow me to share just one."

Darlene nodded.

Trina felt compassion well up in her as she began to speak: "Psalm 34:18 says, *The Lord is close to the brokenhearted; He rescues those whose spirits are crushed.*"

"No one ever rescued me," she spat out.

"Whoever called 911 did. I'm here to try to rescue you."

"So, you think your God wants to rescue me?"

"I know He does. He wants to redeem you out of your life of hopelessness and sin. He's the only one who can do that."

"So how does this God do that?"

"Well, it all depends on you, Darlene. If you're truly sorry for your sins, confess them to God and ask Him to forgive you, He is faithful to do just that. He will forgive you—I promise. And He will set your feet on a new path; you will become a new creation. Your old sinful life will lose its grip on you and you will begin to enjoy an entirely new life."

"It sounds way too easy." Trina thought she was losing her at that point, but Darlene's voice softened and she whispered, "But I guess I'm desperate enough to believe it."

"Then, can I pray with you?"

Darlene looked away once again, but surprisingly answered, "Yes, I guess so."

The room fell silent, except for the sound of her roommate's labored breathing. Trina was about to pull the privacy curtain closed when the old lady extended her hand, "Please, pray for me too."

"Certainly."

As Trina prayed, time stood still as the peace of the Lord blanketed the room. The normal hospital sounds of shuffling feet in the hallway, call bells and elevator doors all briefly went silent. When Trina later reflected on those few precious moments, she could only describe it as being in a holy bubble, doing God's work.

Chapter 29

As the Trayor sisters pulled up to the beach house, Leah noticed one of the Henderson cars. She wondered if Luke drove up with his parents; his car was nowhere in sight. They pulled their overnight bags out of the trunk and turned, nearly tripping over Vinnie.

"Where'd you come from?" Mia laughed as he tightly squeezed her around her waist.

"I was hiding on the porch."

"Where's your pooch?" Leah asked.

"I dunno, think he's with Mom."

"Well, let's go inside and find out."

The three of them climbed the porch steps, purposely bumping into each other as they made their way into the front room. "Hey, where is everyone?" Mia called.

"In the kitchen, honey."

They dropped their bags and headed toward the tantalizing aroma of simmering sauce. "Let me guess, pasta for dinner?" Leah joked.

"And why not? It's delicious and easy to transport," Angie chuckled while stirring the pot.

"So, who's here? I mean, is anyone else coming?" Leah asked.

"Are we not enough for you, fair maiden?" Trina kidded her niece.

"Just wondering how many relatives I have to share those meatballs with?"

"As far as I know, it's just us. Your dad and Uncle Sal just went for a walk on the beach. They'll be back shortly."

Mia was being tempted by those scrumptious looking meatballs; she just had to stab one to taste. "Hey, little lady, no sampling," Angie teased.

"I'm just doing quality control. Isn't that Kevin's standard excuse?"

"Why don't you put your things in the attic bedroom, then come down and tell us all about your internship. Aunt Trina hasn't heard the details yet."

"Okay, be right back," Leah turned, ordering Vinnie to carry one of her bags upstairs. Mia followed them, pinching Vinnie every few minutes to prod him along.

"Hey, quit it," he loudly protested. "Lance," Vinnie yelled, "come protect me from my crazy cousins."

To their surprise, Lance bounded up the steps, nearly knocking all of them into the wall. "Hey, this guy is getting to be a bruiser," Leah exclaimed. But rather than *protecting* Vinnie, he jumped on him, licking his face. Then, satisfied with himself, he jumped onto Mia's bed and seemed to smile at them.

"You know what? Your dog is really beautiful," Leah said, running her hands down his thick fur. "So, Vinnie, what have you been doing these days?"

"Aw, nothing really, until now." He gave her a sheepish grin.

"All right, all right, I get it. We're only here for a few days, but I promise, we'll do something together. Okay?"

"Yess!" And with that, he ran back down the stairs with Lance at his heels.

Later, while working together to put a meal on the table, Leah babbled on and on about her internship at the art gallery. It was completely incredible to her that Mrs. Henderson had actually offered her this coveted spot. Sure, she'd shared that her passion was taking new talent under her wing and watching them blossom, but Leah hadn't come to grips with the reality that *she* was in fact that new talent.

"And, Trina, she's going to get college credit while doing this. Isn't that awesome?" Angie nudged her sister.

"It sure is and you deserve it," Uncle Sal interjected as he walked by.

"I am absolutely thrilled for you, honey. Good job!" Trina fist bumped her niece.

"Thanks, everyone. Just pray that I don't mess up. I want to make her proud and not regret taking me into the gallery."

"Honey, you're not going to mess up. I know you'll succeed at whatever you set your hand to do."

"All right, all right, enough with the fluffing of her ego," Mia interjected. "Let's eat."

Whether at home or the beach house, spaghetti and meatballs was Angie's *go to meal.* It was always a crowd pleaser, and a quick glance at Vinnie's face said he wore it well. "Hey, son, you have more sauce on your face than in your tummy," Sal teased.

"It's yummy. I love it."

A knock at the door interrupted their teasing. "I'll get it," Leah blurted, assuming it would be Luke. She was not disappointed. "Hi, Luke, come in. We're just finishing up dinner. Have you eaten?"

"I'm not hungry, but I'll join you for dessert."

"Who said we have dessert?"

"Ha, when has this family ever *not* had dessert?"

"Hey, everyone, our neighbor is here," she announced, as Luke followed her to the table.

Greetings were exchanged while Sal busied himself with the coffee maker. "Can I interest you in a cup of java?"

"Absolutely."

"And, *yes*, we have dessert. Mom whipped up some pizzelles today."

"So, Luke, please tell your mom how grateful we are for her generous offer. Leah couldn't be happier." Jake said while helping to clear the table.

"Your daughter is very talented. My mom simply saw Leah's potential and capitalized on it. She's a pretty shrewd businesswoman."

"Hey, guys, you do know I'm right here," Leah vigorously waved her hands above her head.

"I couldn't ignore you," he smiled. "As a matter of fact, Mom and Dad sent me over to invite you over for—dessert."

They all looked at each other and laughed.

"What? I can eat two desserts, can't you?" Luke looked at Leah.

"It depends. What's for dessert at your house?"

"No clue, but I'm sure it came from a store. Mom's not much of a baker."

"That's okay, I'll politely have a piece of whatever it is."

Vinnie begged to go with them, but Mia quickly distracted him with an offer to play a board game. "Vinnie, I'm sure they just want to talk about boring business. Let's you and me play some Chinese checkers."

"Okay, and I'm gonna beat you," and he made a dash for the sunroom to retrieve the game.

⁓

Leah and Luke decided to walk along the beach before going next door. It was a beautiful day; the ocean was at high tide, which never failed to captivate her. They stopped to watch the seagulls performing their aerial acrobatics, before gracefully diving for their dinner; it was a dance Leah would never tire of watching. The clouds were moving fast across the sky and the salty ocean smell was almost intoxicating. There was no doubt that the shore was her happy place.

Luke took her hand as they walked. "Do you even know how amazing you are?" he smiled broadly.

"Yeah, I'm totally awesome," she quipped. "What brought that on?"

"Well, I watched you with my mom at the shop; you were so warm to her. And the way you interact with your sister and even your folks—I'm just saying that you are the most well-adjusted, happy person I have ever known."

"Thank you, Luke. But anything good you see in me is because of the work of the Holy Spirit in my life. My folks worked hard to bring us up in 'the fear and admonition of the Lord,' as the Bible says. I simply let Him do his work. Enough about me. Is your mom still sure about this business deal?"

"She sure is. As a matter of fact, she's bragging about you to her colleagues in the art world. You are her newest *project* and she's pretty pumped."

"Really?"

"Really! What do you say we head back to the house; I'm ready for my second dessert. I'm hoping Nina made something really good and sent it with my folks."

"One can always hope."

Angie and Trina brought their steaming hot cups of coffee to the front porch and settled together on the two-seat glider. They had added and removed several pieces of furniture when they bought the place, but everyone agreed the old, really old glider had to stay. Kevin joked, when sitting on it, that it was like being rocked by Mommy, which rewarded him with mocking comments and sideways stares. However, they admitted to understanding his offbeat comment on some weird level.

"So, has Vinnie asked about the *pretty lady* at all?" Angie questioned.

"No, not a peep out of him. I'm not sure he understood what was happening on that awful day at the mall. I am grateful she agreed to let me pray with her and what a bonus to be able to pray with her roommate. Honestly, Angie, only time will reveal if she desires to walk with the Lord and turn her back on her old ways."

"That's all well and good, but what will you do if she starts pressing for custody or starts sneaking around again? I mean, won't that put you over the edge?"

Trina sighed deeply and directed her gaze to the ocean. "I just have to trust God's sovereign plan. He knows what He's doing. My first instinct is to take my little guy and run far away, even though I know that's foolish. I have to accept that we've come this far and God will not allow our family to be destroyed."

A sense of peace came over Angie as she observed Trina's resolve. "You're right. I so agree," Angie smiled.

"Can I join you two?" Mia asked as she came through the door. "Vinnie ditched me for the guys."

"Sure, come on and take a seat."

"I hope I didn't interrupt anything important."

"No, just talking about my son. So, how is that job of yours?"

"Great! I love the challenge and I mean challenge; I'm learning so much and the opportunity for advancement is huge. I've been asked to sit in on meetings with the executive committee more than a few times. It's awesome."

"I'm so proud of you." Trina raised her coffee cup in a mock toast. But the real question is, how are you and Matt getting on?"

Mia blushed a bit, but quickly recovered. "He is terrific, Aunt Trina. Honestly, I feel like I've known him all of my life. Except for Leah, he's my best friend; we can discuss just about any subject."

"That is won—"

"He's smart and he's so kind."

"I'm thinking you two—"

"He never ceases to amaze me; he's always so thoughtful and so good to me."

Attempting to finish a sentence, Trina tried again, "Well it sounds like you are two peas in a—"

"Maybe I'll bring him by your house next week, so you and Uncle Sal can really get to know him."

They sat quietly for a moment when Angie and Trina burst into laughter.

"What?"

"Sweetheart, you are totally hooked, as in line and sinker hooked," Angie blurted.

"Yup, your eyes light up when you talk about him and you can't stop jabbering on and on about the guy," Trina pointed out.

Mia looked down, but soon admitted, "You guys are right. I really, really like him."

"Well, your dad and I like him too."

"I hoped that you did. Mom, we like the same things and he listens to me."

"Oh, here we go again. I'm just teasing. He's a wonderful young man. Is he coming this weekend?"

"No, he's busy with his grandpa. But he's taking me to a Red Sox game next weekend. I can't wait."

"For the game or to see Matt?"

"Well, I always love being at Fenway, but honestly being with Matt trumps Fenway."

"You don't say?" Angie kidded her daughter. "You don't say?"

Chapter 30

Luke was not disappointed; Nina had indeed sent a scrumptious apple galette along with his folks. He'd never known her to boast about her culinary skills and, in her unpretentious way, offered that this dessert was nothing more than a glorified apple tart. Luke frequently walked into their kitchen to find her rolling and shaping this rustic-looking tart. He could definitely manage to eat a second dessert, since she had taken the time to care for his family in such a delicious way.

"That was amazing," Leah dabbed the corners of her mouth. "Please tell Nina that I'm her newest fan," she smiled.

"I will pass along your compliment," Mrs. Henderson acknowledged. "But it's even better fresh out of the oven. I cannot resist the taste or aroma of cinnamon," she admitted.

"I thought I detected the light scent of cinnamon in your gallery."

"You did, indeed. It makes the atmosphere a bit more homey, don't you think?"

"I do."

"Well, would you like to sit on the porch?" Mr. Henderson asked, already standing. "Or do you youngsters have other plans?"

"Dad, we're hardly youngsters, but no, we have no plans."

"You're young to me." He winked at his wife.

"If you don't mind," she said, "I'm going to head upstairs? I have several articles that I must read before my meeting on Monday."

Mr. Henderson gave her a kiss on the cheek as she left the table. "This was supposed to be a relaxing weekend, Blanche."

"Yes, Rodney, I know. Please forgive me just this once," she protested with a smile.

Things certainly look healthier in the marriage department, Leah mused.

The three settled themselves on the front porch. Of course, Leah had seen their porch before, but never really had the opportunity to take in its decor. The lovely wrought iron furniture, although uncomfortable, was impressive looking. She was certain the set was quite old, yet in marvelous condition. *These cushions are as deep as my mattress*. It wasn't just the thickness of the cushions that struck her, but the vivid burst of colors in their floral pattern. It reminded Leah of her grandmother's garden. Neighbors walked by her yard just to enjoy the spectacular display of colors and fragrance. Somehow, her grandmother managed to coax various flowers to bloom from spring until late into the fall.

"Are you comfortable?" Mr. Henderson asked.

"Yes, thank you." Leah began to feel a sense of foreboding, or maybe it was expectancy.

"Are you enjoying your classes?"

"They're fine. I think this fall semester is going to be a killer, though. I've got a heavier load than last spring."

"Leah, you're a *brainiac*," Luke teased, "and I mean that in the most complimentary way possible. You've got it under control. I'm sure of it."

"Thanks, Luke. I appreciate your faith in me."

Except for the sounds of the ocean, there was a long, awkward period of silence. Mr. Henderson cleared his throat and fidgeted in his chair, causing Leah to think, *Here it comes! He's going to forbid me from seeing his son or drop some other bomb.*

At last he broke the silence and turned to face Luke. "Son, I want to talk to you both. I've wanted to explain something for a while; tonight is as good a time as any."

Oh no! That apple galette was not worth what's coming.

Warily Luke answered, "Sure, Dad. What's up?"

"I need to tell you a story; it may be ancient history to you both, but it's part of me. It impacted me and greatly influenced who I eventually became and I'm not the least bit proud of who I became—at least not until Jesus redeemed me."

"Okay, Dad—shoot."

Mr. Henderson cleared his throat, fixed his eyes on the ocean for a long time, then began, "You know I love this place, always have. Although at times it has been very painful for me to sit here, painful simply to look at that seascape."

"Why is that?"

"Well, here's the ancient history part. Please don't be shocked, but long before I met your mother, I was head over heels in love with another girl."

"Really?" Luke sat forward in his chair, genuinely surprised; his interest was piqued.

"We were very young, but nevertheless—it was love." He turned to face Leah, "She and her family lived in your beach house."

"They did? Wow, so I guess you saw her every day." Leah glanced at Luke with a smile.

"Yes, every day that we were both here at the shore. We were *an item*, as they say."

"So what happened? Who broke off with who?" Luke asked.

"It wasn't like that, son. We never would have ended it on our own. Never—" his voice trailed off. "Her father didn't approve of me and

295

forbade our relationship. My family was clearly labeled *conceited new money* while their family's status was very much the old money of New England; those *old money socialites* held the power. Anyhow, Elena and I continued to secretly see each other, whenever and wherever we could."

"You snuck around?"

"Yes, we did. It was so difficult with her right next door. Keep in mind we had no cell phones or even landline phones in our cottages back then. Her father went to the extreme of hiring a nanny to prevent us from meeting."

"So you eventually broke up?"

"No, no, we didn't, but we did keep a low profile for a long time. We'd hoped he would change his mind or soften as time passed. One night after her nanny fell asleep, she snuck out. We sat on this very porch and planned our escape. We were going to elope. I even gave her a ring, which at the time I couldn't afford without tapping into my savings. It was a beautiful ring, custom-made especially for Elena."

"But, Dad, how could she wear your ring? Wouldn't her father have noticed pretty quickly?"

"Her plan was to lock her bedroom door and wear it to bed every night, then she planned to keep it hidden during the day. I only saw it on her finger that night—only that night," he whispered.

"I hope her nanny wasn't the snoopy type." Luke smiled, trying to lighten the mood.

"The nanny was released from her duties the very next day."

"Why?"

At this point, Mr. Henderson obviously became uncomfortable. He went to the porch railing and stood silently for a while. Leah and Luke exchanged glances, waiting for him to continue.

"At dawn, Elena managed to sneak out the house for a short swim. She had done it many times over the past two summers." He stood, motionless, "No one knows . . . whether she got a cramp or the undertow pulled her down—Elena drowned that morning."

"Aw, Dad, that's so sad. I'm sorry you went through that."

With tears in his eyes, Luke's father turned to face them. "It was the worst day of my life. I was inconsolable. Her father wouldn't even allow me to attend her funeral. I said good-bye in my own, private way. I know it sounds silly, but I wrote her letters; it helped me to express my love and my sense of loss."

Luke reached over and touched his father's hand. "But something snapped in me that day. I vowed that I would become successful, powerful and rich. In my messed-up thinking, I would never allow that kind of personal rejection to rob me of something I wanted. Unfortunately, I became a driven man and ultimately grew to be just like the man I had despised. As I became more and more successful and powerful, I too looked down my nose on virtually everyone. I'm sad to say, even your family, Leah."

Leah could not open her mouth, she couldn't respond. Soon a wave of compassion swept over her for this sad, damaged man. She now understood. It wasn't personal, it was a private bondage from his past.

"I now know that she did manage to hide the ring from him."

Leah looked down at her ring and immediately knew. "My ring—this is the ring you gave her?" she whispered, bringing her other hand to her mouth. "Oh, Mr. Henderson!"

"Dad, does Mom know all this?"

"Yes, she does and it freed her up to forgive me for my past behavior. I am so very sorry."

Leah reached for the ring and slowly twisted it off her finger. "Here, Mr. Henderson, I want you to have this."

"No, no. It is yours, please keep it."

"No, I could never keep it now. Elena would want you to have it back."

Luke moved closer to his father. "Dad, you could sell it and set up a scholarship or internship—in her name."

Mr. Henderson's head jerked up. "Son, that is a wonderful suggestion," he was visibly processing that idea. "Yes, I believe that Elena *and* your mother would wholeheartedly approve of that gesture."

A while later, still somewhat surprised by the events of the evening, Luke walked Leah back to her cottage. He hugged her on her front porch. "I am so glad we're free to become *an item*, as they say."

"Me too, Luke, me too," snuggling comfortably into his embrace.

Chapter 31

"You have to bundle up, Vinnie," Trina warned. "Believe me, it gets brutally cold on those bleachers. I turned into a giant Popsicle more than once when frigid winds blew across that football field."

Vinnie giggled at the mental image of his mom turning into a giant Popsicle. "But I have so many clothes on—I can hardly move," he whined.

"You will thank me; I know you will." Trina stepped back and looked at her son. *He looks like Ralphie's poor little brother from A Christmas Story.*

"Aw, Mom, I'm sweating."

"Are you ready, son?" Jake came bounding down the stairs, looking like he was heading for the frozen tundra. "We have to pick up the boys in twenty minutes."

"I'm ready," he managed. "Who's Lawrence High playing, Dad?"

"North Andover, but the game is at the Lawrence stadium, so let's shake a leg."

"Do they have a chance to beat them?" Trina asked.

"I doubt it. North Andover has a great team this year. See ya, sweetie," he planted a big noisy kiss on Trina's cheek.

She laughed at their antics. "Have fun you guys. Vinnie, stay with your dad—you hear me?"

"Okay, Mom!"

The Agosti family were rabid sports fans, which included supporting local high school football. *I'll have to chip the ice from them when they get home.* Trina looked down at her golden retriever, "Well, Lance, it's just you and me today." This started his heavy tail moving: thump, wag, thump, wag.

She decided that a nice pot of New England clam chowder would be perfect once they returned from their adventure. After pulling all the needed ingredients from the refrigerator, she began chopping the celery and onion. The familiar sound of the mailman at the front door spurred Lance into action. He was comical to watch; his daily routine involved growling at the slot as the mailman shoved the mail through the opening. He never once chewed the mail once it dropped to the floor. She assumed his growling was meant to protect his family from every potential intruder. *But he's such a loving dog, he'd probably just lick the bad guys until they surrendered.*

She fanned through the usual mail: bills and advertisements, but then noticed a letter addressed to Miss Trina, not even a last name. She looked at it curiously; her street address was correct, but the zip code was omitted. Her first impression was that the sender was a child, but who?

Sitting down at her breakfast counter, she carefully slit the envelope, pulled out a tattered piece of stationary. She instantly knew who had written the child-like printed letter.

Dear Miss Trina,

It has been a long time since you visited me in the hospital. I don't know if I thanked you for coming to see me. Anyhow, I'm sorry for making you worry. I just had to see my son, I'm sorry—your son. I need to tell you that I'm glad he is with good people. God knows if he'd even be alive if I kept him hidden with me on the streets—so many bad people there. I've made lots of wrong decisions, but I now know that giving him up was a good one. So, thank you for not pressing charges against me and for pulling strings to get me in another rehab. I thought it would be a waste of time, but I'm doing good in this one and I am trying really hard to stay clean. This time I can lean on Jesus. I want to also tell you they have made plans to transfer me to a rehab center in Washington state. I have a cousin, she's a Christian, who wants me near her. She's going to help me to get a new start. Her church has a big ministry to help people like me. I want to go—she's my only relative and we were close as kids. Trina, thank you for giving me a second chance. Take care of *our* son. You will never hear from me again—I promise. Someday, will you please tell him that his first mama loved him enough to give him a real life?

Darlene

Trina was overcome with emotion. She was so thankful that Darlene, with the help of the Lord, was going to get her life back.

She hadn't realized she was carrying a weight of fear and uncertainty, until it was lifted. If Darlene was being truthful, they would no longer have to look over their shoulders.

She just had to share this with her best friend. "Angie, is your whole family at the game?" she said into the phone.

"Yup, the girls even dragged their boyfriends along. I opted for my cozy fireplace and a good book. Why?"

"I'm coming over, I've got to share something awesome with you. I'll be there in a few minutes."

Angie looked at the phone, realizing her sister had just hung up on her and would soon be at her front door. *What could she possibly need to tell me that couldn't wait until our dinner —tomorrow?*

Angie and Trina rejoiced together at the good news—her sister truly couldn't have been happier for their family. "Isn't it amazing how God worked that whole bad situation out to a good outcome?" Angie said. "Just amazing!"

"It sure is. I feel like a boulder has been lifted from my spirit."

"So, I have some news too," she stated. Ever since she was a kid, Angie loved to share a secret or at least be the first to tell a story.

"Okay, your turn," Trina leaned forward, silently wondering what kind of news her sister wanted to share.

"Ellie told me that a couple of extra guests were joining us for dinner tomorrow."

"Who?"

"You remember Ginger Wright—you know, the Maureen O'Hara look-alike?"

"Sure, her son and Vinnie are good buddies now. We've set up a few playdates for them. I didn't know that Ellie knew Maureen, I mean Ginger."

"Well, here's the deal, Sammy gave a little speech to the older kids on Career Day. He knew the principal from his college days and it seems the guy was looking for an engineer to round out the school's program. You know how Sammy loves to talk about his work, so he accepted. Ginger was asked to monitor the kids at the middle school that day. They met over refreshments and I guess they just clicked. They've been dating ever since."

"Sammy and Ginger? That's awesome, she's a lovely woman and a great mom."

"Ellie admitted that they were beginning to think Sammy was destined to be a bachelor. He is kind of picky about women."

"I imagine that flaming red hair really snagged him. Now I'm *really* looking forward to our dinner—and Vinnie will have a playmate. Awesome."

They visited for a while longer, but Trina knew she needed to finish her chowder. The boys would be home before long. She stood, hugged her sister, "Thanks for sharing in my joy; see you tomorrow."

Sal and Vinnie were met at the door by their exuberant pal; wagging, jumping and whining was the typical greeting for the family he loved.

"How was the game?" Trina asked as she helped Vinnie peel off his winter layers. "Daddy said we won a goose egg."

"Huh?"

Sal smiled at her, "We lost forty-one to zero—goose egg."

"Aw, that's too bad, but when Vinnie is preoccupied I have some good news to share with you. Very good news."

Chapter 32

That year the fall foliage drew a record number of tourists to the area; the colors could not have been more vibrant. But as always, it ended too quickly. Winter was already upon them, as evidenced by the piles of boots in the corner, as well as the coats, and hats hanging from the old-fashioned coat rack. As harsh as the winters could be, Joey still loved the four distinct seasons of New England weather. He understood why many elderly flew south for the winter, but he would never be one of them. Over the years, he'd worked on dozens of cars for his Florida-bound customers, but a few snowflakes (well, maybe more than a few) would not scare him into hibernation or a change of address. He prided himself on being of hardy stock.

"Uncle Joey, how's it going?" Mia brightly called as she tapped the bell on the front counter. "Hi guys," she added when Ricky and Anthony poked their heads around the vehicles they were working on.

"Hey kiddo," Anthony returned. Ricky responded with a quick nod and returned to his work.

"There's my princess," Joey acknowledged. "What brings you here? Everything okay?"

"Oh sure, everything is great. I took a personal day today; I had a dentist appointment and a few other things to do. I just thought I'd pop in and say hi, it's been quite a while since my last visit. I don't want you to forget what I look like." She flipped her long, thick hair over her shoulder and struck an exaggerated pose.

"No worries there," he smiled. "I'd hug you, but . . ." A glance down at his greasy coveralls said it all.

"No, that's quite all right. That grease is impossible to remove and this coat is brand-new."

"How's your buggy running?"

"Just fine, no problems. But it's due for inspection soon; can you fit me in?"

"Today? Uh uh, can you bring it in Saturday?"

"Yup, what time?"

"How about eight?" he started to write it in his appointment book.

"In the morning?"

He laughed at her. "Yes, in the morning. You really are a princess, aren't you?"

"No, it's just that Matt and I are going into Boston Friday night and it might be a late night. He's taking me to a new restaurant and maybe dancing. Isn't that awesome?"

"Yup, just awesome. Well, maybe I can squeeze you in around ten," he conceded, erasing the original appointment.

Mia idolized her uncle and knew he had a soft spot for her too. She remembered her high school days, working part-time on the counter and cash register. Grandpa Vincent was so proud to have his family working here with him. She looked around the garage, not much had changed, including a calendar that was four years out of date.

"Uncle Joey, don't you think you need a new calendar?" she mocked.

"Naw, that one is vintage, it lends a certain *character* to the old place."

"Well, I think Grandpa Vincent would be so proud of what you've accomplished here, except for the calendar. All this new equipment, new services, and your expanded customer base, you've done the family proud."

"Thanks, sweetie."

"Well, I'm outta here. I still have a few errands to run. See you Saturday morning. I love you, Uncle Joe."

As if rehearsed, all three yelled, "See ya, kiddo."

Leah loved puttering around the gallery; simple things like dusting and rearranging pieces of artwork was very satisfying. She had a keen eye for balance; it was uncanny how she was able to place certain pieces in exactly the right spot. Mrs. Henderson never failed to lavish praise upon her young intern after she'd successfully showcased newer pieces, yet managed to strategically place older pieces throughout the gallery.

Leah turned at the sound of the doorbell, anticipating a customer, but was surprised to see Mia. "Hi, sis! I just stopped by to see how you're doing and coax you into grabbing a bite to eat with me?"

"What a nice surprise! I take it you played hooky today? And sure, I'd love that; just give me a minute to let Mrs. Henderson know I'm leaving for the day."

Mia walked around the gallery, taking in the beautiful pieces on display. Her eyes were quickly drawn to her sister's photographs. *I am so proud of this kid; she really has what it takes.*

"Okay, I'm ready. What do you think of all this?" Leah said, sweeping her hand in a circular motion.

"I think your work is amazing, you've done a terrific job here. I hope they appreciate you."

"Shh, she's in the back room."

Smiling at her kid sister, "Come on, let's go."

Looking like the Bobbsey Twins, they walked to an upscale corner café, simultaneously pulling their scarves more tightly around their faces against the whipping wind. "Wow, it's getting cold. Are we supposed to get a storm?"

"I didn't think so, but it sure feels like it. Here we are," Leah said, stepping into the warm café.

Mia scanned the one-room café, small but charming with all its nooks and crannies. "Oh, this place is adorable, makes me feel like I just stepped out of a time capsule," she said, pulling off her scarf. The decor was beautifully eclectic, strongly accented with sturdy early American pieces.

"Is the food good?"

"Simple, but very good. So, what are you up to today?"

The waitress was quick to bring water and menus; she rattled off the specials of the day, and promptly left them to decide.

"So, as I was starting to say, I didn't know you were taking a personal day."

"It was a spur-of-the-moment decision. I had a dental appointment and my car was due for inspection."

"Ugh, dentists," Leah shivered. "I just hate sitting in that chair."

"I hear you, but it was just a cleaning, so no biggie. Then I visited Uncle Joey and the guys."

"How long did you have to wait for your car inspection?"

"He couldn't do it today, so I'm bringing it back Saturday morning."

Just then the waitress came back to take their orders and disappeared behind a mysterious wall.

"Matt and I are going into Boston Friday night for dinner, and if I can persuade him, some dancing. Would you and your guy like to join us?"

"Oh, sounds like fun, but we're working late at the gallery. His mom needs help with several new display cases. She and I tried to maneuver them ourselves, but they were just too cumbersome and heavy; we need Luke's muscles."

"Bummer. It would have been a fun foursome. Maybe we can do something together next week."

"Let's do that," Leah firmly declared. "So, did Mom tell you that Luke's folks have already set up a scholarship fund with the proceeds from the sale of the ring?"

"No, I knew it was in the works, but . . . "

"Well, they did it and they're committing additional monies to it on a yearly basis. I feel like we played a small part in helping young women achieve their goals."

"No, honey, *you* played a part. I simply watched you wrestle with that monster dresser. So, tell me the details."

"It's an annual scholarship, which they've named The Elena Scholarship. It will be based on financial need and awarded to a female who has expressed interest in an advanced degree in the arts. It's being established through her high school and will be presented at the time of the recipient's graduation."

"That is wonderful. Do you miss wearing the ring?"

"No, not at all. Right from that day at the beach, I had an inkling that I was simply a guardian until its home was found."

"I think it was a sad love story, but at least some good will come out of it, all these years later."

"Don't you look adorable," Angie stood back to admire her daughter. "What's the big occasion?"

"Nothing special. Remember I told you that Matt and I are going to a fancy French restaurant in Boston, so I thought I'd look fancy."

"Well, you look terrific," Jake tenderly kissed her forehead. "Where has my little girl gone? I don't like this growing up stuff."

"Too late, Dad. I'm already there."

"Indeed you are."

Leah came running down the stairs, but unexpectedly stopped. "Whoa, you look amazing. Can I borrow that dress for New Year's Eve?"

"We'll see. I may need it then myself."

"Not likely. You wouldn't wear the same dress twice with Matt."

"Sure I would."

"Would not."

"I would."

"Girls, girls, I take back my *grown up girls* statement," their dad teased.

Angie laughed at their antics, grateful for their close relationship. "Hey, anyone up for Christmas shopping tomorrow—with their dear mother?"

"Do I get a free lunch out of it?" Leah asked.

"If we're still shopping by one o'clock, lunch is my treat."

"Hold on, I have to get my car inspected at ten. What time were you planning to leave?"

"Why don't we leave right after Joe is done, then we can shop until dinner—still my treat."

"I have a better idea," Jake interrupted. "How about I meet you for dinner—my treat?"

"Deal!"

"Deal!"

"Okay that's settled. Thank you, sweetheart."

Leah pulled her coat and hat out of the closet. "Luke should be here any minute. Have fun! Don't forget, we're double-dating next weekend."

Jake saw Luke walking up the front walk so he quickly opened the door, motioning for him to enter.

"Oh thanks." Looking back over his shoulder, he said, "This guy seems to be following me."

Matt jokingly pushed him over the threshold. "Right behind you, buddy."

They both looked at Mia, but Luke spoke first. "You're all decked out, where's the party?"

"No party. Matt and I are going out to eat."

Matt couldn't take his eyes off her. "You look fabulous. Emerald green is definitely your color. Although you look great in any color," kissing her cheek.

"Well, thank you. Shall we go?"

"I'm ready. Are you sure you don't mind us taking your car? I'm not comfortable driving mine with my wipers acting up. I'll get them replaced tomorrow."

"No, I don't mind, as long as you drive."

"You two have a fun time," Angie walked them to the door.

She turned to Leah and Luke, "Kevin and Cindy are coming over with the baby. Would you like to stay for pizza before heading off to the shop?"

Luke shrugged his shoulders. "My mom's expecting us in less than hour. Besides, I think she's planning to order in for us."

"Okay, another time."

Luke and Leah weren't gone for more than a few minutes when Kevin pulled in the driveway. Angie went straight for little Emma. "Oh, sweetie, I've missed you," hugging and kissing her.

"Mom, Mom, you saw her a couple of days ago."

"I know, but she's my little pumpkin."

"Oh, brother!"

"Never mind pumpkin, let's go get that pizza," Jake interrupted. "Kevin, you want to ride over with me?"

"Sure, where are we going?"

"Is Napoli's okay?"

"More than okay, my first choice," Cindy said.

———✦———

The wind was picking up and the swirling snow was sometimes blinding on the drive home. Driving out of Boston, traffic on route 93 was always congested during the day, but it was still surprisingly heavy considering the hour and the inclement weather.

"Matt, that dinner was out of this world. Thank you. Where did you hear about that place?"

"One of my coworkers recommended it. He assured me that you'd be impressed."

"Impressed is a major understatement. It was beyond fabulous."

"Good. I'm glad you liked it. I hope you're not disappointed that I wanted to skip the dancing."

"No, I understand. This weather is getting worse by the minute, it makes perfect sense to get home. We can go another time, or maybe we can dance in my living room."

"Whoa, in front of your folks? I don't think so."

"You know they like you a lot."

"I like them too, but I like their daughter a whole lot more."

"Yeah, Leah is a sweetheart," she joked.

"Funny girl, I really do love being with you, Mia."

"The feeling is absolutely mutual," she smiled, but noticed he was somewhat distracted. He seemed to be tensing up. "What's wrong, Matt?"

"I just hit another icy patch, that's all. We're all right now," but she knew he was trying to concentrate on the road and not frighten her.

"I didn't hear anything about a storm, but it sure feels like a nor'easter is brewing out there."

"I'll say. It's getting awfully slick and I haven't seen one sander truck. I think we should pull off the highway. Your car is good in the snow, but I'm still fighting this wheel."

"Sure, pull off wherever you can. It will take longer to get home, but we'll probably be safer on a secondary road—"

Without any warning, an eighteen-wheeler attempted to pass them, jackknifed and clipped Matt's left rear bumper. It hit hard, spinning them on the snow-covered highway. Mia screamed in reaction to the violent careening; she screamed again as headlights from oncoming cars came closer and closer, at too high a rate of speed. It all happened so fast: the dizzying lights, the sound of metal on metal, the shattering of glass and then the silence, complete and utter silence.

Mia was drifting in and out, in dreamlike awareness. She was cognizant they'd been hit multiple times; she pictured herself as a rag doll being tossed to-and-fro. "Matt, Matt," she tried to cry out, but no sound came.

Matt shook his head, desperately trying to bring his vision into focus. *What's that smell? My chest, my chest; am I having a heart attack? No, it's got to be the air bags.* Finally his thoughts began to crystallize; he turned to his right, "Mia, Mia, are you okay? Talk to me!"

He was crying and somehow she knew he was crying, but she couldn't respond to him. *God, am I dead? No, I can't be dead or I'd see Your beautiful face.*

"The blood, there's so much blood," he mumbled. "Mia, Mia, please open your eyes," he began to panic. He heard a distant siren—too far away. He tried to take hold of her hand, but she was in such an awkward position that he couldn't grasp it. *She's not moving. Is she breathing?* "Oh, God, help us!" he cried.

A loud bang on the window jolted him, "Hey, buddy hang on, we're going to get you out of there. Just relax, don't move."

Everything was jumbled: red flashing lights, blue flashing lights, muted voices, distant sounds. He couldn't zero in on exactly who was speaking to him. *I'm being loaded into an ambulance. Wait, get Mia! Get Mia!* Darkness.

Chapter 33

"Thanks, Mom and Dad. We had a nice time," Kevin was wrestling with Emma's snow jacket. "I hate taking her out in this lousy weather. We probably should have left an hour ago."

"Why don't you stay? The Pack 'n Play is already set up, we have plenty of room and I'd love more time with this munchkin." Emma was rubbing her eyes and nuzzling into her daddy's chest.

"She's pretty much out for the count tonight, but she'll be all spunky in the morning. Sure, I'm okay with a sleepover," Cindy said.

"Okay, the ladies have spoken. We'll stay! What's for breakfast?" Kevin grinned.

"You're a bottomless pit," Angie joked. "Cindy, does he ever get filled up?"

"Nope! I'd better get this little lady into bed before she gets her second wind, then we're all in trouble."

"Cindy, I'll come upstairs with you. I have pajamas that will probably fit you and I'd like to freshen your bed," Angie said.

The sound of the telephone pierced through Angie like a knife; late night calls always unnerved her. *This can't be good. I hope the kids haven't broken down.* Her heart began to race as she walked to the phone. "I'll get it," Jake yelled, but she was beside him in a flash, studying his facial expression as he listened to a nameless voice.

"What is it?" He held up his hand as if he could stop Angie's questions. "Jake, who is that?" Still he listened and nodded; then hung up the phone. His face turned ashen, his eyes glistening as he attempted to speak. Angie knew, but needed him to say something, anything.

"Angie, we need to get to the hospital. Mia and Matt have had an accident."

"Oh dear God, are they all right?"

"Get your coat, Angie. Let's go." He hadn't answered her question.

"Dad, I'm going too," Kevin insisted. "Cindy, stay here with Emma. I'll call you later."

"Of course, you go, I'll call Joe and Trina."

Joe and Ellie got the call and were out the door in seconds. His mind was racing, thinking back to Mia's recent visit to the shop.

"What a horrible night to be on 93. That highway is wicked on nice days, but tonight . . . " Ellie murmured.

"Why were they out in this storm?"

"They went for dinner, but Joe, you've got to admit this came up fast and unexpectedly. I think it even surprised our weather forecasters."

Their car began to skid, but he quickly brought it back under control. "It's like a skating rink out here; I'm guessing the highway is much worse."

The wind was battering them as they ran through the emergency entrance. Joe stopped short, scanning the waiting area, but didn't see his family. "Where do you think they are?"

"Maybe in with the kids? Let's ask."

Turning toward the desk, they heard a familiar voice behind them. "Joe, wait up."

Trina and Sal came through the entrance right after them. "Where's Angie?" Trina asked.

"We just got here, let's go to the desk and find out."

"Where's your little guy?" Ellie asked, looping her arm into Trina's.

"My neighbor is watching him. She's a gem."

Kevin was the first to reach the desk and was making his presence known, "Miss, we need information about my sister, Mia Trayor, and her boyfriend, Matt Bertolino. We were just called; they were brought here after an accident. Where can we find them?"

The nurse looked to be in her sixties and possessed the demeanor of the *wicked witch of the north*. She scanned their little group over the top of her glasses, then moved toward her desktop computer. "And these are her uncles and aunts," he added a bit softer.

Taking off her glasses, the nurse glared at Kevin, "She's still being worked on in the emergency room. Please take a seat."

Looking at each other rather anxiously, "No!" Kevin blurted out. "I want to see my sister," he almost shouted at the nurse, which caused her to take a step back. He felt Joey's hand on his shoulder, obviously meant to steady him.

"Please, Miss, can't at least one of us see her?" he pleaded in a more controlled voice.

She stared between Joe and Kevin for a rather tense moment, before softening her attitude. "All right, just one of you may go in." She locked eyes with Kevin. "Follow me."

There was no question Kevin was the one; he needed to see his sister. He was right on the nurse's heels as she moved away from the desk and opened a door. She pointed, "Go directly to that desk and ask there."

When the nurse returned to her post, Joe asked, "Can you tell us anything about her condition, her boyfriend's condition?" The nurse coldly stated she was not allowed to share that kind of information.

They turned back to the waiting room, frustrated by the lack of information, when a burst of frigid air drew their attention to the front door. Leah and Luke rushed through the double doors, "Cindy called me, how are they?" Leah's voice quivering. "Have you seen her yet?"

Joe pulled her close, "No, honey, not yet. Kevin just went to check on her, but the nurse insists only one person is allowed."

"No way! I'm going to see my sister," she demanded, but just then Kevin came through the door waving the group to join him.

"Excuse me," the nurse protested. "Please wait until the doctor comes to speak with you."

"No, *excuse me*! I'm attorney Kevin Trayor; I've just spoken with the hospitalist and he wants our family—now!" The nurse quickly backed off and watched them parade through the same door she'd guarded.

The emergency room appeared to be fully occupied, causing a serious flurry of activity for the medical staff. The Agosti family later learned a nine-car pileup had occurred on route 93, not far from Matt and Mia's accident. Many of the injured were also brought to this hospital.

"There's Angie," Joe pointed to his sister. They rushed to Mia's bedside, while respectfully staying out of the staff's way. Trina was familiar with the hospital's emergency room regulations; she fully expected they'd be asked to leave at any moment. Surprisingly, no one paid them the slightest bit of attention.

Joe and Trina went directly to Angie; Kevin and Leah came around to the head of the bed, hoping to talk with their sister. Mia's eyes were closed, her breathing quite shallow. Leah looked up to her mother, "Mom? What did the doctor say?"

Angie, blowing her nose before attempting to answer, prompted Leah to impatiently asked again, "Mom?"

Jake scanned everyone and asked them to move closer so he didn't disturb the patients adjacent to his daughter. "The doctor just left. She and Matt have been here for a while so their examinations have been completed."

"By the way, where is Matt?" Luke asked.

"He's at the end of this row; his folks haven't arrived yet, but he's more stable than Mia," Jake answered.

Leah was growing impatient. "Mom, please tell us about Mia's condition?"

"Dad, she doesn't seem to be responding to us," Kevin questioned.

"No, she doesn't," Jake said, causing Angie to burst into deep sobs. "The doc hopes all of our voices, familiar voices, might rouse her. He believes she can still hear us."

"But, that doesn't seem to be happening," Trina hugged her sister a bit tighter. "So what does that mean?"

Angie burrowed her face into her husband's chest. Jake waited a moment before calmly saying, "It means that she has some degree of traumatic brain injury," prompting multiple gasps. "Even though the air bags were released, she took some pretty direct hits. Apparently, her brain is swelling and if it continues to swell—"

"Oh no! God no, please!" Leah covered her face and wept.

Even with multiple lacerations, Mia was still a beauty. Her gorgeous black hair was spread out across the pillow; it triggered Trina's childhood memory of the classic story—*Sleeping Beauty*. If only the answer was as simple as a kiss on her lips. No one spoke for a long time, each was deep in their individual thoughts with their own questions.

"So, Mom, I have to ask, can't they do *anything*?" Kevin whispered, fighting his own emotions.

Clearing his throat, Jake answered for his wife. "The doctor told us that it's a waiting game, they can't make any promises or give a definitive prognosis," sniffles beginning to drown out his voice. "Listen, guys, isn't our God able to stop that swelling? He and He alone can heal her?"

That simple challenge sparked their faith, putting fear to flight—for now. Angie turned, stroking her daughter's face. "She's going to be all right, isn't she, Jake?" He nodded, squeezing her hand.

"Dad, I think we should take turns staying with her, round the clock," Leah said. "When she wakes up, one of us should be here." She took her sister's hand. "I'm staying tonight, but first, I want to see Matt."

"I'll walk down with you," Luke said. Matt's parents and sister had arrived. Leah and Luke had met them several times over the previous months. "Hey, bro," Luke extended his hand to Matt. "You don't look too bad. How are you feeling?"

"Like I was hit by an out-of-control truck. What was that guy thinking, passing on such a rotten night? Luke, please, tell me about Mia? No one will give me any information. My dad said she was resting when they walked by her bed."

"I'm sorry, Matt, she seems to be in a coma, unconscious."

"Unconscious?" he murmured, covering his eyes with his forearm. "She's going to be okay though," which sounded like more of a question than statement.

"The doctors can't give us anything definitive, but I know in my gut she'll be just fine. She has to be!" Leah said. "She has to."

Matt looked at his mom, eyes glistening, "Mom, I love her! I was going to tell her tonight."

His mom placing a comforting hand on his shoulder, tears rolled down her own face.

"Matt, I'm sure she knows you love her, but you're going to tell her that yourself," Leah said. "I need to get back, I'm staying the night. I'll check on you later."

It was getting late, yet no one wanted to go home. They'd laid hands on Mia several times between tears and conversation, fervently praying, still no one made any move to leave. "Mom, you really should get some sleep," Leah prompted. "I don't feel the least bit tired, so why don't all of you go?"

"You're probably right. We'll be back first thing in the morning," Angie stated. "Hey, I don't see her purse, I wonder if it was left in her car?"

Joey's head shot up. "They were driving Mia's car?"

"Yes. Matt's windshield wipers were acting up, so it was smarter to take her car; she asked him to drive. Why?"

Joe didn't answer, but became quiet.

"Leah, I'll stay with you for a while longer," Luke offered, when the family stood to leave. Angie and Jake leaned in to kiss their daughter, not really wanting to leave.

Joey and Ellie, bone-weary, slipped into bed, neither expected to sleep. She leaned over to reassure him that his niece would come out of this, but was startled when he burst into tears. "What's wrong, Joe? You've been so quiet?"

"Honey, what if this accident is my fault? What if Mia doesn't make it?"

"What on earth are you talking about? How could it be your fault?"

He sat up, looking gaunt and pale. "Ellie, listen to me, Mia came to the shop this week to get her car inspected, but I put her off until *tomorrow*. God, what if something malfunctioned on her car, something I could have caught before they drove into Boston? What if I could have prevented it? Ellie, I'll never forgive myself. I'm supposed to watch over everyone, I'm the head of our family."

"Stop it, Joe! That's nonsense, I'm sure her car was not the problem. Remember how we skidded driving to the hospital; you're talking crazy."

Abruptly, he changed the subject, "I know where those wrecks are brought; I've seen dozens towed in over the years. I've got to check out her car, first thing in the morning. Call my sister and tell her that I'm going to look for Mia's purse."

Joe didn't sleep a wink and was out the door before first light. He was a mess. Ellie picked up the phone at a reasonable time, but no one answered. *Of course, they're probably already at the hospital. There's no keeping this clan away from each other at times like this.*

Leah jumped at the touch on her shoulder. "Honey, we brought coffee and muffins," Jake whispered.

"Hi, Dad. Where's Mom?"

"She's talking to the nurse in the hallway; she was Mia's high school friend. And how are you doing? You must be exhausted?"

"I'm okay, I actually slept a little."

"Here, have some coffee, then go home to your comfy bed. You can come back later."

Angie came in, went right to the head of the bed and began stroking Mia's face. "How was she? Have you seen the doctor yet?"

"No different. Only nurses have been in, but it's still pretty early."

As if on cue, the admitting doctor entered, quietly greeted them and began a cursory examination, lingering as he examined her eyes. They silently watched and waited.

"Well? What can you tell us?" Jake asked.

"I wish I could give you something new, something positive, but I'm afraid I don't see any significant improvement; it's still a *wait-and-see* kind of thing."

Jake instinctively pulled Angie close, knowing those words were breaking her heart.

The doctor removed his glasses. "Continue to speak to your daughter, touch her, maybe even read to her; communicate the best you can, that she's not alone."

"Yes, of course we will. She has a large, loving family. We're here for her."

"Good. I'm having her moved to a private room today; it will give your family plenty of space."

They couldn't think of one question to ask as the doctor turned and moved on to his next patient.

Soon after Mia was settled in her new room, Ellie appeared. "Can I come in?"

"Of course. Are you alone?" Angie asked.

"Joe went to retrieve any personal items from Mia's car; he's familiar with those junkyards. He'll be along soon. Sammy and Anthony will be here later."

"Dad, can I take your car? I really do need some sleep, but I'll be back around dinner," Leah said.

Handing over his car keys, "Sure, honey. We'll be here all day, except for grabbing meals in the cafeteria."

She kissed Mia. "You know that I love you, don't you?" Not expecting an answer, she was out the door, unashamed of the tears that were streaming down her cheeks.

It wasn't long before Joe arrived. Ellie looked at him with inquisitive eyes, but he ignored her, knowing exactly what she'd want to know. He moved past them to his niece. "Hey kid, your favorite uncle is here. I don't know if you can hear me, but I'm gonna tell you anyhow—I love you! I need one of your special hugs, you know, just like when you were a little squirt . . . " He choked up, unable to finish. He stayed next to her for a long time, then continued, "I found your purse in that beat-up old buggy of yours."

Ellie placed her hand on his back, hoping against hope that the car had not malfunctioned. He would never, ever forgive himself.

Angie reached out to take Mia's purse from her brother. "That was nice of you to retrieve it for her, for us. I'm assuming there was nothing else in the car?"

"Nothing of any value. So, any new information on her condition?"

Angie repeated everything the doctor told them. "You were exactly right to talk to her. It's just what we should be doing."

"Anthony is taking my scheduled repairs, so I can take second shift with her or stay the night. What do you say?"

"Sure, Joe, that would be great. I'd feel so much better knowing you're here with her tonight."

Joe couldn't take his eyes off his niece. "I'd like to visit Matt. Is he still in the emergency room?"

"He's also been moved; he's right across the hall. His mom told me he's doing better today."

"Good, good. I'll be right back."

Ellie offered to go with him, "I'll be right back, stay and talk to our princess."

He found Matt sitting up and alone. "Hey, buddy, how are you doing?"

"Hi, Mr. Agosti, I'm doing okay, better than my girl."

Joey looked down, overcome with compassion for this young man. "Have you seen her yet?"

"No, they won't let me out of this bed. I told my doc that I'm crossing that hallway with or without his permission."

"Hold on, son, maybe they know something about your condition that you don't know. You'll see her all in good time."

Moving slowly, Matt tried to adjust his position. It was obvious his injuries were more severe than they appeared, causing him to flinch with every movement.

"Matt, can you tell me how the accident happened?"

"Sure, but some of it is a bit hazy." He went on to explain how the truck jackknifed as it was passing him, causing the multiple car accident; it was the second crash of the evening on that stretch of highway.

"No braking problems? Nothing weird with the car?"

"No, no, nothing like that. It was reckless driving by the trucker—on some very treacherous roads."

Joe leaned back, exhaling long and slow. It was clear, even to Matt, that a weight had just been lifted off his shoulders. They visited a while longer before Joe stood to leave. "I'll be staying with Mia through the night, so I'll stop by again."

"Mr. Agosti, has she opened her eyes yet?"

"No, son. No yet."

Trina and Sal had just arrived and were standing by Mia's bed when Joey returned. They too brought coffee and donuts. "How is he?" Trina asked as she embraced her brother.

"He's hurting, but I'd say he's very fortunate that none of his injuries are life-threatening."

It was quieter in the room than was the norm for this family. Trina pulled a small radio from her purse, set it on Mia's side table and tuned it to her favorite kind of music; the sound softly permeated the room. Trina's professional background taught her this type of external stimulation was helpful for someone in Mia's condition.

Trina leaned into her niece. "Now listen to me, my sweet girl, you cannot lay around here all day. Vinnie wants you to come over and play; he's counting on it, he's waiting for you. You know how he loves you; you're his number one buddy." She thought a tear formed in the corner of Mia's eye, but couldn't be sure so she said nothing.

Throughout the day, family and friends wandered in and out, each hoping for some kind of response from Mia; some tiny reaction to their greeting and prayers, but it never came. By five o'clock, the head nurse suggested Angie and Jake go home and get some rest. "We'll take very good care of your daughter—I promise."

"Thank you for your concern, we'll be going shortly; my brother will be right back. He plans to spend the night with her," Angie replied.

"That's not necessary, Mrs. Trayor. She won't be neglected in any way," the nurse protested.

"Please don't be offended, we are a strong, tight-knit family. When one of us is hurting, we're all hurting. We take care of one another, whatever that takes." Angie turned back to Mia and continued reading a passage of Scripture. She stopped when Leah walked in and went directly to her sister, grasping her hand.

The nurse smiled, "No offense taken. Mrs. Trayor, I certainly do admire your family." She quietly slipped out of the room.

The hospital's neurologist explained that the longer Mia remained unresponsive, the graver the situation became. As they had done countless times in the past, they turned to God, this time pleading for the life of their beautiful girl. Their church also undergirded them with twenty-four-hour prayer coverage. Angie knew in her heart that Mia's every breath was bathed in prayer by this faithful body of believers.

Leah convinced her family to go home; she planned to stay with Mia until Uncle Joey arrived for the night shift. She was beside herself; Mia was not only her sister but her best friend. She begged God, as she awkwardly wrapped her arms around her sister, to manifest His healing touch. Leah whispered private, funny, secret memories they'd shared; memories meant only Mia's her ears. She tucked her sister's chilled hands under the blankets and began softly singing a childhood song, one they'd made up as kids.

"Hey, kid. I think you should go home," Joey gently interrupted.

"Hi, Uncle Joey, you're here. I'm okay. I want to stay again tonight—with you."

"Kevin is going to stay with me for a while; you go home. I bet you haven't had much sleep."

"I slept a little last night. I tried today, but I couldn't shut my brain down. Uncle Joey, I'm just so scared."

"I know, sweetie. I know."

Kevin finally convinced Leah to let him drive her home; she needed sleep. He returned to the hospital with loads of snacks; enough to sustain them for their overnight vigil. Joe had to laugh at his insatiable appetite. "I'm surprised you're so skinny, wait until you get a few more years on you," Joe patted his own belly.

Kevin borrowed an extra chair from another room and settled on one side of his sister, Joe sat on the other. They conversed over her, hoping to trigger a reaction; it didn't happen. After a few hours, Kevin slouched down for a little catnap. Joe was going to suggest he head home, but left him alone. An hour or so later Kevin was jolted awake for no apparent reason. He looked around the room, trying to figure out where he was.

"Okay, that's it, grab us some coffee, then get yourself moving. I really don't mind being here alone, honest," Joe said.

While Kevin was on a coffee run, Joey leaned in close to his niece. "I love you, so quit playing possum. I know all your tricks; you always did love room service," he whispered, his tears beginning to flow. But then he noticed a tear in Mia's eye. He gently wiped it away. "You're still in there. I know it. We all love you, honey. You know we do."

When Kevin returned, Joe asked him to stay a minute while he visited Matt. "Sure, take your time. I'm just going to nibble on these Cheetos." When Joe left the room, Kevin pulled himself closer to his sister, "Mia, you know I'd do anything for you?" he soberly whispered. "I'd take your place, if I could—I really would. You've got to get better; this family needs you."

It was late, so the halls were deserted, even the nurses' station was quiet. Joe crossed the hall and quietly knocked on the door, not wanting to startle or wake Matt.

"Oh, hey there, Mr. Agosti, how is she? The staff still won't tell me anything—stinking privacy laws."

"Well, she's about the same, but I wanted to know if you've been in that wheelchair at all? Or are you bed-bound?"

"They had me sitting in a wingback chair this afternoon. Why?"

"If you're okay with it, I'd like to help you visit Mia."

"Yes, please. I asked Nurse Ratched earlier this afternoon about it, but she just blew me off."

"I don't want to attempt this on my own and I sure don't want to further aggravate your injuries, so I'm going to request help from the nurses' station."

Joey was on a mission; he flashed his beautiful smile, somehow managing to convince a couple of nurses to bring Matt across the hall for a very short visit. "It would be good for both patients," he reasoned.

Kevin's eyes opened like saucers when they wheeled Matt in, positioning him as close to Mia as possible. Matt, likely overcome with seeing her in such poor condition, sat stock-still, then took hold of her hand and brought it to his lips. He struggled to hold back tears as he spoke words of endearment to her. Kevin and Joe respectfully backed away, giving him a few private moments.

Some time passed, but still Matt clung to Mia's hands, speaking in hushed tones. It was heart-wrenching to watch. Joey began to wonder if this was such a good idea, but when he looked at Mia's face, it was—different. Her cheeks now seemed to have a tiny bit of color or was he just wishful thinking?

Matt whispered, "Mia, I wanted . . . I'd planned to tell you the night we went to dinner. I was going to tell you at dinner, but I got cold feet. Then the accident happened; if you can hear me, Mia—don't leave, me. Please don't leave me—I love you. I have from the moment we met at the beach. Mia, do you hear me? I love—"

Joey came closer, were Mia's eyes were fluttering? They didn't open, but they were definitely moving. "I'm getting the nurse—keep talking to her," Joey excitedly blurted. "Matt, keep talking to her!"

Kevin was so excited, he couldn't talk straight, but immediately began thanking the Lord. "You are answering our prayers. Thank You, Lord."

Matt, wincing in physical pain, moved even closer to Mia. "Mia, I know you can hear me. I love you. Open your eyes—please—I know you can do this." Her eyes did not open, but did continue to flutter ever so slightly.

The nurse was indifferent, she did nothing but plump her pillow and check her pulse rate. "The doctor will be notified, but I can't promise what time he'll arrive. I must return Mr. Bertolino to his room."

"No, wait, I'm fine. Please let me stay until her doctor arrives."

"I'm sorry, but you need to return to your bed. If your physician is in agreement, one of the nurses can bring you back on the next shift." And with that she brusquely pulled Matt back away from the bed.

Joe and Kevin were completely frustrated by the nurse's lack of sympathy. Kevin called after Matt as he was being removed from the room, "I'll keep you in the loop, buddy."

Joey looked at Mia, then Kevin, "I know what I saw," he firmly stated.

"Me too, but let's wait until morning to call my folks. I don't want to needlessly raise their hopes."

"Kevin, please stand with me in faith. I believe that God is healing Mia—I just know it!"

Chapter 34

Sunday morning dawned bright and cold. Leah jumped out of bed. Still in a slight fog, she ran to her parents' bedroom—empty. She scurried down the stairs, soon realizing she was alone in the house. *They're already at the hospital! How could I have slept in? I need to be with Mia.*

It was still early enough to make it to church, but she knew her pastor would understand their family's absence. She spotted a note stuck on the refrigerator: 'At the hospital—Love you!' Leah wasted no time in grabbing the phone. "Luke, could I impose on you for a ride? I—" He cut her off before she finished.

"Of course, I was going to call you and offer to pick you up." She knew he was smiling into the receiver.

"You're the best! I'll be ready in fifteen minutes, but come whenever you can."

"I'll be there in twenty," he cheerfully answered.

It was sunny, but brutally cold, so they stopped to pick up a few cups of coffee to share. She knew her family would appreciate it. Luke also ordered cinnamon buns, insisting they'd be eaten by *someone*.

Juggling the pastries and trays of almost hot coffee, they went directly to Mia's room. Leah was surprised that her Uncle Joey was still there, along with her folks. "Hi, sweetie, I didn't want to wake you; you were so exhausted. I figured you'd call for a ride when you were ready."

"That's okay, Mom. It was a good excuse for me to see this big lug. Coffee and cinnamon buns, anyone?"

"Did someone say cinnamon buns?" Sal asked as he and Trina rounded the corner.

Joe was still wrestling with whether or not to tell his sister what had happened during the night; he agreed with Kevin against giving any false hope. But then Kevin, wandered into the room, "Hi, guys!" Looking directly at his uncle, he blurted out, "Did you tell them?"

"Tell us what?" Jake asked, reaching for a cup of coffee.

As each sipped their coffee, Joey shared what had happened the night before. Looking at Mia now, he was beginning to doubt what he'd witnessed.

As the rest of the family listened, hope ignited their spirits. Joe knew they believed him.

Kevin was the first to look around. "What's that?"

"What's what?" Angie started, but then she heard it too. A group of people were gathered on the sidewalk outside Mia's window. Their pastor and his wife, along with twenty or thirty church friends, were signing a hymn, a beautiful hymn. They stood in the bitter cold, in the strength of their faith, singing one hymn after another; those few moments could only be described as a gift of encouragement. These faithful brothers and sisters were linking their shields of faith with this family they so loved.

Everyone, except Leah, went to the hospital cafeteria for lunch, with the promise of bringing her a sandwich. She just wasn't excited about food; her appetite had diminished over the past couple of days. She settled into the well-worn chair, opened Mia's newest fashion magazine and began to have a one-sided conversation with her sister. "Mia," she whispered, "look at this dress. It's almost identical to the one you wore—the other night. You looked terrific in that dress." She just stared at her sister, suddenly feeling foolish for talking into the air. "You know, it's going to be a horrid Christmas," she choked out. Leah laid her head on Mia's open palm and wept.

Leah was well aware that some nurses were staring at her; she didn't care, she was staying right there, close to her sister. She wasn't sure exactly how long she'd been in that position, laying on Mia's hand, but suddenly Leah felt something. She stayed perfectly still—there it was again. *This is definitely not my imagination!* Leah felt movement in her hair, which had fallen over Mia's arm and hand. *Is she moving her hand? Is she trying to stroke my hair?* Leah's head shot up; Mia's eyes were fluttering, her feet were twitching. "Mia, you're coming back to us! Mia—" she cried out.

It seemed like an eternity, but it was only minutes before her parents returned from the cafeteria. "Mom, look!" she rushed to her mother.

Angie's hands flew to her mouth, dropping Leah's sandwich. "Oh, sweetheart! Jake, look at our girl."

Jake didn't answer, instead he ran to get a doctor, or at least a nurse. When the nurse came to her bedside, she cautioned Angie, "This sometimes happens; please don't get your hopes up."

Angie simply responded to the nurse, "Our hopes are already up."

Throughout the rest of the day, Mia's eyes occasionally fluttered; her feet continued to twitch, but nothing else happened. It was getting late; Jake and Angie decided to grab some dinner and then stay with Mia for the night.

Trina was hugging her sister goodnight when she looked over Angie's shoulder—Mia's eyes were fully opened. It was almost imperceptible, but there it was—Mia's dimpled smile.

Everyone was excitedly talking at once when the doctor walked in and pushed through, politely asking them to quiet down and wait in the hallway.

He was taking too long, Angie was about to barge back into Mia's room when the doctor appeared in the hallway, smiling broadly. The family surrounded him, waiting. Literally scratching his head, he said, "I do not say this very often, but I believe you have just experienced a miracle," after which a collective gasp was heard. "I can't explain it, but this young woman is obviously a fighter and she has beaten some very grave odds."

"So what's her prognosis," Jake pressed.

"Her prognosis is very good. Of course, it will take weeks for her fractured collarbone and ribs to heal, but I believe your daughter is on the road to a full recovery. I'm confident, with the help of her loved ones, she will be just fine."

They turned at the sound of gasping sobs. Matt was seated in his wheelchair in the doorway; he'd heard the whole, wonderful report. Luke went to him, "Are you okay, buddy?" He laid a hand on the back of Matt's neck.

"I am more than okay," he excitedly fist pumped in the air. "I am so grateful to God that she's on her way back to us."

Luke pushed Matt into Mia's room and they gathered around her, watching, waiting for her to talk a blue streak. That did not happen. But slowly she focused on each and every face, smiling, her eyes glistening. This tender scene playing out before them brought the final act of the *Wizard of Oz* to Trina's remembrance. Dorothy was finally home with the ones she loved and those who loved her.

Mia's words came back to her slowly but steadily. Leah later admitted to being wrong about one thing; Christmas was not horrid, it was in fact, a beautiful celebration of life. As was their tradition, the family gathered on Christmas day to give thanks for the birth of their Savior, but also to praise Him for bringing Mia back.

Weeks later, on a snowy New England evening, as the family sat by the fire, Leah noticed her sister was a million miles away. "A penny for your thoughts?" Leah asked. "You seem—troubled. Are you okay?"

"I'm fine. Actually, I'm really good."

Leah smiled at her sister, knowing she'd talk when she was ready. She leaned forward, "Remember when I was in la-la-land?"

Angie half laughed. "How could I not remember?"

"Why?" Jake pressed.

Mia winced a bit, as she attempted to change positions on the overstuffed sofa, "I can't remember everything after the accident, but a few things are starting to pop into my head."

"What kind of things?" Leah asked.

"I seem to remember you talking about my new dress."

"I did talk to you; I told you that you looked smashing in it."

"Is that the most significant thing you remember?" Leah probed.

"It may be wishful thinking or maybe I'm still confused—oh, forget it."

"No, I won't forget it. I know you know. Come on, spit it out."

She looked at her sister and shyly smiled, "I love him too."

"We all felt so badly for Matt," Angie said. "His heart was breaking."

"And . . . and there was singing. Leah, you sang—you sang our secret silly song to me—the one we made up as kids. I remember now."

"You weren't dreaming or imagining that, but, honey, our church choir and some of your crazy family sang to you, too, rather off key, but we sang."

Mia leaned back, her thoughts far away, "Yes, yes, but guys—I heard—angelic voices."

Jake and Angie exchanged glances, but Leah just smiled at her sister.

"I definitely heard angelic voices! And there's something else—Don't think I'm crazy, but angels were hovering over me, singing. I heard *songs in the night*. And you know what—God used those songs to draw me out of that dark place." She closed her eyes and smiled, "Hmm, beautiful, angelic songs in the night."

From Mama's Kitchen . . .

Buon Appetito!

2-Day Pizza Dough

2 teaspoons active dry yeast
1 tablespoon sugar
1 tablespoon olive oil
2 teaspoons Kosher salt
5 to 5 ½ cups flour

Dissolve yeast into 2 ¼ cups warm water (100 degrees). Add sugar and olive oil. Let stand until bubbly, 5 to 8 minutes. Combine 5 cups flour with 2 teaspoons Kosher salt in stand mixer, using paddle attachment. Add yeast mixture, on medium-low, adding a little flour or water until a rough sticky ball of dough forms (about 1 minute). Let rest 5 minutes then mix on medium-low until no longer sticky (1 more minute). Transfer dough to floured surface, knead 10 to 20 times. Let rest 5 minutes, briefly knead again. Place in oiled bowl, cover with plastic wrap, refrigerate 8 hours or overnight. 2 hours before making pizza, divide dough in half, place on floured surface, covered with plastic wrap, let stand at room temperature for 2 hours. Stretch dough onto lightly oiled pans, then let rest 15 minutes. Bake just a few minutes to firm up surface of dough, then spread sauce and desired toppings, drizzling olive oil over exposed crust and sauce. Bake 475 degrees until nicely browned. Makes 2 large pizzas.

Chicken Parmesan

2 chicken breasts
1/2 cup flour
1 beaten egg
1 cup Italian breadcrumbs
1/4 cup Parmesan cheese
Grated black pepper
Homemade or prepared marinara sauce
Parmesan cheese, for sprinkling
Mozzarella cheese, shredded, for sprinkling
Approximately 2 tablespoons olive oil and 2 tablespoons canola oil for frying

Pound the chicken breast between sheets of plastic wrap until thickness is fairly uniform, can cut into smaller serving sizes.

Blend Italian breadcrumbs, Parmesan cheese and black pepper, onto wax paper.

Dip chicken breasts into flour, shake off excess. Dip into egg, then coat with breadcrumb mixture.

Pour the blended oils in large skillet and heat to medium.

Fry until golden brown on each side, place on paper towels to remove excess oil.

Place them in 9" x 13" casserole, spoon sauce on each one. Sprinkle with shredded mozzarella and grated Parmesan cheese.

Bake 350 degrees until cheese is bubbly and browned around edges. 18 to 20 minutes.

Chicken Piccata, Light

1/4 cup flour
1/4 teaspoon pepper
1/2 teaspoon paprika
2 boneless, skinless chicken breasts, halved and sliced across to reduce thickness
2 tablespoons canola oil
1/4 cup chicken broth
2 tablespoons lemon juice
2 tablespoons drained capers

Combine flour, pepper and paprika on waxed paper. Dip chicken breasts into mixture, shake off excess. In large skillet heat oil over medium heat. Cook breasts approximately 3 minutes on each side being careful not to overcook. Transfer to a warm serving plate. Add chicken broth to skillet, scraping up browned bits from pan. Stir in lemon juice and capers and heat through. Pour sauce over chicken. Serves 4

Porchetta

Rub ingredients:
3 finely chopped garlic cloves
2 teaspoons fennel seeds
16 fresh sage leaves, chopped or 1 teaspoon dried sage
2 teaspoons chopped fresh rosemary
1/2 teaspoon Kosher salt
Fresh ground pepper to taste
Grated zest of 1 lemon
Chicken broth
3 pounds boneless pork shoulder

Blend all dry ingredients together.

Spread open pork shoulder, spread rub all over, leaving some for exterior of pork. Roll up and tie snugly with butcher's string.

Place pork in either a Crock Pot or in heavy covered pot, such as a Dutch oven. Cook 275 degrees for approximately 3 to 4 hours until very tender, adding enough chicken broth to keep meat very moist. Remove string and serve hot.

Leftovers make great hot sandwiches on toasted Italian rolls.

Risotto

3 tablespoons butter
3/4 cup chopped onions
12 to 16 ounces sliced baby bella mushrooms
1 1/2 cup Aborio rice (no substitute)
1/2 cup dry white wine
32 ounces good quality chicken broth (keep warm)
1/2 cup Parmesan cheese
2 to 3 tablespoons butter
1/2 pint heavy cream or light cream

Melt butter in large skillet or heavy pot; sauté onions and mushrooms for a few minutes.

Add rice and wine, simmer slowly until liquid is absorbed, approximately 3 minutes.

On low heat, add small amounts of warm broth to rice mixture, stirring until broth is absorbed. Continue adding small amounts of broth until all the broth is incorporated. This should take 20 to 25 minutes. Then add Parmesan cheese, butter and heavy or light cream. Serves 4 to 6

Optional: at the end, you may add one of the following—rotisserie chicken, roasted butternut squash or grilled shrimp.

Scacciata (Italian Meat Pie)

2 pounds Italian sweet sausage, removed from casings
1 pound lean ground beef
1 tablespoon olive oil
1 or 2 medium onions, chopped
4 garlic cloves, minced
14 to 28 ounces canned San Marzano tomatoes, peeled
1 cup seasoned Italian breadcrumbs
1/2 tablespoon fennel seeds
2 tablespoons chopped Italian parsley
1/3 cup grated Parmesan or provolone cheese
Kosher salt, to taste
Fresh ground pepper, to taste
2 beaten eggs

Frozen bread/pizza dough, thawed or homemade pizza dough (that would make two 12" pizzas)

In large skillet, brown meat, breaking up until cooked through; remove meat with slotted spoon. In remaining fat, sauté onions and garlic. Remove onions and garlic and add to reserved meat. Drain off any remaining fat, reserving for later use. Squeeze tomatoes into the skillet, breaking them up. Return meat mixture to skillet. Add breadcrumbs, fennel, parsley, cheese, salt and pepper. Mix well. Add eggs and mix again. (Mixture may be chilled at this point for later use.)

Stretch half the dough to fit a greased 9" x 13" (or a slightly larger) casserole dish. Spoon meat mixture onto dough, (optional *layer provolone cheese on top of meat.) Fit second half of dough to cover meat. Crimp edges to seal and brush with reserved fat from skillet or olive oil. Let rise for half an hour, pierce with fork to vent steam. Bake 375 degrees 30 to 40 minutes or until nicely browned. Let stand 10 minutes before cutting.   Serves 12

Angeletti (Italian Lemon Cookies)

1/2 cup vegetable shortening
2 eggs
3 cups flour
1 cup sugar
1 cup milk
7 teaspoons baking powder
1 teaspoon lemon extract
pinch salt

Beat shortening and eggs until well blended. Add remaining ingredients, beat just until blended. Drop mounded teaspoons of mixture on lightly greased cookie sheet. Bake at 375 degrees, 8 to 10 minutes. Cool before frosting.

Frosting:
3 cups confectionary sugar
1/4 cup water
1 teaspoon lemon extract
Optional: decorate with sprinkles

Biscotti

2 cups sugar

6 eggs

2 sticks melted butter

2 teaspoons vanilla extract

3 teaspoons anise extract

6 cups flour

5 teaspoons baking powder

Beat sugar and eggs together. Add melted butter, and extracts.

Blend flour and baking powder together, then add to egg mixture, mix well.

Knead mixture slightly on floured surface. Keep hands well-floured, dough may be sticky. Cut into 6 sections and shape into 6 loaves, approximately 1 1/2" x 10" each. Line 2 large cookie sheets with parchment paper, place 3 loaves on each sheet. Bake 350 degrees 20 to 25 minutes. Dough will double in size.

Cutting at an angle, cut into 1" sections. Place cut side down and bake for 3 minutes longer. Turn each piece to other side and bake 3 more minutes.

Cool and dust with confectionary sugar.

Italian Ricotta Cookies

2 sticks butter, softened
1 3/4 cups sugar
3 eggs
2 teaspoons vanilla
15 to 16 ounces ricotta cheese
4 cups flour
1 teaspoon salt
1 teaspoon baking soda

Cream butter and sugar together. Add eggs, vanilla and ricotta. Add remaining dry ingredients, mix well. Drop heaping teaspoons of dough on parchment paper covered cookie sheets. Bake 350 degrees 10 to 12 minutes.

Cool and frost.

Frost with pastel tinted butter cream frostings or cream cheese frosting. May decorate with sprinkles.

Roman Tri-Colored Cookies

1 cup shortening
1/3 cup softened butter
1 1/3 cup sugar
2 eggs
1 teaspoon almond extract
4 cup flour
2 2/3 teaspoon baking powder
1/3 cup milk

Cream shortening, butter and sugar. Add eggs, cream well. Add extract. Add remaining dry ingredients, alternately with milk.

Divide dough into three parts. Put red food coloring in one part, green in second part and leave third part plain. Take a pinch of each color and gently roll into 1" balls, keeping colors distinct (handle as little as possible). Roll each ball into approximately 1 3/4 cups finely chopped walnuts or almonds. Place on ungreased cookie sheet or parchment paper. Bake 350 degrees for approximately 15 minutes. Bottoms should be lightly browned. Makes 6 dozen

Order Information

REDEMPTION
PRESS

To order additional copies of this book, please visit
www.redemption-press.com.
Also available on Amazon.com and BarnesandNoble.com
Or by calling toll free 1-844-2REDEEM.

CPSIA information can be obtained
at www.ICGtesting.com
Printed in the USA
LVOW12s0325270617
539400LV00002B/447/P